Delores Fossen, a *USA To[day]* [bestselling author of] over 150 novels, with milli[ons of copies sold] worldwide. She's received [...] RT Reviewers' Choice Best Book Award. She was also a finalist for a prestigious RITA Award. You can contact the author through her website at deloresfossen.com

Juno Rushdan is a veteran US Air Force intelligence officer and an award-winning author. Her books are action-packed and fast-paced. Critics from *Kirkus Reviews* and *Library Journal* have called her work 'heart-pounding James Bond–ian adventure' that 'will captivate lovers of romantic thrillers.' For a free book, visit her website: junorushdan.com

Also by Delores Fossen

Renegade Canyon
Her Baby, Her Badge
Deputies Under Fire

Saddle Ridge Justice
Protecting the Newborn
Tracking Down the Lawman's Son
Child in Jeopardy

Silver Creek Lawman: Second Generation
Targeted in Silver Creek
Maverick Detective Dad

Also by Juno Rushdan

Ironside Protection Services
Big Sky Slayer
Big Sky Safe House

Cowboy State Lawmen: Duty and Honor
Wyoming Mountain Investigation
Wyoming Ranch Justice
Wyoming Undercover Escape
Wyoming Christmas Conspiracy
Wyoming Double Jeopardy
Corralled in Cutthroat Creek

Discover more at millsandboon.co.uk

TEXAS BABY RESCUE

DELORES FOSSEN

BIG SKY SHOWDOWN

JUNO RUSHDAN

MILLS & BOON

First Published in Great Britain 2025
by Mills & Boon, an imprint of HarperCollins*Publishers* Ltd
1 London Bridge Street, London, SE1 9GF

www.harpercollins.co.uk

HarperCollins*Publishers*
Macken House, 39/40 Mayor Street Upper,
Dublin 1, D01 C9W8, Ireland

Texas Baby Rescue © 2026 Delores Fossen
Big Sky Showdown © 2026 Juno Rushdan

ISBN: 978-0-263-42015-9

0126

MIX
Paper | Supporting
responsible forestry
FSC™ C007454

This book contains FSC™ certified paper and other controlled sources to ensure responsible forest management.

For more information visit: www.harpercollins.co.uk/green

Printed and Bound in the UK using 100% Renewable Electricity at CPI Group (UK) Ltd, Croydon, CR0 4YY

TEXAS BABY RESCUE

DELORES FOSSEN

Chapter One

The cribs were empty.

That was the first thing Deputy Judson Docherty noticed when he hurried into the nursery of the Horseshoe Ranch. Even though he had been expecting the empty cribs because of the warning that he'd gotten during the phone call, it was still a jolt to realize the caller had been right.

Get here fast. The babies are missing.

That call had come ten minutes earlier, just as Judson had been heading home after a long shift at Renegade Canyon Sheriff's Office, and the caller, Addie Jansen, hadn't stayed on the line. After blurting out that dire announcement, she had hung up on him, no doubt to do a frantic search for the babies.

But where the hell was Addie now?

Judson hadn't seen her when he'd driven up to the ranch. Nor when he'd bolted inside through the already-open door of the house. And she hadn't responded the multiple times he'd called out for her.

Pushing aside that something really bad had happened to Addie and the babies, he raced through the sprawling house that was normally filled with the sounds of foster kids. Lots of them.

But tonight, there was nothing.

It was eerily quiet, and that was in part due to there being only two babies currently in care here, six-week-old twin girls Lily and Rose Alcott. But Addie and at least one of her helpers should have been around.

"Addie?" he called out again.

And this time, Judson thankfully got a response. It hadn't come from Addie, though.

"Out here," someone shouted, and silver-haired Etta Jean Milford stuck her head in through the back door.

Judson had known Etta Jean most of his life, since she had been the cook and caretaker way back when he'd been a foster kid at the ranch, nearly thirty years ago. And even though she was now in her late sixties, she was still going strong and usually looked as steady a proverbial rock. But not at the moment. Her face was tight with worry and barely controlled panic.

"The babies aren't here," the woman told him as she stepped into the kitchen, only to turn around and go to the back porch. Her breath was gusting, and she was wringing her hands. "I've looked through the whole house, every inch of it, and they're gone." Etta Jean's voice cracked on that last word, and she began to sob.

Judson hated those tears, hated that the woman was an emotional wreck, but he couldn't take the time to soothe her. That would have to wait for later.

"Where's Addie?" he demanded.

Etta Jean pressed her fingers to her trembling mouth and shook her head. "I'm not sure. She thought she saw some tracks in the backyard, and she started following them out into the pasture. She told me to wait here until you showed up. We have to find them," she tacked on.

Yeah, they did, and that was Judson's main concern, but at the moment, so was Addie. If someone had taken the babies, he didn't want her going after a kidnapper alone.

"Call the police station," Judson instructed, already heading out the back door. "Have the sheriff send out more deputies and do an Amber Alert on the twins."

That alert might have to be canceled within minutes if he found Addie and the babies right away, but in case that didn't happen, putting out the word on the missing babies would get a lot of resources in motion to try to locate them.

He didn't bother taking the steps. Judson jumped off the side of the porch and hurried through the yard, jogging and looking at the ground for any of those tracks that Addie had mentioned to Etta Jean. And he soon saw them.

Footprints in some mud.

It had rained just a couple of hours earlier, a good soaker that'd left the ground a soggy mess and had put a damp chill in the mid-October air. Not cold, exactly, but it sure as heck wasn't ideal conditions for babies to be out in this unless they were wrapped in blankets.

Would a kidnapper have done that?

Judson had to push that concern aside and just focus on finding Addie. Then he'd know what they were dealing with.

Well, hopefully he would.

Sometimes birth parents came after their kids who had been removed from their care. But that didn't apply in this case. The parents were dead, killed in a car accident shortly after the mother had been released from the hospital and the twins were still in a neonatal unit. The parents had been making a quick trip home to get a change of clothes and had ended up dying in a head-on collision caused by a drunk driver.

Lily and Rose had ended up here at the Horseshoe Ranch with Addie just two weeks ago while the courts were sorting out next-of-kin issues. But maybe the next of kin, whoever that was, had decided to take matters into their own hands and snatch the girls. The odds were higher for that than abductions orchestrated by a stranger.

"Addie?" he shouted once he made it to the barn.

Again, there was no answer, but he saw more of those tracks in the mud. Not one set but two. Hell. Addie was following the kidnapper.

Judson picked up the pace, running now while keeping an eye out for more tracks and listening for, well, any damn thing.

Every bit of this pasture and the thick woods beyond it were familiar ground to him. Addie and he had spent a good chunk of their childhoods here, since she'd been in foster care as well. Those days, Mellie and Frank Carsten had run the place and had run it well, but after they'd died, Addie had stepped up to continue their legacy. And Judson knew Addie would do anything to protect the kids in her care.

Anything.

That's why he had to get to her.

Because she would absolutely confront a kidnapper if it meant getting the babies back. A confrontation that could get her hurt or killed.

He kept moving, even faster now. Kept following the tracks that led into the woods. There were old ranch trails threading through the trees and thick underbrush, and Judson headed toward the trail that was closest to the pasture. Again, he knew it well since it had become a favorite make-out spot for Addie and him when they were teenagers.

"Addie?" he tried again after he reached the trail.

This time, he got a response.

"Here," a voice said.

Relief flooded through him, robbing him of some breath, but it also got him moving in the direction of her voice. She was alive. That answered a whole bunch of his prayers, but Judson figured this ordeal wasn't over.

And it wasn't.

He soon saw that when he bolted through a cluster of trees and spotted Addie. She was standing on the trail, her gaze volleying in each direction. She stopped glancing around long enough for her gaze to land on him.

Judson saw the tears in her eyes, some on her cheeks, too, and there was a sense of sickening dread coming off her.

"I have to find them," she muttered, her voice a tangle of nerves and raw fear.

"We will," he said, though at the moment Judson had no idea how they were going to do that.

Addie looked so distraught. So broken. He wanted to pull her into his arms, to try to comfort her, but the best comfort he could give her was to figure out what had happened to the babies.

"Give me any details you have," he insisted, moving up the trail so he could look for more tracks. He saw some footprints but no signs that a vehicle had recently been here.

Addie moved, too, heading off the trail, her attention pinned to the ground. "I was, uh, getting the mail. Etta Jean was in the laundry room with the monitor while the twins were sleeping," she started but then stopped. "God, Judson. Rowena's out of jail."

That got his attention, not in a good way, either, and he whirled back around to face Addie. He didn't have to ask who she meant—Rowena Matthews was Addie's mother.

Except she wasn't.

When Addie was six, the truth had come out: that Rowena had stolen Addie when she'd been only a few weeks old. And Rowena had killed Addie's bio mom during the abduction.

"How the hell is Rowena out of jail when she's serving a life sentence?" Judson asked. "Did she escape?"

Addie shook her head. "No. She was released. I don't know the details, but someone from the parole board sent me a text. I got that about a half hour before I realized the twins were missing."

Damn it. That was tight timing. Of course, Rowena could have gotten out days ago and managed to set all of this up. Still, the woman had been in prison for twenty-eight years, and Judson would have thought her first move wouldn't have been to abduct another child.

But it was something he had to consider.

His phone dinged with a text, and he saw his boss's name on the screen. Sheriff Grace Granger. "The Amber Alert has been issued," he relayed to Addie after reading the message. "And Grace and the other deputies are on their way."

That didn't put any relief in Addie's eyes, probably because she understood it was going to take time to get a proper search organized. Time when the kidnapper could be whisking the babies away so they would never be found. That's why Addie and he needed to keep on looking, because every second counted.

While he kept moving, he also listened for any unusual sounds, along with firing off a text to Grace. Rowena Matthews is out of jail. We need an APB on her.

Grace might not immediately recognize the woman's name the way Judson had, but it wouldn't take his boss long to figure it out. And Grace wouldn't have any trouble getting an all-points bulletin or maybe even an arrest warrant for someone with Rowena's criminal history.

"You go that way," Addie said, pointing to the left. "And I'll go there." She then pointed to the right.

Judson definitely didn't like that plan. If it was Rowena

who had done this, she had killed before and might kill again. Besides, the trail on the right led to the road, which was about a half mile away, and that was their best bet. The kidnapper could have left a vehicle there.

"We go together toward the road," he insisted, and to save Addie from arguing with him, he took off running in that direction.

Thankfully, Addie followed, staying right behind him. He definitely didn't want her out of his sight if they were dealing with Rowena. Or any other kidnapper, for that matter. Someone willing to sneak into a foster home and steal kids was probably desperate enough to kill anyone who got in their way.

This part of the trail was just that—a trail—no more than a foot wide in some places, and it was littered with fallen leaves, twigs and rocks. Unfortunately, there was no mud here to showcase footprints, but Judson thought he saw some spots where someone could have stepped.

"Other than Rowena, who might have done this?" Judson asked. "Have you had any run-ins with anyone?"

It wasn't an out-there question. Sometimes birth parents and family members threatened foster caregivers and social workers.

"No," she insisted as they kept moving.

"What about the twins' next of kin?" Judson pressed. "Any threats from any of them?"

"No," Addie repeated. "Just the opposite. Child Protective Services has located a couple of distant relatives, but none of them is interested in taking the girls. They're basically wards of the court for now."

So, an abduction likely wasn't linked to anything to do with the next of kin. But that left other possibilities. Bad ones. And Judson had to push those aside, too. He refused to even consider that the babies had been harmed.

He stopped when he reached a mudhole, and Judson spotted footprints—headed straight toward the road. That confirmed that Addie and he were heading in the right direction.

Judson paused to send Grace another text so she could get some deputies to that particular part of the road, but he stopped when he heard something. At first, he thought it could be some small animal, so he lifted his head and kept listening.

He heard it again.

And this time he was certain of something. That it wasn't an animal. It was a baby, and it was crying.

Addie's gaze sliced to his for just a split second. There was both shock and some relief in her eyes that Judson was sure was mirrored in his.

Without a word, they both took off running in the direction of the baby's cries, but they'd barely made it a few steps when Judson heard something else. Something that had his stomach twisting.

A car engine.

And it was speeding away.

Chapter Two

Addie ran as if Lily's and Rose's lives depended on it. Because they did. The babies could be in danger. Their kidnapper could be fleeing the scene and taking them heaven knew where.

Judson was flat-out running, too, and he raced past her, his arms pumping and his legs moving much faster than hers were capable of doing. Both of them had clearly gotten heavy slams of adrenaline. Both knew what was at stake.

If they didn't reach the babies in time, they might never see them again.

They might never know who had them or what was happening to them.

The possibility of that ate away at her like acid, and Addie wanted to scream. She didn't want any child to be put through what had been done to her—abducted and kept hidden away for six years by a woman who had claimed Addie as her own child before the truth had come to light.

No. Addie didn't want that for these precious babies. And she had to make sure history didn't repeat itself.

Just ahead, she saw the country road that led to both the town of Renegade Canyon and the interstate, depending on which direction you went. What Addie didn't see was the blasted car. Where the heck was it? Were they too late? Had the driver already managed to get away?

Still on the move, Judson ran to the end of the trail, coming to a skidding stop right at the edge of the road. His gaze whipped in both directions, and he must have seen someone or something, because he shouted.

"Stop!"

He continued to yell that one-word order, taking out his phone and clicking a photo before he started running again. This time on the road and to the left.

The direction of the interstate.

Addie got to him as fast as she could, and she soon saw what he was chasing. A black car. It was indeed speeding away, and in a blink, it disappeared around a steep curve.

"No," Addie shouted, and she started running again.

She was nowhere near close to catching up with the black car or Judson when she heard the sound of a vehicle behind her. For a moment, Addie thought it was the black car, that a miracle had happened and it had turned around so the driver could bring back those precious baby girls.

But it was a Renegade Canyon cruiser.

Addie instantly recognized the driver—Deputy Livvy Walsh, her foster sister—and she saw that Livvy's face was tight with nerves.

"Where's Judson running?" Livvy asked, lowering her window.

"After a black car," Addie blurted. "The babies are in there."

At least she hoped they were and that the black car wasn't some kind of decoy to get them searching in the wrong direction. But that was possible. Anything was at this point, and it occurred to her that the kidnapper could still be somewhere on that trail, hiding and waiting for a chance to escape.

"Get in," Livvy insisted. She reached over to open the passenger's door, and Addie practically dived inside.

Livvy took off, slamming her foot on the accelerator, which caused the tires to squeal against the asphalt. Judson no doubt heard it, because he spun toward them, already drawing his weapon, ready to respond to a possible threat. He quickly reholstered his gun, though, when he saw this wasn't a threat but rather help in the form of his fellow deputy.

Judson hurried toward them, and Livvy slowed so that he could jump into the back seat. The moment he was in, Livvy gunned the engine again and took off.

"Did you see the driver?" Livvy asked.

"No," Addie and Judson said in unison.

It was Judson who continued. "But I got a picture of the license plate. I'll call it in now."

Good. Addie wanted every cop in the area looking for this monster who'd taken Lily and Rose.

"I thought I saw someone in the back seat of the black car," Judson muttered. "But maybe not. It could have been a shadow or even the seat headrest."

Maybe the picture he'd taken would show that, but when Addie glanced back, she saw that Judson had only captured the license plate and part of the car's trunk.

The cruiser's tires squealed again when Livvy took the curve way too fast, and she had to fight to keep the cruiser on the asphalt. Because of the winding rural road, she immediately had to negotiate another curve, then another before they finally reached a straight stretch.

And Addie's heart dropped.

Because she couldn't see the black car. She couldn't see any vehicle. It was possible that the driver was going so fast that they'd already managed to get out of sight, but there was also a chance that they'd pulled off onto a side road or a ranch trail.

"Keep watch," Livvy ordered them. "See if you spot it. I'm going to keep driving."

Addie did keep watch, but the scenery was practically flying by, and some of the trails were canopied with thick trees. If the driver had gone far enough down the trail, it could be impossible to see them from the road.

"The kidnapper and babies could still be on the southeast ranch trail," Addie managed to say. The muscles in her throat were so tight, it was hard for her to speak. "That's where Judson and I were when we heard one of the babies crying and the car engine."

Livvy nodded and used a voice command on her phone to contact dispatch. "I need someone to check the trail on the southeast side of the Horseshoe Ranch. That's the last known location of the missing infants."

"Will do," the dispatcher assured her and ended the call.

"The car is registered to an Yvette O'Dell," Judson relayed to them in between the conversation that he was having with someone at the sheriff's office.

Addie continued looking for the vehicle, but she also repeated the name several times to see if it was familiar. "That doesn't ring any bells. Who is she? And why would she take the babies?"

"Not sure yet," Judson replied.

Addie heard the hesitation in his voice and glanced back at him. "What?" she demanded.

There was some fresh worry in his already intense dark brown eyes. "Yvette has a record for being drunk and disorderly, and she got three DUIs before she lost her license. And her kids. Twins."

"Oh, God," Addie managed to say.

"No, the kids, her son and daughter, are alive," Judson was quick to add, cutting through what would have been some horrible worst-case scenarios for Addie. "They're in their early twenties now and were adopted by what appears to be a stable family, but Yvette lost custody of them when they were infants." He paused again. "For a while, her kids were fostered at the Horseshoe Ranch."

Addie groaned and fought back both fresh tears and a hot fury over this happening. Two decades ago, both Judson and she had been at the ranch in foster care, and kids came and went all the time. Sometimes they would be there for only a couple of days before their adoptive parents or other family members came to get them.

The Horseshoe hadn't changed much in those decades, so Yvette would likely have known not only the location of the ranch but where in the house to find the nursery. Added to that, the news and social media had been jammed with reports and comments about the orphaned Alcott twins. Yvette would have had all the info she needed to pull off this abduction.

But why?

Was she trying to replace her own kids? If so, why wait all this time? Or did Yvette have a personal connection to Lily and Rose?

Addie desperately wanted the answers to those questions, but for now, she focused on keeping watch, looking for that black car. Livvy continued to drive, slowing when they reached a four-way intersection. Then stopping. Livvy cursed and smacked her palm on the steering wheel. Addie totally understood her frustration.

Four roads and not another vehicle in sight.

A hoarse sob tore from Addie's mouth. This was crushing her heart, but she had to keep focusing. Had to keep thinking.

"Do you have a phone number for Yvette?" Addie asked.

"Getting it now," Judson replied.

Addie wanted to talk to her, wanted to try to convince the woman to surrender both herself and the babies. They were still so little, preemies, and they needed special formula every three to four hours. Addie thought if she could just speak to Yvette, she could make her understand the harm she might be doing.

"Got the number," Judson said, "and I'm calling it now."

From the back seat, Addie heard Judson's phone that was now on speaker. Heard the ringing on the other end of the line. The sound of each ring echoed through the cruiser. But there was no answer, and the call went to a generic voicemail, saying to leave a message.

Addie saw the debate Judson was having with himself. If he left a threatening message, Yvette might panic and do something even more horrible than she'd already done. Instead, Judson hung up and rang the police station again to request the contact info for both of Yvette's kids.

"It might not even be Yvette in the car," Livvy said, taking one of the concerns right out of Addie's mouth.

Yes, someone could have borrowed or stolen the vehicle, and if it was the latter, then that was only going to complicate the search. Addie didn't want more complications. She wanted those babies safely back at the ranch.

"I'm going to drive toward the interstate," Livvy let them know. "I'll have Grace contact the county sheriff's office so they can check these other routes."

Livvy took off again, using her hands-free function to call Grace. Addie tuned that out and instead listened to the info Judson was getting. He apparently had the phone number for Yvette's daughter, Jennifer Rankin, and he tried to call her. Addie prayed Jennifer would answer.

And someone did.

"Hello," the woman barely managed to get out before Judson started talking.

"I'm Deputy Judson Docherty from Renegade Canyon PD," he said. "Is this Jennifer Rankin?"

"It is," she verified, and there was instant concern in her voice. "What's happened? What's wrong?"

"I'm looking for your bio mother, Yvette O'Dell. Do you have any idea where she is?" he asked.

"Yvette?" she questioned, and now there was some surprise mixed with the apprehension. "No, sorry, I don't know. I thought you were calling about my brother, Shane. I've been trying to reach him all morning, and he's not answering—" She stopped. "Wait, is he with Yvette?" And that concern skyrocketed. "Did Yvette do something to him?"

Addie's gaze snared Judson's. Their concerns were soaring even more as well.

"I'm not sure if your brother is with Yvette or not," Judson let Jennifer know. "I'm trying to locate her about another matter. When's the last time you saw her?"

"Last night," she said on a heavy sigh. "Before that, I hadn't seen or heard from her in weeks. But last night she just showed up at my apartment shortly after I got home from work. She was crying and going on about how sorry she was for what happened when Shane and I were kids. She does this about once a year, usually on our birthday. Today is our twenty-second birthday."

Oh God. Had that been some sort of trigger for Yvette to abduct the twins?

"What has Yvette done?" Jennifer asked, the dread coating her voice.

"We're not sure yet," Judson replied, obviously not spilling any details, "but it's imperative that I get in touch with her. If she contacts you, don't mention I'm looking for her. Just try to find out her location and then call me or the Renegade Canyon Sheriff's Office."

"Has Yvette done something bad?" Jennifer pressed. "Something to do with that foster ranch where Shane and I stayed before we were adopted?"

Everything inside Addie went still, and she waited for Judson's response. "Yvette's car was spotted near the Horseshoe Ranch," he finally said after a long pause. "Do you have any idea what she would have been doing there?"

Jennifer paused, too. "I'm not sure, but considering her state of mind last night, she might try to confront the woman who ran the place when Shane and I were living there."

Yvette couldn't have spoken to Jennifer's former foster mom, since Mellie was dead, but Addie was certain that Yvette, or anyone else for that matter, hadn't come to the door to ask about Mellie. They'd had no visitors all morning at the ranch.

Well, no visitor who'd rung the doorbell or paid a normal visit.

Obviously, someone had gotten in. Probably Yvette. And the fact that the car had been hidden on a trail meant the person hadn't had good intentions.

"Call me if you hear from Yvette," Judson repeated, and he ended the call with Jennifer. "I'm going to try to call Shane now," he let them know.

They didn't get lucky this time, because the call to Jennifer's twin brother went straight to voicemail, but Judson did leave a message asking the man to call him back immediately.

Livvy finished her call with Grace and continued the

drive toward the interstate. With nothing else she could do, Addie kept looking for the black car. And tried not to give in to the panic that was building, building, building. She was fighting the tears again, too, when her phone rang.

The sound was so unexpected that she gasped, and because her hands were still trembling, it took her several moments to yank her phone from the pocket of her jeans. She didn't recognize the number on the phone, but she answered it right away on speaker, praying this was Yvette.

"Addie Jansen?" the caller—a woman—immediately asked.

"Yes," Addie verified, and she held her breath.

"I'm Courtney Mora, a social worker from San Antonio."

Addie's hopes vanished as quickly as they'd come. It wasn't unusual for her to get calls from social workers, and San Antonio was less than an hour from Renegade Canyon. Those calls were usually inquiries about possible placements for babies and kids that CPS had taken into custody.

"I'm sorry, but this isn't a good time," Addie muttered.

"I understand," Courtney replied. "I just saw the Amber Alert on the missing babies, and I might have some information."

Addie practically snapped to attention, and from the corner of her eye, she saw Judson have a similar reaction. "What information?" Addie couldn't get out fast enough.

"Yvette O'Dell," the woman said, and just hearing the name gave Addie another slam of those raw nerves. "I was the social worker who removed her kids over two decades ago. Needless to say, I made an enemy of Yvette when I did that. She's tried her best to destroy me and my career."

This recap might be necessary, but Addie was anxious to get to the reason why Courtney had called. "Did Yvette come after the twins that I'm fostering now?" Addie demanded.

"Yes, I believe she did," Courtney replied. "Just yesterday, she showed up at my office to rant about how I ruined her life. I had security escort her out, but she had a wild look in her eyes, and I was worried she would try to do something reckless to get back at me. Perhaps she turned that recklessness on those babies."

Maybe, but again, motive wasn't as big a concern right now as finding Lily and Rose. "Do you have any idea where Yvette might have taken the twins?"

"I might. All those years ago when I took her children into custody, Yvette had them in an old fishing cabin. It used to belong to one of her father's friends. Anyway, if the cabin is still there, that's where she might have taken them."

"What's the address?" Addie pressed.

"I thought you'd ask for it so I looked it up before I called you. It's number three West Betterton Road, just outside of Bulverde."

From the back seat, Addie heard Judson phoning in the address so that someone could respond to the location. Since Bulverde wasn't that far away, only about ten miles, it was possible that Yvette could soon be there with the babies.

Livvy stopped, put the address in the GPS and started in that direction. They weren't far away, either, and would be there in under ten minutes. Sooner, Addie amended, considering the speed Livvy was driving.

"Thank you," Addie told Courtney.

"Glad I can help. I believe Yvette could be a very dangerous woman, and she needs to be stopped. I hope you can stop her. But be careful. There's no telling what she's capable of," she tacked on before ending the call.

Addie tried not to dwell on that *very dangerous* part and instead pinned her focus and attention on the road. Judging by the GPS, they'd be taking a lot of turns to get to the cabin.

Livvy slowed to take one of those turns, but then she slammed on the brakes. Clearly, she'd spotted the same thing Addie had: a red truck pulled just off the side of the road. There was a woman standing outside the vehicle, and she was waving to get their attention.

Addie's first thought was that the woman had broken down and needed help, but she looked more frantic than just a breakdown would warrant. Then again, she might have been out here for a while, and she might have seen the black car if it'd passed this way.

"Is that Yvette?" Livvy asked.

"No," Judson was quick to say. "Yvette's only forty-eight, and according to her latest DMV photo, she still has brown hair."

This person had to be in her late sixties, and her hair was pure gray. The moment Livvy stopped, the stranger hurried to the cruiser.

"She sped off before I could stop her," the woman said, her words rushing out with her racing breath.

"Who sped off?" Livvy asked. "And who are you? What's your name?"

"Nan Fredrick. My farm is just up the road a piece." She motioned behind her. "And as for the woman in the black car, I don't know who she was. Never saw her before in my life. I'd stopped to gather up some dried twigs to make a wreath, and she pulled up beside me. I was about to ask if something was wrong, but she got out and picked up two babies from her back seat."

Oh, mercy. The twins. They'd been here, right here.

"She shoved them into my arms and sped off," Nan went on. "I was about to call 911, but then I saw the cruiser and flagged you down."

Addie's breath had vanished, and she was glad Judson

was able to voice what she wanted to know. "Where are the babies now?"

She pointed to the truck. "I laid them on the seat so I could use my phone. They were squirming, and I was afraid I'd drop them. I put my purse on the edge of the seat so they wouldn't fall off."

Before Nan had even finished her explanation, Addie heard a welcome sound. Actually, two sounds—fussing babies.

Addie bolted from the cruiser, sprinting toward the truck and throwing open the door the moment she reached it.

And there they were.

Lily and Rose were cuddled together in a pink blanket.

Chapter Three

Judson watched from the doorway of the den as Addie and Etta Jean each eased a sleeping baby into the pair of bassinets that had been set up in the room.

The change of location had been a necessity since the nursery itself was still being processed by the CSIs. Every inch of it would have to be checked for fibers or trace evidence to confirm that Yvette had indeed been in that room and had been the one who'd taken the babies.

Even after Addie and Etta Jean had the babies settled in, neither woman was eager to move away from the twins, and he figured it'd be a long time before Addie would want to let them out of her sight.

Especially since Yvette was still at large.

That's why some serious precautions had been taken, including posting a deputy with Nan Fredrick in case Yvette returned to try to get the twins from her. That probably wouldn't happen, since Yvette would likely assume that Nan had called the cops. Still, Yvette might be desperate enough to take the risk and return to the spot where she'd handed off Lily and Rose to the woman.

Another precaution was Judson had already decided that he'd be spending the rest of the day and the night at the Horseshoe Ranch. Because he, too, intended to keep an eye on Lily and Rose. Also on Addie and Etta Jean. It was just too risky to leave them alone, and despite Addie's now fairly calm demeanor, she was no doubt still going through an emotional upheaval.

Still, they'd gotten damn lucky. The twins had not only been found, but they'd also both gotten two thumbs-up from the pediatrician who'd examined them and said there wasn't a scratch or a mark on them. Getting that exam, and the clean bills of health, had required a trip to the hospital before Addie and he had finally been able to bring the girls back to the foster home shortly after noon.

As Judson had expected, Addie and Etta Jean continued to stay by the bassinets even though the babies were now sleeping after being fed, changed, burped and rocked to sleep. The last part of that hadn't taken long, since the girls had drifted right off despite having their routines, and their safety, shot to hell and back.

Judson had to tamp down his fury over what Yvette had done to them. Yes, the babies were safe and they hadn't been harmed, but any number of bad things could have happened, and Judson intended to make Yvette pay for what she had put them all through.

After several more minutes, Addie finally turned away from the bassinet, automatically reaching for the baby monitor that had been moved into the den along with other baby supplies. Then she shifted to look at Judson, their gazes connecting and holding.

Normally, when Addie and he had that kind of eye contact, he could see the heat there. The old chemistry between them. It'd been around for a long time, since they were teenagers, and more than once they'd given in to that lust and had kissed.

Later on, those kisses had escalated, and they'd landed in

bed a couple of times, but afterward, something had always pulled them apart. First, it'd been his stint in the military, and when he'd come home to sign on as a Renegade Canyon deputy, it'd been her brief engagement to another guy. After that particular relationship ended, the pulling apart had been instigated by them having to deal with Mellie's murder.

With Addie and him, it had always felt as if they were star-crossed, always something preventing them from even attempting something more than the occasional sex. That didn't stop the heat from coming, though. It was there, right now, but there was also something else. Judson could see the exhaustion and the worry etched all over Addie's face.

She went to him and walked straight into his arms. Definitely not something she usually did because of that attraction. But there was nothing normal about this day, about this moment.

Judson pulled her to him and hoped it helped. He hated seeing Addie eaten up like this.

"I know I need to give a statement to one of the deputies," she muttered. "But I don't want to go into the police station. I don't think Etta Jean does, either."

Both Etta Jean and Judson made a sound of agreement. "Grace said you could tell me the broad strokes of what happened," he let them both know, "but the official statement can wait until tomorrow now that the babies have been found."

Addie relaxed a little, but he still felt a lot of tension in her body.

"I'll stay in here with the babies if you two need to talk," Etta Jean offered. She seemed to relax some as well. "Then I can give you my statement. You can watch the twins on the monitor," she added to Addie.

Until Etta Jean said that last part, Addie seemed to be

digging in her heels, ready to insist that she was staying put. But the conversation Judson and she needed to have would be emotional. Addie would likely cry, and he would almost certainly continue to get calls and texts about updates on the search for Yvette. All that chatter and noise could end up waking the babies before their naps were done.

"All right," Addie finally agreed.

Judson muttered a thanks to Etta Jean and eased back from Addie so he could take hold of her arm and lead her out of the den. Addie kept a firm grip on the monitor and pinned her attention to the screen as he took her up across the hall and into the living room.

"We don't have to talk in there," Addie said when she realized what direction they were going. "It's not a good place for you."

It wasn't. In fact, it held some hellish memories of where his unstable druggie mother had dumped him when he'd been just seven years old. Plenty old enough to catalog memories that no seven-year-old should have. Of the ugly names she'd called him. Of the rage that had twisted her face. That and the drugs had made her look like some kind of monster straight out of the fairy tales.

And she had indeed been a monster.

That'd been the reason Judson was removed from her custody, and her rage hadn't been because he was being placed in care but because she would no longer get the monthly payments from his late father's Social Security. Without the kid, she didn't have the money to feed her drug habit.

Thankfully, though, Frank and Mellie had quickly gotten the monster out of the house, so that had minimized the memories. Still, they were there, lurking around like ghosts, and it was the reason he usually avoided this room. Not today, though.

"The living room's close to the twins," he reminded her. And he would endure lots of ghosts, monsters and memories to give Addie the peace that'd come from only being steps away from the babies.

He had her sit on the sofa so he could take the spot right next to her. Judson also didn't want to be too far away from her when the tears started again.

And he didn't have to wait long for that.

They came right away, accompanied by a sob that tore from Addie's throat. He pulled her into his arms again and just let her cry it out.

"This is all my fault," she said in between the sobs. "I didn't lock the door, and I was distracted."

"Not your fault," he insisted right back. "An unlocked door isn't an invitation for Yvette to come in and take the twins."

It was true, but he doubted Addie would believe it. No. She would continue to blame herself when the blame sat solely with the woman who'd abducted Lily and Rose.

"When you can, tell me what was happening right before you realized the twins were missing," Judson said, keeping his voice calm despite the tornado of emotions whirling inside him. It was hell watching Addie go through this.

"I had just fed and put them down for a nap," she started after wiping away some of the tears. "It was my first time doing it solo. Usually, Etta Jean and I each take one. But I wanted to do it by myself just to make sure I could. That way, it'll free Etta Jean up to do other things, and with twins, there's a lot that needs to be done. Laundry, sterilizing bottles and such."

"And afterward?" he prompted when her voice cracked. "What happened after you put the twins down for their nap?"

"Uh, after I made sure Lily and Rose were asleep, I took the monitor and stepped outside to get the mail. As I was coming back into the house, I got that text from the parole board to let me know Rowena was out of jail. I was upset," she added to that, and he knew that was a huge understatement. It had likely shaken her to the core. "I wanted to call the parole board, so I gave the monitor to Etta Jean to watch."

"And she was in the laundry room," Judson said.

Addie nodded. "I should have remembered to lock the front door, and I should have carried the monitor with me," she muttered on a groan.

"But you couldn't have watched the monitor and concentrated on the call you needed to make," Judson reminded her.

Again, Addie didn't seem to buy that, but she continued. "It took me a while to get through to someone, and I finally spoke to the head of the parole board, who told me that Rowena had been released for medical reasons. She apparently has cancer."

Prison officials sometimes did that, arranged an early release for an inmate with a terminal condition. But Judson would be looking deeper into Rowena's specific case. Rowena had been in jail for murdering Addie's mother, and even though that had been over three decades ago, it wasn't nearly enough time to serve for taking a life.

And putting Addie through hell and back.

As far as Judson was concerned, Rowena should have lived out her last days in prison. But the parole board obviously didn't agree. Judson knew that because he'd made some calls shortly after they'd gotten the babies back to the ranch, and he had been able to confirm that Rowena did indeed have pancreatic cancer, and her prognosis wasn't good. Supposedly, she had less than six months to live.

Judson had also been able to confirm something else: Rowena hadn't been anywhere near the ranch at the time the twins had been taken. She had been at a clinic in San Antonio, nearly an hour's drive away.

The sound of a car engine caused Judson's attention to shift to the windows, and he saw Livvy pull the cruiser to a stop in front of the house. He immediately got to his feet, hoping this was good news. Hoping that they'd found Yvette and had arrested the woman.

But then Judson saw that Livvy wasn't alone.

There was a tall, lanky, dark-haired man with her, and Judson recognized him from the photo that he'd pulled up when they'd been searching for the babies.

This was Shane, Yvette's son.

Good. Despite his sister's concern, Shane seemed unharmed, and he might be able to give them answers as to the whereabouts of his mother.

Judson went to the door to let them in, and he immediately looked at Livvy for an explanation for the visit.

"Shane, this is Deputy Judson Docherty," Livvy said. "And Addie Jansen," she added when Addie stepped up behind Judson. "After Shane heard about the APB on his mother, he came into the station."

"Pleased to meet you," Shane said, not actually looking at Addie and him but at the house. His gaze was sweeping over it, taking it all in. "Wish it were under different circumstances."

"Where's your mother?" Judson asked, well aware that he sounded abrupt. But the sooner they caught Yvette, the better, and he didn't want to waste time on small talk.

Shane sighed, shook his head and finally turned his gaze toward Addie and him. "I don't know where my mom is, but we need to find her." He opened his mouth, closed it and seemed to rethink what he'd been about to say. "We should probably sit down and talk."

Judson agreed, and he stepped back for him to enter, but Shane paused in the doorway, glancing around the foyer. "So, this is where CPS brought Jennifer and me when we were babies?"

"Yes," Addie murmured.

"I thought I might feel something. Some sense of recognition. But I don't." Shane shrugged. "I was just a baby, and I guess we didn't stay long. Just a couple of months before we were adopted."

That meshed with what Judson had read in the files that he'd managed to access while Lily and Rose were being examined at the hospital.

"You never came back here, just to have a look around?" Judson asked, and then he went with the question he actually wanted answered. "Maybe you came with Yvette?"

Something flashed through Shane's cool blue eyes. "No," he said. He didn't add anything else until they were in the living room, and then he turned to face them. "And I'm not sure my mother has been here recently, either."

Livvy didn't seem surprised by the comment, which meant Shane had likely already discussed this with her.

"I have a photograph of your mother's car fleeing the scene," Judson was quick to point out. "And the woman she left the babies with ID'd Yvette from a photo the cops showed her."

Shane nodded, slipped his hands into the pockets of his khakis. "My mother is a wonderful, loving, trusting woman," he said.

That didn't mesh with the info in the files. "She had a record, and she lost custody of you and your sister as kids," Judson argued.

"She did, but all her problems were caused by alcohol and drug abuse. Once she got sober, we reconnected, and I forgave her for what happened. And I love her," he tacked on to that.

That confession made Judson wonder if Shane was looking at this through rose-colored glasses. Maybe he wasn't able to see his mother's faults. Judson had gotten a totally different vibe about Yvette from Jennifer.

"You love her," Judson repeated. "Yet your sister was worried that Yvette had done something to you."

Shane rolled his eyes. "Jennifer always thinks the worst of our mother. Apparently, so do you, if you believe she stole those babies."

"If she didn't take them, then who did?" Judson demanded, wanting to hear this theory.

"Her husband, Trevor Cates," Shane supplied. He said both the title and the name as if they were the deadliest kind of venom.

"Husband?" Judson challenged. "There was nothing in Yvette's records about her being married."

"Because she married the son of a bitch just two weeks ago," Shane spat out. "Trevor, or Trev as she calls him, is a low-life gold digger who Mom met in rehab. My mother had just received a huge settlement that she got for being injured on the job, and I believe Trevor married her so he could get his hands on it. And I also think he might have taken the babies to try to set her up so that she'd be either arrested or killed."

Judson took a moment to process what Shane was saying, and looked at Livvy to get her take on it. "I ran a background check on Trevor," she said. "He's got a record for DUI and extortion, but there are no red flags to indicate he'd arrange a double kidnapping."

"He did it," Shane insisted. "I think Trevor coerced my mother into coming here. Maybe even used drugs or booze. He could have taken the babies and then fled with Mom and them."

"The witness didn't see anyone else in the car with your mother," Judson let him know.

Shane had a quick answer for that. "Trevor could have been hiding in the back seat. Or by then he could have had Mom drop him off somewhere."

Judson had to at least admit that those were possibilities. After all, he'd thought he had seen that shadow or something, but there was no proof that anyone else had been with Yvette.

"There has to be an easier way for Trevor to get his hands on your mother's money," Judson reminded Shane.

"Well, he can't outright kill her, because then he wouldn't be able to profit from his crime. I'm in law school," Shane added. "Trevor could also have triggered a relapse, something to send my mother over the edge, but he wouldn't necessarily get the money if she was back in rehab." He paused again, his forehead bunching up. "I think Trevor hoped the cops would kill her and then he'd be her beneficiary."

"Do you have any evidence whatsoever that would back up any of this?" Judson asked.

Shane sighed again and shook his head. "But I know in my gut that he's bad news and wants her dead. That's where I've been all morning, out looking for her. I wanted to find her and try to convince her to leave Trevor. I need you to talk to him. I need you to force him to tell us where my mom is and what he did to her."

"We'll contact him and see what he has to say," Judson assured him. "Do you have his address?" he added to Livvy.

She nodded. "It's just outside of Bulverde. Grace and

two deputies are on the way there now. They should be there soon."

Good. Maybe they would find Yvette and could arrest her.

"My mother wouldn't have taken those babies without some kind of prodding," Shane insisted. "I'm sorry they were taken, sorry for the hell you must have gone through when they were missing, but my mom's not responsible."

The words had no sooner left his mouth than Judson's phone rang and he saw Deputy Eden Gallagher's name on the screen.

"Excuse me a second," Judson said, stepping out of the room to take the call. "Eden," he greeted when he was out of earshot. "Please tell me you found Yvette."

"Not Yvette, but there's a lot of blood," Eden replied. "And a big, bloody butcher knife. From what I can see, someone could have been seriously injured or even murdered here."

"But no body?" Judson pressed.

"No, no body, but the place isn't empty. There's someone here who might be able to give us answers." Eden paused. "Her daughter, Jennifer. FYI, Jennifer has blood on her hands, and she was holding the knife when we found her."

Chapter Four

Addie tried to focus just on taking care of the babies and not on the phone conversation that Judson had relayed to her a half hour earlier. But it was impossible for her to shove aside such important details.

Neither the Renegade Canyon PD nor the county sheriff's office had found Yvette's body. Or Yvette herself, if she was indeed alive. But they had found lots of blood at the woman's house. And since they had also found Yvette's daughter there as well, they were bringing her in for questioning.

Had Jennifer murdered her mother when she'd discovered that she'd abducted Lily and Rose? If so, then where was the body? Hopefully Jennifer would confess to that during interrogation, because as long as there was no concrete proof that Yvette was dead, the twins were still at risk. Yvette could return to the Horseshoe Ranch and try to take them again.

Of course, Addie wouldn't let that happen now that she was aware of the possible risk. Neither would Judson. He had stayed with her throughout this horrific ordeal, and he showed no signs of leaving.

Addie was beyond thankful for that. She wanted all the protection she could get for the babies. But as usual, whenever she was around Judson, part of her brain always shifted to the attraction between them. It was always there, a not-so-gentle tug in her body that just wouldn't go away. Well, not until her brain shifted to something else.

To their pasts.

Specifically, to conversations they'd had as teenagers.

They'd made a pact of sorts that they wouldn't have families of their own because of the brutality of their own nightmarish childhoods. Instead, they had agreed to focus on helping other troubled families and kids. It was the reason she became a foster parent and Judson had become a cop.

Addie didn't think either of them was anywhere near ready to ditch that pact and risk the fallout from those memories. Because, simply put, it was still too hard to deal with their pasts and keep up with the good things they hoped to accomplish in their lives.

The sound of footsteps yanked her out of her thoughts. Footsteps that she recognized before Judson even appeared in the doorway of her bedroom. Only fifteen minutes earlier, they'd moved the bassinets and some of the babies' things in here. With the CSIs still in the house, the cops coming and going, and the stream of phone calls and texts, Addie had wanted a quieter space for the twins. At six weeks old, Lily and Rose had endured enough upheavals and disruptions to last them a lifetime, and she wanted to eliminate more if possible.

Judson looked at the baby she was holding, then at the other infant, Lily, who was already asleep in the bassinet. Rose was asleep as well, and since both girls had already been fed and changed, they might nap for another hour or two. But Addie had wanted to hold the baby for a while longer. Correction: She needed to. And she would need to do the same with Lily after her next feeding.

For now, though, Addie could tell that Judson had something to tell her, so she eased Rose into her bassinet. She picked up the baby monitor even though she wasn't planning on going far. *Better safe than sorry* was her new motto. And she stepped into the hall with Judson.

"Did they find Yvette?" Addie whispered immediately.

He was equally quick in giving a response. Judson shook his head. "But there are still two teams out searching the area, and a sample of the blood has been taken to the lab. Both Yvette's and Trevor's DNA samples are on file, because they have criminal records."

"Trevor," she repeated on a heavy sigh.

Addie certainly hadn't forgotten about Yvette's husband, but she hadn't considered that the blood might be his. It could be, though, since after all, it was his house. The man wasn't responding to any attempts to contact him, so he was essentially missing. But did that mean Yvette or Jennifer had killed him? That was possible, but Addie was hoping the blood belonged to the woman who was the threat to the babies—Yvette.

"Has Jennifer made it to the police station yet, and has she said anything?" Addie asked.

Another shake of his head. "Eden texted that Jennifer seems to be in shock and just keeps muttering her mom's name. So Jennifer will need to be examined by a doctor before she can be questioned. They're at the hospital."

Addie groaned. She knew that couldn't be helped, that the cops had to follow the letter of the law on this, but an exam could delay Jennifer's interview. That meant a delay in getting the answers they needed.

Lily stirred a little, causing both of them to hurry back into the room. But the baby didn't wake. After squirming around, she smiled and then settled.

"They're both beautiful babies," Judson muttered, "but they're even more beautiful when they smile."

Addie didn't tell him that it was probably a reaction to gas. Or that's what some experts thought, anyway. But she chose to believe it was the real deal and that it meant Lily was happy and content being home.

"Home," she heard herself whisper.

She hadn't intended to say that aloud, but it was a word she'd been giving a lot of thought to since the twins had arrived. So, Addie went with the rest of what had been on her mind before Yvette had come into the picture.

"I want to adopt them," she admitted.

Judson tore his gaze from the baby and looked at her. She saw the surprise in his eyes, which was the exact reaction she'd expected. She had worked at the Horseshoe Ranch for nearly a decade, and before that, Addie had been a social worker assisting couples who fostered. Not once during all those years had she considered adopting a baby.

Since she'd already given this plenty of thought, Addie figured that her quickly approaching thirty-fifth birthday was playing into her decision. She wasn't past the point of having her own biological children, but she also didn't want to wait much longer. But the biggest player in the decision was Mellie's murder. Life had suddenly felt way too short for Addie not to latch on to what she wanted.

"Uh, can you adopt them?" Judson asked.

"Legally, yes. No next of kin has stepped up to claim them, so eventually they'd be put up for adoption."

Of course, there would be plenty of people—couples— who would want them. And there might be a mark against her since the babies had been kidnapped while under her care. Addie prayed that wasn't the case, but she had to accept that it could play out that way.

"I'm not saying I want to adopt them because of nearly losing them," Addie went on. "I'd been giving it some thought since Lily and Rose were placed here." She paused. "You're thinking about that pact we made about never having our own families."

Judson shifted toward her, studying her, and made a sound of agreement. "I was also thinking you'd be a great mother."

That warmed her from head to toe. She hadn't realized how important it was for her to hear that from Judson. But it was.

"And that pact was made when we were hardly more than kids," Judson tacked on to that.

True, but it had made sense at the time. They had needed to focus on healing. On helping others. They still needed to do both of those things, but Addie felt she could do that while also being a mother to Lily and Rose.

"If you do adopt them, what will happen to the Horseshoe Ranch?" he added a moment later as he gently brushed his fingers over Lily's blond baby curls.

"I'll keep it going." That would mean hiring some extra help, but Addie was okay with that. "Mellie left me the ranch in her will, so legally it's mine, and this place is her legacy."

But there was one other important factor. The Horseshoe Ranch was her home, and it wouldn't feel like a real home without children around.

Addie's phone buzzed, and she stepped away from the bassinet and into the hall again. As she expected, Judson went with her, and both of them frowned when they saw Unknown Caller on her screen. Normally, calls like that were spam, but it occurred to her that this could be someone connected to the investigation.

She answered it, putting it on speaker, but she didn't even say any kind of greeting. She just waited to see what the caller would say.

"Addie?" the woman asked.

Even though it'd been a very long time since she had

heard that voice, Addie instantly recognized it, and her heartbeat and her breathing thundered into overdrive. Because the voice belonged to the woman who'd kidnapped her and murdered her mother.

Rowena.

Oh, the memories came. Of course, they did. Impossible not to think of, or in this case hear, Rowena and not recall the horrible things she'd done. Some Addie had only read about. Others she had experienced firsthand.

Both before and after the abduction.

For a woman who had seemingly wanted a child badly enough to kill, Rowena hadn't known how to deal with motherhood. There had been lots of screaming at Addie. Cursing her. Belittling her.

And even more.

In those final months, Rowena had ended up pulling Addie from school and keeping her in a locked room. That had been the woman's downfall, because the school and neighbors had spoken up about not having seen Addie, and that in turn had launched an investigation, which, in turn, uncovered Rowena's crimes.

"How did you get my number?" Addie snapped.

Even though she felt plenty unnerved, she flat-out refused to let that show in her voice. Thankfully, she had enough anger as well, and she did let that come through.

Rowena sighed. "A friend got it for me."

"A friend," Addie repeated, and it came out in a snarl. "You mean someone you met in prison."

"Yes, please don't be mad at her," Rowena said. "I told her I needed to speak to you and try to make peace with you before... I, uh... I'm dying, Addie. I only have a few weeks to live."

"You can't make peace with me *ever*," Addie let her know

and didn't give Rowena a chance to respond. She hit End Call and immediately blocked the number.

Now, she let out the emotions. The stormy mix of anger and the bitter memories. Suddenly, her legs felt way too shaky, and Judson must have noticed that, because he hooked his arm around her waist and pulled her to him.

She felt the instant relief go through her body. Felt his strength, too. And while this closeness might come back to haunt them, Addie gave in to it and sagged against him.

"I can get a no-contact restraining order," Judson murmured against her ear. "Or I can have the local cops go have a word with Rowena and tell her to back the hell off."

There was a firestorm of emotions in his voice, too, and again he was trying to protect her. That only fueled the closeness. Barriers that had always stood steady between them were coming down fast, and she wasn't going to try to stop it. Addie just stood there, taking every bit of the comfort he was giving her.

"It's okay," Addie let him know. "The blocked number should take care of her trying to contact me again."

She hoped so, anyway, and she made a mental note to find out if Rowena was well enough to attempt a visit to the Horseshoe. One thing was for certain: Addie wouldn't be emotionally blackmailed into seeing the woman.

"I don't need closure with Rowena," she spelled out to Judson. "I shut her out of my life when I was six, and I'm not letting her back in."

"Good. Because I remember all those times she'd manage to call you or sneak a letter to you when you were a kid. It always ripped you apart."

It had, and Rowena had managed to do that three times before Mellie had made a trip to the prison and threatened the powers that be with legal action if they didn't stop the woman from contacting Addie in any way.

There had been no more letters or calls after that.

Until now, that is. And Addie refused to let even a sliver of Rowena climb back into her life.

Addie jolted when she heard the soft buzzing of a phone. Not hers this time, but Judson's, and it wasn't from an unknown caller but rather Livvy. Even though Addie was still feeling plenty shaky, she welcomed it, since this could be good news.

As Addie had done with her call from Rowena, Judson answered it, put it on speaker and alerted Livvy that she was listening in. However, he kept his attention pinned to Addie, no doubt checking to make sure she was okay.

She wasn't. Not yet.

But she was getting there. Every second that she spent being shaken up seemed like a victory for Rowena, and Addie didn't want to let the woman win.

"Just wanted to give you some updates," Livvy started the moment she was on the line. "Jennifer's being examined, and she seems to be coming out of the shock. She says she wants to give a statement. All we have to do now is wait for the okay from the doctor and we can take her to the station."

"Did she say if she killed her mother?" Judson asked, taking the question right out of Addie's mouth.

"No, and we advised her not to say anything about that, not until she was medically cleared," Livvy explained. "We didn't want a confession to be inadmissible if it turned out she wasn't declared competent to understand her rights."

Of course, that made sense, but it was still hard to wait. When Jennifer finally was able to be interviewed, maybe she would also spill about the location of Yvette's body.

"Will the two of you be coming into the station to observe Jennifer's interview?" Livvy asked.

Until Livvy mentioned that, Addie hadn't considered it. But she knew it was something she wanted to do. She wanted to hear firsthand what the woman had to say and maybe even speak to her afterward.

But Addie rethought that when she glanced at the babies. So did Judson, and she saw the concern on his face. She also figured he was champing at the bit to hear that interview.

"I don't want to risk leaving the twins," Addie muttered.

"Understood," Livvy was quick to say. "And I spoke to Grace about that. If Judson and you want to be here, Grace can send two deputies to the Horseshoe to do protective duty while you're away. Before you answer, I'll sweeten the offer by letting you know that you'll also likely be able to observe an interview with Shane."

"Shane?" Judson questioned. "Why are you bringing him back?"

"That's the next thing I need to tell you. I got a call about him," Livvy explained. "Remember when Shane said he'd never been to the Horseshoe as an adult? Well, that was a lie. Or a partial lie, anyway. He might not have actually gone there, but he was damn close. Holly Dennison was on her way into town and spotted a car turning on to the ranch road. A man in a small white car. Shane owns a white Ford Focus."

Addie knew Holly well since hers was the closest ranch to the Horseshoe. Holly was also observant, so Addie didn't doubt the validity of what the woman had seen. But why had Shane been here?

And better yet, why had he lied about it?

"Holly said she didn't think anything of it at the time," Livvy went on. "She thought it might be someone visiting a foster kid, but after the Amber Alert and APB were issued, the news media ran Yvette's pictures. One of them put up a photo of Yvette and her kids, and Holly recognized Shane as the man she saw taking the turn to the Horseshoe."

"When did she see him?" Judson pressed.

"Holly estimates that it was around nine this morning. That would have been before the twins were snatched. Yeah," Livvy muttered, no doubt anticipating the questions Judson and Addie had about that. "Trust me, I'll be asking Shane about that when he comes in for an interview. Not sure exactly when that'll be. He didn't answer when I tried to call him, but I left a voicemail and told him to come into the station right away."

Good. Because if Shane had played any part in the abduction, Addie wanted him to pay and pay hard for his actions.

"Hold a sec," Livvy said. "I have an incoming call from the lab."

Livvy put them on hold, giving Addie some time to think. Judson was obviously doing that, too, but neither one of them had much thinking time, because it was less than a minute before Livvy came back on the line.

"Well," Livvy said on a heavy sigh. "We've got a problem." And she continued after both Addie and Judson groaned. "The blood found in Trevor and Yvette's house doesn't belong to either of them."

"What?" Addie blurted. "Then whose is it?"

Livvy sighed again. "We're not sure. But according to the ME, there was enough to conclude that whoever's blood it is, that person is almost certainly dead. Now we need to find out who was probably murdered in that house."

Chapter Five

Judson watched as Addie gave each of the babies a kiss on the cheek, and while he figured she was trying to keep her nerves in check, he could tell she was worried about leaving them.

So was he.

With Yvette at large, Trevor missing and a possible unidentified dead body, there were a lot of moving parts in this investigation. But Judson was hoping that Jennifer and Shane would be able to fill in enough blanks for Renegade Canyon PD to figure out what the hell was going on.

"The twins will be safe," Judson heard Addie mutter, trying to reassure herself.

Judson couldn't promise Addie that nothing bad would happen—even if they stayed by the babies' sides. But he could promise that his fellow deputies Rory McClennan and Bennie Whitt would protect the girls with their lives. Added to that, Rory's brother, a wealthy rancher, had sent over two of his ranch hands, who would patrol the grounds.

Again, it wasn't foolproof, but everything was in place to make the situation as safe as possible.

"I won't leave this room even for a second while you're gone," Etta Jean promised Addie. She was standing by the bassinets, and she had a fierce, determined look on her face.

"Go," the woman added. "Help them find Yvette so we can put all this behind us."

Judson hoped both things were possible. Finding Yvette was key, and then the healing could start. Still, it was going to be a long, long time before Addie would be able to stop looking over her shoulder for a possible threat.

He hated that. Hated that someone had shattered the peace and calm that Addie had worked so hard to find after Mellie's murder. She'd get that peace and calm back. And she'd find her new routine. But at the moment, it probably didn't feel like that.

Addie gave the girls yet another kiss, and she finally stepped away from the bassinets, turning toward him. Their gazes locked for a couple of moments. He didn't voice any reassurances or make any promises about the babies' safety. No need. Addie knew him through and through, and she was already aware that he had every possible precaution in place.

Including the cruiser parked out front.

Rory and Bennie had arrived in it just minutes earlier, and Addie and he would be using it to drive the short distance to the police station. The cruiser was bullet resistant, and even though Yvette hadn't fired any shots during the abduction, Judson had wanted the extra protection in place for Addie in case the woman came back for round two.

Judson's phone sounded with a text from Livvy, and he relayed the message to Addie. "Jennifer has just arrived at the station, and Shane is on his way."

Addie nodded, giving the babies one last look before she went to Judson. She added a thanks to both Rory and Bennie, who were already standing by to take up protection duty. Since both deputies had kids of their own and were experienced lawmen, Judson was hoping there wouldn't be any problems.

He didn't give Addie or Etta Jean an estimated time for their return. Too many unknowns there. It would depend on what Jennifer and Shane had to say in their respective interviews.

Or didn't say.

But if either of them were trying to hold on to their secrets, then maybe Grace and Livvy would get them to confess.

When they reached the front door, Judson used the keypad to unlock the cruiser, and moving fast, he got Addie outside and into the front seat. Best not to be in the open or on the roads any longer than necessary, so he pushed past the speed limit when they reached the highway.

Addie's phone rang, and he heard her sharp intake of breath. Probably because she thought it might be Rowena, but her shoulders relaxed when she saw the caller's ID. What she didn't do was take the call. She let it go to voicemail.

"It's my attorney who's handling the adoption," she let him know. "I'll need to talk to her, but not now. I'll call her back once the interviews are over and I'm home."

That made sense to him. Hard to focus on a phone conversation when watching to make sure someone wasn't about to shoot you.

"I didn't realize you'd already gotten a lawyer," Judson commented.

She made a sound of agreement and looked at him. "Does that bother you, that I want to do this?"

"No," he couldn't say fast enough. "Like I told you earlier, you'll make a great mom."

"Do I hear a *but* in there?" she came out and asked.

"No." Again, he said it fast. "You've got a lot on your plate right now, and I'm guessing the twins are like the bright lights waiting for you at the end of this ordeal."

She smiled, and it was good to see. Too bad it didn't last, because as Judson pulled in front of the police station, the smile went south.

"Move fast," Judson reminded her.

As he'd done back at the ranch, he hurried her inside to the chaos that went along with such a high-profile case. There were three different phone conversations going on from deputies in the bullpen. Another was going on in the sheriff's office. And another still at the receptionist's desk. A printer was chugging out something and making plenty of noise while doing it.

Despite all the noise and activity, Judson had no problem tuning it out and tuning in to the conversation taking place between Livvy and Shane.

"I didn't go to that damn ranch," Shane spat out, and he must have been alerted to Judson and Addie's arrival, because he shifted in their direction and repeated what he'd just said. This time, though, he added some more profanity.

"Deputy Walsh here is accusing me of lying and God knows what else," Shane went on, clearly in rant mode. "She thinks I kidnapped those kids. Well, I didn't."

Livvy looked as if ready to roll her eyes, but instead she motioned for Shane to follow her toward the interview rooms. She added a nod for Judson and Addie to come as well.

The change of location didn't cause Shane to hush. He just continued with his anger-filled tirade. "I was looking for my mother. That's why I was near that place. I turned in to the road, and when I didn't see her car, I made a U-turn and went looking for her elsewhere."

"I've already Mirandized him," Livvy said over her shoulder to Addie and Judson. "So he knows he has a right to have a lawyer and the right to stay silent. He's definitely

not staying silent and has said he'll call in an attorney if
and when he damn well pleases."

Livvy sounded more than a little satisfied about that not
staying silent part despite the tongue-lashing Shane was
giving her. And Judson understood why: Chatty suspects
often spilled a lot more than they planned.

But the question was—did Shane have something ille-
gal to spill?

Earlier at the ranch, Shane had admitted he'd been out
looking for his mother, so that could explain why he was
in or near Renegade Canyon. Another explanation, though,
could be that he'd been there to assist his mother in committing a felony. Or to try to clean up after the one she'd
already committed.

With Judson and Addie right behind them, Livvy led
Shane to the second interview room. The door to the first
one was closed, and Judson was betting that's where they
had Jennifer waiting. Shane didn't go into the room, though.
He whirled around to face the three of them.

"Look, all this is nonsense and a complete waste of your
time and mine," Shane went on.

Neither Judson nor Livvy asked any questions, since any
answers the man might give right now could perhaps be
challenged later by his lawyer. But if it was info that Shane
volunteered, even after being Mirandized, then it could turn
out to be something the cops could use to prosecute him.

Shane huffed and folded his arms over his chest. "I was in
that area because Mom talks about it a lot. She went through
hell when CPS took Jennifer and me away from her. She
was always going on about the Horseshoe Ranch and how
the woman there, the manager, wouldn't let her see us kids."

The manager, Mellie, would have needed permission
from the courts for a visit like that to happen, so Mellie

had just been following the law. Along with protecting the children.

"Mom's been talking even more about that ranch lately," Shane continued. "I'm not sure why." He stopped, and some of the anger seemed to fade from his face. Either that or he was putting on an act. "Mom hasn't been herself since she hooked up with Trevor," he said in a barely audible mumble. "And I just didn't want her to do anything stupid, something she'd regret."

Judson didn't spell out that the evidence did point to Yvette kidnapping the twins. That wasn't in question since the farmer Nan Fredrick had seen Yvette with Lily and Rose. The big question now was had Yvette had an accomplice, and was that accomplice the man standing in front of them right now?

Shane seemed to stay in deep thought for several moments, and then he huffed as if frustrated that they weren't responding. "I'll call my lawyer after all," he snapped, going into the room and shutting the door behind him.

"You believe what he just said?" Addie asked, volleying glances at both Livvy and him.

Judson had to shrug. "It's possible that Yvette did talk about the Horseshoe, but why would Shane search that area? Why not go to his adoptive parents' house? Or his sister's? I'm sure Yvette talked about them, too."

"I'm hoping I'll find that out once his attorney shows," Livvy said, and then she motioned toward interview room one. "Jennifer hasn't lawyered up, so we'll be able to start with her…now," she amended when they heard the sound of footsteps and saw Grace making her way to them.

One look at his boss's face, though, and Judson knew she wasn't solely here for the interviews, that she had some news for them. And that the news wasn't good.

Grace launched right into that news. "I just got off the phone with the lab guys, and they ID'd the blood found in Trevor Cateses' house. It belongs to a social worker, Courtney Mora."

Addie gasped, and with her eyes wide, she snapped toward Judson. She obviously remembered that was the woman who'd called them earlier when they were searching for Yvette and the twins.

"She's the person who told us that Yvette was probably the one who'd taken the babies," Addie said.

Grace nodded. "Yes, I read that in Judson's preliminary report. I'm getting her phone records, but can you tell me where Miss Mora was when she made that call to you?"

Judson mentally went back through the conversation and had to shake his head. "She didn't say, and she sure as hell didn't mention she was on her way to the Cateses' house."

"She didn't say anything about that to anyone in her office, either," Grace replied. "In fact, she didn't show up for work today, and her boss was getting concerned. It was definitely out of the norm for her."

Hell. She must have taken it on herself to go to the house, looking for Yvette, and then…what? Yvette had killed her and left the knife behind for Jennifer to find and pick up?

Maybe.

Courtney had mentioned that Yvette hated her and had tried to ruin her life because she had been the social worker who'd removed Yvette's kids and placed them in foster care. So, maybe Yvette had returned from her canceled kidnapping plot to find a woman she hated in her home. But if that's what had happened, then where the heck was the body?

And where were Yvette and Trevor?

"What about Courtney's vehicle?" Addie asked. "Was it at the Cateses' house?"

"No," Grace answered. "There were no vehicles in the garage, and the one in front of the house belongs to Jennifer."

Then, that was another question that needed to be answered. It was possible someone had dropped Courtney off, or, heck, maybe she had even managed to get an Uber or a taxi to take her that far. But if she'd taken those particular forms of transportation, there should be a record of it.

"Along with finding the blood and Jennifer at the Cateses' house," Grace went on several seconds later, "the CSIs also found some drugs. Rohypnol and Valium."

"That's a strange combination." Judson shook his head. "The date rape drug and anxiety meds. Any idea who was taking them? Or who was giving them to someone else?"

"Don't have a clue yet, but they were in the nightstand drawer of the main bedroom, so the CSIs might be able to determine through prints who used that drawer the most. Or whose prints are on the actual plastic bags that contained them." Grace checked her watch. "It's going to take an hour or two to get those phone records or any other info from the CSIs and ME. Let's get moving with interviewing Jennifer so you two can get back to the Horseshoe. How are the twins doing, by the way?"

"They're fine," Addie assured her. "They don't seem to be experiencing any kind of trauma."

They weren't, and Judson hoped it stayed that way. He had no idea what babies that young could experience, but he hoped they never sensed or remembered any part of that ordeal.

"The Bulverde cops are on the way to Miss Mora's next of kin to tell them about the blood that was found," Grace went on. "So, I don't want to specifically mention the social worker by name until I'm certain her family knows. But I do intend to bring her up in a roundabout way to Jennifer, just to see what she has to say." She paused. "Because it's possible Jennifer killed her, and I want to know why."

It was indeed possible, since Jennifer had been found at the scene with a knife and blood on her hands. And Jennifer might have had motive to commit that murder if she also blamed Courtney for Shane and her being taken from Yvette's custody. The one problem with the theory was that during their earlier phone conversation with Jennifer, the only animosity she'd shown was toward Yvette. So why would she be so upset about being removed from her home all those years ago?

"Does Jennifer know her brother is here?" Judson asked.

Grace shook her head. "I don't want the two of them speaking until after their interviews. She has asked for him," Grace added. "For her boyfriend, too."

"Elijah Banks," Livvy provided. "He's a personal trainer at a gym in San Antonio, and an amateur boxer. We're trying to get in touch with him now."

Good. Maybe the boyfriend would be able to give them some insight into all of this.

"If Jennifer says something you want me to press her on, just send me a text. I'll see what I can do," Grace told Addie and him, and then she and Livvy went into the interview room.

Judson led Addie to the small area next to interview. It wasn't much bigger than a closet, but it had some chairs and a small table with a laptop. The screen was blank at first, but when Grace engaged recording, the feed from the interview popped up. Judson could see Jennifer pacing. And seemingly ready to jump out of her skin.

"I didn't kill anyone," Jennifer immediately blurted.

Grace motioned for the woman to sit, and Livvy and she took the seats across from her. Judson and Addie sat as well. Side by side. Or rather hip by hip, since that was all the space they had.

"I didn't kill anyone," Jennifer repeated, but again Grace motioned for her to hold off while she recited the case number, time, date and those present.

"Jennifer, Deputy Walsh has already read your Miranda rights, but could you state for the record if you understand them or if you want them repeated?" Grace instructed.

"I understand them and don't need to hear them again." Once more, Jennifer's words were rushed, running together and filled with her heavy breaths. "I just want you to put down in your record that I didn't kill anyone. I was framed."

Grace eased back in her chair. "I'm listening."

Jennifer nodded and seemed to mentally throttle back a little. "I, uh…" she began but then stopped. "I guess I should start with the phone call I got from one of your deputies. Docherty, I think, was his name. He asked where my mother was. I didn't know," she insisted. "But as soon as I got off the phone with him, I started driving out to her house. Or rather, *Trevor's* house."

Judson noted that like Shane, there was some venom in Jennifer's voice when she mentioned the man's name. It made him want to dig harder and deeper to find this Trevor. Then again, he could say the same for Yvette. It was possible the two had fled together and were in hiding.

"Since no one knew where Shane was," Jennifer went on, "I was worried that Yvette had done something to him."

"Like what?" Grace pressed when Jennifer fell silent.

Jennifer sighed and pushed some strands of long blond hair from her face. "I don't know." But it didn't take her but a couple of seconds to amend that. "All right, I thought she'd convinced him to do something that could get him hurt. Shane can be…gullible sometimes. I thought maybe Yvette had talked him into helping her take those babies." She paused again, looked at Grace. "Is that what happened? Did Shane help her?"

As Judson expected, Grace didn't respond to that question. Nor did she mention anything about Shane being seen in the area around the time of the abductions. Instead, Grace flipped through her notes as if checking some kind of details.

"So, you went to the house looking for Shane and Yvette. What happened then?" Grace pressed.

"Not especially looking for Yvette," Jennifer corrected. "But my brother, yes. When I got there, there were no cars in the driveway, and that's where Shane would have parked had he been there. Still, I wanted to check for myself, so I went to knock on the front door. That's when I saw the door was slightly ajar. I eased it open a little more and called out for Shane."

Jennifer stopped, and she pressed her fingers to her mouth. Probably to stop the sob that made it past her lips anyway.

"I saw some blood on the floor," the woman continued. Both she and her voice were now shaking. "Blood on the walls, too. God, it was everywhere," she added on another sob. "I thought it was Shane's, that Yvette had done something to him, so I ran through the house, screaming out his name. No one answered. No one was there. Just all that blood."

"How did the knife get in your hands?" Grace asked.

"I, uh, picked it up," Jennifer admitted. "I thought maybe if it was Shane's blood, then Yvette, or if not her, someone else could be hiding in the house. I wanted to look for them.

Wanted to look for Shane. And that's what I was doing when you and the deputies showed up."

Judson was nowhere near convinced Jennifer was telling the truth. But it was possible Jennifer had killed Courtney because she'd mistaken her for Yvette. Though that felt like a huge stretch. After all, it was broad daylight, so both women would be easy to recognize. Still, it could have happened that way.

Maybe.

But if Jennifer was a killer, then why hadn't she disposed of the knife at the same time she had the body?

"Is Yvette dead?" Jennifer came out and asked. "Was that her blood all over the house?"

"We're looking into that," Grace settled for saying. "Who do you think might have had the motive to do that?"

Jennifer laughed, a single burst of air, but there was no humor in it. "Yvette was a 'recovering' drug addict and alcoholic." She put *recovering* in air quotes. "I'm sure she's made a lot of enemies over the years."

"Including you?" Livvy asked.

"Including me," Jennifer verified. She paused for what seemed like a full minute. "And Shane."

"Shane?" Grace immediately questioned.

Both Judson and Addie moved closer to the monitor. Obviously, neither of them had expected Jennifer to admit that.

Jennifer dragged in a long breath before she said anything else. "Shane didn't want Yvette involved with Trevor. He thought Trevor was only after Yvette's money. I agree with that, by the way. But Yvette couldn't seem to see that, and she refused to have him sign a prenup or try to protect her assets in any kind of way." Another pause. "She and Shane argued about that."

"Did you actually hear any of these arguments, or is this something Shane told you?" Grace asked.

"I heard two phone conversations he had with her. Shane made those calls when he was pleading with her to do the prenup or else sign over half of her estate to him so that he could keep the money safe from Trevor. We're talking nearly a half million dollars," she explained. "But Yvette flat-out refused, and Shane was furious."

"Furious enough to threaten her?" Livvy pressed.

Jennifer didn't jump to deny that, and she finally nodded. "Shane said some harsh things to her. Things she deserved."

Then Grace asked the question that was flashing through Judson's head. "Did he threaten to kill her?"

Jennifer groaned and shook her head, but the headshake didn't seem to be a denial. "Yes. But he didn't mean it," she was quick to add. "I know he didn't."

The woman didn't seem at all convinced of that last part. And neither was Judson. Money was always a powerful motive. But that was a motive for murdering Yvette, not Courtney. Unless…

"If Shane helped his mother set up the twins' abduction, maybe Courtney found out about that," Judson muttered.

Addie's immediate sound of agreement let him know she was thinking the same thing. "Shane and Yvette could have been talking about it, or arguing about it, when Courtney showed up. If she heard something they hadn't wanted her to hear, they might have killed her."

She stopped, her forehead bunching up, and made a sigh of frustration as something else seemed to occur to her.

"It could have played out a different way," Addie concluded. "If Courtney had indeed heard that Shane had had a part in taking the twins, then Jennifer might have wanted to silence her to protect her brother."

Yeah, Judson could see that happening, too. And that meant they were essentially back to square one in this investigation.

"I really need to see Shane now," Jennifer pleaded. "And Elijah. He'll be worried about me."

At the mention of the boyfriend, Judson was reminded they possibly had another key player in this case. One who wasn't responding to attempts to contact him. Was that because he had something to hide? Of course, it could also be that he didn't care enough about Jennifer to want to get caught up in this.

Grace's phone made a sound dinging sound, and when she glanced at the screen, she immediately got to her feet. "Interview paused," Grace said, heading toward the door.

"Sheriff Granger is exiting the room," Livvy added for the benefit of the recording.

Addie and Judson stood, too, and came out of observation just as Grace was stepping into the hall.

"The search team found Courtney in her car about a half mile from the Cateses'," Grace let them know. "She's alive."

"Alive," Addie said through a rush of breath.

"Barely," Grace qualified. "The EMTs are rushing her to the hospital now, and that's where I'm heading. I want her to tell me who left her for dead."

Chapter Six

Addie sat in Grace's office, as Grace had instructed, while Judson worked at her desk. The sheriff was driving to the Bulverde hospital to try to question Courtney.

The waiting was hard, but Judson was making good use of the time while going through reports and doing some paperwork. In fact, all the deputies were doing that, including a reserve cop who Grace had called in to assist with the extra workload.

She imagined that Grace was seriously shorthanded, what with multiple facets of an investigation going on. That's why Addie was thankful Grace had given Judson the time off to do personal protection detail. Addie hated to add to Grace's manpower burdens, but she hated more that the twins wouldn't have someone around who could protect them. The two deputies with them now were a good substitute, temporarily anyway, but Addie didn't trust anyone more than Judson when it came to keeping Lily and Rose safe.

At the thought of the girls, Addie checked her phone again and reread the last text she'd gotten from Etta Jean. It'd come just fifteen minutes earlier, and there'd been one a half hour before that. Addie was thankful for each and every one of the messages, but especially this one, since Etta Jean had included a photo of the babies, sleeping peacefully in their bassinets.

"The CSIs are going over Courtney's car now," Judson relayed, obviously reading from a text update he'd just received. "Her clothes will be processed, too, once the EMTs are able to bag them. It's hard to stab someone and not leave at least a little of your own DNA behind."

Addie hoped that was the case here. Or better yet, she hoped that maybe Courtney herself would be able to give them that info. That was the reason Grace had decided to keep Jennifer in custody a while longer. There wasn't enough evidence to actually arrest her, but that could change in a blink if Courtney named Jennifer as her attacker.

"The CSIs also checked for prints on the two plastic bags of drugs," Judson went on. "There are some smudges and what appear to be paper fibers on the outsides, as if someone tried to wipe the bags clean. Still, the lab might be able to enhance them enough to get a match."

She considered that a moment. The drugs were yet another question mark in an investigation crammed with questions.

"How much access did Jennifer and Shane have to the Cateses' house?" Addie asked.

"Shane was there recently. Jennifer claimed she'd never been there before today." He paused. "You're thinking one of them could have planted the drugs."

She nodded. "Maybe to set Trevor up and make it look as if he was drugging Yvette. Or could they have done that to discredit him in Yvette's eyes?"

"Possibly. Both Jennifer and Shane have made it clear they despise their stepfather. There's no evidence, though, that Yvette was ever given or took the drugs. And by that, I mean no witness statements or tox reports."

That was true, and Addie would have given that more thought as well if the sound of approaching footsteps hadn't caught her attention. She was still on edge enough to get to her feet, ready to defend herself.

A moment later, Livvy stepped into the doorway, and she wasn't alone—Shane and his lawyer were right behind her. Addie recalled the lawyer introducing himself as Ira Covington when he'd arrived at the police station shortly after Grace had left for the hospital.

"Grace texted and said she's decided to reschedule Shane's interview," Livvy let them know.

"The cops have no grounds whatsoever to hold my client," the lawyer piped up, causing Livvy to roll her eyes. Obviously, she was tired of dealing with the attorney's complaints.

"The cops have rescheduled your client's interview for tomorrow morning at eight," Livvy replied, mimicking the same snappy tone as the lawyer's.

"I'd like to see my sister before I leave," Shane said, aiming that request at Judson.

"I've already told him no," Livvy volunteered.

"Then you won't be seeing her." Judson aimed that remark at Shane.

Shane huffed. "But if there's no cause to hold me, the same applies to her. You should have her come back in tomorrow, too. For now, I can take her home so she can get some rest."

"The same doesn't apply," Judson was quick to point out, but he didn't elaborate, holding on to the details of Jennifer being found with a knife in her hand. "And the reason you're not speaking to her is because we don't want her statement skewed by any outside information. It needs to be an accurate account from her perspective of what actually happened."

The lawyer stepped into the doorway, bumping Livvy as if trying to nudge her aside. But Livvy held her ground.

"Are you saying you believe my client and his sister will

fabricate something if they have a simple conversation?" Covington demanded.

Judson gave him a hard stare. "Yes. I'm saying it's possible. And it might not even be intentional or with criminal intent," he added, cutting off what appeared to be the start of a rant from the lawyer. "It's best if Jennifer gives us a clear account of what happened at her mother's house. We don't want her to add or draw conclusions from anything that anyone else says. That includes her brother."

Clearly, neither Covington nor Shane cared much for that answer, but they must have sensed the deputies weren't going to change their minds. The lawyer muttered something about seeing them in the morning and motioned for his client to follow him out of the building.

Because Addie kept her attention on them, she saw the beefy man with sandy-brown hair approach Shane and Covington just outside the door. She couldn't tell what the three were saying, but it was obvious Shane knew this man.

Obvious, too, that the man was furious.

After a short conversation with Shane, the man practically threw open the door to the police station.

"Where the hell is Jennifer?" he snarled.

"That's Elijah Banks, Jennifer's boyfriend," Judson informed Addie. "I recognize him from his DMV photo."

Both Livvy and Judson turned to face the man. Addie moved as well, positioning herself right behind them and looking over their shoulders so she could see Elijah try to storm toward them.

Try but fail.

Deputy Garrison Zimmer blocked him and tipped his head to the metal detector. "Walk through there," Garrison ordered.

Elijah looked ready to argue with that, too, but, muttering obscenities under his breath, he finally went through. And immediately set off the alarms. Garrison drew his gun, and while he didn't actually aim it at Elijah, it caused the young man to thrust his hands in the air.

"There's a sign on the door that reads, 'No firearms or knives allowed on these premises except for law enforcement officers,'" Garrison pointed out. "There's even a picture of a gun with a red line drawn through it."

"I didn't notice it, all right," Elijah snapped. "All I was thinking about was getting in here to see my girlfriend."

"Using just two fingers, remove your weapon and place it there," Garrison instructed, motioning toward a box on the table next to the metal detector.

Elijah glared at him, but did as he was told and produced a small handgun from the back waist of his bulky cargo pants. He put the gun in the box and lowered his other hand.

While Garrison dealt with locking up the gun in the box, Judson walked through the bullpen to reach Elijah.

"We've been trying to reach you for hours," Judson told the man. "Where were you?"

"At work," Elijah said without hesitation. "And then training for a boxing match." He tapped a bruise on his right cheekbone. "I don't answer my phone or check my messages when I'm at the gym or in the ring. Good way to get your face busted. When I finished and listened to the voicemails, I drove straight here. Now, I want to see Jennifer."

"I'm sorry, but Jennifer can't have visitors," Judson informed him. "And Shane probably told you that when you saw him outside."

Elijah cursed. "Shane's a wimp. I figured he didn't press hard enough about that." He rammed his thumb against his chest. "But I will see her."

"You won't." Judson returned the fierce stare the man was giving him. "I can have her contact you after her interview."

Oh, Elijah didn't care for that, and the fury raced through his stormy gray eyes. "Is Jennifer under arrest?" he demanded to know.

"Not at the moment, but she's been detained for questioning," Judson replied.

"Why?" the man insisted. "What is it you think she did?"

"I'm not at liberty to discuss that with you" was Judson's reply.

Elijah cursed some more. "Did that train wreck Yvette have something to do with this? If so, you shouldn't believe a word she says. The woman is a walking, talking bag of... lies," he finally finished, but Addie thought he wanted to use much stronger language to describe her.

That clearly got Judson's attention. "You know Yvette?"

"Of course I know her. She's always trying to worm her way back into Jennifer's life. Always boo-hooing about *forgive me, baby*," he said in a mock-pitiful voice. "As if. That woman has put Jennifer through hell and back over the years."

"What about Trevor?" Judson pushed. "Has he done that, too?"

Elijah had a surprising response. His glare shifted to a smirk. "Trevor's lazy and worthless, and he'll suck every penny out of Yvette. Personally, I hope he does. That'll be exactly what Yvette deserves."

So, maybe that meant Jennifer wasn't concerned about Trevor's possible gold-digging. Unlike Shane, who seemed to want his share of his mother's money.

"Any idea where Yvette and Trevor are?" Judson asked.

"Hell if I know. Last I checked, I wasn't their keeper." He paused again. "Did one of them do something to hurt Jennifer?"

Judson turned the question around on him. "What makes you ask that? Has one of them hurt her before?"

Elijah opened his mouth. Closed it. "I don't know. Let me speak to Jennifer's lawyer," he tacked on to that.

"She doesn't have one," Livvy provided.

"And you're hounding her anyway?" Elijah howled. He started shaking his head. "No, no, no," he strung out. "That's not gonna happen. No more questions until she has a lawyer."

"That's not your call," Judson said.

"We'll see about that," the man snapped, already taking out his phone. He turned and headed back toward Garrison and the metal detector. "I want my gun, and I'll be back when I get Jennifer the legal help she needs."

Once Elijah was on the other side of the metal detector, Garrison picked up the gun, but he didn't hand it back to Elijah until the man was outside the door. Then Garrison tapped the sign about no firearms.

Elijah gutted out a single word of raw profanity and walked away while he scrolled through his phone. No doubt to contact a lawyer. He apparently found what he was looking for, because he made a call as he got into his dark blue truck and drove away.

Judson cursed as well. "If a lawyer shows up, the interview probably won't happen today. There'll likely be lots of legal wrangling…well, unless Jennifer flat-out refuses to have legal counsel."

"She probably won't refuse if she knows Elijah arranged it," Livvy pointed out. She sighed and glanced at both Addie and Judson. "Why don't you two go back to the ranch? I figure you're anxious to be with the twins."

Addie was indeed anxious, so when Judson nodded, she was ready to go despite the hesitation Addie saw on his face. He no doubt felt swamped with the amount of info that needed to be processed.

"Send me some of the workload," Judson told Livvy. "I'll go through any and all reports and summarize them for the rest of the team."

"I can do that," Livvy said. "It'll free me up to try to find Trevor and Yvette. And to deal with Jennifer. I'm not sure how long she'll sit in interview without putting up an argument."

Yes, and coupled with a potential attorney, Addie could understand why the interview likely wouldn't happen anytime soon. It was possible a lawyer would demand a thorough psychological eval of his client rather than relying on the expertise of a small-town ER doctor. Especially a doctor who would know all the members of the police force.

"I'll get my purse," Addie said, heading back into Grace's office where she'd left it. However, she'd barely made it a step before Livvy's phone rang.

"It's Grace," Livvy muttered, and she immediately took the call, putting it on speaker. "I'm here with Addie and Judson, who are listening in. Garrison, too," she added when the other deputy joined them.

"I made it to the hospital in Bulverde," Grace started, and Addie's stomach automatically clenched. Because she could tell from Grace's tone that this wasn't going to be good news. "Courtney died before the EMTs could even get her out of the ambulance."

Addie groaned. The three deputies each did some cursing. "Did Courtney manage to say anything to the EMTs?" Judson asked.

"No. She never even regained consciousness." Grace's heavy sigh came through loud and clear. "So, this is officially a murder investigation. *Ours*," she emphasized. "The area where Courtney was found is in the county sheriff office's jurisdiction, but since this is possibly connected to the twins' abduction, the county is handing it to us. I'm heading back to the station now to create a file on it. What's going on there?" she tacked on.

"We got a visit from Jennifer's boyfriend," Livvy let her boss know. "I can brief you on that since Addie and Judson were about to leave."

"Good," Grace said. "No need for them to be there, and they'll be better off at the ranch. Once you're back at the Horseshoe, just send Rory or Bennie back to the station. One of them can stay there for a while until…well, until things are more stabilized than they are right now."

"Thank you," Addie and Judson said together.

Addie took her purse, and she and Judson headed out while Livvy got started with the recap of Elijah's visit. Grace probably wasn't going to be any happier about it than the rest of them were.

They were only steps from the door when a landline phone rang, and seconds after Garrison answered it, the deputy called out, "I have Trevor Cates on the line."

That stopped them in their tracks, and they hurried back to the desk. "Put the call on speaker," Judson instructed the younger deputy, and Livvy moved closer, holding up her phone so that Grace could no doubt hear as well.

"This is Deputy Judson Docherty," he said.

"Trevor Cates," the man replied, and he sounded all frantic nerves. "I've been camping. There's no cell service out there, and I just saw all the missed calls. Some from Jennifer, others from Shane and three from Renegade Canyon PD. What the hell is going on?"

Addie figured Judson had plenty of questions, but he went with a simple one. "Where are you right now?" he asked.

"On the way back to my house. I pulled over when I finally got out of the dead spot and was able to check my phone," he explained. "When I saw your messages, I called right away."

"Don't go home," Judson insisted, and he dragged in a long breath. "A woman was attacked in your house, and there's a team of investigators inside and on the grounds."

"What?" Trevor blurted, his voice practically a shout now. "What do you mean? What woman was attacked? Was it Yvette?"

Again, Judson took his time answering. "Where is your wife, Mr. Cates?"

"Uh, I assumed she was at the house. At our home," he amended. "Isn't she? God, is she hurt?"

"We're not sure. We've been looking for your wife but haven't been able to contact her."

"Wait, hold on," Trevor insisted, and now there was some panic rising in his tone. Maybe the real deal. Maybe fake. Addie couldn't tell. "Just wait," he repeated. "I'm going to try calling Yvette now."

Judson didn't stop him from doing that. Trevor put them on hold, hopefully to make that call and not flee. Addie also hoped that once he came back on the line, he'd have answers about Yvette's location.

But that didn't happen.

"She's not answering," Trevor relayed several seconds later. The panic in his voice had gone up significantly. "Is my wife all right?"

"Like I said, we don't know. We need to speak to both of you," Judson informed him.

"Of course," Trevor muttered, and he repeated that several times. "But I want to look for her. I want to try to find her. I have to know if something happened to her." He stopped, groaned. "You said a woman was attacked in my house. Was it Yvette?" he demanded again.

"No," Judson replied, "it was someone else, but I can't discuss the details with you. Best if you come in and give that statement."

"Okay," Trevor said after a long pause. "But can it wait until morning? It'd be dark before I could get to Renegade Canyon, and I have trouble driving at night. Plus, I guess I need to find some place to stay since my home is a crime scene." His voice broke on those last two words.

Livvy and Judson exchanged a long look, probably trying to decide the timing for the interview since Shane would be coming back in at eight. Jennifer might possibly still be here as well.

"Have him come at 8:00 a.m.," Livvy mouthed.

Judson gave a quick nod, indicating he wanted the same thing. "Be here at eight tomorrow morning," he told Trevor. "And if you do hear from or find your wife, call us immediately."

"Will do," Trevor assured them, and he ended the call.

"It'll be interesting to see how Shane reacts to Trevor and vice versa," Livvy muttered.

"Yeah, and maybe by then, we'll know where Yvette is," Judson added, and they started for the door again. "I also want to verify some things about Trevor. The camping trip, for one thing. I want to make sure he was where he said he was. And that bit about him not being able to drive at night. He's only forty-nine, and that's not usually something that happens to someone in his age bracket."

Addie agreed, but she didn't ask the questions on her mind until after Judson and she were in the cruiser and driving toward the ranch. "I understand why Trevor might lie about the camping. He could be using that as a sort of alibi to make us believe he was nowhere near Yvette or Courtney today. But why would he lie about the driving to stall the interview?"

"Maybe he wants to find Yvette first." Judson stopped talking, scrubbed his hand over his face and groaned. "Or, hell, maybe he's telling the truth and has no part in any of this. It's hard to trust the guy based on what Yvette's kids have said about him, but none of what they spilled could have been the truth."

It was frustrating not knowing if Trevor was a killer, but maybe something incriminating would come out during the interview. If not incriminating about himself, then maybe for one of their other three suspects—Elijah, Shane or Jennifer.

Addie's phone sounded with a text, and she saw it was from Etta Jean. No actual message, just a photo of the twins side by side on a quilt on the floor, awake and alert. Etta Jean had even managed to catch Lily smiling. Addie smiled, too, and texted the woman that Judson and she would be home soon.

Judson took the turn to the ranch, and she spotted one of the ranch hands patrolling the fence that was next to a deep ditch. The other was in the backyard between the house and the barn. Addie appreciated the extra eyes, and guns, and made a mental note to thank Rory's brother for sending them.

Judson pulled to a stop directly in front of the house, parking the cruiser so that she was only a few inches from the bottom porch step. He didn't repeat his *move fast* order. No need. Addie knew what she had to do, and added to that, she was anxious to get inside and see the babies.

She threw open her door. Across from her, Judson did the same, and he barreled out of the cruiser. So did she. But she had made it up only four of the eight steps when the sound of a gunshot ripped through the air.

Judson had no trouble hearing that gunshot. Or seeing the bullet slam into the post right next to where Addie was standing. But before he could even shout out for her to get down, another shot came toward them. Then, another, with all three coming too damn close to Addie.

Hell, they were under attack.

Judson didn't look for the shooter. He'd do that later, when Addie was safe. If that was possible. But at the moment, any of those shots could turn out to be deadly.

He tried not to think of that and focused on what he could do. Staying low and using the cruiser for cover as much as he could, he drew his gun and scrambled toward Addie. Thankfully, she had already dropped down and was trying her damnedest to flatten her body against the steps, but the wood porch wasn't going to provide much protection.

"The babies," Addie called out.

Yeah, Judson had already considered them and everybody else in the house. It was wood, too, and the bullets could go through the walls. The shooter didn't seem to be interested in doing that, though, since all the shots were aimed at the two of them.

That was both good and bad.

Addie and he were the targets. No doubts about that. And

they could keep the gunfire and attention on them by not trying to get into the house. If they did, that's almost certainly where the shooter would turn their attention.

A bullet skipped off the top of the cruiser, ricocheting heaven knew where and giving Judson a spike of fear and more adrenaline that he definitely didn't need. He just had to concentrate. Had to make this work so that everybody except the shooter got out of this alive.

"Get the babies and Etta Jean into the bathroom," Judson shouted to Rory when the deputy opened the front door.

"Bennie's doing that now," Rory replied, and then he had to immediately duck back inside when a shot slammed into the doorframe.

"Don't do anything to make the bullets come your way," Addie pleaded. "No shots in the house."

So, Addie had worked that out as well, that they needed to keep the gunman's attention solely on them. Judson only wished he were outside alone. That he was the sole target and that Addie was somewhere else.

Someplace safe.

More shots came, all of them hitting the porch posts. Despite the fact that the sun was setting and the light wasn't optimal for target shooting, their attacker had a decent aim, only missing the mark by a fraction, and that's why Judson had to move Addie now.

He caught the first part of her that he could reach, her foot. And even though it would likely give her a few bruises and scrapes, he yanked her down the steps toward him.

Not a second too soon.

Because the shooter finally got the angle right, and the next bullet slammed into the spot where Addie had just been.

Judson dragged Addie closer to the cruiser and silently cursed that she hadn't left the door open so they could dive inside. Of course, she hadn't known there'd be an attack. But he sure as hell should have anticipated it and done a better job of stopping her from being in harm's way.

"Who's doing this?" he heard her say over the loud, thick blasts.

"Don't know yet," he had to admit, and then Judson focused on trying to pinpoint the shooter.

He could hear the shouts of the ranch hands who'd been guarding the place, and he hoped they'd taken cover as well. Judson was positive that neither of them was firing, but the shots were coming from the area at the front of the ranch near the fence.

Near the drainage ditch, too.

But not in it.

Judson had played there plenty enough times when he was a kid to know it was deep enough to conceal a shooter, but he was pretty sure the shots weren't specifically coming from there.

So, he waited. Listened. And all the while he prayed that he could get Addie out of this alive.

For now the best he could do was try to shield her with his body, so he rolled over her, shoving her right against the cruiser. "Get underneath it," he ordered.

Addie's gaze shot to his, and he saw exactly what he'd expected to see in her eyes. The fear. Yeah, it was there. But part of that fear was for him.

"You get underneath, too," she insisted.

"I will, later. After I've done some things."

That was possibly an outright lie. If they got the chance to stop or pursue the shooter, he would. But he couldn't even start doing that until he had Addie out of the direct line of fire. Of course, a bullet could still reach her, but it would make the shooter's job much harder.

"Later," he repeated, and to hurry things along, Judson used his body to muscle hers beneath the cruiser.

He tore his gaze from hers. Had to. And Judson also had to shove aside the hurricane of emotions roaring through him. The fury over this SOB's attempts to kill them. The danger the gunman had brought right to the ranch's doorstep, putting the babies in harm's way yet again.

Yes, he had to put all of that aside and try drowning out everything but the way the barrage of shots was slamming into the porch and cruiser.

And he finally thought he had the location.

There was an old barn just on the other side of the road, and while he couldn't actually see anyone, he figured their attacker was perched in the hayloft, shooting through the spaces between the boards.

Plenty of room for a sniper to slip the barrel of an assault rifle through one of them and start shooting.

It wouldn't have been hard for the gunman to get there, either, since no one lived in the house that was about fifty yards from the barn. The elderly owner had died three years earlier, and there was a battle going on to determine ownership. From what Judson had heard, none of those involved in the legal wranglings had visited the place in over a year.

Even though the shooter was out of range for him, Judson levered himself up enough to send a shot in the gunman's direction. He probably missed by a mile, but at least it caused a pause in the gunfire. But only a pause. The shots started right back up again.

And that gave Judson an idea.

"Text Rory," he told Addie. "I want him to get a message to the ranch hand by the fence. The hand needs to stay down, but if he's able, I want him to start shooting into the barn. Have him aim high."

That last part was a safety precaution so that someone who just happened to be driving by wouldn't get hit by friendly fire.

From the corner of his eye, he saw Addie send the text, and Judson fired at the barn again. And again. Since that was giving him the lull he needed, he kept it up until Addie got a response.

"Rory's texting the ranch hand now," she relayed. "And he says backup is on the way. Two of them will be heading to the barn."

Good. But Judson knew that backup couldn't just come charging in. They'd have to hang back, wait for an opportunity to go after the shooter.

It wasn't long, only a couple of seconds, before Judson heard a welcome sound: gunfire, but this time it was coming from the ranch hand. And unlike Judson, he was in firing range to put a permanent end to this SOB.

But he immediately rethought that.

If possible, he wanted the shooter alive. Alive and talking so that Addie and he would know why someone was trying to kill them.

Judson reloaded and added his own gunfire to the mix of the ranch hand's, and as he'd hoped, the shooter stopped firing. Maybe because some of the hand's bullets were tearing through the old wood of the barn. Judson still didn't see any movement from the hayloft area, but that didn't mean the guy had been hit. He could be just lying low, waiting for an opening to start shooting again.

In the distance, he heard the wail of police sirens. Neither Judson nor the ranch hand stopped firing. They both kept pulling the triggers until Judson finally saw something.

A blur of motion at the back edge of the barn.

He caught just a glimpse, but it appeared to be someone

dressed in dark clothes. Clothes that blended with the twilight. One thing was for certain, though.

The SOB was running.

Escaping.

And Judson had to do something about that.

"Stay put," he warned Addie, but Judson didn't give her a chance to respond. Definitely not a chance to try to talk him out of what he was doing.

He leaped up and took off running.

"Hold your fire," he shouted to the ranch hand, and the man immediately stopped.

That cleared the way for Judson to pick up the pace to a sprint while he kept his gun gripped in his hand. Kept his attention on that blur of motion, too. If the man, or woman, turned around, Judson wanted to be able to take cover rather than be gunned down.

Running as fast as he could, Judson reached the road just as he saw the cruiser approaching the turn for the ranch. He paused only a second to make sure the driver, Livvy, wasn't going to plow into him. When she slowed, Judson bolted across the road, vaulting over the pasture fence.

And he kept running.

His heart was thundering now, and his pulse was crashing in his ears, but thankfully he had yet another slam of adrenaline. The mother lode of energy that got him to the barn in no time flat.

He had to slow again, though, as he approached the barn. Slow down and keep watch in case this idiot tried to ambush him.

But he didn't see any signs of that. No signs of the shooter, either.

Not at first, anyway. Not until Judson picked through the darkness and saw the figure racing past the house. Clearly, the shooter had gotten some adrenaline, too, because within a blink, the person was out of sight, disappearing into a cluster of trees in front of the house.

Judson got moving, racing toward the snake. He was still a good twenty yards away when he heard a different sound. Not gunfire. But an engine.

He kicked up the pace again, trying to get to the shooter, trying to stop him before he escaped.

But he was too late.

Judson caught sight of the taillights as the car sped away.

Chapter Eight

Addie sat in the rocking chair in her bedroom, a sleeping baby nestled in each arm, while she waited for Judson. Waited and tried not to give in to the sickening dread that just wouldn't let up.

So much dread.

For the babies. For the danger they'd been in during the attack. For the possibility that the attacks weren't over, and that the gunman could strike again.

Yes, that was the fear all right, and Addie was hoping that Judson might be able to steady her nerves and give her some much-needed assurance once she was able to talk to him. She hadn't managed to have more than a couple of seconds with him before he'd run off toward that barn and the person who'd been firing those shots.

She knew he was busy with the aftermath of the attack. So were Rory, Bennie and Livvy. Rory and Bennie were staying close to the house in case the worst happened and the shooter returned, but Livvy and Eden were out looking for the person who'd tried to kill Judson and her.

Kill.

That was definitely a word, and a dread, that wasn't going away anytime soon. The shooter had been very determined to finish them off. Nearly had, too. And it was beyond frustrating that they still had no idea why this was happening. That was one of the big answers that Judson and the other cops were trying to find, and if they managed to catch the shooter, that would the start of getting answers.

In the meantime, they all had to take precautions. That included keeping the curtains drawn so a sniper couldn't pinpoint their location. There'd be no going outside for Etta Jean, the twins or her. Basically, they'd be prisoners in their own home while Judson and so many others were risking their lives. That didn't sit especially well with Addie, but priority one was the babies, and she had no intention of leaving them until this shooter was caught.

"Want me to help put the babies down?" Etta Jean asked.

That yanked Addie out of her doom-and-gloom thoughts, and she welcomed the reprieve. She glanced at Etta Jean, who was perched on the edge of a chair in the sitting area of the bedroom. Clearly, she was battling nerves and dread, too, but she seemed to be holding it together. So would Addie, for the sake of the twins. But she still wanted to see Judson.

Addie shook her head. "I want to hold them just a bit longer." She snuggled her face against Rose's baby curls and drew in that wonderful scent. "Thank you for protecting them," she added to Etta Jean, and she voiced something that she'd been afraid to say. "Were Lily and Rose scared during the shooting?"

All that noise had to be terrifying. Or rather, it had been for Addie. Because any of those shots could have gone into the house.

"I don't think so," Etta Jean replied after a slight hesitation. "Lily was crying, but I think that's because I gave her a jolt when I scooped her up, ran into the bathroom and climbed into the tub with her. She'd been sleeping," she explained. "Rose was awake, and Bennie was right by her bassinet, talking to her. She didn't fuss when he took her and followed Lily and me."

Addie's imagination was far better than she wanted. She could see all of that playing out. Lily crying. The sheer terror that Etta Jean and Bennie had to have been feeling as they put the babies in the tub and no doubt protected them with their own bodies.

Judson had done that for her. He had shielded her by having her move under the cruiser while he'd stayed in the line of fire. Addie hated that he'd done that. Hated that he had put her life ahead of his. But she was beyond thankful that neither of them, nor the ranch hands, had been shot.

Addie's head whipped up when she heard footsteps, and she tried not to show her disappointment when it wasn't Judson who stepped into the doorway but Livvy.

"Judson will be here soon," Livvy volunteered, letting Addie know that she obviously hadn't succeeded in hiding the disappointment. "He's finishing up giving his statement to Grace. I just wanted to drop by and check on you before I head back to the station."

"Any signs of the shooter?" Addie asked, already knowing the answer. If they had found him or her, then Livvy would have led with that.

Livvy shook her head, the frustration all over her face. "But the CSIs are in the barn, looking for anything that might clue us in to who fired those shots." She glanced at the babies and then at Etta Jean before her attention went back to Addie. "How's everybody holding up?"

Addie decided to go with a lie. "Okay." Because if she said that lie enough, she might start to believe it. Or better yet, it might start to be true.

Livvy made a sound to indicate she didn't quite believe

that, but she didn't push and then went for a change of subject. "The cops who notified Courtney's parents about her death said they were ripped to pieces, but they were able to give them some info. Apparently, Courtney talked to them a lot about Yvette, and there was plenty of bad blood between the women. Over the years Yvette has filed more than a hundred complaints against Courtney."

"That many?" Addie shook her head. "For what?"

"Lots of things. Yvette apparently liked to follow Courtney, so she's reported her for everything from speeding to jaywalking to littering. Yvette has even contacted plenty of Courtney's clients, trying to get them to have the woman fired or file a joint lawsuit against her."

It took plenty of anger for Yvette to do something like that. But then, the woman did blame Courtney for losing custody of Shane and Jennifer, and that was motive for murder. Not just for Yvette, but maybe for Jennifer and Shane, too. Jennifer might not have good things to say about her bio mom, but that didn't mean she wouldn't feel compelled to protect her in some way.

"Has the lab found anything in Courtney's car or on her clothes to link her to Yvette?" Addie asked.

"No." Livvy sighed again. "But it's getting priority treatment, so we might have something soon."

Livvy didn't add more, probably because she heard more footsteps coming up the hall toward them. And this time, it was the person Addie wanted to see.

Judson.

He stepped around Livvy, walking straight to Addie. He gave the twins a long look over before his gaze met hers. "We should talk. Are Lily and Rose ready for bedtime?"

Addie silently groaned. She didn't want to hear more bad

news, but she also didn't want Judson keeping anything from her, either.

"Yes, they're ready for bed," Addie muttered.

And they were. Despite everything, or maybe because of it, Etta Jean and Addie had already gotten them bathed and fed. They were wearing their footed pj's with Lily in her usual pink and Rose in yellow.

Judson eased Rose from her left arm, taking her to her bassinet while Addie did the same to Lily.

"I'll stay with them while you talk," Etta Jean said, making the same offer she had earlier that day.

That day, Addie mentally repeated. Had it only been that morning when the babies had gone missing? It felt like a couple of lifetimes ago. And while the day was technically over, the night certainly wasn't. With the gunman still at large, that wouldn't make for restful sleep.

Addie thanked Etta Jean and added a hug that lingered for several moments when she felt the tension in the woman's muscles. It was going to take them all a while to get past the trauma of what had happened.

"Call me if you need anything," Livvy offered as Judson and Addie went to the door.

"I will," Addie assured her and gave Livvy a hug, too. "And thank you for everything."

"Anytime," Livvy replied, and she walked away.

Judson took hold of Addie's hand and led her in the opposite direction. Not toward the front of the house, where there was so much chatter and activity still going on. He took her to the kitchen. When they found Bennie and one of the ranch hands there, Judson made a detour to the small sewing room that had once been the maid's quarters when the house was first built, over a hundred years ago.

The moment they were inside, he shut the door. And Judson pulled her into his arms.

Addie welcomed it. Mercy, did she. She needed this, and even though it brought on the inevitable heat, she didn't care. She just held on and let his arms ease some of the tight tension in her body. Only after she'd steadied herself did she say what had been flashing like neon lights in her head.

"You could have been killed," she blurted. "You put yourself between a shooter and me, and you could have died."

Judson had an odd reaction. The corner of his mouth lifted into a smile. It only added character to that amazing face that had way more character than a man had a right to have.

"I would tap my badge to remind you I'm a cop," he drawled. "But if I move my hand between us now, I might end up touching something of yours that I shouldn't."

For some stupid reason, that made her smile, too. It didn't last. But the old attraction came, and parts of her were certain she would enjoy Judson touching her. Well, if it weren't for the fact they'd nearly died and were in the middle of hunting for a killer.

"You wanted to talk," she managed to say, hoping it would get her mind back on track.

But she was instantly sorry for the change in subject. His smile vanished, and she saw the cop standing in front of her. A cop who eased back from her.

"Here's the bottom line," he started. "We don't know squat about who fired those shots. There are no visible tracks and so far none of the recovered shell casings have had fingerprints on them."

Her heart sank. She had been hoping that the CSIs or deputies would find something.

"You got a look at the shooter," she reminded. "Could it have been one of our suspects?"

"I got a couple of glimpses," Judson corrected. "And, yes, it could have been Elijah, Shane, Trevor or, hell, even Yvette. The only person it couldn't have been is Jennifer. She was at the police station at the time of the attack."

True. Jennifer had an airtight alibi, but that didn't mean Elijah hadn't been acting on her behalf.

"Elijah was furious when he left the station," she pointed out. "He could have fired those shots to get back at us for not letting him see Jennifer. Or he could have done this to try to make it seem as if she's innocent, that we're looking at the wrong person for Courtney's murder."

"Yes, he could have done it for either of those reasons, and trust me, Grace will be talking to him about that. To Shane and Trevor, too, when they come in for interviews in the morning." He paused. "You'll hear this soon enough, but all of our suspects have had firearms training."

Sweet heaven. It twisted at her to think of how easy it would be for one of them to try to come after them again.

"I don't want to leave the ranch," Addie said. "I want to be with the babies, but I want them to be safe."

Judson sighed and moved closer to her again. Not hugging her, but he did take her hand. "This all started with someone abducting the twins. The shooting today could have been another attempt to do that."

Oh, God. She hadn't even considered that. Those shots had been aimed at Judson and her, so Addie had assumed this was some sort of retaliation. But it could have been to eliminate them.

"We're beefing up security around here," he spelled out, obviously noticing the fresh round of fear in her eyes. "It's too risky to bring in someone from a security company right now, since we can't be sure our attacker won't use that as a chance to sneak onto the grounds. But the ranch hands will continue to patrol, and we'll keep all windows and doors locked."

She shook her head. "Is that enough—"

"And I'm sleeping in the room with you and the twins tonight," Judson interrupted.

"All right," she said, noticing his tone and body language. The muscles in his jaw were having a battle with each other. "You don't sound especially pleased."

Judson opened his mouth, closed it. Then sighed and cursed. "I'm doing it. I want to stay here and protect all three of you." He paused. "But I'll admit that it won't be easy."

She knew what he meant. What he felt. Because she was feeling the same exact things. All this close contact was testing those barriers again. It was tearing the pact to shreds. But at the moment she was having a hard time remembering why that would be such a bad thing.

And that's why she leaned in and kissed him.

She immediately felt the jolt. A sizzle of heat like electricity firing through her. It was always this way with Judson. So intense.

So hot.

But somehow it also managed to feel both wrong and right at the same time. *Damn pact.* They'd made that pact for good reasons, but those reasons and pretty much all logic went out the window whenever they kissed.

For now, Addie just settled on the part that felt right. The heat. The pleasure of his mouth and taste that set her on fire. Judging from the moan that came from deep within his throat, he was feeling the same thing.

He didn't throttle back. Didn't try to cut the kiss short. Just the opposite. The kiss became hotter, and he slid his hand to her waist. Definitely what her body wanted. His touch coupled with the kiss. And that's what she got.

Judson kept his hand in place for a couple of heartbeats before he hooked his arm around her back and drew her to him. So close. With a lot of him touching a lot of her.

That amped up the heat even more, and Addie felt herself sinking deeper and deeper into that fire. She wanted to give in to it. Give in to Judson. She wanted to drag him off to bed. But thankfully there was just a sliver of reasoning coming through in her foggy brain, and that reasoning started to tick off why sex couldn't happen.

And it had nothing to do with the pact.

The house was full of cops, and there was an intense search going on. Even if they could be sure they'd have some uninterrupted time to sneak off to a bed, or the floor, it wouldn't be right. They needed to be helping with the investigation so they could stop any further threats.

Judson must have remembered that, too, because he tore his mouth from hers and stepped back. What he didn't do was curse or show any signs that the kiss had been a huge mistake.

Just the opposite.

Addie thought he might be on the verge of saying something about putting this on hold, but he didn't get a chance to actually voice that. Or anything else, for that matter. Because his phone rang.

"It's dispatch," he relayed to her, and he put the call on speaker.

Addie appreciated that. She didn't want to be kept in the dark about anything, but she tried to steel herself up since any contact from the dispatcher or his fellow cops could be another round of bad news.

"Judson, I've got someone on the line who wants to talk to you," the dispatcher said.

"Who is it?" he asked.

"She won't say, but she insists she had to talk to you. I can try to push her on giving me her name. Or I can have her contact Grace. You know we always get crackpot calls when there's any kind of investigation going on."

Judson made a sound of agreement, and his forehead bunched up while he no doubt considered what to do. "Put the call through," he finally said.

It took only a couple of seconds for the dispatcher to do that, and before Judson could get out a greeting, the woman's frantic voice poured through the room. "I tried to save those babies. I swear, I tried to save them."

Addie's chest went tight. But then she made herself remember that this could be a hoax.

"Who is this?" Judson demanded.

"Yvette Cates," the woman blurted.

Judson and Addie exchanged a glance, and his was tinged with some skepticism. "There's an APB out on Yvette Cates, and there are a lot of details about her on social media—"

"I'm Yvette," she insisted. And she began to rattle off details like her birth date and those of her two kids. Then she added, "My kids' names are Jennifer Alise and Shane David."

That seemed to convince Judson that she was telling the truth. And it caused the tightness in Addie's chest to increase. They were talking to the woman who had kidnapped the twins. Before Addie could blurt out a demand as to why Yvette had taken those precious babies, Judson voiced a demand of his own.

"Where the hell are you?" he snapped while he hit the record function on his phone. He also sent a text to dispatch to try to have the call traced.

"I'm not sure, but as soon as I can, I'll get to a police

station so I can give them my statement. Just promise me I won't be arrested."

Judson huffed. "I'm not promising that. You kidnapped two infants and endangered them—"

"No, I was trying to stop them from being hurt," Yvette insisted.

The woman was sobbing now. And whispering. Was she doing that so she wouldn't be overheard? If so, why?

Addie listened for any background noise. For any signs of a possible threat. But no one was shouting at Yvette or firing shots at her.

"The only person who put the twins in danger was you," Judson argued. "Now, tell me where you are."

Yvette did more sobbing before she spoke again. "Someone was going to take them," she said as if choosing her words carefully. "So, I took them first. I tried to get them to safety."

The skepticism skyrocketed big-time in Judson's eyes. "Who was going to kidnap them?"

"I… I can't say. Just believe me when I tell you that I was doing what I thought best. Are they all right?"

Judson seemed to debate his answer, or else he was stalling with the hopes of getting the call traced. "I can give you an update about them when I see you. Where are you?" he repeated.

Yvette didn't answer. Not with words anyway. But seconds later, there was a sound.

A bloodcurdling scream.

And the line went dead.

Chapter Nine

Judson stood in the shower in Addie's bathroom, hoping the hot water would perform some kind of magic. And fast.

He needed the cobwebs clear from his head. Cobwebs caused by the lack of sleep since he hadn't managed more than a couple of hours throughout the night. Hard to sleep while worrying about Addie and the twins' safety. Also, by being in the same room with her, mere feet away.

Yeah, that hadn't been easy.

His body hadn't let him forget how close she was or the lingering effects of that kiss they'd shared. Nope. No forgetting that. It was just as powerful as the other things going on in his mind and body.

Including the flashbacks.

Not just of the attack against Addie and him but also the call from Yvette. He could still hear the sound of her scream echoing through those cobwebs. It had seemed genuine. Like the woman had been terrified for her life.

But there was a problem with that.

They didn't know where Yvette was because they hadn't been able to trace the call. So, if she had indeed been screaming because of some horrible threat, her attacker could already have killed her and silenced her for good.

Being a cop all these years had made him enough of a

cynic to believe this was all some ploy to make herself appear innocent. It wouldn't work. If Yvette was alive and they could find her, she was going to pay for what she'd done.

Judson heard the dinging sound of a text, so he got out of the shower and glanced at his phone on the vanity. It was from Grace, updating him on the schedule. It wasn't his boss's first text of the day. She had sent one an hour earlier to let him know that Shane's and Jennifer's interviews were still on for the morning and that she'd be talking to the ME about Courtney's autopsy.

Yeah, plenty going on, but so far, they still didn't have the answers they needed to get a break in the investigation.

Judson texted back a thumbs-up emoji to Grace and gulped down the rest of the mug of coffee that he'd taken into the bathroom with him. Not his first cup, despite it being barely 8:00 a.m. He'd had that first one as he sat with the twins while Addie showered, and as soon as he made it back to the kitchen, he'd be tanking up on yet more caffeine.

He dressed in the clean clothes that Livvy had had brought over, putting on his holster and weapon, before he went into the bedroom. Addie was right where he'd left her, in the rocking chair with Rose. The baby had finished her bottle, though, and Addie was burping her.

"I heard your phone," Addie said, the worry in her eyes.

Of course, the worry had been there since the start of this ordeal, and sadly, it likely wouldn't be going away anytime soon.

"It was a text from Grace," he explained, going to the bassinet to check on Lily. She was still sacked out. "Trevor is on his way here. Grace decided to do the interview with him here rather than the police station. This way, she doesn't have to split the manpower and we can continue to show a strong police presence here."

"In case of another attack," Addie finished for him.

Judson had to make a sound of agreement. "Right now, there are three cruisers parked out front and four cops inside the house. Grace, Livvy, Bennie and me. The shooter might think twice before trying to come at us again."

Addie no doubt mentally played out what would happen later today. Grace, Livvy and Bennie couldn't stay here indefinitely, and the shooter could just wait for an opening. The danger wasn't over and wouldn't be until the killer and/or their attacker was caught.

"Trevor will be thoroughly searched before Grace allows him to step foot inside," Judson explained. "And she's going to ask if he'll submit to having his vehicle searched as well."

If Trevor refused, then Grace would get a search warrant. Trevor wasn't automatically guilty by association with his kidnapping wife, but simply being married to her should be enough to convince a judge that the cops needed to take a harder look at the man.

"Did Grace say anything about Yvette?" Addie asked in a whisper.

Judson shook his head. "No update on her."

Because they hadn't been able to trace the call, they had no idea where the woman was. Basically, they had to wait for Yvette to call them again. Or for someone to spot her.

Or for her body to turn up.

Despite the hell that Yvette had put Addie through by abducting the twins, Judson didn't wish the woman dead. Just the opposite. They needed Yvette alive and talking, especially if she'd been telling the truth when she claimed she had taken the babies to try to protect them.

That claim had cost Judson some sleep and was even now going through his head. It was too bad Yvette hadn't spilled more info and named names. And Judson had given that some thinking time, too. Yvette likely would have been reluctant to rat out her own kids and her husband, so who did that leave?

Courtney?

There was no proof whatsoever that the social worker had wanted to kidnap the twins. And that no proof applied to anyone else. There hadn't been any threats and there wasn't any chatter on the dark web about abducting the babies. Of course, that didn't mean such a threat hadn't existed, but at the moment, everything still pointed to Yvette as the perpetrator of the crime.

Addie sighed, drawing his attention back to her, and she got to her feet. Like her sister, Rose was sleeping, too, and she didn't even stir when Addie eased her into the bassinet.

"What about Jennifer and Shane?" she asked, still whispering. "Please tell me they didn't disappear."

It was a valid worry, since Grace had cut both of them loose for the night. For Shane, there'd been no grounds to hold him, and his lawyer had put up enough fuss for Grace to allow Shane to leave with the promise he would return to the station in the morning to answer more questions.

Jennifer's situation had been different since she had been found at the scene with a knife and Courtney's blood, but there was still no evidence that she'd been the one to attack Courtney. In fact, the lab hadn't been able to find any of Jennifer's DNA on Courtney or in her vehicle. It was enough for Grace to allow the woman to leave—again with the stipulation that she return for an interview.

"They haven't disappeared," Judson assured her, but he didn't get a chance to add more because there was a soft tap at the door.

"It's me," Etta Jean said.

Since the door was locked, Judson crossed the room to

let the woman in. Like Addie and him, there was plenty of fatigue and stress on Etta Jean's face, too, and she was carrying two mugs of coffee.

"I figured you could both use this," she immediately said, handing the mugs off to them. "There's also plenty of breakfast stuff in the kitchen. I made some bacon, eggs and biscuits and left it all warming on the stove."

"Thanks," Judson said after he'd gulped down some of the coffee.

He was sure his fellow cops and the ranch hands would appreciate the food. He would, too, since he'd need to fuel up to help with the fatigue, and he might be able to convince Addie to eat something as well.

"I'll stay with the babies as long as needed," Etta Jean added. She paused. "Any idea when we'll know…something?" she settled for saying.

Judson had to shake his head. "But there'll be at least three interviews this morning, and we might get something from one of those."

Etta Jean nodded, sighed and patted his arm. "Let me know the second you learn anything."

He assured her that he would, and Judson got Addie moving out of the bedroom and toward the kitchen. Apparently, others had had the same notion of fueling up and grabbing coffee, because they stepped in to find Grace and one of the ranch hands, Ty Matheson.

"Morning," Grace greeted, stepping to the side to make room for them at the stove. "How are you holding up?" she asked Addie.

Addie made a so-so motion with her hand. "The twins slept well enough."

"But not you." Grace sighed. "Eat up, because you're going to need it. We have a long day ahead of us." She was chowing down on a biscuit that she'd stuffed with bacon and scrambled eggs. "Trevor's ETA is fifteen minutes," she tacked on to that.

Not much time, so Judson made two of the breakfast sandwiches and handed one to Addie. Grace motioned for them to sit at the massive kitchen table.

"I didn't put it in the text, but the background report came through on Elijah," Grace started. "This will probably come as a surprise, but the man has no criminal record."

It was indeed a surprise. "His hot temper hasn't gotten him into legal trouble," Judson commented.

"Oh, it has," Grace corrected while Judson and Addie both took a bite of their sandwiches. "He was detained after a bar fight a year ago, but no one pressed charges after he agreed to pay for the damages. Elijah doesn't come from money or have a huge settlement like Yvette," she added. "Nor does he have a high-paying job. Still, he somehow managed to come up with the cash."

"Maybe he got it from Jennifer?" Judson suggested, washing down his sandwich with more coffee.

Grace lifted her shoulder. "Possibly, but she's not exactly rolling in dough, either. In fact, both Elijah and she are pretty much broke."

"Which could be motive for kidnapping babies," Addie piped in. "Yvette said she took the twins to protect them." She stopped, shuddered. "Maybe she was protecting them from Elijah."

"It's possible," Grace admitted. "Elijah doesn't have an alibi for, well…anything related to the investigation. Not for the kidnapping or for the attack. So, he could have planned to take the twins for ransom, thinking either you or Yvette would pay it."

During those sleepless hours of the night, Judson had

considered that. And more. "If Elijah planned to abduct Lily and Rose for a payout, there would have likely been easier targets. Targets closer to his home, anyway. So, maybe this wasn't about getting a ransom. Maybe it was about getting his hands on Yvette's settlement money."

Addie was quick to mutter an agreement. Obviously, she'd done some nighttime thinking about this as well.

"If Elijah made Yvette believe he was going to take the twins," Addie spelled out, "then he could have been hoping that Yvette would steal them herself and that she would perhaps be killed or at least incarcerated in the aftermath. Then, he'd be a big step closer to getting his hands on Yvette's money either through receiving a ransom demand or convincing Jennifer to hand it over to him."

She stopped, sighed. And Judson knew why.

"Elijah would have had an obstacle or two, or three, to flat-out inheriting the money," Judson spelled out. "Trevor, for sure. Also, Jennifer and Shane. I can't imagine Trevor or Shane just giving him Yvette's money the way that Jennifer might."

"Same," Grace said. "And it's why I'm trying to get a copy of any will that Yvette might have. That might give us some answers."

Yes, it could, but it was a shame they couldn't question the woman herself.

"Are we certain there's actually money?" Addie asked. "I mean, we know Yvette received a settlement, but could she have already spent it?"

Grace shook her head. "There's money. I got her financials, and Yvette has every penny of it stashed in CDs. She hasn't tapped into any of it, and it's accumulating a nice chunk of interest each month."

That was indeed motive, then, for Elijah, Jennifer, Shane or Trevor. But motive didn't mean any of them had actually done anything wrong. In fact, the only guilty person was Yvette. An eyewitness had put her with the babies, and the woman had confessed to taking them.

And that brought Judson to more of his late-night thoughts.

"Yvette could have orchestrated it all," he said. "The anniversary of losing her kids is coming up. Along with it being their birthday, that could have triggered something in her. Or if she's using drugs, she might have become delusional, thinking that the twins were actually hers. She could have taken them and then gotten cold feet about what she'd done."

"Yes," Addie said, taking up the explanation. "After she left the babies with the farmer, she possibly could have rushed home to get things to make an escape and then run into Courtney."

Grace nodded. "If Yvette killed her, then the attack and that phone call could be about covering her tracks. If she could pin all of this on someone else, like Elijah, for instance, then she could walk away a free woman."

That would wrap everything up in a neat little package. Or rather, it would have been neat if they actually had Yvette.

Judson heard some voices at the front of the house, and at the same time, Grace got a text. "Trevor's here, and he's being frisked," Grace relayed to them, already getting to her feet.

She stopped and seemed to be considering how to handle this. "Why don't the two of you come with me to *greet* Trevor? If Yvette didn't stage that attack on you, then maybe Trevor did. I'd like to see how he reacts to seeing you."

Judson wanted to see that as well. Too bad he couldn't hook Trevor up to a lie detector or dose him with truth serum, but he was at least hoping he'd get some kind of vibe from the man. Because if Yvette had enlisted anyone for help, it would likely be the man she'd married.

The three of them left their coffee and breakfast and headed toward the foyer, where Judson immediately saw Bennie, Livvy and a beefy man in jeans, a white muscle tee and a brown leather jacket that was almost the same color as his hair. Judson knew from the bio he'd read on Trevor that he was forty-nine, but he looked at least a decade younger than that.

"No weapons," Bennie announced.

Livvy added, "And I've given him the Miranda." Livvy also made introductions.

Trevor didn't acknowledge anything that Livvy or Bennie said. Nor did he look bothered about being frisked and treated like the suspect that he was. Instead, Trevor's attention was on Addie.

"Addie," the man finally said, aiming his weathered blue eyes on her. "I recognize you from the media reports," he quickly added when he must have noted the alarm on Addie's face. "I'm so sorry. I can't believe Yvette would have taken those babies from you."

So, the man wasn't going to defend his wife and proclaim her innocence. Interesting.

"Have you heard from Yvette?" Addie asked, not bothering to address the man's comments.

Trevor sighed, shook his head. "No. And I can't find her. None of her friends have heard from her, either." He stopped. "You don't remember me, do you?"

Addie pulled back her shoulders, practically coming to attention, and her gaze combed over his face. "I don't," she admitted after a long pause. "How do you know me?"

Trevor's mouth turned into a slight smile. "You were just a kid, and it was a long time ago."

"How do you know me?" she repeated, this time her voice a snap, when Trevor didn't continue.

The man's smile faded, but he kept his attention on Addie. "When you were four or five, I went out with your mother a couple of times. With Rowena."

Because Addie's arm was against his, Judson felt her muscles tense. "She's not my mother."

"Yes, of course," Trevor was quick to say. "I wasn't aware of that at the time. Rowena introduced you as her daughter, and I had no idea what she'd done. *Murder*," he added under his breath. A look of disgust tightened his face. "Trust me, I wouldn't have had anything to do with her if I had known the truth. I didn't find out until a year or two later when I saw it on the news."

Judson considered all of that, and he'd need to try to figure out if what happened back then had anything to do with what was going on now. It seemed a stretch since it would have been almost thirty years ago, but it was an eerie coincidence that Judson didn't like.

"Mr. Cates, do you understand the Miranda rights that Deputy Walsh recited to you?" Grace asked, clearly shifting the subject. Maybe because she could see how uncomfortable Addie was.

That got Trevor's attention, and he finally turned toward the sheriff. "You're the one who arrested my stepdaughter."

"I didn't arrest her," Grace was quick to point out. "However, she is being questioned. So is your stepson."

Trevor nodded as if he'd fully expected that. "Jennifer doesn't get along with her mother. And I'm certain she despises me." He stopped. "Did Jennifer do something to Yvette? Is that why no one has heard from her?"

"We did hear from her," Grace said.

The silence settled over the foyer, and Judson watched the alarm go through Trevor's eyes. "When?" he snapped. "Where is she?"

"I'm sorry, but I'm not at liberty to get into the details," Grace said. "But we'll talk about that during the interview. I've set that up in the formal dining room, if you don't mind."

"I don't mind," he muttered, almost absently. His focus was clearly still on the contact they'd had with Yvette. "What did my wife say?" Trevor asked. "Did you tell her I was worried sick about her?"

Again, Grace dodged the question and motioned for them to follow her. She started walking at a very slow pace toward the dining room.

Trevor muttered some profanity. "Yvette has to be terrified. I really need to talk to her. If you'll just tell me where she is—"

"So, is this your first visit to the Horseshoe Ranch?" Grace asked. Maybe it was more question dodging, or Grace could possibly want to learn if Trevor was familiar with the house and the grounds.

"My first," Trevor grumbled. They stopped outside the dining room, but none of them went in. Instead, he shifted back to Addie. "My wife's a very troubled woman. If you saw her or spoke to her, you'd know that."

"Troubled? How?" Addie questioned, sounding a whole lot like a cop.

Trevor certainly didn't jump to answer. He seemed to be calculating how to handle this. Maybe because he was worried that Yvette had said something incriminating about him.

"Losing her kids has stuck with her," he finally said. "It's an obsession for her."

"What do you mean?" Judson pressed. "She lost the kids years ago."

"And she's never gotten over it," Trevor insisted. He

stopped, groaned and scrubbed his hand over his face. "Look, I love my wife, but I can't always understand why she does the things she does."

"Like kidnapping two babies?" Grace supplied.

After several more of those long moments, Trevor nodded. "It's as if she can't get past what happened. As if she needs to relive it, with the illogical hope that she can somehow change things."

Addie and Judson exchanged a glance, and he could see she was just as confused as he was. Judging from Grace's next question, she clearly was, too.

"Explain that," Grace demanded. "And then we can begin the interview and get all this and more on the record."

For a moment, Judson thought that would get Trevor to back down, to try to wave it all off. But he didn't. "Yvette is obsessed with reading everything she can about the Horseshoe Ranch," he said. "Random mentions in the press, for instance. She'll print out and save those articles."

That did seem obsessive, considering that Jennifer and Shane hadn't spent much time here before being adopted.

"Over the years, Yvette's contacted any and all parents who had kids who ended up here," Trevor continued. "She tries to talk to them about their experiences. A sort of therapy, I guess you could say. But most don't want her pushing them about stuff like that. They've moved on. Yvette hasn't."

"Did you ever try to get your wife help for this?" Grace asked. "Maybe have her see a counselor?"

"Yes," he said on a heavy sigh. "I've tried many times, but she always refuses to go."

"Yet you married her," Judson pointed out in case Trevor was exaggerating Yvette's mindset.

"I did because I loved her. Still love her," he amended. "But love doesn't blind me to her faults. To this obsession she has with the Horseshoe Ranch and her kids. And I'm worried all this now caused her to go over the edge. When I'm done here, I need to make a few more calls so I can try to find out where she is," Trevor added a heartbeat later.

"Who else could you contact that you haven't already?" Grace pressed.

Trevor lifted his shoulder. "Yvette has a file with the names and phone numbers of those people I told you about, and she's in touch with a lot of them. Parents who lost custody of their children. Especially mothers," he said, turning back to Addie again. "Like yours."

Everything went tight inside Judson, and he saw some of the color drain from Addie's face.

"What do you mean by that?" Addie asked. "Are you saying Yvette has been in touch with Rowena?"

"That's exactly what I'm saying," Trevor confirmed.

Addie made a soft sound, part gasp, part moan, but Judson figured there was nothing soft about what she was feeling right now. Just the mention of Rowena was enough to trigger some god-awful memories for her.

"Yvette visited Rowena in prison many times," Trevor went on. "In fact, that's how I met Yvette. Apparently, Rowena mentioned me during one of those visits, and Yvette looked me up."

Judson was going to have to check into Trevor's relationship with Rowena, but that tidbit didn't mesh with anything Jennifer, Shane or Elijah had said about Trevor. Then again, the three of them might not know that Rowena and Trevor had once dated.

"Rowena," Trevor repeated, and he snapped his fingers as if recalling something. "I was leaving for my camping trip, and the last thing Yvette said to me was that she was on her way to visit her. It's possible that's where Yvette is now."

Chapter Ten

Addie felt as if someone had punched her. When this hell-ish ordeal with Yvette had started, she certainly hadn't ex-pected Rowena to be added to mix.

"Come on," Grace told Trevor, leading him into the din-ing room. "Let's get all this on the record." She had him sit at the table and then went back to join Addie and Jud-son in the hall.

"This might not be true," Grace said, obviously noticing that Addie had gotten that gut punch. "Yvette could have made it all up. Or Trevor could be the liar. Just don't jump to any conclusions yet."

Too late. Addie had already made that jump, and she was coming up with a very disturbing possibility. Had Rowena been the one to spur Yvette into kidnapping Lily and Rose?

"First things first," Grace went on, shifting to Judson. "Call and find out where this Rowena is and if Yvette is with her."

Judson nodded and stepped to the side to make the call. Grace stayed with Addie and took hold of her shoulders, forcing her to make eye contact. "Tell me about Rowena. When's the last time you saw her?"

It took Addie a couple of seconds to drag in enough breath to speak. "I haven't seen her since I was six. But yesterday, she called to tell me she was dying and that she wanted to see me." She stopped, had to, because she got another of those punches. "Rowena could have set up the kidnapping as a way to force me to see her. She could have arranged for Yvette to bring the babies to her."

"I won't rule that out," Grace said, "but at the moment just focus on the details. If Rowena's in jail—"

"She's not," Addie interrupted. "She's been released and is in some medical treatment facility in San Antonio. Judging from the route Yvette was taking to escape with the twins, she could have been heading in that direction."

Grace cursed under her breath. "All right. I'll get someone out there right away to check on—" But she stopped when Judson finished his call and came back over to join them.

"I just spoke to the director at Serenity Springs Care Facility, where Rowena is a patient," Judson explained. "Yvette isn't there. In fact, Rowena hasn't had any visitors since she arrived two days ago."

That eased some of the knotted muscles in her stomach and chest, but Addie was nowhere near ready to relax. "Rowena and Yvette could have worked out the kidnapping when Rowena was still in jail. The two could still be in contact."

Grace's forehead bunched up while she glanced at Trevor. "Okay, let me do this interview, and then I'll drive to San Antonio and have a chat with Rowena."

The words had no sooner left her mouth than Judson's phone rang, and Addie saw the name of the treatment facility on his screen. That bad feeling returned with a vengeance.

Judson moved them farther away from the dining room, no doubt so Trevor wouldn't be able to hear, and he took the call on speaker. "This is Deputy Judson Docherty," he said.

Addie expected to hear the facility director's voice, maybe telling them that Rowena escaped. But it wasn't.

It was Rowena.

"I understand you just contacted Serenity Springs about me," Rowena said, skipping any greeting. "I was in the room with the director when she got the call," she added. "Yvette isn't here."

"When's the last time you saw her?" Judson was quick to ask.

But Rowena certainly wasn't quick to answer. "I won't get into that over the phone, but I will tell Addie and you in person. I'll tell you anything you want to know."

Now, it was Addie who cursed, and it wasn't under her breath. "That's blackmail," Addie spat out.

"Yes, it is," Rowena readily admitted. "But I need to see you, and if this is the way I can make that happen, then I'll use it."

"This is Sheriff Granger." Grace spoke up, the anger rising in her voice. "I can charge you with obstruction of justice and aiding and abetting a fugitive. You'll be sent back to prison and take your dying breath there."

Rowena coughed. "You could do that, and then I'll take what I know about Yvette to the grave. I've got nothing to lose, Sheriff Granger, by staying silent, because no matter what I do, I'll be dead in a couple of weeks."

"Fine," Grace snarled. "I'll send someone from SAPD over there now to arrest you."

"Wait," Addie mouthed, not saying it aloud since she didn't want Rowena to hear it. "Mute your phone," she told Judson and didn't add anything else until he had done that. "I can go see her."

"You can't," Judson snapped just as Grace insisted, "No need. I'm calling her bluff."

"It's not a bluff," Addie muttered. "Her one and only

goal is to see me, and she'll risk going back to jail to get a chance at that happening."

Grace groaned and did more cursing. "You don't have to do this," she told Addie.

"I know," Addie replied, but it didn't exactly feel like an option. "As long as Yvette is at large, the babies are likely in danger. Judson and me, too. Heck, anyone around us as well. If Rowena has any inkling of where we can find Yvette, then it's something I need to do."

Grace didn't look convinced. Judson certainly didn't, either. And while Addie was dreading this, dreading it all the way to her bones, she would do it for those precious babies. She'd face down the monster who'd killed her mother and kidnapped her and hopefully get the truth about Yvette.

"All right," Grace said after what felt like an eternity of hesitation. "The two of you go to San Antonio. And take Livvy with you."

Addie shook her head. "No. I want her to stay here. I want all the protection possible for Lily and Rose."

Grace shook her head, too. "I'll be here. So will Bennie and two of the ranch hands. But there's no way I'll send Judson and you out there alone without backup. Go and have Livvy follow in a cruiser. That way, if the killer sees two cop cars, he or she might think twice about launching another attack."

Addie wanted to argue with that, but then she remembered this wasn't just about her. Judson would go with her, she had zero doubts about that, and it meant he'd be in danger.

"All right," Addie agreed. She turned to Judson. "Can we leave now? The sooner we get this done, the better. I don't want to sit around here thinking about it."

His expression morphed from deep concern to anger, which she didn't think was directed at her but rather Rowena. "Okay," he finally said. "But I stay with you during the visit. You're not doing that solo, even if Rowena insists on it."

Addie had no trouble agreeing to that. This visit would be beyond hard, but without Judson, it felt impossible. Besides, Judson was the cop, and this could serve as an official interview.

"Just let me give the babies a quick kiss goodbye," Addie insisted, hurrying toward her bedroom.

She stepped into the room and found them both asleep. Etta Jean was folding laundry on the bed, and she must have seen something in Addie's expression, because she immediately asked, "What's wrong?"

"I just have to visit someone," Addie settled for saying. "Judson's going with me. If you need anything, let Bennie or Grace know. And call me if there's any sign of trouble."

Etta Jean gave a shaky nod and kept her gaze pinned to Addie as she gave each baby a kiss on the cheek. Addie gave Etta Jean a hug, too, and then hurried back out to find Judson waiting for her at the door.

"The cruisers are ready," he let her know.

Clearly, he still wasn't convinced this was the right thing to do, but he didn't hesitate getting them out of the house and into the waiting cop car. Livvy was already in her vehicle, and they took off, heading toward San Antonio.

"Should I call the treatment center and let them know we're coming?" Addie asked.

"No. I don't want anyone there knowing our plans. Especially Rowena. She could call the person who attacked us."

Oh, mercy. Addie hadn't even considered that, but it was a possibility. Rowena had made it seem as if she'd wanted to say goodbye, but the woman could have something sinister in mind.

Like trying to kill Addie for rejecting her.

"If you want to change your mind about this visit, I can turn around and take you home," Judson offered.

"No." Addie steeled herself up and mentally repeated that a couple of times. "I want to find out anything Rowena knows about Yvette."

Judson's jaw muscles tightened, but he didn't turn around. However, he did keep watch around them as they headed toward the interstate, and he used a voice command to call the prison where Rowena had been an inmate. It took him several minutes to work his way to the warden.

"Curtis Sanchez," the man said when he came on the line.

"Deputy Judson Docherty from Renegade Canyon PD. I'm pressed for time, and I'm hoping you can help me. Rowena Matthews's name had come up as connected to a fugitive wanted for abducting two infants. Yvette Cates."

"Yes, I saw that on the news," Sanchez said, but then he paused. "How's Cates connected to Rowena?"

"It's possible they were friends. I need you to tell me if Yvette ever visited Rowena while she was incarcerated?"

"Hold on a second and I can check that." They heard the clicks of a keyboard in the background, and it didn't take long for the man to come back on the line. "Yes, she did. Lots of times. Three visits in the last two weeks. Before that, Yvette came about every other month."

So, something had caused those visits to increase. But what? Had the women been planning the trip to the Horseshoe Ranch to get the twins, or was this about something else?

"Were the visits monitored?" Judson pressed. "In other words, were they recorded?"

"Supervised but not recorded," Sanchez admitted. "Rowena wasn't considered a flight risk. In fact, while she was here, she was a model prisoner, which was why she was granted medical release. Why? Do you think Rowena had a part in the abduction of those babies?"

"I'm not sure. What about other visitors?" Judson pressed. "I'm specifically looking at other parents who might have lost custody of their kids and were taken into care by CPS."

"Well, I wouldn't have that info, but I can send you a list of names of her visitors. Would that help?" Sanchez asked.

"It would. Text it to my phone, and I'll share it with my boss, Sheriff Granger. We can dig through the names and see if anything pops." Judson paused. "By the way, for what it's worth, Rowena isn't being a model citizen now that she's out," he explained. "She's refused to give the cops vital information about Yvette unless she speaks to the woman she abducted as a child. It's down and dirty blackmail."

"I'm sorry to hear that." And the man sounded genuine. "I can call and speak to her if you think that'll help."

Judson seemed to consider that and then said, "No, but thanks for the offer. I'll be in touch if I end up filing charges against her. Then, you can decide if you want to try to revoke her release."

The warden thanked him, and Judson ended the call. With the silence filling the cab of the cruiser, there was nothing to interfere with her thinking, and dreading, this face-to-face. Addie wouldn't change her mind, but she could feel the tension building, building...

And then it stopped when Judson took her hand and gave it a gentle squeeze. That was all it took to settle some of her raw nerves. All it took to lower that barrier between them another notch.

"Just think about the babies," Judson said, his voice oh so calm. "Think about holding them, feeding them." He paused. "Think about how many times they'll wake us up tonight." He grinned at her.

The moment seemed way too light, considering everything that was going on. But it also seemed intimate. And it was. After all, they might be sharing a bedroom again, and the intimacy between them was building, too.

It'd been years since they'd been lovers. A lifetime ago. Yet, all those memories came flooding back to her now. Of the hot kisses on the seat of his pickup truck. The touching. The need. So much need.

The making out had escalated until they'd finally done the deed. And repeated it throughout the summer right before he'd left for the military and she had left for college.

Sometimes, like now, she wondered what would have happened if they'd both stayed in Renegade Canyon. Would they have ditched the pact they'd made and hooked up for good?

Maybe.

And that's what Addie decided to focus on. That and her future with the babies. She let herself sink right into the images and stayed there until Judson drove into San Antonio and to the Serenity Springs Care Facility.

"It doesn't look like a prison," Addie remarked when she eyed the two-story redbrick building with the white columns. "Or a hospital."

It looked more like someone's home. An expensive one. And it seemed way too luxurious to house a killer.

Judson pulled to a stop in one the visitors' spots, and Livvy parked right next to him. He didn't get out. He turned in the seat to look Addie straight in the eyes.

"I'm not changing my mind," she let him know.

"I figured as much. I was going to say, don't let her get to you. Keep the conversation on Yvette and the present. Don't let Rowena drag you into the past."

It was good advice. Easier said than done, but still good, and that's why she leaned in and brushed her mouth over his. For the advice and because she knew, like his touch, the kiss would soothe her.

And it did.

It aroused her, too, but Addie figured she could embrace the heat while they made their way out of the cruiser and inside.

With Livvy right behind him, they stepped into the facility, and while the foyer didn't look much like a hospital, either, it smelled like one. That antiseptic smell seemed to coat everything from the high plastered ceilings to the marble floors.

Judson immediately went to the reception desk to deal with the woman in pale blue scrubs who certainly wasn't welcoming them. In fact, she seemed ready to send them on their way. Judson showed her his badge, followed by a murmured conversation.

The woman gave Addie a long look before she called someone, and she continued to scrutinize both Livvy and Judson while she spoke to whoever she'd called. Probably the director. Heck, maybe even Rowena.

After she ended the conversation, she typed in something on her laptop and used her phone to take a photo of Judson's badge. She also had him sign something before she finally stood.

"This way," she said. "The patient has agreed to see you."

Yes, Addie would bet Rowena had, and she was probably fist pumping in triumph at getting her way. The thought of that disgusted Addie even more.

The receptionist led them down a long hall and stopped outside a room across from a nurses' station. The nurse manning it was on the phone, and he barely spared them a glance before they went inside.

Definitely a hospital room.

Not just the scent but the bed and the equipment that surrounded it. And in that bed sat Rowena, looking considerably older than the last time Addie had seen her. Looking considerably older than her age, too. It was obvious the cancer had taken a toll on her, as her face was very thin. Her head was wrapped in a bandanna that had been fashioned into a cap.

"Addie," Rowena said, her voice a hoarse rattle. She lifted her hand and motioned for Addie to come closer.

She didn't.

Addie stayed put, and she didn't even attempt to soften her glare of disgust. That disgust went up a notch when she spotted the photo of herself on the nightstand. Definitely not one that Addie had given her, but rather one that had been printed out from an online newspaper article that had been done about the Horseshoe Ranch when Addie had taken over running it.

"Deputy Judson Docherty," he said, breaking the cold silence that had settled in the room. He hitched his thumb to Livvy. "Deputy Walsh. Now, start talking, Rowena," he added. Judson certainly wasn't toning down his venom, either. "Babies are at risk, and I don't want to waste a second with these sick mind games you're playing."

Rowena finally tore her stare from Addie and shifted to Judson while she shook her head. "No mind games. I needed to see my... Addie."

Even though the woman hadn't said the d-word, *daughter*, Addie knew she was thinking it. And that upped Addie's anger even more.

"I needed to say I'm sorry," Rowena went on, shifting her attention back to Addie. "I'm so very sorry for taking you, and while I don't expect your forgiveness—"

"Good," Addie snapped. "Now, tell us about Yvette so we can get the heck out of here."

Rowena sighed, and for a moment Addie thought the woman was going to keep the conversation on the past. But she didn't.

"I had no part in taking those twin baby girls," Rowena finally said. "I want you to know that up front. And I had no idea that Yvette would do it, either."

Judson put his hands on his hips and aimed narrowed eyes at Rowena. "You'd better tell us a hell of a lot more than that, or I'll be filing charges against you. I've already spoken to the warden, and he's considering revoking your release."

That put some alarm in Rowena's eyes, and she gave a shaky nod. "There's more. I just wanted you to understand that I didn't know what Yvette was going to do. If I had, I would have tried to talk her out of it."

Judson made a circling motion with his finger for Rowena to continue when she fell silent.

"Yvette started visiting me years ago," she went on. "She was furious that her kids had been taken from her, and she blames CPS and anyone connected with the Horseshoe Ranch." When her voice cracked, she reached for a container of water and had a few sips. "Recently, Yvette was worried that someone had been drugging her."

"Who?" Judson demanded.

"She didn't know, but she thought it might be Trevor. Or Jennifer's boyfriend, Elijah."

That got Addie's attention, and while she didn't go closer, she was very interested in this part of the conversation.

"Yvette thought Trevor or Elijah might be trying to kill her so they could get their hands on her money," Rowena added.

"Did she have any proof?" Judson pressed.

Rowena shook her head and sighed. "And I'm not sure it was actually happening. Yvette seemed to be having some kind of breakdown. I think maybe because of the rift between Jennifer and her. She loves her daughter very much, and it was tearing her apart that Jennifer was being so hostile."

Addie kept up the glare and intensified it when Rowena

looked at her. The woman was clearly applying Yvette's situation to her own.

Or trying to, anyway.

Addie wanted to blurt out a reminder that Rowena was a killer and a child abductor and deserved hostility, but she didn't want to give this woman anything. Not her words, not her anger. Not her attention. And that's why Addie shifted her gaze to a spot on the floor. No more eye contact.

"Is that it?" Judson asked. "Did you drag us all the way out here for that?"

"There's more," Rowena was quick to say. "Shane also believes Trevor could have been drugging his mother. If he was, then maybe Trevor used the drugs to manipulate Yvette into taking those babies."

"Wait," Judson said. "You've talked to Shane, or is this hearsay from Yvette?" Addie definitely wanted to know the same thing.

"Not hearsay," Rowena insisted. "I've spoken with Shane plenty of times. At first, Yvette brought him with her when she visited me in prison. Then, later, Shane started coming alone."

Addie didn't like the sound of that. What would Shane have wanted with a convicted killer? It certainly wouldn't have been just to accompany his mother, since he'd done solo visits, too.

So, what had Shane been doing there?

Unfortunately, Addie could think of a reason. If Shane was angry about being placed into foster care, then he could have been thinking it was time for payback, against CPS and the Horseshoe. It chilled Addie to the bone to consider that was why Courtney had been murdered and the twins had been taken. Yvette and Shane could have come up with this sinister plan together.

But did Rowena play into that plan in any kind of way?

"I'm guessing Shane didn't have any proof that Trevor or Elijah was drugging Yvette?" Judson asked.

"No," Rowena replied. "But Shane despises both men and thinks they're after his mother's money. He said his mom and sister were weak and naive for getting involved with the likes of those two. He was also worried that Jennifer might try to get back at Yvette for the miscarriage."

"What miscarriage?" Judson snapped.

"Jennifer's." She paused. "You didn't know," she muttered. "Jennifer had a miscarriage last month, and she told Yvette that she believed the stress caused it. Stress her mother caused by being with Trevor."

Addie had no idea if that kind of anxiety could cause a woman to miscarry, but if Jennifer had believed that, it might be motive for her to get back at Yvette in some way. But there were a lot simpler ways to do that than threatening to kidnap the twins and spurring Yvette to try to "rescue" them.

"The last time Shane and I spoke," Rowena went on, "he was trying to convince Yvette to cut Trevor and Jennifer out of her will. He thought if Jennifer couldn't inherit, then there'd be no threat to Yvette from Elijah."

Addie considered that, and she could see Shane's point. That would eliminate possible threats if the two were indeed trying to get Yvette's money. But Shane could have also wanted Yvette to cut them out of the will so he could inherit it all.

"Any ideas where would Yvette be hiding out right now?" Judson asked.

"She usually just talked about her children and husband, but she did mention a fishing cabin that Trevor owns."

That was the place where Trevor had claimed to be during

the twins' abduction. Addie knew from the updates she'd read that the cabin had already been searched, and there'd been no sign of Yvette.

"Anywhere else?" Judson asked when once again the woman fell silent.

"No. I'm sorry. Like I said, Yvette kept the conversation on her kids and what she'd gone through with CPS. I can't imagine she'd go anywhere without telling Shane, though. Yvette seemed very devoted to him."

Well, if Yvette had told Shane, he wasn't volunteering the info. Hopefully, though, that might change since both Jennifer and Shane could still be in interviews at the police station in Renegade Canyon.

"Is that it?" Judson asked. "You've got nothing else to tell us about Yvette or her husband and kids?"

More silence followed. "Nothing more about Yvette and Shane," Rowena finally said. "But I want to talk to Addie. Just give me five minutes so I can say my piece," she added in a plea.

That snapped Addie out of her thoughts about the investigation and gave her a cold, hard reminder of where she was. The anger came. Mercy, did it, and she had to clench her fists to stop herself from storming across the room and ripping up that photo of her.

But even that would be giving Rowena the attention that Addie didn't want her to have. In fact, she wanted to give this woman exactly what she deserved.

Which was nothing.

Absolutely nothing.

Without even sparing Rowena a glance, Addie turned and walked out.

Chapter Eleven

Judson didn't say goodbye to Rowena or thank her for talking to them. He was still way past being riled that the woman had forced Addie to go through this to give them those scraps of info. As far as he was concerned, those scraps had come at too high a price for Addie, and Rowena had put Addie through hell and back, all so she could see her.

Livvy and he followed Addie out of the room with Rowena calling out, "Addie. Just forgive me before it's too late."

Addie didn't respond. She just kept walking and only paused for them to catch up when she made it to the front door. Judson didn't linger. It was obvious that Addie needed to get the heck out of there now, so he scanned the parking lot of any signs of a threat. When he didn't see one, he hurried Addie out of the building and got her into the cruiser.

"Give me a second," she muttered while she gulped in some long, deep breaths. She was clearly trying to steady herself.

"Take all the time you need," he assured her.

Judson didn't touch her. Didn't pull her into his arms to try to comfort her—something he truly wanted to do. But he figured there was nothing he could say or do right now that would make this easier. So, he just sat quietly and waited her out.

Addie didn't cry, but she did mutter some ripe profanity under her breath. She also groaned and squeezed her eyes shut.

His phone sounded with a text, and he saw the message from Livvy pop up on the dash screen. On the drive back, I'll put more pressure on Yvette's lawyer to give a copy of her latest will.

Good. Judson sent her a thumbs-up emoji. Seeing the will would confirm if Yvette had indeed written her daughter and husband, Trevor, out of it. Of course, that didn't prove squat. Even if Yvette had basically disowned Trevor and Jennifer, they might not have even known about it. The will wouldn't necessarily be motive for drugging Yvette and pushing her to become mentally unstable.

But Yvette might not be the unstable one.

Jennifer could be, and while he hated to believe anything Rowena had just told them, he had to at least consider that Jennifer had indeed blamed Yvette for the miscarriage and that everything that'd happened in the past twenty-four hours had been orchestrated to get back at Yvette.

He considered texting Eden and Rory to find out if they'd learned anything in their interviews with Yvette's kids, but he dismissed that. If there was anything relevant, it'd soon be coming in a report. Something he'd need to do as well to fill Grace and the others in on the conversation with Rowena.

"You might think I should have just said I forgive her," Addie said, her voice cutting through his thoughts.

"I don't think that at all," he was quick to say. "Today proved that she's manipulative and self-centered. It was all about what she wanted, and she had no consideration for what a visit would put you through."

He saw some of the tension fade from her shoulders and face. "Thank you for that."

"Just stating the truth," he assured her, and because the timing felt right, he went ahead and pulled her into his arms.

Addie made a sound, sort of a sigh mixed with a soft sob, and she dropped her head on his shoulder. Judson tightened his grip around her, but he also kept watch. Making sure they weren't about to be attacked. He was certain Livvy was doing the same thing. Sitting here was a risk, but he wanted to give Addie these moments to try to settle from the emotional ordeal she'd been through.

"She is self-centered," Addie muttered. "And narcissistic. She made my life a living hell long before I even knew she'd murdered my mother and kidnapped me. I had to be perfect. My hair, my clothes, my manners. Everything. I had to present the perfect child to her so-called friends."

Over the years, Addie had mentioned bits and pieces of her life with Rowena. She'd been forced to perform in pageants, and Rowena had even put Addie on severe diets when she'd been only five years old.

"She was never violent with me," Addie went on. "She never physically hurt me the way she did my mother." The venom, and the hurt, spiked in those words. "But there was abuse."

Yeah, there had been, and while Judson hadn't wanted to pry into that part of Addie's life, once he'd become a cop, he had taken a look at the case file and reports after Rowena's arrest. Along with the diets and strict training routines for the pageants, Rowena had basically isolated Addie, not allowing her to make friends and even pulling her out of school so that Addie stayed right by her side. Rowena's generous inheritance from her late parents had allowed her to have that lifestyle.

And to basically keep Addie a prisoner.

Addie lifted her head and met his gaze. "Thank you," she said.

Judson felt he should be the one doling out the thanks for allowing herself to be put through this, but he didn't get the chance.

"Just please get me far away from her," Addie insisted. "I need to get back to the ranch and see Lily and Rose."

He needed that as well. Not just to put some distance between Rowena and them but because it was safer for Addie to not be out in the open like this. Plus, seeing the twins would settle both of them.

The moment they both had on their seat belts, he pulled out of the parking lot, and with Livvy behind them, they headed home. From the corner of his eye, he saw Addie text someone. Probably Etta Jean to let the woman know their estimated time of arrival.

Judson had barely made it out of San Antonio when his phone rang and Eden's name popped up on the screen. He went ahead and took the call on speaker, hoping this wasn't bad news.

"Should I ask how the meeting with Rowena went?" Eden said the moment she was on the line.

He waited and let Addie respond to that. "Rowena didn't give us any new info on where we might find Yvette, but she did mention the fishing cabin."

"She's definitely not there," Eden confirmed. "Well, not unless she showed up after the crime scene team left about an hour ago." She paused, and Judson heard what he thought was Eden texting someone. "I'm having one of the county deputies go back and have a look just in case."

That was a smart move. Yvette had to be somewhere. Well, unless she was dead. And if she was alive, she might try to hole up in a familiar place rather than risk checking into a hotel.

"Did you get anything else from Rowena?" Eden asked.

Again, Judson let Addie take that question. "Nothing more on possible locations, but Rowena told us that both Yvette and Shane visited her in prison and that she believes either Trevor or Elijah are trying to eliminate Yvette so they can inherit her money."

"Interesting," Eden muttered. "During my interview with Jennifer, she pointed the finger at Trevor, too. And at her brother."

No surprise there. If money was indeed the reason to get Yvette out of the picture, then Trevor, Shane, Elijah and Jennifer all had motive. But all these accusations were muddying the investigative waters. What they needed was proof.

"Did anything come out in Rory's interview with Shane?" Judson asked Eden.

"Not really. Shane certainly didn't mention anything about having visited Rowena," she explained. "We had to cut Shane loose about a half hour ago, but we can call him and ask him about that."

"I'll do that," Judson heard Rory say in the background.

Good. Because Judson wanted to hear what Shane had to say about those trips to the prison.

"What about Jennifer?" Judson asked. "Is she still there?"

"No. Grace said not to hold her, and we didn't. She left shortly before her brother did. Elijah picked her up."

Again, that wasn't much of a surprise. Grace didn't have the evidence to arrest Jennifer, and of course, she would have wanted her boyfriend to get her the heck out of there.

"Did Jennifer say anything about her recent miscarriage during the interview?" Judson added.

"She did. Said it happened about six weeks ago." Eden paused. "Why? Is it important?"

"Could be." Judson stopped and decided to rephrase that. "According to Rowena, it's important, anyway. I don't have a clue if Rowena is telling the truth, though. If she is, then Jennifer blames her mother for creating the stress that caused her to lose her baby."

"Wow," Eden muttered. "That could be a game changer and maybe give Grace enough to make an arrest, since it speaks to motive."

Yes, it did, but Judson wasn't sure they'd be arresting the guilty party. "What was your gut feel when you interviewed Jennifer?" he asked Eden. "Do you think she could have done the whole deal? Drug her mother and provoke her into abducting the twins so she could get back at Yvette?"

"My gut feel is she probably couldn't have done it solo," Eden said on a sigh. "She's an emotional wreck, likely suffering from some lingering trauma from her miscarriage. FYI, during the interview, Jennifer said a couple of times that the baby would have made her relationship with Elijah stronger. When I pushed on that, I got the impression that she's worried he's about to dump her."

Judson was giving that some thought when Addie voiced a question that was forming in his own mind. "When did Elijah and Jennifer start seeing each other?"

"Shortly after Yvette was awarded all that money in her settlement," Eden admitted. "But that's also around the time Trevor and Yvette hooked up. The timing is so coincidental that I understand why Shane thinks they could be gold diggers."

Shane just might be right about that, too. "Grace should

soon be finished interviewing Trevor," Judson commented. "What about Elijah? Is Grace bringing him back in, too?"

"Yep. This afternoon," Eden verified. "And Grace is already done with Trevor, and he's left the ranch. Grace is doing a report, but the gist is that Trevor didn't admit to any wrongdoing. He put it all on Yvette, and he swears up and down that he doesn't know where she is or why she took the twins."

Convenient, since the woman wasn't around to give her side of the story. But Judson was glad of one thing—that Trevor was no longer near the twins. It didn't matter that the man hadn't been armed, he was still a suspect, and Judson wanted him far away from Lily and Rose.

"Hold on a second," Eden muttered.

In the background, Judson heard Rory say something he didn't catch, but Eden relayed it a second later. "Rory wanted me to tell you that Shane didn't answer when he tried to call him. Rory left him a message."

Judson didn't care much for all their suspects being in the wind, again, but that only made him want to work harder to get to the bottom of what was going on.

He took the turn off the interstate, and since he'd made this trip so many times over the years, he knew they only had about ten miles before they made it to the ranch. If Grace was still there, he'd catch her up and then start diving into the reports of the interviews to see if there was some kernel of info he could use.

When he heard Addie draw in a quick breath, Judson glanced at her and saw that she was looking at the spot where they'd found the twins. Nan Fredrick wasn't at the end of the road today. No one was. But Addie must have gotten a jolt from the memory of what had gone on here.

Once they were past the farm road, Addie tore her gaze

from it and looked at him. For only a couple of seconds, anyway. They seemed to spot the movement together as Judson rounded a curve.

A woman.

Hell. What was this? Some kind of trap or diversion so the killer could attack them? Maybe. But the woman was real. And there was blood on her face. Judson had no trouble seeing that or the fact she was running up the road straight toward them. In the distance he could see a black car in the ditch.

He hit the brakes, thankful that Livvy reacted quickly, too. If she hadn't, the cruiser would have slammed into them, and Judson might have hit the woman.

"Help me," she shouted just as a text lit up his dash.

I'm calling this in, Livvy messaged. Any idea who she is?

It was hard to tell with all the blood, but the car in the ditch was damn familiar. "I think it's Yvette," Judson said.

Addie made a sharp sound of surprise and moved to the edge of her seat, no doubt to get a better look. That look was made considerably easier as the woman continued to come closer.

Yeah, it was Yvette, all right.

And judging from the blood streaming down her face, she had some kind of head injury. Either that or she had staged this to make it look as if she was hurt.

Judson didn't open the door to her, not even when Yvette shouted, "Help me." But he'd soon have to do that if for no other reason than to take her into custody.

The woman was firing glances over her shoulder as if looking for anyone who might be following her. Judson couldn't see anyone, but that didn't mean an attacker wasn't in that ditch, waiting and ready to strike.

In case another vehicle came barreling toward them, Judson turned on his lights and siren. Behind him, Livvy did the same. That didn't slow Yvette. Not a first, anyway. But after another glance over her shoulder, she stopped and turned, her attention zooming toward a cluster of trees just off the road. Judson thought he saw the start of a trail there, too.

"Does she see someone?" Addie asked. "Or is this some kind of ploy?"

Judson didn't know, and he didn't have time to figure it out because there was a loud blast that he had no trouble recognizing.

A gunshot.

And it'd come from those trees.

Yvette screamed, a bloodcurdling sound that ripped through the air, and she dropped to her knees. Judson couldn't tell if she'd actually been shot, but he knew he had to do something. If Yvette truly was in a danger, she could be killed right in front of him.

"Get down in the seat and stay in the cruiser," Judson told Addie while he threw the car into Drive and moved up closer to Yvette.

It wasn't easy, since the road was so narrow, but he turned the cruiser sideways to make it easier to reach Yvette through the driver's side door. That wasn't a huge precaution, considering that someone had already tried to kill Addie and him, but it was better than him just bolting out where he could be gunned down.

Judson threw the cruiser into Park and opened his door. He drew his gun and automatically braced himself for the sound of another bullet.

But none came.

However, even over the sirens, he could hear Yvette moaning, and she was now clutching her chest.

Livvy moved her cruiser, too, parking so that she was

right next to the passenger's side where Addie sat. Hopefully, Livvy would be able to protect her if things went to hell in a handbasket.

And they did.

Damn it, they did.

The gunfire blasted out from the trees. A spray of shots that slammed into the cruisers and the pavement. They would have likely slammed into Judson, too, had he not dropped down, using the front end of the cruiser for cover.

Judson considered leaning out, trying to pinpoint the shooter, but the bullets were coming too close to him. Pinning him down.

"Stay low," Livvy shouted a split second before Judson heard more gunfire.

From Livvy this time. And he cursed when he glanced behind him and saw that Livvy was behind her cruiser door and was returning fire. She only managed a couple of rounds before the shooter shifted his aim and sent some shots her way.

Cursing, Judson levered himself up and fired where he thought their attacker was, and he did some praying. Praying that Livvy and Addie weren't getting hit, since bullets could eventually get through both the window and the body of the cruisers. He also added a prayer that he could get Yvette out of this alive. Even if she was working with the gunman, she could give them answers as long as she wasn't dead.

But she wasn't screaming.

And she was moving.

Judson could see the blood spreading out from her, sliding across the pavement. There was way too much of it, and if he didn't do something soon, Yvette would bleed out.

"I'm driving closer to her," Judson let Livvy know.

He jumped back in the cruiser, giving Addie just a glance. He wanted to make sure she was all right, wanted to give her some kind of reassurance, but there wasn't time for that.

"Call for an ambulance," he told her. Not just to give her something to do, either. If he could get Yvette into the cruiser, they'd need EMTs out here right away.

Addie's hands were trembling when she took out her phone, but she made the call while Judson pulled up closer to Yvette. As close as he could get without hitting her. He aligned the back door with the woman and glanced at Addie again.

"Stay down," he repeated.

Just as a shot slammed into the window right above her head.

The glass cracked and webbed but held. Still, it could break at any second, and that's why Judson knew he had to move fast.

"All the way down in the seat," he told Addie, but she was already heading in that direction.

"You, too," she managed to say. She must have known, though, that wasn't something he could do. Not yet, anyway.

Behind him, he heard Livvy returning gunfire. Bullet for bullet. And he hoped Livvy would keep this SOB occupied while he got to Yvette.

Judson bolted from the cruiser again, staying low while he scurried toward Yvette. She still wasn't moving or speaking, but when he latched onto her arm, he saw her eyes open just a slit.

Alive.

For now, anyway. She wouldn't stay that way for long, though, with all that bleeding.

Even though it appeared the woman was seriously injured from a gunshot wound to the chest, Judson still took the time to make sure she wasn't armed. No signs of a weapon. Her hands were empty, and she didn't have a purse. However, she did have pockets in her jeans, and he patted them down while he dragged her to the cruiser and out of the line of fire.

The gunfire shifted, no longer being aimed at Livvy but rather coming at Judson. He didn't take the time to return fire. He just kept moving until he got Yvette to the side of the cruiser.

It was possible that just moving her had made her injuries worse. But he hadn't had a choice about that. Their attacker had fired at least two dozen shots, and many of them could have hit Yvette.

Hoisting Yvette up, he laid her on the back seat, and, staying low, Judson did another weapons check. But nothing. The keys were in the ignition, but the woman didn't even have a phone on her.

"The ambulance is on the way," Addie relayed to him.

Good. But whether it would make it there in time was anyone's guess. Added to that, the EMTs wouldn't be able to approach the scene until the threat from the gunman had been contained.

Judson decided to contain it.

He pulled out his backup gun from a slide holster and handed it to Addie. "If Yvette tries to hurt you, shoot to kill. Understand?"

Addie gave a shaky nod.

Since he could be leaving Addie with a killer, he hated dumping all of this on her, but he didn't have a lot of options. Livvy couldn't get to their cruiser unless she took a major risk of being gunned down. Judson couldn't let that happen.

Readying his gun, he got out of the cruiser again, and in the same motion, he took aim over the roof. And straight toward those trees. Judson fired and fired and fired.

From the corner of his eye, he saw Livvy rejoin the attack after she reloaded, and she sent her own rounds in the direction of the shooter.

Finally, their attacker stopped firing.

And Judson had no doubts, none, that he or she was getting away. Unlike the attack at the ranch, though, he didn't go running in pursuit this time. He couldn't take that risk.

Not when it would be Addie's life he was putting in yet more danger.

He shoved aside the notion of catching the gunman and instead focused on getting the identity of the SOB from Yvette.

"Who shot you?" Judson demanded, getting right in the woman's face. "Who were you running from?"

Yvette stared up at him with eyes full of shock and pain. She opened her mouth, but nothing came out for what seemed to be an eternity.

"You have to stop him," the woman finally said. "He'll kill her." Yvette's words were all breath and had barely any sound.

Still, Judson heard her loud and clear. "Stop who?" he demanded.

She opened her mouth again, but this time, nothing came.

"Stop who?" he repeated, shouting the question at her.

But Judson was talking to a woman who couldn't answer. Her breath rasped in her throat, and her eyelids drifted down.

Yvette was dead.

Chapter Twelve

Addie sat at the dining room table at the ranch and read through the statement she'd just given Grace. A necessary statement in what was now another murder investigation, but Addie had hated going through it all over again.

Still, she would have gladly given the statement if she'd thought this would put an end to the danger. An end to the nightmares the attacks and abduction had caused. But it wouldn't.

No.

She knew the memories of seeing Yvette die would stay with her for the rest of her life.

"Thank you," Grace said when Addie did an e-signature on the laptop screen. The sheriff stood. "Is there anything I can get you? Other than Judson, that is?"

Despite everything, Addie managed a weak, short-lived smile. She did indeed need Judson, but because of those legal necessities, they had been placed in separate rooms of the house to be interviewed. Bennie had been tapped to take Judson's statement, and Addie knew that Grace would now be shifting rooms to take Livvy's.

"I want to see Judson and the twins," Addie muttered. In fact, at the moment that was all she wanted.

Grace nodded as if that was the exact answer she'd expected. "He should be in the kitchen." But then she tipped her head to the front of Addie's shirt. "I'll need that first so the lab can analyze it. Let me grab an evidence bag from my cruiser."

Addie glanced down and saw the blood. Not hers. But rather Yvette's. It hadn't come directly from Yvette, either, but from Judson, who'd transferred it to her when he'd pulled her into his arms shortly before the ambulance and backup from the county had arrived.

"I'll be right back," Grace said, heading to get that bag.

Addie went in search of Judson and found him where Grace had said he'd be, in the kitchen. And he was in the process of stripping off his clothes. She nearly whirled around to give him some privacy, but after everything that'd happened, privacy seemed like too low-level of a concern. So, she waited.

And watched.

It was hard to tear her gaze away from him as he took off everything but his boxers. More memories came.

Not of death and blood this time.

But of Judson and her together. Even now, it was impossible for her not to notice that he still had an amazing body. One that caused the heat and the old need to start simmering between them.

"I need his jeans and shirt," Bennie said, his voice and expression filled with apologies. He held up an evidence bag and put the items in it when Judson handed them to him.

Judson kept his gaze pinned on her, searching her face to see how she was doing, while he fumbled around in his go-bag for the change of clothes.

"Grace needs my shirt, too," she said, managing to get her throat unclamped. She didn't know if that was because the emotion was catching up with her or because she was in the kitchen with a nearly naked Judson.

She decided it could be both, and once Judson was dressed and had pocketed his keys and phone and reholstered his weapons, Addie walked into the adjacent laundry room to grab a clean top. Since Etta Jean had been doing laundry when this whole abduction nightmare had started, several of Addie's shirts were already out of the dryer and folded.

"I'll step out for a minute," Bennie said, obviously getting out of the way so she could change.

Thankfully, Judson went into the laundry room with her. Thankfully, too, he didn't give her any privacy, because she didn't want him to. She wanted him right by her, and if seeing her without a shirt caused that heat and need to ripple again, then so be it. Addie didn't want him out of her sight.

She pulled off the top, taking a clean one off the top of the folded stack, and the moment she pulled it on, Addie stepped into his arms. Mercy, she needed this. She needed him, and Judson gave her that steadying comfort that no one else could. In the back of her mind, she knew she was falling hard for him all over again, but she couldn't stop it.

Correction: She didn't *want* to stop it.

He continued to hold her and brushed a kiss on the top of her head. Addie probably would have lifted her mouth to his to make it a real kiss, but the sound of footsteps stopped her. A moment later, Grace appeared in the doorway of the laundry room.

"Sorry," she muttered, holding up the evidence bag.

Addie stepped away from Judson so she could get the top and hand it to Grace. "What happens now?" Addie wanted to know.

"The clothes will go to the lab to see if there's any trace or fibers to tell us where Yvette has been the past twenty-four hours," Grace explained. "That, in turn, could tell us if she had an accomplice."

"An accomplice," Addie repeated in a mutter. "You mean Trevor, Jennifer, Shane or Elijah." She stopped. "Well, maybe not Jennifer. When Yvette was running, she shouted out, 'You have to stop him. He'll kill her.'" Those words were still repeating like gunfire in Addie's mind. "If she was referring to Jennifer, then the *him* could have been one of the three men."

Grace nodded. Then shrugged. "Or Yvette could have been talking out of her head. Perhaps in shock."

Maybe, but that didn't feel right to Addie.

"It's also possible that Yvette was talking about someone she hired. The accomplice angle again," Grace tacked on to that. "Yvette could have hired someone to attack Judson and you here at the ranch. Then, the hired gun could have turned on her for some reason and killed her. Yvette could have been worried that this person might go after her daughter."

Addie tried to envision any of their suspects doing just that. And she decided any one of them could have. Of course, it was equally possible that Yvette had acted alone in the abduction and attack at the ranch. Still, someone had murdered her, and that someone had tried to do the same to Judson, Livvy and her.

"While you were giving your statements, Eden managed to get her hands on Yvette's will," Grace continued a moment later. "Apparently, she made a new one less than a week ago, and she left everything to her kids. She specifically stated that no one else was to inherit anything. That *no one else* included a husband."

Well, that was interesting, and it made Addie wonder if Yvette had had her suspicions about her husband. Or had Yvette done this simply to try to repair her relationship with her daughter? Either way, Trevor wasn't going to care much for that.

"Who knew about the new will?" Judson asked.

"Not her family," Grace provided. "Well, not unless Yvette told them herself. The lawyer said the will had just been signed and processed and that he hadn't even given Yvette a copy of it yet."

Neither Shane, Jennifer, Trevor nor Elijah had mentioned the will, so it was possible Yvette had kept it to herself. But if she hadn't, if Shane and Jennifer knew about their inheritance, then it strengthened their motive for murdering her.

Grace had just finished bagging the shirt when both her phone and Judson's sounded with texts. They both looked to see what the message said.

"Group message from the CSIs," Grace relayed. "They're going over Yvette's car now, and they found something." She stopped, looked at Judson. "Apparently, a suicide note."

Of all the things Addie had thought the sheriff might say, that wasn't one of them. "Yvette was running for her life when we got to her," Addie pointed out. "Is the note real or something her killer planted?"

"We might soon find out," Grace murmured just as another text arrived.

Because Addie was still right next to Judson, she saw this message was a photo attachment. "The note," he said, holding his phone so they could both see it.

This wasn't some pristine, typed letter but something that appeared to have been hastily scrawled on a napkin from a fast-food place.

"'I'm so sorry,'" Addie read aloud. "'I can't live with what I've done.'"

That was it. Not even a signature. Definitely no last words for her kids. And that made Addie instantly suspicious.

"Yvette would have told Shane and Jennifer she loved

them," Addie remarked, and she got immediate sounds of agreement from both Grace and Judson.

"So, either she was coerced into writing this, or she didn't get a chance to finish it," Judson concluded. He glanced up from the photo to meet Grace's gaze. "I got a look at Yvette's car, and it'd been run off the road. There were skids on the pavement from where it looked like she tried to stop."

"That was Livvy's impression, too," Grace said. "The person who shot Yvette could have maybe hoped to make her death look like a suicide. When that failed and when she started running and you guys showed up, the killer had to resort to shooting her. And trying to eliminate any witnesses by shooting Livvy and the two of you."

Yes, all of that was possible.

Grace opened her mouth to say something else, but the sound of raised voices stopped her. Judson automatically stepped in front of Addie, and he drew his gun. Grace did the same. Addie might have pushed them both aside to try to get to the babies, though, if Bennie hadn't stepped into view.

"Elijah, Shane, Trevor and Jennifer just arrived," Bennie let them know. "They're demanding to speak to you," he added before he hurried off. No doubt to make sure the visitors didn't barge in.

Grace sighed and looked back at Addie. "When I called to do the death notification, I told them to meet me at the station. I didn't want them here around you or the twins."

Addie got that. She didn't especially want the trio around the babies, either. But she did want to see something.

"Will you tell them about the will?" Addie asked Grace. "Because I'd like to see how they react to that."

The corner of Grace's mouth lifted into a smile. "Oh, yes, I'll definitely let them know, and I won't be having that conversation in the house but rather on the porch, so you'll both be able to watch and listen. The babies are tucked away safe with Etta Jean?" she asked.

Addie nodded, but she sent a text to Etta Jean to tell her to take the twins into the bathroom. Yes, she wanted to see the reactions to the will, but Addie didn't want that info to come with any additional risks to Lily and Rose.

"Do any of the four have alibis for the time of Yvette's shooting?" Judson asked Grace as they all made their way to the front of the house.

"Nope. I asked them that when I did the phone notification, and all claimed to be at home or on their way home. We'll check and see if that can be verified."

"I will see her now," Shane shouted, his voice so loud that it would have drowned out anything else that Grace said.

Elijah wasn't exactly being quiet, either. He was yelling out a demand to see Grace and Judson. Trevor was in the mix, too, shouting at the top of his lungs. Addie couldn't hear Jennifer at all.

When Judson, Grace and she made it to the front door, Addie saw Livvy and Bennie were blocking Shane and Elijah from coming in. She spotted Trevor on the porch steps, and Jennifer was by the gate. Jennifer was the only one of the four who looked grief-stricken, and it was obvious the woman had been crying.

"What the hell happened to my mother?" Shane demanded when his attention landed on Grace. The man also shot looks of disgust at Judson and Addie. "Did those two kill her?"

"Throttle back now," Grace snapped through clenched teeth. "Or I'll arrest you on the spot."

"Yeah, yeah, and kill me, too," Shane taunted. "Just like they murdered my mother."

"They didn't kill Yvette," Grace said, moving between Livvy and Bennie to face Shane head-on.

"Then, damn it, who did?" That came from Elijah. Like Shane, his face was tight with rage.

"We're looking into that." Grace aimed a warning finger at Elijah when he took a menacing step toward her. "If I have to arrest you for threatening a police office, trespassing and other assorted charges, it'll mean hauling you down to the station. It could be hours or days before you get any info from me. Or you could all just shut the hell up and I'll tell you right now what I know."

That silenced Trevor and Shane, but Elijah still looked ready to push Grace. He seemed to rethink that after sliding glances at the three other cops, who were clearly ready to back up their boss.

"All right," Grace continued once they'd all hushed. Well, their shouts and accusations had stopped, but Shane and Elijah were still doing some glaring. "Yvette was shot and killed by an unknown assailant. She appears to have been fleeing from that assailant when she died."

"Unknown assailant," Elijah snarled in a *yeah, right* tone. "You can't make me believe those two didn't want her dead because she took those kids." He turned his glare on Addie and Judson.

Grace shrugged. "Believe what you will, but they didn't kill her, and there's a manhunt for the person who did. To rule yourselves out as suspects, I'm asking you all to submit to GSR testing."

That brought on more cursing from Shane and Elijah, but Trevor stepped forward. "I'll do it," he said.

"So will I," Jennifer agreed.

Elijah tossed her a *what the hell* look, clearly not approving of her cooperation. If it was cooperation, that was. Jennifer could have still been the shooter, but maybe she was certain there wouldn't be any residue on her clothes.

"I want to know what happened to my mother," Jennifer added, showing some defiance of her own against Elijah. She shifted her attention to Judson and Addie. "Did she say anything before she died?"

Addie heard the question, but she focused on the reactions of the three male suspects. All of them seemed to have a second or two of stunned silence while they considered that.

Or feared that.

Were they worried that Yvette had said something to incriminate one of them? Maybe.

"She did say some things," Grace admitted. "We're going to analyze it further and try to enhance the dash-cam feed."

That sent Shane on a cursing spree. "What kind of doublespeak is that? Tell us what she said."

"Sorry, but I'm not at liberty to disclose that," Grace fired back. "But as soon as the analysis is done, I'll be in touch. Trust me on that."

It sounded like a threat, and while her expression, tone and badge had Elijah backing up a step, Shane held his ground.

"However, I can give you some other info," Grace went on a heartbeat later. "It's about Yvette's will." She paused, waiting until all four were staring at her. "Did any of you know that Yvette redid her will last week?"

Trevor groaned and muttered something under his breath that Addie didn't catch. "I told her not to give in to Shane's demands."

So, he'd known the change to the will was possible, and it made Addie wonder if Trevor had used those drugs to try to stop her. In fact, the drugs might come up if Trevor decided to challenge the will.

"Yvette left everything to her kids," Grace let Trevor

know. "She purposely excluded anyone else, including a husband."

Elijah smiled. Actually smiled. Until he must have realized that wasn't an appropriate response and shut it down.

Trevor certainly wasn't smiling. He was riled to the bone, and, cursing, he stormed off the porch, headed to his car and then sped away.

Addie shifted her attention to Shane, who wasn't smiling but did appear more than a little shocked. It was the same for Jennifer, who began to cry again.

Elijah hurried off the porch to go to her, and he tried to put his arm around her, but she stepped away from him. The man didn't show any irritation over the rejection. Instead, he turned back to Grace.

"How soon will Shane and Jennifer be able to settle Yvette's estate and get the money?" he asked.

"Stop it, Elijah," Jennifer snapped before Grace could respond. Well, respond other than rolling her eyes and making a loud huff. "Just go wait in the truck for me," Jennifer ordered.

Now, the irritation came, but Elijah didn't push back. Probably because he figured out that badgering Jennifer wouldn't help him get his hands on her dead mother's money. Kicking at a rock that was on the pathway, Elijah went to the truck, slamming the door behind him after he got in.

"I did encourage my mother to cut Trevor out of the will," Shane admitted. "I still believe the man was solely after her money." He paused. "And I believe he could have been the one who killed her."

"Maybe," Grace said, not sounding at all convinced of that. "He agreed to the GSR test. What about you?"

The muscles tightened in Shane's jaw, but he finally nodded. "I'll be tested, too."

"Good. Then, go to the police station and one of the deputies will take the swab. The results come back like that." Grace snapped her fingers. "And you might be surprised at how hard it is to wash off gunshot residue. A shower and change of clothes usually aren't enough."

Shane stood in silence for a couple of seconds before he nodded and walked away, heading to his car. Jennifer, however, didn't budge. Not until her brother had driven away, and then she came up the porch steps toward them.

"Did, uh…are you sure someone killed my mother?" Jennifer asked. "Are you sure she didn't take her own life?"

Those questions seemed like giant, waving red flags, and none of them jumped to respond. Grace hadn't said a word about a suicide note being found in Yvette's car, but maybe Jennifer hadn't needed to be told.

Maybe she already knew.

"Did she take her own life?" Jennifer repeated. Her hands trembled while she wiped away more tears.

"Why do you think that?" Grace finally asked.

Jennifer didn't give a quick answer. She squeezed her eyes shut a moment, and a sob made its way from her throat. "Because I think Mom was considering it. Ending things," she added in a hoarse whisper. "She was depressed. Or something. I think she was using drugs."

"Did she say that or did you see her use them?" Grace pressed.

Jennifer shook her head. "No, but something was off this past week or so. She left rambling messages about when she'd lost custody of Shane and me. In one of them, she said this place was evil, that the people here basically stole children from their loving parents."

Good grief. Addie had to bite back the anger and frustration over that. Yes, mistakes could and did happen in the foster system, but Mellie had worked hard for the children in her care.

"You didn't mention any of this during your interview," Grace reminded Jennifer. "Why not?"

For a second, Jennifer got the deer-caught-in-the-headlights look, but she shook it off. "I, uh, didn't remember until now." She paused and glanced around as if to make sure no one else was listening. "I think someone's trying to kill me," she whispered.

"Who?" Grace demanded.

"My brother, I think," she admitted after wiping away more tears. "I believe Mom told him about the change in the will. He was the one pushing for it. Him and Elijah," she added, her voice dropping to a whisper again.

"Has Shane done something specific to make you think he might want to kill you?" Grace asked.

Again, no quick answer, but Jennifer took out her phone and handed it to Grace. "I recorded Shane. And, no, I didn't tell him I was doing it, so I guess that's not exactly ethical."

"It's not," Grace agreed, but she took the phone. "What's on the recording?" she pressed.

"Just listen to it," Jennifer insisted. "And when you're done, maybe it'll be enough to arrest my brother for murder."

Chapter Thirteen

Judson sat in the makeshift office area that Addie and he had set up in her bedroom and checked to see if an update of Jennifer's recording had arrived on his laptop.

It hadn't.

But he knew something like that could take time. It wasn't just the accessing it from her phone but having the lab techs do thorough tests to make sure the recording didn't contain a virus.

And that it was real.

With all the advancements in AI, it was getting easier for people to do realistic fakes of such things, and Jennifer had a motive to do something like that. Well, she had motive if she wanted to cut her brother out of any inheritance from their mother, and a half a million was plenty of motive for her to want to do exactly that.

Since he didn't yet have the recording, Judson moved on to the latest report from the CSIs while he did some multitasking. He was keeping an eye on the twins, who were now asleep and listening for Addie in the shower. Thankfully, Addie was taking her time in the bathroom, and he hoped it was helping to ease her knotted muscles as it'd done for Judson when he had finally been able to wash off the remnants of Yvette's blood.

Now, listening to the water running and hearing her move around in there, he had tried not to think of Addie washing away blood. Tried not to think of her fighting the images of a woman being gunned down in front of her. Part of him wanted to go into the bathroom and try to soothe her. To check and see if she was all right.

But that would be playing with fire.

A naked Addie would be far too tempting, and an attempt at comfort might turn into full-blown sex. She didn't need that now.

Probably not, anyway.

And he admitted that wasn't a good thought to let stay in his head. He tried to shove it aside and focus on the report. Judson soon saw that it was dashcam footage not just from his cruiser but also the one Livvy had been driving when they'd come around that curve and seen Yvette.

Hell.

The camera had captured the woman dying.

Yeah, that was a way to yank his attention away from Addie and shower sex. It was the exact reminder he needed. They were in the middle of an intense murder investigation, and it needed his focus.

Judson watched the dash-cam feed frame by frame as it all played out again. Yvette running on the road toward them. The terror on her face as she begged for help. Help that hadn't come in time, because one of the slowed images showed the impact of the shot slamming into her body.

But another of the frames showed something else.

And that's what Judson zoomed in on now.

As that part of the road had just come into view, there was some movement in the trees to the right. Just a blur of motion, really, but judging from the location, it had almost certainly been Yvette's killer.

According to the memo attached to the report, the lab techs were in the process of trying to enhance the blur, trying to come up with any small detail that would help them identify who it was. Judson certainly couldn't tell from that smeared image, but he was hoping for something of a miracle. They needed to know who'd fired those shots so they could arrest him or her and put an end to the violence.

Judson swiveled around in his chair when he heard some movement in one of the bassinets, and he got up to check. Lily was wiggling and kicking her feet, but her eyes were still closed.

Still sleeping, well, like a baby.

It wasn't a surprise, since it was something that Addie had said the girls would do for at least another two hours. He was hoping Addie herself would do the same soon and get some rest or at least eat some of the sandwiches that Grace had had delivered from the diner in town.

He went back to his work area, sitting and using the keys on his laptop to freeze the screen on that blur.

On the killer.

And he played around with enlarging it and trying to change the colors and pixels enough to coax out some more details. He stopped again though when he heard Addie turn off the water in the shower. She didn't take long to dress because what seemed like less than a minute later, she came into the room wearing loose gray jogging pants and a black T-shirt.

Addie looked at him, their gazes connecting for a couple of heartbeats before she went to the bassinets to check on the babies. Then she turned, her attention settling on his laptop screen.

"What is that?" she asked, her eyes widening as she began to take it in. Addie headed straight toward him.

Judson sighed. Not that he could have kept this from her, but he'd hoped it could wait until the techs had managed to clean up the image. Maybe then he could have given her good news.

"It's the feed from the dashcams in the cruisers," he let her know and added, "You don't want to see this."

"Probably not," she murmured. "But I need to."

Hell. He debated if he could talk her out of this and decided the answer to that was no. So, Judson rewound it to the starting point of when he'd driven around the curve.

"Yvette," she said, leaning in closer to the monitor.

He made a sound of agreement, and before they got to the part where the woman was shot, he reversed the feed again and froze it on the shooter.

Again, Addie went even closer, studying it and no doubt doing what he'd done. Trying to figure out who the heck that was.

"The techs are trying to clean this up," he explained. "We might have something soon."

She seemed to latch on to that, and he saw some hope creep into her eyes. But that hope apparently wasn't going to get her to change her mind about continuing to view the footage where she would soon be seeing a woman murdered.

Judson was ready to let her take a look at all of it when his phone vibrated with a text. He'd shut off the sound so as not to wake the babies, but it still made a noise when it skittered on the surface of the desk.

"It's from Rory," he relayed to her. And then he saw the attachment. Not the dash-cam footage but something else that he'd been waiting for. "It's the recording that Jennifer gave Grace."

Judson welcomed the interruption and figured the recording wouldn't be nearly as gruesome as the dash-cam footage. At least he hoped it wasn't. But then, Jennifer had accused her brother of trying to murder her.

"The lab has authenticated it," he continued, reading through the info that Rory had sent along with the attachment. "It's real, and they've confirmed it's actually Jennifer and Shane speaking on the recording. The techs were able to do a voice analysis using the statements they both gave during their interviews."

"When did Jennifer record this?" Addie asked.

Judson found that in the notes, too. "According to the time stamp, it was one week ago today."

He adjusted the volume so it would be loud enough for them to hear but hopefully wouldn't carry to the bassinets. When he clicked the play function, he immediately heard Shane's voice.

"I repeat," Shane snarled. "We have to do something to snap Mom back to her senses. She's letting Trevor rule the roost, and if that continues, you and I are going to be flat broke."

"It's Mom's money," Jennifer replied.

"Yeah, but we're her kids, and if we don't do something and do it fast, Trevor will spend every last dime of it. If Mom was thinking straight, she'd want her own flesh and blood to have an inheritance."

Jennifer huffed. "She's got a blind spot when it comes to Trevor. She'll never choose us over him."

"She will if she has no choice," Shane spat out.

"What do you mean?" Jennifer asked after some hesitation.

"I mean, we have to do something. If she starts using again or drinking, then we can have her declared incompetent. We can take control of her estate. It'd be easy enough to tempt her into going back to her old ways. All I need is you to back me up. Us against Trevor."

Jennifer was silent for several seconds. "What are you saying, Shane? Are you planning on pushing Mom to use drugs or start drinking again?"

"It would only be temporary," Shane replied, as if he were certain that something like that would be reversible and not just flat-out wrong. Or dangerous if Yvette overdosed. "And then after we have her estate under our control, we can give Trevor the boot and get Mom into rehab. Once she's free of Trevor, she'll understand we did all of this for her."

"You're doing it for you," Jennifer snapped. "So you can get her money." She groaned. "I can't believe you'd consider drugging her."

"I didn't say I'd do it," Shane fired back. "But she could be…nudged in that direction. Maybe nudged into doing some other things that would help us get her declared incompetent."

"You are truly despicable." Jennifer added some harsh profanity to go along with that. "I won't help you ruin a woman so you can get her money, and if you try it, I'll tell her what's going on."

Now, it was Shane who cursed, and even though Judson's phone vibrated with another incoming text, he continued listening to the recording.

"Right, go whining to Mommy about me," Shane taunted. "You don't speak to her for weeks. You shove her away when her emotions catch up with her, and now you want to protect her. Do it," he stated like a threat. "And you'll be sorry. I'll come after you with both barrels and manage to convince Mom that you're lying. She'll believe me over you any day."

"I can make her see what you are," Jennifer said, but there wasn't a whole lot of conviction in her voice.

"Do that, *sis*." The word came out like the deadliest of venom. "Just remember, both barrels. I'm not going to let you get in the way of what I need to do to fix this mess she's gotten herself into."

With that, the recording ended, leaving Judson to wonder if it was truly the end of the conversation between the siblings or if Jennifer had only provided them with what she'd wanted them to hear.

The part that would incriminate her brother.

"This could be Jennifer's way of getting Shane out of the picture," Judson commented. "If he's locked away for his mother's murder, then he won't be able to inherit any of her estate."

He'd give that plenty more thought later, but for now he shifted his attention to the new text he'd gotten from Rory. Judson cursed after reading it. He had hoped this would be good news that could ultimately lead to an arrest.

"Rory got the results of the GSR tests," he explained. "Jennifer, Elijah and Shane all tested negative."

"And Trevor?" she asked.

Judson shook his head. "He didn't show up at the station. Grace is having him tracked down."

Blowing out a long breath, she sank down in the chair next to him. "You think he could be on the run?"

"Yes, if he's guilty," Judson replied.

That was a big *if*, though, because as far as Judson was concerned, it could be Jennifer, Shane or Elijah who was behind this. Hell, Elijah and Jennifer could be working together.

He saw the frustration and worry roll over Addie's face. She groaned, squeezing her eyes shut a moment. "I just need this to end," she muttered. "It eats away at me to think the babies are in danger."

Yeah, Judson was right there with her on that. They weren't his children, but, damn it, he loved them and he wanted them safe. Right now, it didn't feel they were close to making that happen.

When he saw Addie blinking back tears, he leaned over and put his arms around her. She didn't pull back. In fact, she moved out of her chair and onto his lap, pulling him into a hug as well. This felt right.

And wrong.

Addie was on an emotional edge. They both were. They certainly didn't have clear heads. But he didn't pull back, either, when Addie lowered her head and put her mouth on his.

Nope.

He just stayed put and let the heat do its thing. That soft kiss definitely packed a punch. Then again, just about everything Addie did had had a similar effect on him since they were teenagers.

"I know the timing is bad," she muttered with her mouth still against his. "But please, just go with it. Give us these minutes."

There'd been no need for her to add that *please*. No need for her to even justify what they were doing. Judson had been hot and ready from the moment this had started. And despite the timing, despite whether it was right or wrong, he was going to finish it.

He snapped her to him, letting the heat dictate the intensity of the kiss. And it was intense, all right. Scalding hot. Deep. French. It was also filled with plenty of that need that was building by the second.

She tasted good, like all the things he'd ever wanted in his life. Like Addie. A taste that worked with the kiss and the body-to-body contact to amp up the inferno that was driving them both to find some release.

Judson wanted to slow things down. Wanted to take the time just to savor her. But that didn't happen. The kiss got even hotter. Even deeper. And Addie turned, moving until she was straddling him.

That shot the need straight through the roof.

Judson ditched the notion of slowing down, especially when Addie pressed her center to his. Especially when the kiss didn't stop. Especially when that need took on a raw urgency that made his body push toward getting her naked.

He didn't move her away from him, but Judson reached between them and somehow managed to locate the bottom of her shirt. Hard to do since she was in the process of trying to do the same to him. Still, he succeeded, stripping off the tee and the sports bra beneath, and with her breasts bare, he levered her up so he could take her nipple into his mouth.

She moaned, her voice silky and low, and she threw back her head, letting him taste her. Giving them both this moment while the hot storm continued to build and build.

Apparently, the building became too much for her, because she cursed him and went after his shirt again. Since she was clearly on a mission to remove their clothes, Judson decided to help with that.

It wasn't easy to shuck him out of his holster and shirt, but once his torso was bare, Addie returned the kissing favor by putting her mouth and tongue on his chest.

Judson heard himself groan. Felt the new surge of heat and need. Felt the urgency go up even more. He had to have her, and it had to be now.

He got up from the chair, sliding his hands around her bottom to hold her in place while he carried her to the bed. Because she wrapped her arms and legs around him, they both landed on the mattress together.

And the kissing started all over again.

There was a frantic edge to it now. Hell, there was an edge to everything with the need heightened. With their bodies both pushing hard for release.

Judson peeled off her sweatpants. Then her panties. He couldn't resist dropping some kisses on her stomach. And lower. He got to hear Addie make another of those long moans, but she definitely didn't let him finish her off with his mouth. She clearly had a plan for the finishing, and that was for him to be inside her.

"Please tell me you have a condom," she said through gusts of her breath. She went after the zipper of his jeans.

"I do," he let her know. It was in his wallet, but it wasn't easy to get at it with Addie clearly on a mission to finish undressing him.

All the touching and wrestling around continued to hike up the need so by the time Judson located the condom, he was beyond ready. His jeans were suddenly the enemy, and he fought along with Addie to get them off. She didn't waste a second ridding him of his boxers as well.

"Now," she demanded.

He was right there with her, and the moment Judson managed to get the condom on, he rolled on top of her.

And into her.

The pleasure shot through him. Every inch of him. So hot, so strong that it robbed him of his breath. He didn't care. At the moment he didn't seem to need breath. He only needed Addie.

He pushed hard and deep into her as she lifted her hips, finding a primal rhythm that would help them find that release. Again, Judson tried to slow things down. Tried to hang on to each second of this. He managed it despite all the tight heat of her body that was trying to coax him into surrender.

Judson held on, kissing Addie again. Sliding his hand between them and touching her again. Building the need again and again. Until he felt the climax ripple through her. Until he saw the pleasure of release on her face.

It was perfect.

The right moment with the right woman.

With his body begging for its own release, Judson gave her one last kiss. And let himself go.

Chapter Fourteen

Addie was floating between waking up and a wonderful dream. Floating and experiencing a nice buzz from having sex with Judson.

Of course, this hadn't been their first time together. That first time had been awkward, fumbling, but still amazing. This latest one hit the amazing mark and then some without the other stuff.

Her body was practically still humming, and while part of her wanted to hang on to the dream, she decided to hang on to the man instead. She was hoping he not only had a second condom but that they could get in another round of sex before the babies woke.

She turned in the bed, her hand hoping to land on a still-naked Judson. But it didn't. And when she felt around the mattress and realized he wasn't there, her eyes flew open. Oh, God. Had something happened?

Since the only illumination was coming from a night-light clear across the room, it took her a couple of frantic moments to spot him. He was fully dressed in his jeans, boots and shirt and was sitting in the rocking chair feeding Rose from one of the premade formula bottles they'd stored in the room.

"I didn't hear her wake up," Addie blurted, throwing back the covers and getting out of bed. Good grief. She must have slept hard not to hear the babies. She usually woke if one of them stirred even a little.

Judson smiled at her and gave her a long, lingering look with his gaze sliding over her body. That's when she realized she was bare naked. Considering the amazing sex they'd recently had, that shouldn't have alarmed her, but it didn't seem right to be in her birthday suit with one of the babies awake. Addie snatched her clothes up off the floor.

"Why didn't I hear you, or Rose, get up?" she muttered.

"Because you were getting some much-needed sleep," Judson was quick to say. "And besides, Rose didn't actually make much of a sound. I'm a light sleeper, and when I heard her moving around, I slipped out of bed, changed her diaper and got her a bottle. I've seen you feed the twins often enough that I know how to do it."

He did indeed know how, holding the tiny bottle at the correct angle, and Rose seemed perfectly content being in Judson's arms.

Addie glanced at the clock and was surprised to see that it was already after midnight. She had figured both babies would wake up sooner than this, since it was rare for them to go longer than four hours. Apparently, they'd needed their sleep as much as Addie had. That sleep for Lily was soon coming to an end, though, since the little girl was already beginning to wiggle.

Rather than wait until Lily broke into a cry, which she would almost certainly do any second now, Addie picked her up and kissed her. She took a few extra moments just holding her before she changed Lily's diaper and took out another bottle of formula. The timing was perfect, since Rose had just finished her feeding, and Judson stood to do the burping and uptime against his shoulder with the baby while Addie settled in the rocker with Lily.

This seemed odd. But normal, too. And she tried not to allow herself to slip into a fantasy of this being their usual routine. There were way too many unknowns for that, so she pushed this warm, fuzzy feeling aside.

"Did I miss anything else while I was asleep?" she asked. Though she figured if he had good news, he would have already told her.

"I've gotten a few texts," he admitted while he gently patted Rose's back. "I had to specifically ask Grace to send them to me, though. She was trying to give me some time to rest, but I wanted to be kept in the loop."

"So do I," she let him know. "I'm guessing from the way your jaw muscles are stirring that we still don't know who shot and killed Yvette."

"We don't," he verified.

Which meant the killer was still at large. And they weren't safe.

"You said that you just needed this danger to end," he reminded her. "But it might not happen any time soon. We might have to stick with these arrangements for a while."

Part of that suited her. The part with Judson being here with her and the twins. But Addie knew she couldn't live like this. If they didn't identify the killer soon and make an arrest, then she might have to ask Judson and Grace about setting up some kind of lure or trap to catch them.

"I saw a note on your nightstand," he went on a moment later. "It's a reminder for you to return a call to your adoption attorney."

Addie nodded. Then she sighed. "Yes, she tried to contact me yesterday when I was waiting to give my statement about Yvette's murder, but I let the call go to voicemail. I wasn't in the right frame of mind to talk to her," she settled for saying. "I listened to the voicemail, and it, uh, wasn't good."

Judson stopped walking and stared at her. "What do you mean?"

She gathered her breath and snuggled Lily just a little closer. "The lawyer wants me to hold off on the adoption petition until after the killer is caught and I can guarantee that the babies are safe. Added to that, she believes I should include a statement in my petition outlining future safety measure I'll take to make sure there's no repeat of what happened."

He continued to stare at her. "Will the abduction affect your application for adoption?"

Addie wanted to say no but couldn't. "Maybe," she admitted and then went with the truth. "Probably." She had to take a moment to tamp down the churning in her stomach over the possibility of not being able to become a mother to these babies. "There's no doubt others want them, and the adoption agency might consider them to be better parents than I can be."

"No one would be better than you," Judson was quick to assure her.

He believed that. And she hoped it was true. But Addie couldn't forget that they'd had sex just hours earlier and that might be playing into his assessment of her. Heck, their entire past together certainly colored his thoughts.

"The powers that be might not see it that way," she muttered.

Judson started walking again and stopped right in front of where she was sitting. "I'll marry you if you think that'll help your petition."

Addie's mouth dropped open, and while she was stunned, she was pretty sure that Judson was, too. She was betting he hadn't given that a lot of thought before he'd thrown it out there like that.

"Marry," she repeated, and because she didn't know what else to say, she repeated it a couple more times.

"That proposal isn't about the sex," he spelled out before she could manage to say just that. "It's about Lily and Rose. And, I mean, it's not as if we don't know each other."

"So, it is partly about the sex," she said.

He looked ready to shrug and then seemed to remember he had a baby on his shoulder. A burping one. The sounds added a bit of lightness to the serious tone that'd settled over the room.

"All right," Judson conceded. "The sex plays into it. Things are…good between us in that department."

They were better than good. However, she could practically hear the *but* to follow that. Good sex was a start, but it shouldn't be the foundation for a marriage, one that included a ready-made family with preemie twins who were going to need a lot of care, love and attention.

"I appreciate that," she told him. And she voiced that *but*. "It's a bad time for either of us to be making big decisions about our future." Then she spelled out another issue. "And I don't want to tie you into a relationship for the sake of the babies. It's honorable, yes. Very honorable," she amended. "But if you're honest with yourself, you'll see it isn't what you really want."

She frowned and felt the stir of fresh emotions. Disappointment was leading the pack, followed closely by the dread that she'd just shut down something she shouldn't have.

Something she wanted.

She did want Judson. Addie wanted him, marriage. Heck, a bright, rosy future together with their twin girls. But this wasn't a fantasy she could force or lure Judson into. If he truly proposed, she wanted it to be for the right reasons.

For love.

Judson opened his mouth to speak, and Addie held her breath. Then she heard the silent profanity in her head when his phone vibrated doing its little dance across the desk.

Talk about lousy timing, but when he walked to the desk, looked at the screen and muttered, "It's Grace," Addie knew the phone call could be more important than the personal stuff going on between them.

Because until this investigation was over and the killer was caught, any and all personal plans had to be on hold.

Judson eased Rose into her bassinet and took the call. Thankfully, he didn't step out of the room so she wouldn't be able to hear, but instead he moved closer to her and put the call on speaker.

"Addie's here with me and listening in," Judson let his boss know right off the bat.

Grace sighed. "I was hoping she'd be asleep."

"I slept some," Addie piped in.

"Good. We'll all need a long sleep once this ordeal is over," Grace replied. "And we might be closing in on that. Finally." Addie was ready to cheer or at least blow out a breath of relief, but then Grace added, "There might have been another murder, though."

Judson bit off the profanity that he started. "Who?"

"Possibly Trevor," Grace was quick to let them know. "After he didn't show for the GSR test, I had two reserve deputies go to the hotel where he was supposed to have been staying. When they arrived, the door was ajar so they entered, and they saw blood on the floor. But no sign of Trevor."

Addie had to stop herself from cursing, too. She wasn't a fan of Trevor, but if he'd been murdered, that meant the killer wasn't stopping.

But why?

It was beyond frustrating that they still didn't know the motive for these deaths, the two attacks on Judson and her, and now the blood found at the hotel. Heck, they didn't even know if Courtney's murder was connected to Yvette's. It could have been two different killers.

Or even a single killer working with a hired gun.

Shane, Jennifer and Elijah didn't have huge bank accounts, but Addie figured the money might not play into it. There were other ways to entice an accomplice.

Such as the babies.

It crushed her heart to think that someone wanted to get their hands on the twins so they could offer them up on the black market. If Yvette had had any part in setting that in motion, then Addie wished the woman a thousand deaths. She felt the same way about anyone else who had that as their motive.

"How much blood did the deputies find?" Judson asked, yanking Addie's attention back to the conversation.

"Nowhere near the amount found at the scene where Courtney was murdered," Grace answered.

So, maybe Trevor wasn't dead after all. And it was possible that it wasn't even his blood. Trevor could have been the attacker, and the blood could belong to someone else. Maybe that accomplice. Or even one of their other suspects.

"There's some spatter and maybe cast-off on the walls and floor," Grace continued a moment later. "That could indicate some kind of blunt-force trauma. And before you ask, the hotel didn't have any security cameras except in the lobby. The manager is handing over the feed to the techs as we speak, so they might be able to see Trevor and/or the killer coming and going."

Good. And Addie hoped that feed was better at capturing the image of the attacker than the cruisers' dash cams had been.

"What's the time frame for this possible attack?" Judson asked.

Grace's groan was a sound of pure frustration. "Anywhere from when Trevor stormed away from the ranch until about an hour ago, when the deputies found the blood."

Judson echoed that frustration. "I'm guessing Shane, Elijah and Jennifer don't have alibis?"

"They don't. I just had phone conversations with all three of them. Elijah and Jennifer can't even corroborate each other's whereabouts. Apparently, they haven't seen each other since they were at the police station doing the GSR test. Shane claims after he did the test, he went home to grieve his mother's death, saying, and I quote, 'I didn't want an audience for that.'"

So, plenty of time for any of them to have gone after Trevor. Or vice versa.

"Is there any evidence whatsoever that Trevor might have staged the attack?" Judson asked.

"Nothing direct," Grace supplied. "But there's also nothing to rule it out, either. There was some toppled furniture to make it appear there'd been a struggle. *Appear*," she emphasized. "But no one in the hotel heard any sounds of an altercation or anyone shouting for help. Those walls aren't exactly soundproof, so someone should have heard something."

Addie considered that a moment. If Shane, Jennifer or Elijah had come to the hotel room door, Trevor might not have had the chance to call out before it was too late. One blow to the head could have possibly knocked him out and caused the blood loss. After that, Trevor could have been carried or led away from the scene.

Or walked away, if he'd staged this.

If he'd done that, then he was likely in the wind, and Addie thought the main reason he would do that was because he was the killer. But did that mean he was trying to evade capture? Or had he gone into hiding so he could plan another way of coming after them again?

"Now, to the good news," Grace announced. "Well, good for us, anyway."

Addie's hopes soared again, and she pushed aside that possibility of Trevor launching another attack. They needed a break in this investigation, and maybe this was it.

"The lab was able to come up with a partial fingerprint on one of the bags of drugs found in the nightstand at the Cateses' house, and it was enough to get a match," Grace explained. "The print belonged to a woman named Sienna Flanagan, age twenty-six, who...ta-da, is a friend of Jennifer's. They've known each other since elementary school, and Sienna has a record for drug possession. That's why her prints were in the system."

Judson blew out a long breath. "Have you had a chance to talk to Sienna or Jennifer about this yet?"

"Not Sienna, but when she didn't respond to attempts to contact her, I had an APB put out on her. And I got phone records to confirm that Jennifer and she had a conversation as recently as three days ago. Before that, they texted about once a month."

That seemed like a solid link. Despite what Jennifer had said on that recording with Shane, she'd possibly wanted to push her mother over the edge. Maybe so she could be declared mentally incompetent. Maybe just to get her to do something reckless that would get her killed or incarcerated. Going to her old friends for the drugs would have been the first step.

"As for Jennifer," Grace added, "SAPD is sending officers to her place now, but I spoke to her on the phone when I first got the results on that fingerprint. She denies everything and claims she's being set up, either by Shane or Trevor. She also told me that Sienna and Shane are friends, too, but there's no phone record of him contacting the woman. Of course, he could have used a burner or met with her face-to-face, but for now, I'm following the evidence."

"And that evidence points to Jennifer," Judson concluded. "She's got means, motive and opportunity for killing her mother."

Grace made a sound of agreement. "Maybe for killing Courtney if the social worker saw something incriminating when she went to the Cateses' house." Then, she stopped and sighed. "It's all wrapped up in a neat little package except for one thing. Jennifer couldn't have been the one who fired those shots at Addie and you at the ranch."

No, she couldn't have. Because Jennifer had been at the police station at the time of the attack.

"I'll look for phone links between Jennifer and Elijah during that time frame," Grace spelled out. "Or links between Jennifer, Shane or Trevor... Hold on a second. I've got an incoming call from SAPD."

Addie looked up at Judson to get his take on all of this, and she saw the doubt in his eyes. She was sure it was in her own eyes, too. Because even if Jennifer was the culprit, she wasn't in custody. And neither was the person who'd fired those shots at them. So, two people at large if Jennifer was behind this. Of course, if it was Trevor, Shane or Elijah, they could have been working solo.

"A possible problem," Grace said, coming back on the line. "Jennifer isn't at her apartment. But Trevor is." She paused only a moment. "Judson, he's dead."

Chapter Fifteen

Judson wished for a cup of strong coffee as he began to read through the report Grace had just sent him. His head was throbbing, and every muscle in his body was tight to the point of being painful. Still, he didn't want to risk waking Etta Jean, the twins or Bennie, who was sleeping somewhere in the house.

The people he wouldn't have to wake were Rory and the two ranch hands also standing guard, with Rory inside and the others patrolling the grounds. One glance at Addie, and he could add her to the list of those who weren't sleeping. She was sitting right next to him, reading the same as he was.

At least she was eating something—one of the sandwiches from the small fridge that had been moved into the room along with the baby stuff and other supplies. Etta Jean had made sure they had plenty of sandwiches, fruit and bottled water. Two Cokes as well, but they'd finished those off shortly after their phone conversation with Grace two hours earlier.

A call to let them know about Jennifer's impending arrest. And Trevor's death.

Correction: his murder. The SAPD cops had determined that from the sixteen stab wounds on the man's body. A staggering number of injuries for it to have been self-inflicted, and the medical examiner had apparently agreed. According to the first line of Grace's report, Trevor's death had been ruled a homicide.

The murder was in SAPD's jurisdiction, so they would be the primary investigators, but also according to the report, Grace would be looped in and apprised of any developments. Grace, in turn, would update all her deputies, since each and every one of them was involved in hunting down the person responsible for Yvette's murder.

It was possible—hell, it was even likely—that both law enforcement groups were looking for the same killer, but they wouldn't know that until they had more information.

And knew the whereabouts of their three surviving suspects.

That bad news was in the second part of Grace's report. Jennifer, Shane and Elijah weren't responding to any attempts to contact them, and none of them were home. Considering that it was nearly three in the morning, when most people would have been in bed, that wasn't good.

There was the possibility that one or more of them had met an end like Trevor's. The killer could be cleaning house, and that might involve murdering anyone who would link him or her to this string of crimes.

Unfortunately, that cleaning up could involve Addie and him.

Grace hadn't come out and said that in her report, but she had stated that Bennie and Rory would remain there at the Horseshoe Ranch until eight in the morning, when they'd be relieved by replacement deputies. Judson knew that meant their small-town police force was stretched well beyond the thin mark, and basically everyone was on duty until Jennifer was brought in and confessed. Or until they identified the person responsible, if it wasn't in fact Jennifer.

He would be eternally thankful to his fellow cops for diving into this with full force. That might be the very thing that managed to keep Addie and the babies out of harm's way. Of course, the only thing that would guarantee their safety would be for Grace to make that arrest and get the killer behind bars.

Judson ate some chips as he moved on to the second page of the report. This one was filled with the notes Grace had taken while the ME was examining Trevor's body at Jennifer's apartment.

Addie motioned to the part that had already caught Judson's attention. Trevor's head injury. Specifically, a fairly superficial cut and bruise that the ME hadn't believed would cause unconsciousness.

Or even any serious injury, for that matter.

Unlike the stab wounds, the ME stated that the angle of this one could suggest that it might have been self-inflicted. So, had Trevor tried to stage his own attack at the hotel and fled the scene, only to be attacked for real and murdered?

That was possibly how it had all played out, but it still left them with the huge question of why. If Trevor had been the accomplice to the person who'd murdered Yvette and even Courtney, that might make sense, but inflicting that many stab wounds was serious overkill. It implied the killer had been in a rage.

Or had the killer wanted them to think that?

Again, Judson had to go with a *maybe* here. The bottom line was they didn't know who they were dealing with, but these three murders were proof that someone would go to any and all lengths to accomplish their goal. Now, the challenge would be to discover the motive since that could lead them to the killer's identity.

"Why was Trevor at Jennifer's?" Addie asked, voicing

the question that was repeating in his head. "And where's Jennifer?"

Judson didn't have an answer to either of those, only speculation. "They could have been working together. Or Trevor could have been lured there. And not necessarily by Jennifer."

"True," Addie muttered, and then she groaned and scrubbed her hands over her face. She also tried to stifle a yawn.

"You should try to get some sleep," he suggested. But it was more than a suggestion. Addie looked, and no doubt was, exhausted.

She looked at him. "I'll try if you will."

Addie leaned in and brushed her mouth over his. It was one of those barely there kisses that packed a solid punch. Then again, any contact with Addie always did that to him.

"I'll stand a better chance of getting some sleep if you're right there next to me," she muttered. With her mouth still hovering over his, she fluttered her hands toward the bed.

Hell. There it was again. That rush of heat and need. But Judson didn't think of sleep and rest when he glanced at the bed. He thought of sex, and while it would feel damn good to be with Addie like that again, he had to throttle back and stay focused. Not focused on her and great sex, either. But on trying to figure out the puzzle of this blasted investigation.

It took every ounce of his resolve to ease away from Addie. "I want to go back through all the reports again," Judson let her know. "Not just the ones that have come in tonight but those from the moment babies were taken. There might be something in them I've missed."

She nodded, and while the disappointment came through loud and clear, she straightened in the chair and pinned her attention to his laptop screen. "Then I'll go over the reports with you."

Judson sighed and then decided to play a little dirty. Not by kissing her, though that's what certain parts of him wanted to do.

No.

He played the baby card.

"Lily and Rose will probably be up soon, looking to be fed, and they might not go right back to sleep." He'd personally witnessed a few episodes of that when one or both of them would start crying and need some rocking and soothing. "You have to rest to be able to deal with that."

Of course, he would help if the babies were fussy and didn't settle. Heck, he'd help with just a routine feeding, but Judson was hoping that Addie would see the logic in at least one of them getting a little shut-eye.

And she did.

She stood and then did her own version of playing dirty by bending down and kissing him. This wasn't one of those pecks. It was long, deep and hot. And when she finally stepped away from him, they were both smiling. Both aroused, too. But Judson forced himself to stay put at the desk as she made her way to the bed.

Addie kept her gaze on him as she lay down and threw the quilt over her. He began rereading the reports, but he also volleyed some glances at her. Judson smiled again when he saw her eyelids drift closed. Maybe, just maybe, she'd be able to sleep without the nightmares taking over or any interruptions.

But that didn't happen.

She'd been asleep less than ten minutes when Judson's phone vibrated not with a text but a call. He muttered some profanity under his breath, but when he saw Rory's name on the screen, he got up, hurrying into the bathroom to answer it.

He didn't even manage to get the door shut before he heard Addie bolt out of the bed and make her way to join him. Since Addie was obviously awake and would insist on hearing what his fellow deputy had to say, Judson went ahead and took the call on speaker.

"We might have a problem," Rory said, and Judson heard the concern in his voice. "One of the hands, Calvin Hawkins, is patrolling near the front fence, and he says he saw a light in the barn across the road."

Hell. That was the spot where the sniper had set up for the first attack against Addie and him.

"I checked with the CSI head just to make sure it wasn't one of his guys returning to have another look around," Rory added a moment later. "And it's not. It's also not any of the other deputies. Of course, it could be some lookie-loo poking around where they shouldn't, but I wanted to give you a heads-up."

"What do you need us to do?" Judson asked.

"Just stay put for now…" Rory stopped. "Incoming text from Calvin." A second later, Rory cursed. "Take cover," he blurted. "Calvin says there's someone in the barn, and he's pretty sure the person has a rifle."

A RIFLE.

The words punched through Addie and had both her heart and her body racing back into the bedroom to get the babies. She had to get them to the bathroom before the shooter started firing.

Again.

It would be like the earlier attack. Bullets slamming into the house and possibly tearing through the walls. And just like before, the babies would be in grave danger. She had to protect them.

The girls were still sleeping, but she scooped up Lily anyway. Addie had reached into the bassinet to do the same to Rose just as there was a frantic knock on the door. That set Lily to start crying, and Judson hurried to the door to answer it. The moment it was open, Etta Jean rushed in.

"I heard Bennie say there could be a shooter in the barn," Etta Jean blurted. The panic and fear were evident in both her expression and her body language. She rushed to the second bassinet and gathered Rose up in her arms.

"There is," Addie confirmed. But she had to guess that the person was still getting in place since there hadn't been any shots fired yet.

"Rory and Calvin are moving closer to the barn," Judson let them know when he finished his call with Rory. "They both have rifles, too, and they'll see if they can get a visual on the person. And maybe take him or her out."

Addie prayed that Rory and Calvin could do just that. Eliminate the threat before any more shots were fired. But she also understood the necessity of them verifying who the heck this was. They couldn't risk killing someone who had simply been curious and was in that barn to poke around a crime scene. Still, it would be stupid of someone to do that, knowing that everyone on the ranch would be in a state of heightened alert.

"Let's get the babies into the bathroom," Addie insisted, and after grabbing two bottles of the formula, she went in that direction with Lily.

Etta Jean was moving along right behind her, and, keeping a firm grip on Rose, she climbed into the bathtub. Despite the commotion and Lily's crying, Rose somehow stayed asleep.

"Hand Lily to me," Etta Jean insisted. She grabbed a clean towel from the rack, putting it on the surface of the tub like a pallet and easing Rose onto it to free up her hands.

Etta Jean had no doubt made that offer when she noticed Addie firing glances at Judson, who was still in the bedroom. He was on the phone again, probably getting an update from Rory, and she wanted to hear what the deputy had to say.

Addie went ahead and passed Lily to Etta Jean, and the woman immediately opened one of the bottles. The moment the nipple touched Lily's mouth, the baby latched on and the crying stopped. Addie hoped it stayed that way.

She hurried back into the bedroom with Judson and realized that he was still on the phone but no longer had the call on speaker. Addie moved right next to him, hoping to catch the gist of the conversation, but she could only hear murmurings on the other end of the line.

"I'll find some binoculars and have a look," Judson finally said, and then he added, "Stay safe," before he ended the call.

Judson put his phone back in his pocket, but before he could ask, Addie motioned toward the hall. "There are several pairs of binoculars on the top shelf of the foyer closet." Mellie had been an avid bird-watcher and had always kept extras on hand for any foster kids who'd taken an interest in that as well. "Bring me a pair. I want to try to see who's in that barn."

He frowned, and for a moment she thought he was going to refuse to do that last part, but he rushed off. Addie listened to the thuds of his running footsteps. She also heard the soft sounds Lily was making while she drank her bottle. What she thankfully still didn't hear were any gunshots.

She didn't like the notion of having weapons anywhere

near the babies, but she wanted to be able to protect them. Addie went to her closet and took down the lockbox she'd stashed there. It, too, had been Mellie's, and Addie scrolled through the numbers on the lock to open it. She took out the loaded .38, and after making sure the safety was on, she went back into the bedroom.

Carrying two pairs of binoculars, Judson came rushing back in and caught a glimpse of the gun as she was slipping it into the pocket of her jogging pants. That deepened his frown even more.

"I don't want you in the line of fire," he was quick to point out, and he was adamant about it.

"Neither do I, but I want to be able to stop someone if they get past Rory and Calvin. Past Bennie and the other hand inside as well. You know full well there are too many ways in and out of this house, and a killer could slip past all of them."

He didn't dispute that. Couldn't, since he had personally used many of those ins and outs. It was an old Victoria house with side entrances and nearly two dozen ground-floor windows as well as the front and back doors.

"Try to stay out of the line of fire," Judson amended, and after he handed her a pair of binoculars, he crossed the room to the window that would give them a view of the barn.

Well, a partial view, anyway.

She wanted to curse when, after he pushed aside the curtains, she could see there were some trees in the way. Judson ended up dropping onto his knees to try to get the right angle. Addie went to the floor with him, using the binoculars to peer over his shoulder.

Since there was thick clouds blocking the moon and sunrise was still hours away, it wasn't hard for her to spot the faint light coming from the loft area of the barn. She adjusted the binoculars, trying to zoom in, but the only thing Addie saw was that light, and it didn't seem to be moving.

"I'd rather you stay in the bathroom with Etta Jean and the babies," Judson grumbled. Like her, he was making some adjustments to his binoculars, trying to find a possible killer.

"I want to know who we're up against," Addie argued. "And whether it's one of our suspects or a hired henchman, I want to be ready."

Judson opened his mouth, probably to make another attempt to convince her to go into the bathroom, but he stopped and dropped down a few inches more. He kept his attention pinned to the barn.

"There you are, you bastard," he snarled.

"Where?" she couldn't ask fast enough.

"Not by the front of the hayloft. Look toward the back," Judson instructed.

Addie immediately shifted her aim, not onto the light itself but past it. And in the murky darkness she did indeed see something.

A person wearing all black, blending in with the night.

She leaned slightly to the side and saw something else. The light glinting off the barrel of what appeared to be a rifle. But neither the person in black nor the rifle was moving.

"What's he waiting for?" she murmured to herself.

Maybe he or she was trying to determine the best target. With Rory and Calvin out there, she prayed the attacker wouldn't just gun them down.

"I don't like this," Judson said under his breath. "If it's two of them working together, one could be coming closer to the house while we've all got our attention on this one."

Oh, God. Addie hadn't considered that, but it was a strong

possibility. A two-pronged attack to take care of the protectors inside and outside the house.

Judson stood, taking hold of her arm and pulling her from the window. "I'm going up to the roof. I can climb through that old attic door to get there."

They were both very familiar with that spot. He'd climbed up there often as a kid just to look at the stars. Later on, when they were teenagers, she had joined him, and it had become one of their make-out spots. The roof had a panoramic view of the entire grounds.

And that barn.

It would also make Judson an easy target once he was up there. No place to duck and hide from a killer hell-bent on ending his life.

"I need to do this," he insisted.

Yes, he did. But that didn't make things easier. Addie had to force herself not to latch on to him and beg him to stay.

The kiss helped with that.

He lowered his mouth to hers, and along with robbing her of her breath, it nipped any objections she had in the bud.

"Go in the bathroom and stay put," he ordered, giving her one more kiss before he rushed out.

Addie stood there just a moment, trying to force aside the sickening feeling that it would be their last kiss. The last time she laid eyes on Judson.

No.

This couldn't be the last of anything but the danger. She refused to even consider a future without Judson, and she latched on to that thought—that hope—as she hurried toward the bathroom.

Addie had just reached for the doorknob when she heard the sound that she'd been dreading.

A gunshot.

Chapter Sixteen

Judson had just made it to the stairs when the gunshot blasted outside. And the sound punched him like a meaty fist.

Exactly where outside the sound had come from, he didn't know, but he didn't think the shot had hit the house. Still, he was ready to rush back to Addie's bedroom when his phone vibrated with a text.

From Addie.

Hell. His first thought was that Etta Jean, the babies or she had been hurt, and he had to tamp down the panic racing through him. He forced himself to look at his phone screen.

Are you all right? Addie had texted. We're okay here and staying down in the bathroom.

The relief shoved away the bulk of the panic, and he was able to reply with a thumbs-up emoji. A quick, way-too-light response that didn't convey the emotions he was feeling, but it got the job done. He let her know he hadn't been hurt, and now he knew that Addie, Etta Jean and the babies were safe.

Hopefully, they would stay that way if he managed to pinpoint the shooter and stop the attack from escalating. That reminder got him moving even faster up the stairs to the second floor.

Another shot came.

His muscles turned to iron, and his heartbeat began to thunder in his ears. But again, this bullet hadn't seemed to hit the house, and it made him wonder if the gunman was aiming for Calvin or Rory. If so, he didn't want to text and possibly distract them when they were trying to stay alive.

Instead, Judson focused on getting to the center of the upstairs hallway and to the cord for the attic door. He gave it a hard yank, and the ladder unfolded as the door dropped open.

As he'd done countless times as a kid, he scrambled up the rungs, stepping into a massive space that was filled with an equally massive amount of stuff. Furniture that'd been able to fit through the door. Boxes, dozens and dozens of them, filled with all sorts of decorations for any occasion—birthdays, Christmas, Easter, swimming parties, homecoming and bon voyages.

Judson also knew there were thousands of photographs and old magazines, and he'd spent some time looking through those as a kid. The attic had become his sanctuary of sorts, and he was familiar with every inch of it.

Including the ceiling door that led to the roof.

Moving fast, that was where he headed.

It wasn't a standard feature in homes in this area, but he recalled Mellie saying that it had once led to a cupola. Apparently, storms had damaged the structure a century or more ago and it had been turned into a sort of widow's walk, a flat portion of the roof surrounded by a low rail. Over the years, the stairs had fallen down, but the ceiling door appeared to still be intact.

Judson was thankful for that since he needed to try to pinpoint the location, and the identity, of this sick SOB who kept trying to kill them.

He heard another shot outside, but this one sounded as

if it'd come from a different firearm. Or maybe just a different distance. He was hoping that meant Rory or Calvin had been able to return fire.

Pocketing the binoculars, Judson dragged a chair beneath the ceiling door, and, holstering his gun, he opened the door and used both hands and a good portion of his strength to hoist himself up. He immediately felt the chilly early-morning air close in around him, but he kept moving until he was on the widow's walk.

The moment he was through the ceiling door and on the walk, he drew his gun again.

The two-foot-tall railing around the widow's walk wouldn't give him much cover or protection, but it didn't obstruct his view, either. He could see nearly the entire ranch from this vantage point. Better yet, he could see the barn across the road.

Holding his gun in his right hand and the binoculars in his left, he zoomed in on the hayloft again.

And he cursed.

Because he could now see that it wasn't a person at all but rather what appeared to be a black jacket and pants pressed against some bales of hay. There was a rifle propped up beside it, and someone had positioned a flashlight so that it spotlighted the items.

Damn it.

There was only one reason for that setup—to make them focus on the very spot where the killer wasn't.

So, where was the SOB?

With his heart drumming faster now, Judson scanned the yard, the road and the pasture. He saw Calvin behind a sprawling oak. He had his gun, but he wasn't shooting. However, he had his attention pinned to the area across the driveway and in front of the house.

Judson swiveled in that direction, and he spotted Rory. His fellow deputy was crouched down by one of the cruisers, but he wasn't focusing where Calvin was. He seemed to be looking in the direction of one of the ditches.

Another shot rang out, blasting through the silence. And because Judson could see both Rory and Calvin, he knew the shot hadn't come from one of them. It had come from the gunman, and Judson thought he or she was in those trees across from the driveway. So, he turned there to keep watch, but he was well aware there could be two attackers.

One in each of the locations that had gotten Calvin's and Rory's attention.

If so, one of the attackers could be trying to get into the house while the other tried to pin Calvin and Rory down with gunfire. It was a plan that could work, and that's why Judson knew he had to give Bennie a heads-up.

Listen and keep watch for a possible break-in, Judson settled for saying.

Will do, Bennie immediately texted back. You have a visual on the shooter?

No visual, he replied. Just an estimation based on that last shot. Also, there might be two of them.

He imagined Bennie silently cursing when he read that. Cursing but staying vigilant. I'm keeping watch, Bennie assured him.

Judson was about to text Addie to give her the same warning and a reminder to stay put in the bathroom, but his phone vibrated with a text. Not from Bennie but rather Rory.

I think the SOB used the ditch to get closer to the house, Rory had messaged. I caught a glimpse of him, but I don't think he's in the ditch now.

He? Judson questioned.

Or maybe she, Rory was quick to reply. I only got a

glimpse of someone wearing all black. I shot at them, but I think I missed.

Too bad about that. Judson wished that Rory had blown this snake to smithereens.

Watch the house, Judson advised Rory.

And he did the same. Watched and waited. Listened.

The breeze didn't exactly cooperate with his attempts to listen. It came in short bursts, stirring the trees and rattling the shrubs and the leaves on the live oaks. Those little noises were maybe masking other sounds that he should be hearing. Like movement out of the ditch or that area across from the house.

What Judson wasn't hearing was any gunfire, but he wasn't exactly thankful for that at the moment. Of course, he didn't want any bullets going into the house, but if the SOB fired just one more single shot, that would help Judson pinpoint the location. Then he could return fire. Apparently, though, like the wind, the shooter wasn't going to cooperate.

Finally, after what seemed like a couple of lifetimes, Judson caught some movement from the corner of his eye. Not exactly in the area that Rory and he were watching. But rather to the right. At first he thought it could be the shrubs shaking from another gust of wind.

But no.

He spotted the shadowy figure as it darted out of sight. Judson got just a glimpse, and he couldn't tell if it was a man or woman. So, he continued to watch, taking aim in that direction. Readying himself in case he got the chance to put a stop to this.

More seconds passed, dragging by, and finally Judson caught another burst of movement. Someone wearing all black. Someone threading their way through the underbrush.

And toward the house.

He cursed himself for not having already hurried back downstairs so he could be waiting for this clown when he made it to the door.

But the person didn't run toward the door.

Judson shifted his gun, trying to lock his aim on the person, but he or she wasn't staying still. Nor were they moving in a straight line. They were weaving through the trees and bushes, using them as cover.

He pivoted again when he caught another glimpse. But the person darted behind one of the vehicles parked out front.

Judson moved, too, scrambling to edge of the widow's walk so he'd be in a better position to shoot. He was still taking aim when there was more movement. The shadowy figure raced to a tree.

Then another.

Judson fired. And missed. The bullet slammed into the tree just as the SOB raced out from the other side. Straight toward the side of the house.

His heart went straight to his knees when Judson heard the glass shattering. And he knew exactly what that meant. The killer had broken the window and was getting inside.

Hell.

Judson had to get to Addie and the babies *now*.

"Oh, God," Addie muttered.

She had no trouble hearing the sound of shattering glass and thought it'd come from a window on the side of the house. What she hadn't heard was a gunshot, which meant the glass hadn't broken from gunfire.

But rather from someone using different means to gain access to the house.

The killer, no doubt.

He or she was breaking into the house and would be coming for her. That gave Addie a slam of emotions, with fear being right there at the top of the heap. The babies were right here, and a bullet aimed at her—or anyone else, for that matter—could miss and hurt them.

She had to stop that from happening.

The jolt of adrenaline would help with that. So would Mellie's gun. She wasn't a markswoman by any stretch of the imagination, but she could use the gun and go after the killer before he or she made it to this part of the house.

"Wait here," Addie told Etta Jean. "Stay as low in the tub as you can with the twins. That's your best protection."

And Addie had to pray that it would be enough. Thankfully, it was an old-fashioned cast-iron one that might stop any gunfire from getting to them.

Etta Jean had plenty of fear on her face, and she was shaking her head before Addie even finished. "You should wait in here, too. You should stay with us where you'll be safe."

Maybe. But she couldn't. Addie had to put a barrier between the twins and the killer, and if necessary, she'd do that with her own body.

"Bennie's in the bedroom," Addie reminded the woman. "And Judson will be here soon."

She had no doubts about that. Well, he would be arriving soon if he'd heard the window shattering. Or if he'd realized the killer was breaking into the house. If not, well…she didn't want to consider that right now. Addie only wanted to focus on stopping the monster who had put her babies in harm's way.

Addie brushed a quick kiss on the twins' cheeks. "I'll lock the door behind me," she added to Etta Jean.

And with that, she hurried out of the bathroom.

She did indeed lock the door, and Addie immediately

glanced around to find Bennie. He was in the open doorway of her bedroom, and with his gun ready, he was peering into the hall. Or rather, he had been until he heard her behind him, and he threw her a quick look from over his shoulder.

Correction: a quick glare.

Addie could see that even though the only illumination in the room came from the twins' night-light and the light in the hall.

"You're supposed to stay in the bathroom," Bennie reminded her in a hoarse grumble.

That had indeed been the plan when Judson had left to hurry up to the roof. But that was when the attacker had still been outside. The broken window had changed everything.

"I have my gun," she replied. "And there's no window in the bathroom. The killer will have to get through us to get in there."

Bennie muttered some profanity, but he didn't order her back into the bathroom. He just continued to keep watch of the hall. "Rory thinks there could be two of them," Bennie whispered. "So, keep an eye on the windows in here."

Sweet heaven. She had already known that was a possibility, but it shook her to the core to hear Bennie spell it out. Rory and Calvin would also be aware there was a pair of attackers, and that probably meant they wouldn't be coming into the house to help. They were likely looking for the second one before he or she could get inside as well.

Since there could be two of them working together, did that mean this was Jennifer and Elijah? Or, heck, Jennifer and Shane?

Maybe.

But it could be none of them if they'd gone the route of hiring thugs to do their dirty work. That didn't make the situation any less dangerous. Just the opposite. Because they might not be dealing with amateurs but rather trained killers.

That thought was eating at her like acid, so she had to nudge it aside. Addie also had to tamp down her breathing so that she didn't risk hyperventilating.

Her heartbeat was a problem, too.

It was so loud in her ears that it was making it hard for her to hear, which was critical when it came to stopping someone trying to get in through the windows or approaching up the hall.

She kept a firm grip on her gun. Stayed vigilant. Listening. Waiting. She also calculated that it'd been less than two minutes since she'd first heard that sound of the breaking glass.

Not long.

But it felt like an eternity.

If Judson had heard the glass, too, he would have likely made his way off the roof by now and was racing through the attic to get to the ladder in the second-floor hall. So, Addie listened for his footsteps as well.

And she heard something.

After a few more seconds, there was a heavy thud above her. Maybe the sound of Judson dropping from that ladder to the floor. If so, he would have immediately broken into a run, which meant he'd be here in under a minute.

And that caused every muscle in her body to twist and knot.

Mercy. Judson could be running straight into the killer. In fact, the killer might be waiting in the shadows to gun Judson down. Then, he or she would have a clearer path to getting to her.

She was about to call out to Judson, to warn him, but as she opened her mouth, the night-light blinked off. So did the overhead light in the hall, plunging them into total darkness.

Oh, God.

The killer had done this.

Had somehow managed to cut the power. Which wouldn't have been hard to do, if he or she had gotten to the fuse box on the kitchen wall.

But then she remembered something. One of the ranch hands was supposed to be in the kitchen. Had the killer knocked him out? Or murdered him? She prayed not, but if he was capable of it, the hand would have probably called out to let them know there was immediate danger.

Once again, Addie had to try to level her breathing so she could stay focused and listen. And she soon heard something.

Footsteps.

Not someone running. These were slow, cautious steps. And they were coming straight for the bedroom. Maybe Judson.

Perhaps the killer.

Heck, it could be both of them, one coming from the front of the hall and the other from the back that fed off the kitchen. Without any illumination and no windows, the hall was pitch-black. Judson wouldn't be able to see the killer.

And vice versa.

Except maybe that wasn't true.

If the killer had made plans to cut the power, then he or she could have also brought along night vision goggles. Which meant the killer could see Judson and shoot him.

Addie couldn't stop herself from moving closer to Bennie and the door. She wanted to be able to help Judson if he needed it. She also wanted to stop the killer from claiming a fourth victim.

She had to shut out thoughts of Judson dying. Of him being hurt and bleeding out the way Yvette had done. She was trying to shut out everything but the sounds around her. The footsteps.

Yes, she could hear them. From the front of the hall. That would probably be Judson, making his way to them. Risking his life to try to protect them.

Addie could also hear the faint whimpering of one of the babies, and she prayed Lily and Rose weren't frightened, that they weren't picking up on all the danger around them. Also, if the whimpering turned to full-out cries, the killer would have no trouble pinpointing their location.

That got Addie moving even closer to the door, but she came to a dead stop at the sound of the gunshot. It roared through the house, a deafening blast that sent her heart racing and her fears skyrocketing.

Mercy.

Had Judson been shot?

She couldn't accept that. Wouldn't. And she tried to listen for any indication that he was hurt. But all she could hear now were those full-out cries from not just one baby but both of them. Probably from the sound of that gunshot. She hated that the little girls were being put through this.

Addie blinked several times, trying to get her eyes to adjust to the darkness, and she could finally see Bennie. Well, the outline of him, anyway. She couldn't see anything or anyone in the hall, though. It was a black void where a killer no doubt was coming for them.

But where was Judson?

Was he lying in wait, too? Waiting until he could see the killer before he tried to take him out?

There was more movement. Footsteps this time. And she heard Bennie mutter something under his breath that she didn't catch. But she had no trouble catching the next sound.

Another gunshot.

This one seemed even louder than the first, something she hadn't thought possible. Maybe because it was closer? Was the killer right outside the bedroom door? It certainly seemed as if he was.

There was a flash of light. A bright burst of it, and Addie thought of those old cameras with the bulbs. It caused spots in her vision, smears and blurs blending with the darkness. It must have done the same for Bennie, because he rubbed at his eyes with the back of his left hand.

There was another shot.

Even louder, and closer, than the last one.

Bennie made a sound. A sort of grunt, and now that she could see slightly better, Addie saw something she definitely hadn't wanted to see.

The deputy collapsed in the doorway.

God, had Bennie been shot?

Addie couldn't see any blood, but it would have been next to impossible to catch sight of that anyway in the darkness and based on the way he'd fallen. Bennie was curled up in a heap on the floor.

However, she had no trouble seeing the figure that hurdled over Bennie. It happened at the exact second she heard another gunshot. But it wasn't coming from the figure wearing all black and night-vision goggles.

The shot had come from the hall.

Addie brought up her gun, trying to take aim.

But it was too late.

Everything was too late. The killer charged right at her, ramming into her and knocking her to the floor.

Chapter Seventeen

Judson couldn't see squat because of the blinding light that the SOB at the end of the hall had flashed at him. But his hearing was just fine, and he heard all sorts of sounds that had him charging forward despite not being able to see.

The babies were crying.

Then there'd been those gunshots. Followed by someone falling onto the floor. The thud had been unmistakable. But had it been Addie who'd fallen? Had she been shot?

"Addie," Judson managed to get out, and the thought of her being shot got him moving even faster.

But not fast enough.

Despite not being able to see much of anything, he cleared his eyes enough to catch a glimpse of a person jumping over something and into the bedroom.

Hell.

Where was Bennie?

Keeping his gun raised and moving closer to the doorway, Judson soon got the answer to that. Bennie was on the floor, and he was bleeding. Maybe dead. He certainly wasn't moving.

Judson had to shove aside the possibility that his fellow deputy might have been the killer's latest victim. He couldn't deal with that now. First, he had to somehow get Addie, the twins and Etta Jean to safety and then capture the killer. Then he could get Bennie the medical help he needed.

He considered firing off a quick text to Rory, to let him know what was going on, but every second was precious now. Judson knew that in every bone in his body. He knew he had to get to Addie or this SOB would kill her.

If he hadn't already.

Judson made it to the door, stopping by the frame and getting another quick glimpse of Bennie. The man was breathing. That was something, at least. Maybe he could hang on a little while longer.

Maybe Addie could, too.

He peered around the edge of the door, hoping to see her—alive. And he did. But his heart dropped to his knees. She was definitely alive, for now anyway, but there was a person behind her. Someone wearing black clothes and night-vision goggles.

And that someone had a gun pointed at her head.

Damn it. The killer had her.

Now that his eyes had refocused from the burst of light, Judson took in the rest of the room with a sweeping glance. There was a small device on the floor that looked to be an attachment for a camera flash. It'd been simple but effective in temporarily blinding Judson. Heck, probably Bennie, too, which explained how the deputy had gotten shot. He wouldn't have seen the killer coming right at him.

Judson continued looking around and spotted another gun on the floor. Maybe the one Addie had had been using. The killer could have knocked it out of her hand when he'd come at her. So, she wasn't armed and couldn't defend herself without risking a fatal shot to the head.

He shifted his gaze from Addie to the bathroom door, and Judson was glad to see that it was closed. Glad, too, that with the babies crying, he at least knew they were alive. He had to do something to keep them that way.

Had to do something to free Addie, too.

There was only the one person behind her. That didn't mean that someone else, an accomplice, wasn't outside the house. The killer's backup. And it sickened Judson to think that the accomplice might have killed Calvin and Rory. Maybe the ranch hand who'd been in the kitchen as well.

Judson heard some soft footsteps to his right, and he snapped his gaze in that direction. His body braced for an attack.

But it was Rory and Calvin.

Alive, and unlike Bennie, neither of them was injured. Thank God. And the fact they were here told him that this person was probably acting solo.

Judson motioned for Calvin and Rory to stop. He didn't want the killer hearing them and pulling the trigger in panic.

"What do you want with Addie?" Judson shouted out to the killer.

And he was certain this SOB wanted something or Addie would have already been dead. The only reason to hold her like this was for some kind of leverage.

"What I want is some cooperation," the man replied.

Judson cursed. He had no trouble recognizing the voice. Elijah.

So, he was the killer. Maybe. Or he could be the accomplice. Still, even if he hadn't killed yet, he could be willing to start now.

"What I want is fast cooperation so we can all get the hell out of here," Elijah added a moment later.

The man didn't sound scared or on the verge of panic. His hand wasn't shaking, either, and that let Judson know he was dealing with a cold-blooded killer. And it wasn't just Addie in danger. The babies were only a wall away from this snake.

"If you want fast, then spill why you're doing this," Judson snapped.

He stayed partially behind the doorframe so he could duck out of the line of fire if Elijah tried to shoot him. Which he was certain that Elijah would do—once he got what he wanted.

"Two things," Elijah said, still sounding plenty calm despite jabbing the barrel of his gun even harder against Addie.

It caused her to muffle a sound of pain, and while it was barely audible, it made Judson want to tear Elijah limb from limb. Which was no doubt why the man had done it. He likely wanted Judson on the edge, maybe going off half-cocked. That would make him easier to kill.

"First, take out your phone and toss it on the floor toward me," Elijah spelled out as he quickly yanked off the goggles. "I need to delete a picture."

Of all the things Judson had thought a killer might demand, that hadn't even been on his radar. "What picture?"

Elijah made a *yeah, right* sound as if he wasn't buying that Judson didn't know what he was talking about. Still, the man explained it.

"The one you snapped of Yvette's car as she was speeding away from the ranch. I was in the back seat with the brats, and I lifted my head just as I'm pretty sure you took that picture."

Yeah, Judson had no trouble recalling the photo. Or thinking that maybe he'd caught a glimpse of someone in the car with Yvette. But that glimpse had come a split second *after* he'd gotten the picture of the license plate. He had studied and restudied that photo, and there hadn't been even a partial image of anyone other than the driver in the car.

"Do it now," Elijah demanded, and he gave Addie another of those jabs to the temple.

Judson did take out his phone, and he considered hurling it at Elijah and trying to hit his hand. But it was too risky. It might distract him, yes. Might even cause him to drop the gun. But it also could cause him to accidently pull the trigger and kill Addie where she stood.

Instead, Judson leaned down, putting the phone on the floor on the other side of Bennie, and he shoved it in Elijah's direction. Since Elijah was standing in the middle of the room, the phone stopped a good yard short of Addie's feet.

Elijah cursed, and after calling Judson a crude name, he began to force Addie to move toward the phone. "I know the photo didn't go to the lab. I checked. I've got some decent hacking skills," he tacked on to that. "Of course, a county lab doesn't have as much cybersecurity as it should. I saw what was logged in, and the photo wasn't one of the items."

Elijah was right about that. The photo hadn't been sent in because the only thing of value on it was the license plate number. There'd been no glimpse of the back seat or anyone in it, only the trunk and the license plate.

Of course, Elijah wouldn't have known that.

All he would have seen was Judson aiming his phone at Yvette's car. If his image had indeed been captured, it was possible the lab techs could have cleaned up the image and used it to ID him.

So, yeah, in Elijah's mind, getting that picture was critical.

But once he had it, there'd be no reason to keep any of them alive. In fact, just the opposite. He'd want them all dead. Maybe Etta Jean, too, once he discovered her in the bathroom and realized she could have overheard everything they were saying.

"You helped Yvette steal the babies," Addie spat out. She

was probably terrified, but she managed to sound more than ready and willing to make him pay for what he'd done.

"Helped?" Elijah laughed while he kept her moving. "Sugar, I did all the hard work by convincing that dimwit Yvette that the babies were in danger from some fake bogeyman I made up, and I made her believe that the only way to save them was for us to kidnap them. Yvette went right along with everything, including handing the brats off to the first person she saw on the road. Of course, she wanted to keep them, and I had to talk her out of that. Dimwit," he repeated in a snarl.

"I'm sure the drugs you gave Yvette helped convince her," Judson snarled. He wanted Elijah's attention on him.

"Maybe," Elijah muttered, and then amended that with, "Probably. They didn't hurt, anyway. They made her more pliable."

So, he'd been the one to give Yvette the drugs, which had made her more suspicious. What else had Elijah done?

"Why have her take the babies only to give them to someone else?" Judson wanted to know.

"The brats weren't the goal, *Deputy*." Elijah said the title as if it were the worst kind of poison. "Giving Yvette a motive to off herself was. After the drugs wore off and she came to what little senses she had, she was supposed to be so overcome with guilt that she couldn't live with herself. Of course, I would have encouraged her to do that."

That explained the note found in Yvette's car. Maybe the woman had written it on her own, but Judson suspected Elijah had *helped* with that, too. It'd been why it was so impersonal.

"And the visits to see Rowena in jail?" Addie asked. "Did you *encourage* Yvette to do that?"

"I did," Elijah admitted. "I figured Rowena could stir up the old feelings for Yvette over losing custody of her kids."

"But why?" Addie pressed.

Elijah cursed, clearly growing more impatient, but he answered. "I needed that trail," he spat out. "After Yvette was dead and the cops started digging, I needed there to be some kind of reason why Yvette was spurred to take the kids. I figured the cops would think it was because of her conversations with Rowena. I didn't expect Shane to start going with her on those visits," he added in a grumble.

"What about Courtney?" Judson pressed just as Elijah got to the phone.

Hooking his arm around Addie's throat, Elijah reached down, and with Addie in tow, he snagged the phone and shoved it into her hand.

"Sugar, find that picture," Elijah ordered her. He gave her a third jab, no doubt to prod her to be quick about it.

Judson didn't want *quick*. He needed some time to try to figure out how to put an end to this jerk. And all the backup wouldn't help with that. In fact, backup could make things worse for Addie.

"Courtney," Judson repeated. "How does she fit into this?"

"She doesn't. She was collateral damage. A total accident, I swear," Elijah explained, his attention on Addie as Elijah tried to open Judson's phone. "What's your PIN?" he barked out to Judson.

Judson rattled off the four numbers. The real ones. Because while a false answer would buy him some time, it might set Elijah off. The man obviously had a short fuse on that vicious temper.

"Where was I?" Elijah muttered as Addie unlocked the phone.

"You were saying how Courtney's death was a total accident," Judson provided, and no way did he sound convinced of that.

"Oh, yeah. It was," Elijah insisted. "She was there at the

house when Yvette and I got back. I was going to convince Yvette to take her own life and leave that suicide note. But that social worker was there, and she demanded to know if we took the babies. She was going to call the cops, so I had to stop her."

"But you didn't stop her," Judson pointed out. "She got away."

A flash of that quick temper darkened Elijah's face. "She did, but that was thanks to Yvette, who tried to hit me with a damn lamp. She gave me a hard knock on the head, and then she ran off, too. That's when I decided I'd have to find both of them and silence them for good. Courtney died on her own, bless her heart, but Yvette took a little more work."

"You gunned her down on the road," Judson spelled out.

Another shrug from Elijah, but he seemed to be getting more and more frustrated that Addie hadn't gotten to the picture he wanted. Since it was one of the last ones Judson had taken, it shouldn't have taken her long to find it, which meant Addie was stalling, too.

"And now with Yvette dead, Jennifer and Shane will inherit her money," Judson added, hoping to yank Elijah's attention back to him. "Were Shane and Jennifer in on it?"

"No, hell, no. Shane blabbered on and on about doing something to cut Trevor out of his mommy's life, but he's all talk. No way does he deserve a penny of that money. And it'll be hard for him to collect with his sorry butt in a jail cell. There should be enough evidence to point to him murdering Trevor."

"But Shane didn't kill Trevor," Judson said. "You did."

"The man was in the way. He wanted justice for Yvette. Oh, boo-hoo," Elijah mocked. "So, now he'll help make me rich by being dead, and Shane will be going to jail for his murder."

Judson didn't know what evidence Elijah had planted,

but he was sure the CSIs would find it when this was over. And he intended for this to be over with Addie alive and this SOB either under arrest or dead.

"There," Elijah said when Addie got to the picture. "Delete that and check for others taken from a slightly different angle. Then go to his sent folder to make sure he didn't forward them to anyone."

There had only been that one picture, and he hadn't sent it to anyone, but Judson was glad Elijah was searching for others. It bought him more time. Time he needed, because he still couldn't figure out how to get that gun away from Addie's head.

One possible move would be for Addie to drop down, to give Judson a clean shot to take out Elijah. That was a hell of a risk, but anything they did at this point was. Once she made it to the end of the photos and Elijah was certain there hadn't been any forwarded copies, he would kill them.

"You shouldn't have used the drug dealer with a connection to Jennifer," Judson threw out there, unsure if it would distract.

It did.

The man's head whipped up, and he got another flash of that anger. "I didn't know you'd be able to link that to her. I didn't know her friend's prints would be on the bag. And you shouldn't have harassed Jennifer for that." His voice got louder with each word. "I might have just broken into the house to get your phone, but I changed my mind because of way the two of you harassed her."

"We treated her like a suspect because she was found with blood on her hands at Yvette's house."

"She went there looking for Yvette," Elijah snapped. "Jennifer was in shock, and you damn near locked her up."

"You added to making her a suspect by buying those drugs from her friend," Judson pointed out just as fast.

Elijah cursed again, and it was raw and vicious. What he didn't do was take any responsibility for his fiancée nearly being arrested for murder. "I should kill all you idiot cops for going after her like that. Hell, I still might. Go faster through that sent folder," he snapped to Addie.

The man was quickly losing it, and that meant Judson only had seconds to stop him. Judson's gaze connected with Addie's, and he lowered his eyes, hoping she understood that he wanted her to drop down.

She gave a slight nod and stopped scrolling on his phone. "I took a picture of Yvette's car, too," Addie said.

It was a lie. Perhaps a very dangerous one. Because Elijah let out a loud roar, the rage tearing out in that feral sound.

"Where's your phone?" Elijah shouted, punctuating that demand with yet more profanity. He caught onto her hair and snapped her head back.

"It's in my purse in the foyer," Addie managed to say, though she was clearly in pain now.

But she was also clearly thinking straight.

As the last word left her mouth, she dropped, and even though Elijah still had hold of her hair, she fell far enough down that it gave Judson the opening he needed. He stepped into the doorway, and in one quick motion, he took aim.

And he pulled the trigger.

So did Elijah.

Both of them fired, but Judson's shot was a split second faster. Elijah's bullet slammed into the door next to Judson. Elijah, however, had no idea that he'd missed. The man had no idea of anything, not anymore.

Because Judson's shot hit Elijah right between the eyes.

The man was dead before he even hit the ground. And before he hit, Judson had already bolted across the room to Addie.

Chapter Eighteen

Addie lifted her face to the shower in the guest room and kept it there for as long as she could hold her breath. She had to wash away the blood.

Again.

This time, not from Yvette but from Elijah. When Judson had delivered the kill shots that had ended the man's reign of terror, and his life, Addie had gotten hit with some spatter.

It'd been a small price to pay for getting out of the nightmare alive, but she hadn't wanted the blood to stay on her body any longer than necessary. Nor had she wanted to hold the babies until she was clean. That's why she had headed to the shower as soon as Rory had bagged her clothes and taken a brief statement.

And after she'd spoken with Judson, of course.

That had been just quick reassurances that they were alive and unharmed. He hadn't kissed her and hadn't extended the hug he'd managed to give her right after shooting Elijah. That's because they had both wanted to rush into the bathroom and check on the babies.

Lily and Rose had been fine, not a scratch on them, and both girls had already gone back to sleep now that the gunfire had stopped. Etta Jean had looked just as shell-shocked as Addie no doubt had, but the woman was holding up. Addie prayed that continued in the aftermath of this attack.

The flurry of activity had started to swarm around the room and the ranch within minutes after Elijah's death. Priority one had been getting an ambulance for Bennie, but Addie knew that was just the start. The CSIs and ME would be coming in, and Grace and the deputies would be going through Elijah's place and any and all of his things.

Looking for proof to support what the man had confessed to when he'd been holding Addie at gunpoint.

Even if there was no proof, the confession and Elijah's actions in the past hour were more than enough to give him the label of serial killer, along with committing other assorted crimes, including the multiple attempts at the murder of police officers. Since Elijah was also the person responsible for abducting Lily and Rose and putting them in grave danger, Addie wouldn't shed a single tear over the man's demise.

Just the opposite.

Elijah's death brought her the flood of relief that the babies were now finally safe. They would be inconvenienced by having to leave the ranch for a day or two since it was now a crime scene. One that would need to be processed and cleaned up. That move would happen in an hour or two, after the deputies had cleared the grounds to make sure no other threat was lingering around. Everyone was convinced that Elijah had acted solo, but they wanted to be sure.

So did Addie.

She didn't want to take any chances with the twins' safety.

Then, the three of them and Etta Jean would be going to Judson's house for a couple of days. Not ideal, since it meant hauling loads and loads of baby stuff, but it was better than the alternative of being in the house where Elijah's blood was still on the floor. Soon, that would all be cleaned up, and while there would always be those horrible memories of him, there were thousands more good memories to overshadow what he'd tried to do.

Addie lathered up for a third time to make sure there were no traces of Elijah left on her body and wished it would be this easy to rid her mind of the terrifying images that would likely plague her for years to come. Etta Jean and Judson as well. Heck, the entire Renegade Canyon sheriff's office. Elijah had spread this nightmare to so many people.

And for what?

Money, plain and simple. His greed had spurred all of this, and she wondered if that greed would have soon extended to murdering Jennifer as well once he was certain he could have Yvette's entire estate.

Trying to shove aside as many thoughts of Elijah as she could, Addie stepped from the shower and was greeted by an amazing sight.

Judson.

He was in the doorway of the bathroom that she'd left open so she'd hear if anyone called out for her. Especially Etta Jean, since Livvy and she were in the nursery with the babies.

Judson's eyes locked with hers before his gaze slid down the naked length of her. The corner of his mouth lifted into a smile. Something she was glad to see. Right now, she wanted anything that would erase even a small portion of what she'd just been through.

He handed her a towel and watched as she coiled it around herself. "I would pull you into my arms right now, but that could be a little risky," Judson admitted. "I doubt we want to start something when we could be interrupted at any second."

That was true. But Addie risked it anyway. She went to him and let him engulf her in exactly what she needed. She let the feel of his body against hers ease some of her still-knotted muscles. Addie took in his scent, too, and let that fill her with something wonderful rather than the stench of gunfire and blood.

Yes, she needed this.

Addie held on for several minutes, letting herself level out.

"FYI, they just removed the body," he murmured, gently rubbing her back with his fingertips. "So, you won't have to see that when you go back downstairs."

Addie was beyond thankful for that. She never wanted to see Elijah again. She just wanted this moment with Judson and then the babies.

But she didn't get another moment with him, because his phone rang. Groaning, she stepped back, knowing he needed to take the call since it could be important.

"It's Serenity Springs Care Facility," he let her know.

He didn't put the call on speaker, and Addie didn't push him to do that. If this was Rowena, she didn't want to hear the woman's voice.

"Yes," Judson replied in response to what the caller had just said. "I'll tell her," he added a heartbeat later. "Thanks for letting us know."

Before he even ended the call, Addie knew what this was about. "Rowena's dead?"

He nodded, and she saw him studying her face, no doubt looking for any signs of grief. But there weren't any. Just the opposite. Addie exhaled a long, slow breath of relief and nodded.

"It's over," she muttered.

On a sigh, he reached for her again, but reaching was as

far as he got before he got a text. Clearly, fate was not going to allow Judson and her a little alone time. Of course, that was expected with all the various wheels turning in the wrap-up of the investigation.

"From Grace," Judson relayed after looking at his screen. "It's a couple of updates. One about Bennie."

That grabbed her attention, and she steeled herself up in case the deputy had died, but she didn't see dread in Judson's eyes. Only relief.

"Bennie made it through surgery," Judson explained. "He's in stable condition. The doctor is optimistic that he'll make a full recovery."

That eased even more of her too-tight muscles. They had already gotten word that the ranch hand, Delbert Reeves, was doing well, too. He'd been in the kitchen when the lights had gone out, and Elijah had clubbed him with the butt of his gun. Delbert had needed stitches and would require a night's stay in the hospital for observation, but like Bennie, he would recover.

"Good," she managed to say. Elijah hadn't claimed another life. But Bennie, and the rest of them, were also going to have to live with the SOB's actions for a while.

"Grace also found out that Elijah had already managed to add his name on to Jennifer's bank accounts," Judson went on.

"How'd he do that?" she asked.

"Apparently, Elijah had her sign some online forms that Jennifer thought were for payments for her hospital bills from the miscarriage. But they weren't. They gave him full access to her funds."

So, that's how Elijah had intended to get his hands on her inheritance.

Judson looked at her again. Then he picked up the clean

clothes she'd put on the vanity. "Want to go see the babies?" he asked. "They're awake. At least they were about
ten minutes ago."

"Yes," she couldn't say fast enough.

Addie practically yanked on the jeans, T-shirt and slip-
on shoes and started out of the bathroom the moment she
was dressed. Her hair was dripping wet, but she didn't care.
She wanted to hold the babies now and let them soothe her
as only they could.

Since the guest room was on the second floor, they made
their way to the stairs, past the attic ladder that was still
pulled down. Before they even made it to the landing, Addie
heard the chatter of the cops and the CSIs.

Once again, her house was crammed with first respond-
ers, and she hoped this was the last time such things would
be needed. The only cop she wanted filling her home on a
permanent basis was Judson.

That thought gave her a mental pause, and she tested out
the idea of it again. Yes, she wanted that. She didn't want
to lose this moment-to-moment contact, this intimacy, with
him again. She stopped on the stairs, looking up at him since
he was on the step above her.

"What?" he asked, at first frowning, but that faded fast.
Maybe because he saw that need for him in her eyes. Yep,
he saw it all right, because he smiled.

She smiled back, but Addie still didn't tell him what she
was thinking. What she wanted.

What she needed.

Now wasn't the time for her to spill any of that to Judson. But soon. After she held the twins.

When they made it to the foyer, Addie heard yet another familiar voice, but this time it wasn't one she'd expected to hear.
She spotted Grace in the front doorway, talking to Jennifer.

Addie could see the woman had been crying. In fact, she still was. She was swiping at tears as she muttered something to Grace. However, Jennifer's head whipped up, her gaze zooming right to the two of them.

Addie steeled herself, figuring that Jennifer was going to blame them for her fiancé's death. Heck, she might not even believe that Elijah was a killer, so things might get ugly in a hurry. Judson must have thought the same thing, because he stepped in front of her.

Protecting her, again.

Part of Addie thoroughly appreciated that, but she stepped to his side to face Jennifer. If the woman wanted to verbally blast them, Addie would tell her exactly how close Elijah had come to killing them.

But there was no verbal blast.

"I'm sorry," Jennifer said. "So very sorry."

"Jennifer heard about the incident on the news," Grace explained. "She's on her way to the police station to give another statement, but she wanted to stop by here first. I told her she couldn't go inside."

"It's okay," Jennifer quickly said. "I, uh, don't want to go in."

She shivered as if she could imagine the body and the blood of a man she loved. Or had once loved, anyway.

"I swear I didn't know what Elijah was doing. I didn't know he'd killed my mother, Courtney and Trevor." Jennifer stopped and pressed her fingers to her trembling lips. "I mean, I knew he wanted the money. He was always going on and on about that, but I didn't know he would kill to get it. And those babies. He tricked my mother into taking those precious little babies."

Apparently, that had made it to the news reports, too, or

else Grace had mentioned it to her. Clearly, that revelation had shaken Jennifer to the core.

"I've also told Jennifer that she'll likely be cleared of all charges," Grace explained. "Unless, of course, we find something at Elijah's place or on his computer."

"I had no part in this sick plan," Jennifer insisted, frantically shaking her head. "So, if you find anything, it'll be something he set up to make me look guilty."

Judging from what Elijah had said when he was holding Addie at gunpoint, there'd be nothing to implicate Jennifer. Only Shane because he wanted Trevor away from his mother, maybe even dead. And the CSIs and cops would no doubt be able to sort that out.

"I won't keep you," Jennifer said, turning her attention back to Addie and Judson, "but I wanted you to know that I won't be keeping the money from my mother's estate. It doesn't feel right for me to have it when it was my fiancé who's responsible for so much pain. So much hurt." She swallowed hard. "I'll see a lawyer about donating it to the Horseshoe Ranch. Maybe as some kind of scholarship fund for the kids who are fostered here."

That touched Addie. The ranch was self-sufficient, but donations were always welcome. "Thank you," she managed to say around the lump in her throat.

Jennifer nodded and murmured another, "I'm so sorry," before she turned and walked away.

"If Shane shows, I'll send him straight to the police station," Grace said after Jennifer was in her car. "I figure he won't be nearly as tearful as his sister."

Probably not, but at least he was alive and wasn't in jail because Elijah had framed him for murder. Once that sank in, Shane might be plenty thankful for the outcome.

"We'll be in the nursery if you need us," Judson said,

and taking Addie's hand, they headed in that direction. Not taking a direct route, since that would have led them past the room where Elijah had died. Instead, they went out through the side porch to get to the kitchen and the back hall. The moment they reached the door, Addie heard an amazing sound.

Cooing.

She went straight in and saw Etta Jean sitting on the floor with the babies, who were lying on a quilt. Both Lily and Rose were indeed awake, and as Addie approached, they both looked up at her.

Twin smiles.

And no way would she believe that was gas. They were as glad to see her as she was to see them.

Addie dropped down on the floor next to them, giving them both kisses, which brought on yet more cooing. The tears came. Happy ones, of course, and she saw that Etta Jean had them, too.

She gave the woman's hand a squeeze. "We can watch them for a while so you can take a break."

Etta Jean nodded. "I do want to pack some things to take to Judson's." She looked at him as she got up from the floor. "Thank you for letting us all stay there."

"Anytime," he assured the woman, and he pulled her into a quick hug. "We'll leave as soon as Grace gives us the okay."

Another nod from Etta Jean, and she blew out what sounded like a breath of relief. They all needed to get away from the chaos for a while, but Addie was already looking forward to coming back home. To things returning to normal.

Well, her new normal, anyway.

Addie wanted some things to stay exactly the same. But she wanted some changes, too. For now, though, she just savored this moment. Her babies were smiling and making those wonderful sounds, and Judson was right by her side.

"I'll call my lawyer in a couple of hours and ask her to try to expedite the adoption petition," Addie told him. Now that the killer was no longer a threat and there wasn't any next of kin to try to claim them, there shouldn't be any obstacle standing in her way.

Judson smiled and sat down beside her. "Good. The sooner, the better."

She felt the same way. Lily and Rose were a huge part of that new normal. In a couple of months, she wanted to resume taking in foster kids, too, so the legacy of the Horseshoe Ranch could continue.

"Does the sooner, the better work for other things?" Judson asked.

Addie had been playing with Lily's toes, but she turned to stare at him. He wasn't quite smiling now, but there was certainly no gloomy expression on his incredible face. Just the opposite.

And his expression got a whole lot better—hers as well— when he leaned in and kissed her.

Oh, there it was. That dreamy feel of pleasure sliding right through her. The man could perform magic with that mouth.

He upped the magic by slipping his right arm around her and pulling her to him to add a hug to that kiss. It was plenty hot. But fun, too, because both babies were kicking them.

Laughing, Judson eased back from the kiss and gave both Lily and Rose a nuzzle on their cheeks. The girls clearly liked that, because they cooed some more.

"Well?" he said. "Does the sooner work for other things?" he repeated.

Addie hoped he was talking about their future, but just in

case he wasn't, she went ahead and launched into things she needed to say to him. "I've been in love with you for a long time, Judson. Then we made that stupid pact. Not so stupid then, but it would be for us to try to hang on to it now."

Mercy, she was babbling. And she was nervous. Or at least she was until Judson smiled again.

"You're in love with me," he stated.

She nodded. Waited. Waited some more. Then his smile widened.

"Same," he finally said. "I've been in love with you forever, and that pact has dissolved to dust."

Addie would have smiled or cheered, but he kissed her again, and that pretty much robbed her of the ability to make any sounds or facial gestures. The kiss went on for several incredible moments before he eased back and gently nipped her bottom lip with his teeth.

"I'd love to haul you off to bed to celebrate," he said, "but I like this celebration just as much. Well, almost as much," Judson added with a chuckle.

"We'll do the bed celebration soon." Which hopefully wouldn't be too long. "For now, there's just one more thing I need to do."

She kissed him, and she made it way too hot, considering they had an audience of twin babies. Still, Addie had wanted this dizzying intensity from the kiss to give her the courage for what was to come. If Judson rejected her…but she stopped. Nope. She wouldn't go there. She would just spill and let him decide what to do.

"Will you marry me?" she asked. But she pressed a finger to his mouth to stop him from answering just yet. "And FYI, I'm not talking about a marriage of convenience or one simply for the sake of the twins. I'm talking the real deal, an honest-to-goodness marriage—"

"Yes," he blurted. And she caught just a glimpse of the grin he flashed before he hauled her back to him and kissed her as if to seal the deal.

Addie sealed it right back. She melted against him, savoring the moment. Savoring, too, the thought that she wanted many more moments just like this one.

Cooing, kicking babies. A really amazing kiss. And the man she loved. Her future husband.

Yes, this was exactly the new normal that Addie wanted.

* * * * *

BIG SKY
SHOWDOWN

JUNO RUSHDAN

To unsung heroes who make the world a better,
safer place.

Chapter One

The days of running headfirst into trouble were over for Kimi Redbird Wheeler. Or so she thought.

She no longer dated bad boys or partied late into the wee hours when nothing good ever happened. Even traded in her rodeo buckles for a nursing degree. No more barrel racing. No more bronc riding. No more taking the risk of breaking her neck.

For the past four years, she tended to the sick and mended the broken.

After her big brother Jacy died, she got her act together. Now, at twenty-nine, she was finally the woman he'd hoped she would grow into. Grounded. Thriving. Doing her best to stay out of harm's way.

Yet, no matter how hard she tried, she simply couldn't steer clear of trouble.

Or rather, trouble was determined to follow her, regardless of what she did.

Kimi glanced over her shoulder. She only saw ordinary pedestrians on the busy Main Street in downtown Bitterroot Falls. *He* wasn't back there.

Nonetheless, she had that feeling again. The eerie prickling sensation skittered across the back of her neck like a colony of fire ants, making her shoulder blades bunch together in reflex.

Someone was watching her. Tracking her.

Kimi quickened her steps, hurrying to The Beanery. The café was the last stop on her list of errands, after hitting the bank, the home goods shop for a new lamp, and the supermarket. The Beanery was the one to-do that was a must-do because she'd been craving a pistachio latte all day on her shift in the emergency room.

Her vintage chambray-blue cowgirl boots that she loved to wear on her time off when she didn't have on sneakers clacked against the cold pavement. She slid a furtive glance across the street.

Nothing. He was nowhere to be seen. Like the slippery shadow dogging her every move was a figment of her imagination. Two or three times she'd questioned her sanity, wondering if it was just in her head, the way he'd appear and vanish.

She rarely got a good glimpse of the man who had trailed her for three days. But her gut told her he was there. Somewhere.

Whipping another quick look over her shoulder, she scanned the faces of the others on the street. Many she recognized as friendly, law-abiding citizens of the small town of Bitterroot Falls. None she knew well enough to call a neighbor or turn to for assistance without sounding paranoid, or worse, hysterical, because…

She still didn't see *him*.

No sign of her shadow.

Not that she had ever seen his face outright from a full-frontal perspective, but she had spotted him enough times to feel confident he wasn't the short man, sixtyish, with glasses perched on the bridge of his nose and an umbrella

in his gloved hand, or the tall, thin man who had an aristo-
cratic bearing, wearing a red scarf wrapped tightly around
his neck and carrying a brown paper bag filled to the top
with groceries.

Kimi and Mr. Red Scarf had checked out of the supermarket around the same time. Now he and Mr. Glasses were
close behind her.

In the past several days, she'd tried to ignore the feeling of
warning she got every time she caught sight of her shadow.
More than once, she'd dismissed it as a byproduct of listening to too many true crime podcasts, blaming it on an over-
active imagination. But Jacy had taught her to trust her gut.

She worked in Cutthroat Creek, frequented Bitterroot
Falls, and lived in between both quaint, quiet towns where
it wasn't odd to see the same faces over and over again. It
was to be expected. That was normal.

Which was part of the problem.

Kimi could describe Mr. Glasses and Mr. Red Scarf in
detail and, for that matter, most other passersby on the street.
Yet, she'd never quite seen the face of her slippery shadow.
Too elusive.

Perhaps if she could look the man square in the eyes for
a few seconds, without him trying to hide, she might overcome her mounting fear whenever he popped up.

The best description she had was a white male or light-
skinned Hispanic. Taller than average. Facial hair. Dressed
in plain dark clothing. Sunglasses covered his eyes, day or
night. Basically, he looked like a scary thug who intended
to rough her up the first chance he got.

Dread curdled in her stomach.

Why would someone want to hurt her?

She didn't have the faintest idea. Even in her wildest

rodeo days, she hadn't given anyone a reason to follow her with the intent of bodily harm.

Kimi stopped in front of a flower shop, her palms growing sweaty in spite of the frigid January temperature. Disregarding the gorgeous displays of fresh blooms, she used the glass's reflection to survey her surroundings. At six o'clock in the evening, it was already dark outside, and the winter gloom cast a dreary, sinister pall over everything.

No one was lurking suspiciously. It seemed all clear.

But the prickle along her spine flared again. There was no doubt in her mind that he might be out of sight at the moment, but he wasn't far.

Waiting for the chance to do…what?

An icy chill slithered down her spine as her shoulders hitched.

She moved on from the store, hurrying to catch back up to the two older men, Mr. Glasses and Mr. Red Scarf. The street was busy but not crowded. People were dipping in and out of stores. No one was loitering outside, engaged in conversation. Not in this frosty weather.

Her brother Jacy had taught her what to do in such situations.

Keep calm. Pay attention. Go to where there are people.

In her case, stay within shouting distance of people. Since the elusive guy had started tailing her, she carried her cell phone in her coat pocket as opposed to inside her handbag in the event she needed to call the police quickly. One less step to slow her down.

She increased her pace, bringing her closer to the men in front of her.

The cold air had grown damp, the wind whipping up, like a storm was brewing. One that would bring lots of rain rather than snow. She pulled the hood of her parka up over her head.

Her hold on the plastic handles of her bags began to slip. Adjusting her grip on the groceries, she shrugged the strap of her handbag higher on her shoulder.

Two more blocks and she'd be at the Beanery. One decaf pistachio latte would soon be hers.

"And then head home to cook dinner," she muttered, realizing she'd used her outside voice when a couple passing in the opposite direction gave her a curious glance.

Talking to herself was a quirk that had emerged after Jacy's death. He'd been more than her big brother. He'd been her idol, her best friend in all the world. The one person she fell back on for everything, good or bad. Mostly bad until she'd straightened up, but he had been there to clean up her messes. Her mom, Aiyana Redbird, was an artist, off traveling the world, following her bliss, only checking in now and then. Even less once Jacy was gone. It wasn't unusual for months to go by without hearing from her mother. While her dad, Thomas Wheeler, lived in Bitterroot Falls, and he could see her if he so desired. She was just a simple phone call away, but the only thing he cared about was his work. He lived and breathed palladium mining.

When Jacy died on a deployment with the air force as a combat engineer, she had processed her grief by talking to him. Keeping him alive, in spirit. The habit spilled over during times of high anxiety and turned into speaking to herself more than to Jacy nowadays.

"Yep, I'm going to have a sugary drink before dinner," she said low, this time to her brother. Something the old Kimi would have done without a qualm about spoiling her appetite.

One more block and hello pistachio latte.

She reached the corner, thinking about the warm frothy drink that would delight her taste buds, just a ten-second lapse in focus, and she didn't spot him until it was too late. The shadow lunged from the side street that was little more than a dark, dreary alley.

A gasp tore from her lips with the first hard, jarring yank of her purse strap on her shoulder. The man jostled her painfully, like she was nothing more than a rag doll. She should've worn the bag across her body.

It wasn't until she had to free her hands to fight back that she fully grasped the gravity of her situation. The plastic bags went flying out of her grip, the groceries tumbling to the ground. The porcelain lamp crashed on the pavement, shattering to pieces.

"Help!" she cried out, holding on to her purse. She struggled to get back onto the busy Main Street, but the man grabbed her by the hood of her coat, hauling her backward, forcing her deeper into the alley.

He was so strong. So much stronger than her.

The second brutal tug on her purse sent her spinning into a wall. Her cheek smacked against the brick, the breath rushing from her lungs. Pain exploded along the side of her face, and that quickly jolted her out of the momentary shock that froze her reflexes.

"Oh, my God!" someone shouted. "She's being mugged!"

Kimi tightened her hold on her leather strap. The man whipped her around, slamming her into the wall. Her skull snapped back against the solid brick. In the daze fogging her brain, she realized that in addition to the usual sunglasses he also wore a ski mask this time.

Her head cleared, and she threw a kick, the chunky heel of her boot connecting with bone or a kneecap.

A loud grunt sputtered from the man, but he didn't stop.

And neither did she. Kimi gripped her purse strap with one hand and punched with the other.

Let it go, Jacy would've told her.

Just give the man what he wanted, her handbag, and this assault might end. The credit cards could be frozen and the cash in her wallet wasn't worth her life.

Let it go.

But she couldn't. She flat-out refused.

This was her only designer handbag, and her twenty-fifth birthday present from Jacy. The Burberry bag matched the vintage boots. Both had been the *last* things he had ever given her.

And then there was the principle of the matter. She might've buckled down in lieu of winning buckles, but she would never give in to anyone, especially not some two-bit street thug.

The bruiser was built like a tank, square and squat and solid. He had his meaty fist locked around her strap. He nearly ripped the handbag from her desperate grip, and would have had to, if not for timely help from others.

Mr. Glasses whacked him with an umbrella while Mr. Red Scarf wielded a red mesh bag of oranges like a weapon, walloping the guy, blow after blow.

"Call the cops!" someone yelled.

Onlookers at the entrance of the alley pulled out their cell phones. Others held them up as if they were recording, with bright lights shining in their direction.

Kimi held tight to the leather strap, but she managed to grab the man's ski mask and yank it down.

Throwing an elbow back into Mr. Red Scarf and shoving Kimi to the side, her assailant lowered his face away from the cameras and disentangled himself from the free-for-all scuffle. The slippery shadow darted down the dark alley, heavy boots thudding on the concrete. He was running fast for a big guy, but he was getting away. The man skirted a dumpster, rounded a corner and disappeared.

People clustered around her and guided her out onto the sidewalk of Main Street.

"Are you hurt?" one person asked. "Are you okay?"

Nodding, she was breathless from the fight and grateful for the heroic assistance of strangers.

Kimi put a hand on the shoulder of one of her saviors, opening her mouth to thank him, and gasped from the sharp pain that radiated in her jaw. She pressed a palm to the side of her face that was throbbing.

The wail of a siren pierced the air, and she sagged with relief.

But she couldn't help wondering if the man who had been following her for three days would try again. Not that she could let it get that far. To the point of another attempt to mug her. To steal her handbag.

As soon as the thought popped up in her mind like a creepy jack-in-the-box—she never understood why anyone would make such a toy—she felt like she was losing her mind again.

Why would someone follow her just to mug her?

She wasn't rich. Sure, the designer bag was beautiful, but it cost less than a thousand dollars. Not worth the effort to trail a person and try to rob them. Unless he was a junkie.

Drug addicts made poor choices. Desperate decisions that were born out of their need to get their next fix. Even if it made little sense.

That had to be the explanation, right?

Mr. Red Scarf handed her a bag of frozen peas. "Here you go. Put that on your face."

"Thank you," she said, taking the chilled bag. She pressed the frozen peas to her cheek and winced. Her head pounded. She was going to have to forego her pistachio latte and go to the hospital. Ten to one, she had a concussion. "To both of you." She glanced between Mr. Glasses and Mr. Red Scarf. "I don't know how I can ever repay you for what you did. You risked so much by jumping in to help me. A stranger."

They could have been hurt and if her attacker had had a weapon, then much worse might have happened.

"Think nothing of it," Glasses said.

Red Scarf nodded. "This is a good town, with good people. Can't stand by and do nothing." He winced and rubbed his head.

"Are you hurt?" Kimi asked.

"He got me good in the face. I think I'll have a shiner in the morning."

She handed the chilled bag back to Red Scarf. "You've already done more than enough. I can't take your peas, too. Not when you need them."

The sirens drew closer. Police and, most likely, an ambulance would be there soon. Then she'd tell them her story. Maybe they would believe her.

Maybe they wouldn't. There was no way they'd give her a hard time about the attempted mugging since she had plenty of witnesses.

It was the part about this being premeditated that worried her. The part where she couldn't accurately describe him. Or his vehicle, other than it was a black SUV. Or how no one else had seen this man following her.

Once, in the hospital parking lot, she'd been talking to her ex-boyfriend, Danny, an ER doctor, and tried to point out her slippery shadow. Before Danny had seen him, the guy had disappeared.

Poof. Gone like he had never been there.

Like he didn't exist.

"Did anyone see his face?" Kimi asked. "Get it on video? A picture?" She couldn't be sure, but she hoped she had pulled down his mask long enough for someone to have captured his face.

The crowd surrounding her murmured as folks looked at their phones, most likely searching through the photos and footage they had.

"No," one person said, followed by another and another.

Her heart sank.

She knew how this was going to play out. A cop would file a report, tell her to be careful, to be on the lookout for this suspicious man who she couldn't describe and no one else had seen prior to today.

Then she would be left to deal with it on her own.

Unless…

Groaning, Kimi shook her head. "No, I can't go to him."

"Go to who, honey?" a woman asked her, and Kimi realized she had spoken out loud.

"No one." *Just talking to myself again.* Which would only feed into the perception that she was losing it.

Takoda Yazzie would not want to see her, much less help her. The last time they'd run into each other at the hospital—*six weeks and four days ago, and yes, she was counting*—she had asked to speak to him for a minute. Sixty seconds, in private, like two adults. He had stared at her, a muscle ticking in his jaw as her heart stuttered in her chest, waiting for him to respond.

A curt shake of the head. He had grunted and mumbled, *I'm working,* and then couldn't get far enough away from her fast enough. To make things worse, other people they both knew were present, watching and listening. They'd probably thought she had a communicable disease the way Takoda had treated her.

Working. That had been his excuse.

They had been standing in the middle of the emergency room, where she had been wearing scrubs and a nametag because she was working, too.

Sheesh. He wouldn't give her one measly minute.

It had been so humiliating; she had wanted to scream. And not at the universe. Oh, no. She'd wanted to scream at him, in his face, and stab his muscular chest with her finger and give him a piece of her mind.

After that embarrassing encounter, she had vowed then and there that she didn't need him. Not for anything. Didn't even need to speak to him if that was the way he wanted to handle the situation. Seemed immature from her perspective, and she was younger than him by five years.

But she could be just as tough and distant as Takoda if pushed. Even tougher. Colder.

She took a breath, not sure if she was more upset about Tak or the failed mugging.

Go see Tak. The voice in her head sounded so similar to her brother's, it made her heart ache.

Jacy would have insisted that Tak, the friend he'd loved like a brother, was the one person she needed to turn to since Jacy wasn't there to help with this latest mess that she found herself in.

"This is a good, clear video," someone said, handing her their phone.

Kimi pressed Play on the recording and watched the horror she had endured play back. The violence that had unfolded so quickly. The brutality that could have ended so much differently if others hadn't selflessly intervened on her behalf.

Her gut clenched and she wanted to retch. "Do you mind if I send myself a copy?"

"No, of course," the woman said.

"Thanks." Kimi texted herself the video file.

What if that big bruiser came back? What if she didn't have the kindness of strangers to save her next time?

As much as she hated the idea and knew she might regret it, doing what her brother would want was better than the alternative.

She needed to see Takoda.

Chapter Two

Gravel crunched as a vehicle pulled up his driveway. Takoda Yazzie set down the pile of mail he needed to open
along with his beer on the coffee table and got up from the
sofa. He strode to his front window, peeled back the mo-
torized blinds and looked to see who was visiting him at
ten o'clock at night.

None of the guys he worked with at Ironside Protection
Services had called to say they were stopping by, which
they would have done.

Popping up unannounced was considered rude in his circle of friends.

The motion sensor lights on the garage came on, illuminating the sapphire-blue Subaru Forester that parked. Tak
recognized the car.

It was Kimi's.

Every muscle in his body went rigid, and he swore. The
absolute last person he wanted to see on his doorstep, at
night, after he'd been drinking, was Kimimela Anne Redbird Wheeler.

Her full name was a bittersweet mouthful, and the woman
was more than a handful. It was easier to wrangle a wild
bull than to get her to listen. Or cooperate. Or heed pru-
dent advice.

The only way Jacy had gotten her to settle down and grow up was by dying.

A pang of remorse nearly split him open. Four years since he'd died. Sometimes the sorrow, the guilt and the shame felt as fresh as that first day when he'd lost his best friend.

He sucked in a breath. Stared out the window.

The Subaru was still running, headlights on. Why was she sitting in her car?

If she was waiting for an engraved invitation to come inside, she'd be waiting forever because he had no intention of letting her set foot across the threshold.

It would be even better if she reconsidered this drop-by altogether, backed out of his driveway and went home. They did not need to do this. Talk about what happened.

He felt bad enough as it was. For his carelessness. For his selfishness. For making the one mistake that he'd promised Jacy he would never make with Kimi.

Tak didn't even know how it had happened.

Well, yes, he did. They were at the snazzy rooftop bar at the BMH—the Bitterroot Mountain Hotel—sitting under a heater, drinking. He drove her home. On the ride, they were talking about Jacy and discovered a strange coincidence. Sometimes they both heard Jacy's voice in their head, maybe out loud. She started crying. Shared grief pricked his eyes and swelled in his throat. He wiped away her tears, his palm caressing her soft, warm skin, his fingers tangling in her silky hair. Then somehow her mouth was on his and they were kissing.

Really kissing. And groping. His hands slipping into places they did not belong. Her hands finding spots that ached for her touch.

Even worse than breaking his promise to Jacy that he would stay away from his baby sister, Tak had almost messed up things for Kimi. She was a nurse, who was sort of dating an ER doctor, the way her brother wanted. Kimi and her boyfriend had taken a little break, but Doc Dan had asked her to move in with him. Despite the break, she was mulling over the idea of living with the doctor.

To Tak, that was the next logical step. The right move for her. Literally. Then an inevitable engagement would follow.

In a moment of weakness, Tak had almost, *almost,* stopped her from becoming Mrs. Doc Dan one day.

He wanted to slap himself silly and not stop until he could forget about the mistake he'd made. The only problem was kissing Kimi Anne was unforgettable.

She was unforgettable.

Her car door finally opened.

Tak stepped away from the window.

Bracing himself, he established some quick ground rules. *Don't let her in. Keep the conversation short. No touching. And definitely no kissing under any circumstances.*

Compartmentalization was his strongest skill. He just had to stuff all his messy, complicated feelings about Kimi into a steel box, lock it and bury it.

Simple.

His doorbell rang.

"I've got this," he said to himself.

You had better, a voice replied.

He had to look over his shoulder to be certain Jacy's ghost wasn't standing there behind him.

Sucking in a fortifying breath, he moved away from the window and flicked on the porch light. He steeled his backbone and opened the door.

Kimi had retreated down the steps and was standing off his porch, out of the light in the darkness. As though she was prepared for how this had to go.

Wrapping her arms around herself, she shivered, and he would've liked nothing better than to warm her up. But...

Jacy's sister was off limits, he reminded himself.

Keep your hands and thoughts in check, man. Lay a finger on my baby sister and I'll kill you. Jacy had told him that outright eleven years ago. Tak had met Kimi, and his best friend must've seen the unbridled heat in his eyes whenever he looked at her.

Tak schooled his features. "What are you doing here?" he asked, deadpan, but the words still came out harsher than he'd intended. So he added, "At this time of night."

"I'm sorry to disturb you like this." She lowered her head and shook it. "Maybe I should've called first."

"That would've been polite."

She spun away from him, her flared wool skirt whooshed around her, and she marched off down the walkway. Got about midway. Turned around and stomped back to the foot of his porch. "I didn't call because I didn't think you'd answer and, if you did, I knew you wouldn't let me come over."

"Then you thought right," Tak said, his voice steady, formal.

Huffing a breath, she muttered something too low to completely make out, but he caught his name and a dirty word.

"Are you going to invite me inside?" she asked, grudgingly, like mustering the question had taken a herculean effort. "Let me get out of the cold and get warm in front of your fire?"

Bad idea. The innuendo alone of getting warm by his *fire* made it sound even worse.

Crossing his arms, he stepped out onto the porch. "Why are you here, Kimi? Shouldn't you be snuggled up with Doc Dan or is he working?"

"Tactless Tak strikes again." Kimi sighed. "Thanks for

giving me the reception I expected. You could try being a little less predictable."

He gritted his teeth. In business, he was known for his tact. Not only was he a consummate professional, but he'd been raised to handle any unexpected confrontation with a mask of calm control.

With Kimi, things were different. Around her, he tended to forget himself. The way he had the night she had expected him to drop everything and come running to have drinks with her while her boyfriend was working late in the emergency room, busy saving lives. The fool that Tak was, he had, and they had gotten too close, crossing the line. But they hadn't crossed the point of no return. No serious, unfixable damage done. He intended to keep it that way.

"It's cold." He gave her a hard stare. "And I'm waiting."

"I need to talk to you."

"Okay." He shrugged. "So, talk. I'm listening."

Her face was cast in shadows, but he thought he caught the narrowing of her eyes.

"Not out here on your front stoop." She groaned, shaking her head like he was the most obtuse man on the planet. Tactless, thoughtless, as well as discourteous. "I need a friend. Can you be that? Let me in? Let me get warm? Ask me if I'd like a drink? I could sure use one."

That was how the disastrous mistake had played out last time. She'd needed a friend. Wanted to talk, over drinks, about moving in with DD.

This time, he was the one shaking his head. "We've done this dance, kiddo. Fool me once, shame on me. Not happening again."

"Fool you?" She dropped her arms to her sides, hands clenching into fists. "What exactly are you insinuating, Takoda Yazzie?"

Whenever she used his full name, it meant Kimi was getting fired up to light into him. He braced himself.

"That I lured you in?" She sounded aghast. "Tricked you into kissing me?"

"Your words. Not mine. But you did kiss me, and not to offend you, I simply kissed you back."

"What?" Rocking back on her heels, she gaped at him. "That's—that's not how it happened."

"It's how I remember it, kiddo."

"Stop calling me that! I am not a kid," she said, stomping a foot like she was having a tantrum. "I'm almost thirty years old, for crying out loud." She huffed, her breath crystallizing the air.

He was painfully aware that she was no longer a kid. Hadn't been back when they'd first met either. At eighteen, she had been a blossoming young woman.

Now, she was all woman. Filled out with curves guaranteed to wreck him. Black, lustrous long hair and deep brown eyes in a face that was…pure *wow*. And when she smiled, it was like a sucker punch to his soul every time.

But she wasn't smiling now.

"Forget it," she said, waving a dismissive hand in his direction. "I should have my head examined for coming here, thinking that you would help me. Oh yeah, that's right, I already did have my head examined by Danny, who is indeed still working. By the way, I have a concussion. Not that you care. But my brain injury explains my poor judgment in coming here tonight." She spun on her heel and marched down his walkway, heading for her car.

He was off the porch, right behind her, his chest tightening at the mention of her being hurt. "Kimi."

"Look at what you do to me! I came here calm and collected, and you turn me into a raging, unhinged fool. I don't know why Jacy believed you would be there for me. That I could count on you when I needed you the most. He's probably rolling over in his grave with disappointment at how you're letting him down. Letting me down. And if he's not cursing your name, you better believe that I will be," she said, every barb she threw, hitting its mark, straight down to the bone.

"That's a mighty low blow."

"You earned it."

He couldn't disagree.

Kimi opened the car door and hopped in.

Tak grabbed onto the top of the door frame, preventing her from closing it. "Hang on. How did you get a concussion?"

"I won't trouble you with the story or my presence on your property a moment longer." She tried to shut the door.

He held fast to it, moving inside the opening and peering over at her. In the light, the bruises covering half her face were apparent. "Holy hell! What happened to you, kiddo?" He reached for her cheek.

Kimi slapped his hand away. "Don't you dare touch me," she snapped, the look she gave him cutting.

"All right," he said, raising his palm. "Tell me what happened."

"I was mugged. Well, almost. By this big guy. Relatively speaking. You're probably a little bigger."

"Did the cops catch him?"

"No. Witnesses recorded part of the altercation, but his face was covered the entire time. Sunglasses and a ski mask."

"Are you okay?" Leaning closer, he put a hand on her shoulder.

She swatted it from her body. "Don't. After the way you

spoke to me just now, after the way you've been treating me, not taking my calls, avoiding me in public—"

"I didn't avoid you when we bumped into each other at the hospital." That was six weeks ago. Way too long, he admitted to himself. But he'd been trying to give her a wide berth, plenty of space to sort things out with her boyfriend and take the leap at moving in. Part of him wondered if she had. Okay, all of him wanted to know if she was shacking up with the doctor. "We talked that day."

"Talked? You uttered two words to me." She held up one finger and then slowly raised a second. "Two, Tak. That's not a conversation, and the way you looked at me, like you wished I would just disappear. I'm not going anywhere, by the way. Do you have any idea how that made me feel?"

Tak needed more than a slap in the face. He needed a punch to the groin. At the hospital, he'd been a bit brusque to keep her from cornering him.

Hurting her so deeply had not been his intention.

As if it wasn't bad enough that he had dishonored his best friend's wish, broken a promise. Keeping that promise, to never act on any romantic urges—physical or emotional—toward Kimi was the least he could've done.

What was wrong with him?

That made him the worst.

At the hospital, he hadn't been running from her—well, maybe he was just a little—but he was so ashamed of himself. Facing her was a terrible reminder of what he'd done.

Not only for kissing her back, but for what had happened on that last deployment. The truth of how Jacy died.

If only he could tell her. But the words were clogged in his throat.

Kimi glared at him. "You think I want to ruin our friendship. But you're the only person I can talk to about Jacy. The only other person who knew what he was really like. Who can tell me things about him that no one else knows. Who still misses him as much as I do." Tears welled in her eyes, but she dashed them away with the backs of her hands, not letting them fall. "The kiss was a drunken mistake. One that we both clearly regret. Friends should be allowed to make mistakes. To talk about it and be forgiven. Have things move forward beyond the awful slip-up. Like mature adults. But I guess you're not capable of that, kiddo!"

This woman knew how to wound and humble him like no other. "I'm sorry. You're right."

She stared at him, mouth open, beautiful brown eyes glassy with unshed tears. "What did you say?"

Clenching his jaw, he drew in a long breath. "You heard me."

"Could you repeat it? Wait a minute." She pulled her phone from her pocket. "I want to record it."

"Get out of the car." He took her arm, urging her from the vehicle, and then closed the door once she was beside him.

Rain started falling, only a drizzle, but the sky would open up soon. Not letting her go, he ushered her up his porch steps and across the threshold.

Now, he had broken every ground rule. Except for one.

Closing the front door, he let her go and vowed to keep his lips to himself tonight. "Can I get you some aspirin?"

She shed her coat, hung it up and collapsed onto the sofa in front of the crackling fire. "I'd prefer a whiskey."

Another bad idea. "Don't you need to take something for the inflammation?"

"Give me some ice and a drink. I deserve it." She gestured to her bruised face, and he wanted to beat the guy who did that to her into a pulp.

Tak got her an ice pack, two fingers of whiskey, and sat

beside her. Shoving his mail aside on the table, he grabbed his beer.

He reconsidered their proximity and scooted away a couple of inches.

Staring at him, she shook her head. "What? Do you think I'm going to throw myself at you? That you're so drop-dead hot that I won't be able to control myself?" She arched an eyebrow.

Did she think he was drop-dead hot?

No, of course not. She was being sarcastic. He was aware he generally didn't have problems meeting women, but drop-dead hot?

No way. He also knew he wasn't Kimi's type. She went for extremes. Charismatic bad boys that most women drooled over or boring, passive professionals like DD. Tak was squarely in the middle, in looks and temperament.

"You did say that I have an effect on you," he replied, his tone teasing.

Kimi slapped his arm and scooted closer to him. "You have a bad effect on me. Raging. Unhinged. Remember?" She put the ice pack on her cheek. "Not melting in a puddle of desire at your feet. Get over yourself."

He was in no danger of getting an inflated ego. "Tell me what happened," he said. "Start at the beginning. Don't leave anything out."

"Three days ago, I was leaving work and noticed this guy sitting in the parking lot."

"Make and model of the car?"

Shrugging, she sipped the whiskey. "Black SUV. Big. Like a Chevy Tahoe or GMC Yukon. Maybe a Ford Explorer. I don't know. I'm not good with cars."

American make, which was a start. "Same guy who attacked you today?"

"Yes."

"How can you be sure? You told me his face was covered the entire time. Sunglasses and a ski mask."

"I'm sure," she snapped. "Okay? He wasn't wearing a ski mask in the hospital parking lot or any other time I've spotted him. Just sunglasses. Tonight, when he attacked me, he wore a ski mask for the first time. But I managed to yank it down for a moment. It's the same guy."

Deciding to let it go, he nodded and took a draw on his beer. "Okay."

"Anyway, he followed me into Bitterroot Falls."

"And you didn't notice the make of the vehicle behind you?"

"It was dark, all right, and he wasn't close enough. He always keeps his distance."

"But you're sure it was him following you?"

She sighed. "I picked up tacos for dinner and when I was headed back to my car, I spotted him on the street, looking in the window of a store two doors down. Stuff like that kept happening. I'd catch a glimpse of him here and there and then he was gone."

"For the past three days?" he asked, skeptical about the length of time, but she nodded. "Did you point him out to anyone? Notify the cops?"

"Danny and I were talking in the parking lot one night at the hospital. I noticed the guy. Tried to show him. But the man took off before Danny saw him. As far as calling the cops, I didn't know what to say without sounding hysterical or paranoid."

"You didn't see his face tonight because it was covered. In all the times that he's followed you, have you gotten a good look at him? Not a single picture of his face?"

She narrowed her eyes like he was the enemy. "No, but

I'm not making this up. This guy has been like a shadow. Appearing and disappearing. Sticking to me even when I try to lose him. I'm sure that the same guy who has been following me attacked me tonight. I'm certain of it."

"You said he almost mugged you. Did he just go after your purse?" This made no sense. Why would a petty thief interested in mugging a woman and snatching her purse follow her three days? "Did he say anything to you?"

"Not a word. After he dragged me into an alley, it all happened so fast. You can see for yourself. Someone captured part of it on video and shared it with me." She took out her phone, brought up the footage and hit Play.

Watching the video, seeing this guy hit Kimi as she struggled to hold on to that silly bag, and then as others stepped in to fend off her assailant, filled his veins with ice. He didn't even realize he had been holding his breath until the video ended and he handed the phone back.

Irrational as it was, he felt that he should have been at her side, protecting her.

He wasn't her boyfriend and couldn't be with her in the way that he wanted.

But he could keep her safe. If she followed his instructions.

"Thankfully," she said, "some people heard the commotion and came to help me."

He wanted to raise his beer in a toast to Good Samaritans. "Next time, you let a thief take your handbag, your wallet, your jewelry. Better than him taking your life."

"Jacy bought me this purse." She patted the handbag she wore crossbody. "I know it wasn't smart, but I couldn't let him take it."

Looking down at the soft blue-gray bag, Tak remembered Jacy had given it to her for her twenty-fifth birthday, along with the boots she had on now. Jacy had purchased them separately, but the boots and purse had matched, and her brother knew she would love them. So did Tak. Watching her light up after she opened the box was one of his top favorite memories.

Second only to kissing her.

Compartmentalize, man.

"I don't want there to be a next time. That's why I came to you," she said. "Help me figure out what's going on."

Tak frowned. As upsetting and disturbing as her story was, there wasn't much he could do. Maybe he could tail her, see if this shadow turned up again. He had a ton of vacation days that he needed to take and even if he didn't, Chance Reyes, his boss and friend, would give him the time off.

"Listen, I don't want you to go home tonight." He had installed a state-of-the-art security system at her house with help from some of the guys at IPS, Bo and Eli. Bitterroot Falls and Cutthroat Creek were quiet towns, but as specialists with Ironside Protection Services, they handled all sorts of security, investigative and intelligence solutions. One thing they didn't do was take unnecessary chances, especially not with family and friends. They'd hooked her up with surveillance cameras, motion sensor lights and an alarm. The firewall protected her Wi-Fi and smart locks from hackers. A standard set up for themselves and all those in their circle. They'd even installed a generator to ensure everything continued to run during a wicked winter storm that might knock out the power. Still, it was best to act on the safe side. "Unless home is now with Doc Dan," he said, fishing to find out if she was living with her boyfriend.

She stared at him, not saying anything, her eyes growing hard and narrowing to slits. By the twitch of her lips, something unpleasant was simmering beneath her self-possessed surface.

"Until I can figure this out, I don't want you to be on your own. Stay with DD," he said, using the nickname she hated for the doctor.

Lowering her head, she set her glass down on the table with a clink. She dropped the ice pack beside it. "Turn to Danny and rely on him. That's your answer?" She stood and strode to the door.

He trailed behind her, perplexed by why the suggestion would rankle her. Doc Dan was her boyfriend. Staying with him, the same way she had done many nights beforehand, was a sensible idea.

"I don't want you to go home alone right now," he said. "You have floodlights, but there are still pockets of darkness where someone could hide and wait for you to come home." The image of some masked man springing out of the dark, wrapping an arm around her throat and hauling her inside to do only goodness knew what made his heart clench. "I don't know why this guy would go to the trouble if he only wanted your purse. You probably won't see him again, but you should take extra precautions for the next few days while I look into it. Okay?"

Kimi grabbed her coat and put it on. "Yeah, sure."

"Hey." He put a hand on her shoulder, turning her around to face him. "I need you to listen to me and do as I say, for once. Go stay with your lucky boyfriend. Play house with the doctor for a few days. Try it on, see how it feels." It might assuage some of her doubts about taking the next step with the ER doctor and she might realize there was nothing to fear. Doc Dan was established, had a lucrative job, was nice; more importantly, he treated her well—all the things Jacy had wanted for Kimi. Things Tak wanted for her, too. Every happiness with a man who deserved her. "Give me time to sort it out. Make sure you're not in any danger."

She stood at attention, heels clicking together, and gave him a mock salute. "Yes, sir."

Swearing in his head, he knew she wasn't going to listen. "Don't 'sir' me. I work for a living." It was a military thing. Having been enlisted once, he did not want to be confused for someone in the privileged position of an officer who delegated the real work.

"Good night, Tak." She was out the door, her hood pulled up over her head, and running in the rain.

He watched Kimi climb into her car and drive away, his gut hollow with foreboding, his mind roiling with the images from the video of her attack.

Swearing, he grabbed his keys and his coat, then hustled to his car in the downpour. He'd follow her to make sure no one else was.

First thing in the morning, he'd get to work figuring out who was after her and ensure the guy stayed away. His one responsibility to Kimi was to keep her safe.

Chapter Three

Standing at the nurses' station, Kimi lifted her head from the medical chart she was writing on and spotted Dan. He was headed in her direction, his gaze locked on her.

She had done her best to dodge the conversation they were about to have for the majority of her shift. Not that she'd had to try very hard. A nasty six-car pileup on the interstate had packed the emergency room, filling every medical bay. The staff had been hustling for the past four hours.

Things tended to be relatively slow in comparison to today. Cutthroat Creek Community Hospital served folks in the town it was named after, the people who worked at the nearby oil field, and handled overflow from Bitterroot Valley. Plenty of nurses were always available, but they were short on doctors. Hence the reason Danny often pulled extra shifts.

The ER hadn't been this busy since the mass shooting in October. Both Bitterroot Falls and Cutthroat Creek had been rocked to their foundations. During the investigation, the number of casualties had reached an alarming new high. Not only civilians but SWAT team members as well had been treated. The DOJ Division of Criminal Investigation had worked with Ironside Protection Services to apprehend the sniper. Everyone at IPS had become a local celebrity overnight.

Making it impossible not to think about Tak after the incident in his truck, where he had kissed her, not the other way around even though she had welcomed it.

Now Takoda wouldn't talk to her, but he was everywhere. News articles. Featured in magazines. Hosted on podcasts. Doing charity work in the community, something IPS did often. She was forced to see his devilishly handsome face and not be able to talk to him.

Not even when he was on her turf in the emergency room.

"You shouldn't be at work," Danny said, putting a forearm on the desk and leaning toward her. He wore green scrubs that matched his eyes and well-worn sneakers. "You should be resting."

Setting down the chart, she looked over at him and a little pang of regret niggled in her chest. Not for ending their relationship. Regret gnawed at her over the fact she had let things continue for as long as she had, knowing, deep down, that she didn't love him. "It's only a mild concussion. I'm fine to work."

Danny stared at her with an intense look. "I'm the doctor and I disagree." He rubbed her arm, flashing one of his best bedside smiles.

If only she felt hot and bothered, yearning for more when he touched her the way she did whenever Tak's hand was on her, things might've been different.

"I thought you'd go to my place last night," he said. "After I discharged you, that was the agreement. You stay with me so after my shift I could monitor you, wake you every couple of hours, or you had to be admitted."

"If I stayed on your couch, you wouldn't have gotten any sleep. Which you need to function." She dug in her pocket and fished out the house key he'd given her once he finished examining her and put it in his hand.

The chatter at the nurses' station had stopped and they had a captive, not-so-discreet audience.

She touched his elbow and guided him away from the desk, toward an alcove with a water fountain, safely out of the earshot of the other nurses who were eager for a chance to be with him. "I can't be at your place."

"Sure, you can." He cupped her cheek. "I want to be there for you. We're still friends."

"You don't look at me like a friend." Not any more than she looked at Tak as a friend or a substitute big brother.

Affection for her radiated in Danny's eyes. He was sweet and nice and loyal. Good-looking, too. He was everything she should have wanted.

"I'm sorry I'm not more present and that work dominates my life, but I realize I could've made more of an effort." He sighed. "I'm even willing to go to the next powwow with you."

Willing. Like he was doing her a favor and she should be lucky. "We're not a good fit, Danny. It's no one's fault. We just don't click."

"Since we broke up, I haven't been able to stop thinking about you. I miss you, Kimi."

The difficult thing was, she knew that he was truly sorry. For all their missed dates. For how he was constantly tired. For not wanting to go to the Crow Fair Celebration, the largest Native American event in Montana, the biggest powwow in the country. For showing no interest in half her culture. For how everything in his life, his job, his mother, playing golf when the weather was nice, all came ahead of her.

On their first date, he'd been upfront about his vigorous work schedule, which she had witnessed firsthand. He'd claimed he'd had a midlife epiphany on his forty-first birthday and was determined to make changes. Starting with her. That he was ready to settle down.

After four months of quasi dating, things never felt right between them. The desire to make Jacy proud by settling down with a nice, stable guy, her need for intimacy, for an emotional and physical connection, had made her stick it out long past the relationship's expiration date. She'd realized she wasn't settling down, simply settling, and called it quits with him. But Dan had suggested not making it final, taking a break instead. Then, as what she could only assume was a knee-jerk reaction, he'd asked her to move in with him. To consider it, like it was a solution. When she'd talked things over with Tak at that rooftop bar, it dawned on her that Danny didn't need *her*. He wanted someone pretty and flexible, who would squeeze into his life, causing as little disruption as possible.

And that was definitely not her.

Kimi removed his hand from her face and held it. "I care about you and I'm glad you care about me, too. But our time together is done." She gave his fingers a small squeeze before letting him go.

His remorseful expression disappeared, replaced by cool professionalism. "I'm sorry you feel that way. I was hoping you would change your mind. Spare me from going through this dating process all over again with someone new."

The one thing Danny was not—a romantic.

"You've been kind not to rush into dating another nurse. I appreciate it." Even though the real reason apparently was that he had hoped to avoid the hassle. "But you should get back out there. Madison would be a good match for you." The perfect, pretty Lego block. Kimi predicted they'd be married in a year.

Danny gazed at her for a long moment. "Have you gotten back out there? Is that the reason why you didn't come over?"

"No, it isn't. I'm not dating anybody, and I slept alone."

His frown deepened, as though he was skeptical. "I thought you would've gone to Takoda," he said, studying her face. "Had him look after you."

She had confessed to Danny about the kiss with Tak, one all-too-brief kiss, and didn't use alcohol as an excuse. Even though they'd been on a break, they hadn't agreed to see other people. Ashamed of herself for violating his trust, she'd apologized profusely.

Danny had acted relieved that she hadn't slept with Takoda. Hadn't appeared fazed about a kiss. To her, that kiss was still a betrayal. Maybe because it had meant something to her. A whole lot more than any kiss with Danny ever had.

So, she had ended things, for good.

"I don't need anyone to look after me," she said. "What am I, seven? I don't need, nor do I want, a babysitter. I stayed at the hotel. The BMH is pretty nice. Had the front desk call me every three hours and gave them instructions that if I didn't answer, to have someone on staff enter the room and check on me."

"Good. I'm glad you're taking your concussion, which is not mild, seriously." He put a gentle hand on her arm. "We needed you earlier with the victims of the car crash. Things have calmed down. Get out of here. I don't want to see you back in this ER for at least forty-eight hours unless you need treatment for some reason. Doctor's orders. Understand?"

She nodded. "Okay. I'll get out of here."

He patted her arm, and she went to the locker room.

The only time she left the hospital in her scrubs was when she was too exhausted to change or in a rush. Taking advantage of an empty dressing room, she opened her locker and took her time changing into the extra outfit she kept at work. Jeans and a V-neck sweater. She released her hair from the topknot and finger-combed the strands. After swapping her running shoes for her favorite cowgirl boots from Jacy, she threw on her coat and made sure to wear the strap of her handbag across her body. Putting on her leather gloves, she headed out into the brisk night air.

She hurried toward her vehicle, scanning the parking lot for her shadow. Just when she thought it was all clear, a man emerged from a gunmetal-gray truck parked nearby, making her pulse spike. Someone she hadn't been expecting.

Takoda.

The guy had the most irritating habit of materializing out of nowhere. A quality that her slippery shadow shared. She'd have to circle back around to that coincidence.

Wearing a silverbelly Stetson, he strode toward her, his cowboy swagger dialed high, making her breath catch in her throat. He reached her car first and leaned against her door, all six-foot-three of him, hard, honed muscle, blocking her from getting inside. Tipping her head slightly back, she stared at him. His golden-brown complexion and sharp, chiseled features reflected his mixed heritage of African American and one quarter Navajo. His thick black hair was cropped short, and his dark brown eyes were piercing.

The man was one tempting package.

Well, some naive women might find him tempting. After twenty minutes in his presence, they would discover that there was nothing tempting about Takoda Yazzie. Except for his devilishly handsome face.

And his sinfully hot body.

Kimi remembered what it was like to be held in those strong arms, pressed tight against all that warm, solid muscle. She shivered, and not from the frigid breeze.

Just forget about it. Forget about him. She wasn't sure if that was her voice or her brother's.

Not that it mattered. Wanting something, or rather someone, she couldn't have, was an exercise in futility.

Silence hung between them in the bitter cold.

"Well, what are you doing here?" she asked, not in the mood for a staring contest. "You made it clear last night that you weren't going to help me."

"Not true. You don't listen to me, kiddo."

Kimi bristled.

Every time that Tak opened his mouth, he had all the charm and personality of a cantankerous wolverine. Even more off-putting, he never stopped letting her know that he wasn't the least bit interested in her as a woman.

Calling her *kiddo* was a stark reminder of how he saw her.

Kimi folded her arms. "I may not do as you say, but trust me, I listen to every single word that leaves your mouth." Her gaze dipped to his full lips, and to her shame, she ached to kiss him.

"Then you would've heard me when I told you I'd look into it and handle things if you were in any danger."

Her pulse was still thrumming. His unexpected presence outside the hospital flustered her. And when she got flustered, she got snippy. "You ordered me to run to Dan and let him protect me."

Tak had a way of bulldozing people, but she was just as good at standing her ground.

"I'm not here to fight," he said. "We need to talk about a couple of things."

"Not out here." When he didn't budge, she said, "Move." She shooed him aside and, surprisingly, he pushed off her car and stepped out of her way.

She climbed into her Subaru, let the engine warm up, and pulled off. He was in his truck not far behind her.

Now that she had an escort, she could go home in the dark and grab some things without worrying about being ambushed and attacked a second time.

Her house actually belonged to her mother. Kimi had been entrusted with taking care of the place while her mom gallivanted, free of responsibility. Living as she pleased. Loving who she wanted. Having fun. Nurturing her passion. Odd how that had once been Kimi, doing the exact same thing on the rodeo circuit. It was like she'd swapped places with her mother.

Oh goodness, she had turned into Aiyana Redbird. Who had also once been a nurse. How much Mom had changed— really, they both had—after Jacy died.

For the better.

Strangely, Kimi was happier than she had been before. She liked the routine with less risk. Helping people during challenging situations came with its own reward.

Jacy had been right about a lot.

But not everything.

It was nice, putting down roots, serving her community and building friendships. Though all her friends were also Takoda's. Bo Lennox, Eli Easton, Chance Reyes and Autumn Stratton from IPS, along with the rest of the Stratton *season sisters*: Winter, who was in love and living with Chance, and Summer as well as her fiancé, Logan Powell. During Kimi's frosty standoff with Tak, he'd staked claim to all of them.

Maybe their absence from her life was more striking after her breakup with Danny. No one had excluded her from anything. She still received the invitations to their group dinners, the Sunday funday brunches, Logan and Summer's engagement party, and the holiday parties. But she hadn't wanted to endure a repeat of the hospital run-in with Tactless Tak. So, she'd made excuses and gone into self-imposed isolation.

It sucked.

Kimi turned down her road and pulled into her driveway. The floodlights above the garage remained dark. They were motion-activated and should have popped on.

She got out and by the time she closed her car door, Tak was beside her.

"Did you adjust the settings on the lights?" he asked.

"No. I figured there might be a short circuit."

"I thought you'd be spending the night at the hotel again."

She stiffened. "How do you know that's where I was last night?"

His mouth tightened. "How do you think? I followed you because I knew that you wouldn't listen. Why didn't you go to DD's?"

Kimi rolled her eyes. "Stop calling him that." She went around the car and started up the walkway. "I didn't because we broke up. A while ago."

He took hold of her arm, stopping her, and a quiver spread over her as it always did when he touched her. "You should have told me you two weren't together anymore."

"What would've been the point in telling you? Hmm…" she said, and he looked down at her. "Would you have offered to let me bunk with you instead?"

Something flashed in his eyes for a second, a spark that brightened his impassive dark gaze. Then whatever it was disappeared as quickly as it had appeared, making her wonder if she'd truly seen anything at all.

Don't delude yourself, she decided. If that hint of heat had been real, that would mean she ignited some emotion in him other than irritation. Not that Tak, her brother's best friend, wanted her.

Wolverines were solitary creatures. Some never even mated.

Although he had been the one to initiate the kiss that night in his truck, he hadn't done it out of desire. He had kissed her out of pity. Plain and simple.

She'd been crying and he hadn't known how to handle her tears. He'd felt sorry for her. Kissed her to make the crying stop. And it worked. End of the pathetic story.

"Well?" she demanded when he just stood there staring at her. "What difference would it have made? You don't care."

His expression remained a stony blank mask, but the muscle along his jaw twitched. "I care." He cut his gaze from her and glanced around. "None of your security lights are working."

She looked up at the house. The lights around the front of the perimeter hadn't come on either. "Do you think they're all on the same circuit board?"

"Get back in your car," he said, his voice lowered. "Drive to Mr. Simpson's house and wait for me there."

Kimi tensed. Mr. Simpson was her closest neighbor, the only one within shouting distance out there on the outskirts of Cutthroat Creek, where the houses were acres apart. "Why?" she asked, matching his hushed tone. "What's going on?"

"I don't think there's a short in the circuit." Drawing a gun from inside his coat, he nudged her toward the driveway. "If you see or hear anything suspicious, take off and go to IPS. A couple of the guys are still at the office."

Something inside her went stone-cold. "What about you?"

"I'm going inside to look around. Make sure it's safe."

"We should stay together and call the police." She curled her hand around his forearm. "Let the cops search the house."

He shook his head. "What if it's nothing?"

"What if it's something?" she countered.

Tak frowned. "Call 9-1-1 on your way to IPS." He dislodged her clenched fingers from his arm and nudged her again, prodding her to move away from him and toward her car. "Listen for once, will you." His voice was a rumbling whisper. "Go."

He stood there, eyes narrowed, waiting for her to leave.

Kimi stifled the groan rising in her throat, then hurried to her Subaru, jumped behind the wheel and did as he asked. Only because Mr. Simpson lived across the road. Kimi backed into her neighbor's driveway, stopped beside his truck and cut off the lights but kept the engine running. She hoped Mr. Simpson didn't come outside to ask why Kimi was sitting there. At least his dog, Bandit, hadn't started barking yet, alerting him to her presence.

With a clear view of her own house, Kimi watched Tak tread up the steps to the front door. He tried the knob. The door must have been locked, which was a good sign. He started entering the digital code on the keypad to get in. She knew the code for his place as well.

To be used in case of emergencies only.

When he wasn't speaking to her, she had contemplated letting herself into his house. Imagined sitting on his sofa, waiting for him to get home to confront him. Then that fantasy somehow morphed, and she was naked, waiting to kiss him.

So, she'd abandoned the entire idea. A pity kiss was one thing.

Pity sex?

No, thank you. She did *not* want that. Not even if it was with the sexiest man she'd ever met.

Takoda crept into her house, shutting the door behind

him. Maybe she should call the police now, to be on the safe side. It could take them ten to fifteen minutes to get there.

Movement from an upstairs window drew her gaze. The curtain in the guest bedroom slid to the side, and her breath stalled in her lungs. A figure peered through the glass. There was someone else in the house. Whoever it was, they wore a ski mask. In the moonlight, it seemed as though their head canted in the direction where Tak's truck was parked in the driveway.

Did Tak know he wasn't in there alone?

The curtains in the bedroom drew closed.

Panic welled in her chest. She clenched her hands on the steering wheel, not sure what she was going to do.

But she had to do something.

And fast.

Chapter Four

With heightened caution, Tak closed the door quietly and crept deeper inside the house. He reached out for the wall, feeling around for the light switch. Found it. Flicked it up. Nothing.

The place was dark. And cold. All the power had been cut. That meant the generator had been tampered with, too.

He pulled back the curtains in the front room. Moonlight illuminated a shocking sight. Kimi's living room was in a shambles. He moved through the house quickly, but with care not to step on anything that would make noise. Furniture had been turned over. Cushions ripped and torn apart. Delicate items that had once held sentimental value were shattered. Bookshelves emptied and dumped on the carpet. Someone had also busted in the drywall, making huge holes, as though they were looking for something they thought Kimi had. It might explain why, possibly, that same person had tried to snatch her purse.

A cold draft drew his attention toward the other end of the house.

The kitchen had been tossed as well. Cabinets opened. Drawers yanked out. Food and dishes and utensils thrown on the floor. He noticed the back door that led to the small, gated yard was slightly ajar. The wood on the casing near the strike plate was broken. Like someone had kicked the door in. He turned the light from his phone into the darkness outside and glanced around. No one was lurking in the yard and the gate was open. Perhaps whoever had been there had left.

He made his way back through the ransacked house.

Once Kimi saw this mess, she was going to have a conniption. That was fine by him. Her anger he could handle. She used it like armor, hiding other emotions. Hurt, mostly. And sometimes, fear.

She never liked to admit when she was either. Better to be angry and stubborn.

Why was it so easy for him to see through her?

He didn't want to, but it had always been that way. Even when she had acted like an invincible wild thing out on the rodeo circuit. He'd seen it for a lie, a different kind of armor that masked insecurities and doubts and fears.

Tak saw clearly who she was—a complex, beautiful woman who didn't want anyone else to see her vulnerability.

A woman so determined to honor her brother's memory that she'd overhauled her entire life. Went back to college. Became a registered nurse.

A woman he aimed to protect.

With the first floor clear, he headed to the carpeted stairs. Each step he took was steady and soft and silent. He listened on his way up.

No sound of any other movement.

Although it had been a while, Tak had been in the house many times and remembered some of the floorboards upstairs creaked. Reaching the landing, he took a wide step at the top to avoid one plank that squeaked.

Stilling, he paused for a moment. There was no noise from anyone rifling around upstairs.

Maybe the house was empty.

He figured he would start with the first guest room and work his way down the hall. He eased into the bedroom doorway. The curtains were pulled closed, only a sliver of moonlight from the window slicing the darkness.

Taking another step deeper into the room, he noticed it wasn't in disarray like downstairs. Not tossed and searched. It was possible whoever it was had lost steam by the time they'd reached the second floor. Or they hadn't had a chance to search *yet*.

A floorboard groaned beneath shifting weight. Too late, he realized that someone must've been concealed behind the armoire.

He spun in a defensive move, deflecting the blow intended for him. Operating on training and instinct, Tak threw out an arm and snatched the weapon before his attacker had a chance to strike again. It was something long and solid, like a pole. He tugged it hard, trying to knock his assailant off balance. But another blow came from behind him, striking the back of his head.

Pain blasted in his skull, flaring down to his jaw and into his neck. Tak dropped to a knee, fighting to stay conscious. But he kept hold of both his gun and the weapon he had wrangled away from the other man.

There were two attackers in the room with him. Not one.

Loud barking erupted just outside the house.

Tak took advantage of the noisy distraction and swung the pole or stick, striking a leg.

A man swore, but the two assailants made off into the hall.

Harsh whispers, male voices.

"We're running out of time to find it."

"Let's go."

Hurried footsteps pounded on the steps.

Downstairs, the front door banged open, wood slamming against the wall. The distinctive sound of a shotgun cocking, a shell pumping into the chamber. Ferocious barking grew louder, closer, from the entryway.

"Bandit!" Mr. Simpson said, calling his German shepherd. "Sic 'em, boy!"

Panicked footsteps scurried toward the back door. A man cried out. Something clattered to the floor, breaking. A door slammed.

Then a shotgun blast cracked the air.

Tak staggered to his feet, smothering a wave of nausea. He needed to get to Kimi.

An engine roared, a heavy rumble—a full-size pickup truck, Tak guessed—and tires peeled off with a squeal.

He moved quickly into the hall and onto the stairs.

A bright light shone in his eyes and he raised an arm to block it. His face tingled. Spots danced in his vision. His head ached.

"Takoda!" The light lowered. Kimi ran to him, meeting him in the middle of the staircase, and threw her arms around him in a tight hug. "Are you all right?"

"Yeah. I'm fine." He was a bit woozy, not what he would classify as *all right*, but his only priority was getting her to safety and keeping her out of harm's way.

Not letting him go, Kimi kept an arm around his waist as they went the rest of the way down the steps. In the light from the flashlight she carried, he got a good look at the weapon the man had tried to use against him before he'd managed to snatch it. Adorned with genuine leather and hand-beaded craftwork, fur and prayer feathers, it was a Native American walking stick. The crowning feature was a hand-carved bear on the top. It belonged to Aiyana.

Mr. Simpson was in the hallway, crouching down, petting his dog, who was standing on all fours, alert and wagging its tail.

"Is Bandit okay?" Tak asked, hoping the dog hadn't been injured fending off the intruders.

"You betcha. He managed to take a chunk out of one of those burglars. The guy almost shot him, but I opened fire, and the sound of my shotgun made them hightail it out of here." Mr. Simpson patted the dog and stood up, cradling the shotgun in his arm. "This boy is built like a tank. Aren't you, Bandit?"

The German shepherd gave a high-pitched bark that sounded like he agreed.

"Thanks for hurrying over," Tak said.

"Sure thing. Kimi told me there was a problem. That's what neighbors are for. You need me to stick around? Give a statement to the police?"

"You can go home. If the cops have any questions for you, they'll swing by." Tak shook the older man's hand. "Everything you did is much appreciated."

"Good to see you, Takoda. I wish it was under better circumstances. You should come around more often and keep this one company." He pointed a finger at Kimi. "So she doesn't have to be in this house alone all the time. What if she had come home by herself with those two robbers in here? I shudder to think what could've happened to her."

Anger took hold of him at that thought, and Tak nodded. Immediately, he regretted it, pain spreading into his teeth, hammering behind his eyes. Pain he'd accept if it meant Kimi was safe. He wasn't going to give anyone the chance to hurt her.

"This is usually such a quiet, safe town. Heck, I still leave my keys in my car and my front door unlocked. I can't believe someone broke in," Mr. Simpson said. "Probably drug addicts would be my guess. The meth epidemic has spread everywhere. Come on, Bandit." The neighbor left with his attack dog.

Tak rubbed his forehead. The sharp pain in his head was settling into a persistent, pounding throb, but he tried to ignore it.

He turned to Kimi. "I told you to go straight to IPS if there was any trouble. This proves you don't listen."

"I heard you. I just choose to follow my mind rather than your orders after I realized there was someone in the house with you. By the way, you're welcome. But I didn't know there were two of them." Kimi stepped toward the living room and gasped. "Oh, my God. First, I almost got mugged and now my house has been turned upside down. At least the cops won't be able to dismiss this as some random act of violence."

They'd call the police, just not right now. She didn't need to stare at the wreckage of her home for hours while the police did their job. Besides, the longer they stayed there, the more time whoever had broken in would have to strategize while they were aware of Kimi's whereabouts. They might decide to circle back, park, wait for them to leave and follow.

No way in hell Tak was giving them that opportunity. "I want you to pack a bag."

She pivoted toward him. "I have two days of stuff in an overnight bag at the hotel."

"That's not enough. You need to pack for at least a week."

"Why?"

"Come on." Not answering her question, which would only inspire more, he took her by the arm and led her upstairs into her bedroom. The priority was getting her out of the house. Then they could talk. There were still two things he needed to tell her, and it was going to lead to difficult discussion.

Kimi grabbed a bag and gathered some of her things.

He caught the smell of honeysuckle. Vivid, sun-kissed radiance. Easy to recognize since it was Kimi's favorite scent. It was the top note in her perfume and maybe even her shampoo since it kicked up whenever she ran her fingers through the long hair that she always wore loose and free unless she was working. The smell grounded him, helping him shake off the pain, but it also made him laser-focused on Kimi.

Her hourglass silhouette. The way she moved. The intensity she put into everything she did.

How close she came to danger.

"Why do I need so much stuff?" she asked, closing a dresser drawer.

"Because you're not coming back here until we get to the bottom of what's going on. And I'm not sure how long that'll take."

KIMI STOPPED PACKING and stared at Takoda. He wasn't telling her everything.

Something was wrong, besides the fact that two men had broken into her house and torn it apart for some reason. She could hear it in his voice.

He wasn't simply short-tempered and frustrated with her for not following his instructions earlier. There was an edge. A strain in his tone. Worry, not just irritation, and...*pain*?

She set her bag down. Getting closer, she shone the light on him. He squinted and turned his head away. She looked him over. Spotted a suspicious dark patch on his head. She touched along his hairline, behind his ear. He sucked in a sharp breath.

Definitely pain.

Her fingers came away wet with red. "You're bleeding and you've got a nasty lump. You are not fine. We should go to the hospital and have you examined."

"I'll be fine once I get you out of here."

Shaking her head in disbelief, she went to the adjoining bathroom and washed her hands. "Come in here and sit down. I'm not leaving until I clean you up." She needed to be sure the wound wasn't serious.

Huffing a breath, he marched into the bathroom, lowered the lid of the toilet seat and sat while she pulled out a medical kit from the cabinet.

"It's nothing," he said, "really."

"I'll be the judge of that." Slipping in between his spread legs and standing in front of him, she shone the light in his eyes, and he shuttered them reflexively. "Stop squinting," she ordered. "Your pupils aren't dilated, which is good." She aimed the flashlight at the injured spot on his head. Leaning in to see better, she brought her chest close to his face, and he went rigid. She soaked some gauze in saline solution and used it to wipe away the blood.

He flinched with a hiss and clutched his knees.

"Sorry," she said, not meaning to hurt him.

"The sting surprised me."

He had a one-inch-long gash. Not terribly deep. "Provided the bleeding stops, you won't need stitches. But you might have a concussion."

"Probably. But it can't be fixed by going to the hospital."

True.

She propped her knuckle under his chin, tipping his head up. "Any blurred vision?"

"No."

"Weakness or tingling in your arms or legs?"

"No."

"Severe neck pain?" She slid her hand over his cheek and down the side of his neck. "Or how about any nausea?"

His eyes locked on hers in the dim light, and the air between them stirred, charged with electricity.

She wondered which was worse, being attracted to this hunky man or pretending she wasn't?

Maybe if she told him how she felt about him. That she'd loved him since she was eighteen years old when he'd strode into the kitchen and looked at her, turning the power of his smile her way. If she admitted her feelings, he'd probably reject her, but then she might be able to finally move on without wanting him. "Takoda—"

"I'm fine. Are you finished packing?" He set his hands on her waist, setting off a flurry of nerves in her belly, and then he shuffled her backward, out of his way. "We're leaving. Now."

He was up and out of the bathroom before she could process what had just happened.

"What's the big rush?" She put the medical kit away, gathered extra toiletries, and went to her bag in the bedroom.

"One of the things I wanted to tell you was that I followed you today. There was no one else watching you. He, or they, probably figured you'd be at work for your entire shift. So, they were here, searching your house. But you left the hospital early."

She swallowed around the sudden lump in her throat. "What on earth do they want from me?"

"That brings me to the second thing, but I don't want to get into it here. Let's go." He took her bag from her hand, and they headed down the stairs.

"What about calling the police? Don't I need to file a report?"

"I'll call Logan and ask him to handle it," Tak said.

Logan was a detective with the Bitterroot Falls Police Department. Technically, she'd met Logan first, before Takoda had. Kimi had gotten to know the cop and his fiancée last year during a murder investigation that had brought them both to Big Sky Country. The two had ended up moving to Bitterroot Falls. Since Logan and Chance were best friends, it was through Tak and her association with IPS that Kimi had gotten to know the detective and the season sisters better.

Kimi had been invited to Logan and Summer's engagement party close to Christmas, but decided to skip it, dreading the cold bite of another public rejection from Tak. Consequently, she'd spent the holidays alone. The mistake she'd made with Tak, giving in to a reckless impulse and kissing him, had cost her far more than it had him.

Even though the kiss had been mutual. Pity on his side and desire on hers, but they were equally responsible.

They stepped outside the house and he shut the door.

"I guess it's a good thing I still have my room at the hotel," she said.

"You can't stay there. We'll swing by so you can pick up your stuff." He took her arm, his head on a swivel, steering her to his truck. "That guy, your shadow, and his friend searched your place, looking for something. If they didn't find it, they might decide to ask you point-blank about whatever it is."

The image of being cornered and questioned with a gun to her head flashed through her mind. She was not eager to have that scenario play out.

"The hotel isn't safe," he added. "Any idea how easy it is to break into one of those rooms?"

"No."

"Too easy. He could pretend to be hotel staff, delivering room service, a maintenance guy, someone from the front desk dropping off a package. All else fails, he just has to swipe a universal keycard from a housekeeper."

Not one iota of anything he'd just spouted out did a thing to steady her jittery nerves. It only amplified her anxiety.

Tak opened the passenger door for her.

"What about my car?"

"Leave it at Mr. Simpson's. You're going to ride with me."

She climbed into the truck. "But if I can't stay at the hotel, where am I supposed to go?"

"My place."

Did she hear him correctly? "Your place."

He frowned. "Yes."

She stared at him. "I thought you didn't want us getting cozy anymore."

His gaze darkened slightly, then grew strangely blank. "Listen, Kimi. There will be house rules. You'll sleep in a guest room. If we're in a common space, we'll wear appropriate clothing. At the very least pajamas. There will be no getting cozy. Or getting warm by any fires together. No fires at all. Got it?"

Stunned, speechless, she nodded.

His tone softened just slightly. "For Jacy. Okay?"

She nodded again, and he shut her door, hurried around the front end and jumped in the truck.

"Are you okay to drive?"

"I wouldn't endanger you by being behind the wheel if I wasn't." He pulled out of her driveway. "Please, stop worrying about me."

That edge was still there.

"Yeah, okay." But that was easier said than done.

Their first stop was the Bitterroot Mountain Hotel, where

it took less than five minutes for her to grab her things and check out. Tak never left her side. Even though the men who had violated the sanctity of her home hadn't made an appearance, she was grateful not to be on her own.

They headed to Tak's house. He had purchased a property that was only a fifteen-minute drive from everything. Bitterroot Falls. Cutthroat Creek. The IPS office. The Redbird house.

In a haze, she stared out the window, trying to process what was happening. Not the least of which was that she was going to bunk—*correction*, sleep—in Tak's guestroom.

They reached his house. He whisked her out of the truck and ushered her inside. Trudging off down the hall, he dumped her bag in the guest room.

She noted it was the one farthest from his. At least he was letting her stay with him. That alone was an accomplishment. She'd take the win.

Taking off her coat, she let the gravity of things settle in. She plunked down onto the sofa and stared at the cold fireplace.

"Were you serious when you said there wouldn't be a fire?" she asked, rubbing her arms with an exaggerated shiver.

He blew out a heavy breath, strode to the hearth, and built a fire. Once it was going, he sat in one of the leather chairs, facing her. "Happy?"

Not even close. "Thank you."

Now she wanted a drink to chase away the chill flowing inside her, but she wasn't going to push it. Provided she adhered to the rules, there shouldn't be any problems.

Had she packed pajamas?

"Do you have any idea what they were looking for in my house?" she asked.

"No. I was going to ask you the same thing, but that reminds me." He got up, took a folded manila envelope from his inside coat pocket and handed it to her. "That was in my mail yesterday."

She glanced at the return address. There was none, and it was postmarked Monday, two days ago. She peeked inside.

Disbelief rocked through her. She reached in, taking out a bundle of cash. Large bills with a rubber band around the stack.

Holding the wad of money, she stared at him.

"It's ten thousand dollars," he said.

She reeled back. That was an awful lot of money. "Who sends that kind of cash in the mail?"

"There's a note. Look at it. I need to call Logan."

Turning the envelope upside down, she shook it. A slip of paper fell into her lap, and she read it.

Takoda,
I'm hiring you. To ensure you take the job, I've included a retainer for your services. I've gotten myself into a bit of trouble and may have dragged Kimi Anne into it. If anything happens to me, your job is to protect my baby girl.
I lost one child. Another shouldn't go before their time, especially not because of me.
Thomas Wheeler

A chill raked over her flesh—the sting as sharp as frostbite. She read the note two more times.

Tak was still on the phone with Logan.

Kimi took her cell phone from her handbag and tried calling her father. The line rang six times and went to voicemail. She hung up.

On the rare occasions when they did reach out to each other, it wasn't unusual for either of them to leave a message first before deciding to return the call.

But this was different. With someone following her, mugging her, breaking into the house, the note and money sent to Takoda, this was all seriously bad. And her father was the only one with answers. Surely, her dad expected her to contact him.

Why wasn't he picking up?

Tak slipped his phone in his pocket and sat in the chair, facing her. "Logan is going to check out your house, speak to Mr. Simpson, and come over to get our statements. I'll tell him everything when he gets here."

"I don't understand." She held up the note.

"Neither do I. So, I went to ask your dad while you were at work. No one has seen him in the past four days. Not since Saturday."

Her mouth grew so dry so fast it was difficult for her to swallow. "What are you saying?"

Takoda hesitated, and she wished he would just spit it out. "It appears your father is missing. Whatever your dad was wrapped up in is most likely linked to the shadow who has been following you and the two men who tossed your place. Somehow, your dad has put you in danger."

Chapter Five

As Tak roused in his bed, a ray of sunlight from the window hit him in the face, and it was like a hot needle in his eye. He'd designed and built his house to have the bedrooms facing east with breathtaking views of the mountains and stunning sunrises. The blinds on the floor-to-ceiling windows were automated to lower at dusk and rise at dawn. Right now, he was cursing those decisions.

Groaning, he managed to sit up and make it to his en suite bathroom with no sign of nausea. That was good.

A hot shower helped put him back solidly on his feet. He pulled on boxer briefs, pants and socks. Shrugging on a flannel shirt, he left it unbuttoned as another bolt of pain stabbed his eyes. Thankfully, it faded fast.

Heading to the walk-in closet, he threw on his shoulder holster and secured his weapon inside. The Heckler & Koch Mark 23 was his favorite handgun. A preferred choice in the spec ops community. In the air force, when he was stationed at Malmstrom Air Force Base, assigned to the elite RED HORSE Unit—a highly mobile, civil engineering, quick response force—he'd supported contingency operations and worked closely with Special Forces in austere and hostile environments around the world. Difficulty and danger came with each mission. They were airborne—jump qualified—and had vigorous combat training.

Even though they hadn't had a tier-one designator, they'd had to be ready to handle their own under fire, especially *if* things went south and hit the proverbial fan.

Not if, *when*.

Jacy slid into his mind, but Tak didn't have the bandwidth for grief and guilt. Not this morning.

Inside his closet, he entered the code on the digital keypad of the built-in safe and then pressed his thumb to the biometric fingerprint scanner, a dual-layered security feature. The door popped open, and he scanned his collection of tactical knives that were lined up by size. He decided on his MAMU fixed-blade. From slicing and chopping, to piercing and splitting, the knife's ergonomics were top-notch. Also, it had been a gift from his cousin, Aiden Yazzie, who was a US marshal. They'd grown up together in the Navajo Nation, close as brothers after Tak's parents were killed in a car crash. He'd been so little, lucky to survive, but he didn't remember them. His only living relatives were on the reservation, a sovereign territory roughly the size of West Virginia. They shared stories of his parents, particularly of his father. He hadn't been back home in years, not since his aunt, Aiden's mother, had passed away.

Tak slipped the blade in its sheath and clipped it on his waist. Turning to the shelf with his guns, he picked the Ruger LCP Max. A lightweight, micro-compact weapon that was a powerful backup option at close range despite its small size. He strapped on an ankle holster, tucked the Ruger in, and pulled on boots. Before he closed the safe, he grabbed extra loaded magazines.

Thomas Wheeler had opened Pandora's box, and Tak wanted enough firepower to fight a small war if necessary.

He hoped it wouldn't come down to that. Experience had taught him it was better to have a mini arsenal and not need it than to need it and not have it.

He left his room.

The scent of baked goodness hit him in the hall. He made it to the kitchen without another lance of pain.

Kimi glanced up from her spot on a stool at the island, looking right at home in his kitchen. She wore a T-shirt and yoga pants that hugged her legs. Staring at him, she raked a hand through her hair and smiled.

Sucker punch straight to his soul.

"Good morning," she said. "How's your head?"

Kimi had knocked on his door a couple of times throughout the night, waking him to check on him. Thankfully, she'd stayed in the hall and his verbal response was sufficient.

"Better." Still, he went to the cabinet, found the aspirin, and swallowed two pills dry.

"Let me see." She patted the stool beside her.

He'd rather skip letting her get close enough to examine his head again. "No need." Averting his gaze from her, he glanced around. She'd made coffee. A plate of blueberry muffins was on the counter. She'd been busy. "I didn't realize I had any muffin mix in the pantry." He took a mug from the cupboard and poured himself coffee.

"You didn't. But muffins are easy. Basic ingredients. Flour, baking powder, sugar, eggs, butter, salt, milk. I threw in some blueberries from the freezer and added the zest of a lemon. Voila." She spun off the stool and sauntered over to him with the sexy grace of a dancer, her full breasts swaying against the cotton T-shirt.

A bolt of desire pierced him and he struggled to ignore it.

She looped her arm around his and led him to one of the

stools. Putting her hands on his shoulders, she forced him to sit, bringing them eye level.

He set his mug on the counter.

She pushed his legs apart, sliding between his thighs, and he stiffened. A hint of a smile danced on her lips. "Turn your head and look down."

He did. His gaze landed on the soft outline of her breast. Her silky hair brushed his cheek, and a hint of honeysuckle invaded his senses. It was all too much. He ached to touch her, to let go of his guilt and his shame and the promises he never should've made. For just a day, for an hour, for ten minutes— even though it would feel like torture. He would take any amount of time where he could stake claim to this woman.

She was so sensual and sweet, so right and yet so wrong for him.

Clenching his hands, he shifted his focus to the kitchen countertop. The cold, hard, flat slab of quartz. Tak needed to nip this—*whatever this was*—in the bud. If only he knew how.

"No more bleeding." Kimi's fingers were warm and gentle as she examined his head, and his throat tightened. "The lump has gone down, and it's only a cut now."

"One more scar."

Her fingers traced his earlobe and she pressed her palm to his cheek. He glanced at her face, skin bare, with no makeup to conceal her bruises—*still, so beautiful.* She was looking down at his chest. She pushed back one side of his open shirt and ran her other hand over a spot that was tight and shiny, where he had taken a piece of shrapnel. Her touch was hot as a brand on his skin.

"I like your scars." Her voice was a husky whisper, curling up his spine, seeping in like smoke. "You got most of them in the air force, didn't you?"

His throat tightened another notch. "Yeah."

"You and Jacy made it possible for others to do their jobs. For missions to succeed. For wars to be fought and won. Scars are a part of being an unsung hero."

She had no idea. Not one clue.

If she knew the truth—that Jacy's death was his fault—would she still consider him a hero?

She met his eyes, her lips inches from his mouth. "If you smiled more, worked on being less crabby and a bit more charming, you'd be a chick magnet."

"I don't want to be a magnet for women, or anything else for that matter."

She tilted her head, eyeing him like he was a jigsaw puzzle she wanted to piece together. "Not even luck?"

"Luck comes in two varieties." Good and bad. "I'd have to take both, kiddo." At the nickname, she flinched.

He knew it bothered her, but it was the best way for him to remind himself to behave.

"Most men would love to know how to draw women to them," she said, not backing off.

"I'm not most men."

"And I'm not a kid." She slid a palm up his chest. Her fingers danced over his collarbone and brushed across the nape of his neck.

His heart raced while other parts of him hardened. Twelve years of pretending like she was nothing more to him than his best friend's kid sister hadn't done a thing to dampen his desire for her.

Keeping one hand on his neck, she ran the other slowly over his thigh and looked up at him, meeting his gaze.

Blistering need hit him like a bolt of lightning. His restraint frayed. He shook his head, but he didn't move away. "Kimi."

"I know. You're not attracted to me." She dropped her forehead to his. "You probably wish I had never come to you asking for help. Wished my dad hadn't sent a retainer, forcing you to take me on as a job. I know you're only doing this, protecting me and trying to find out what's happening, because you feel obligated."

Is that what she thought? That he wasn't attracted to her? That she was an obligation to him?

If the choice was between him and anyone else on earth protecting her, he'd want her to come to him first, every time. And not because of professional duty or a personal sense of responsibility.

He'd hurt her before by letting her believe something that wasn't true. Letting her think it was easy for him to keep his distance from her. Easy to be near her and not talk to her, touch her. Easy to send her to Doc Dan when it killed him inside because he wanted her right there with him.

Never again would he let her think such things were the truth when it couldn't be further from it.

He longed to kiss her, knowing he shouldn't, but it was going to be the only thing on his mind until he burned it out of his system.

KIMI STOOD BETWEEN his legs, not meeting his eyes, determined to keep her hands on him until he inevitably pushed her away. She braced herself, mustering the strength to tell him how she felt. To throw all her cards on the table, leaving no regrets, on her part.

But then his strong arms wrapped around her waist, his hold on her loose at first. She was too shocked to move, to speak. He slid his hand to her lower back and drew her so close that the gap between their bodies disappeared. So close, the tension could only be relieved by shifting even closer. She pressed her breasts against his hard chest, her pelvis to his, and to her surprise she discovered he was attracted to her.

Heat thrummed off him, and her body responded with a flush of intense awareness.

"I'm always here for you," he said, his voice deep and low, his minty breath tickling her lips. "No matter what. Because I choose to be. Because I want… I want you to be safe and happy."

"How am I supposed to believe that after the way you turned your back on me?"

His callused fingers cupped her chin, tilting her face up. That piercing gaze locked with hers, sending a shiver through her. "Believe this."

Takoda leaned in and she did, too, drawn by a gravitational pull into his orbit, and it was like déjà vu when they met in the middle. Except this time, no tears. His warm lips brushed over hers, tentative and gentle, teasing, almost flirting before he penetrated the seam of her mouth. She welcomed his tongue, savoring the taste of him, lost in the shocking relief of *his* kiss.

The fear, and the worries, and the rest of the world simply faded away. Sliding her fingers around the back of his neck, she arched against him. He tasted so good, felt so warm and solid. His fingers slipped into her hair and his arm tightened around her as though he didn't want to ever let go.

Flutters in her belly went wild. He changed the angle of his mouth, taking it deeper still. Hot and possessive, like he wanted to claim her. She held on to him, relishing the sweet ache of her insides jump-starting since the last time he'd kissed her. A small, needy sound escaped her, and he pulled her in even tighter. That ache coiled through her all the way down to her toes.

The kiss went on and on until she wanted to yank off his shirt. Wanted to pull hers over her head and toss it to the floor.

No regrets. She reached for his belt and unfastened the buckle.

A groan rose in his throat. Gripping her hands, he leaned away, breaking the kiss, leaving her breathless and wanting so much more. "This can't happen."

A cold slap of disappointment hit her, sobering her quickly. He wanted her and she was offering everything, but he… "Why?"

He scooted his stool backward, the legs scraping against the hardwood floor, turned away from her and hopped off. Going around to the other side of the counter, he fastened his belt.

Kimi straightened, staring at him, waiting for an answer. She understood the guys on the rodeo circuit. It had taken a while with Dan, but she'd figured him out and what made him tick. But Takoda was still a puzzle. One she was determined to solve. "Are you seeing someone?"

Keeping any reaction tightly under control, he stared at her. "You should get dressed. We're supposed to meet Logan at your dad's house in less than an hour."

A reminder of her father and the threats to her life was not what she wanted at the moment. "First, answer my question."

"What does it matter?"

The answer was obvious. To her, anyway.

Thank goodness she hadn't made herself any more vulnerable by telling him how she felt about him. Now he was asking ridiculous questions to push her away.

Maybe she needed to push back. "You know everything about my life. About me. It matters. I think it's only fair."

"Oh, hell," he muttered. "I'm not seeing anyone, Kimi. Okay?"

No girlfriend. That was a good start. "The last woman you brought around was Brooke, right?"

"Yep."

Brooke, the waitress. She had dark hair that fell to her waist and bright green eyes, but she hadn't held his interest for long.

"That was what, last year, late summer or early fall?" she asked, casually, as though she couldn't quite remember.

It was mid-September. Takoda had brought her for drinks with the group on the twelfth, and she had been there with Dan.

He nodded. "Yeah."

"Been a while. No one else during the holidays when you were avoiding me?"

Tak sighed. "No."

Then this should've been easy, but for some reason he was making it impossible.

"Surprising for a guy like you." She didn't say anything else, letting the bait dangle, hoping he'd bite.

He picked up his coffee, sipped it slowly. His gaze locked on her. His jaw clenched. "A guy like what exactly?" he asked, unable to resist.

She grinned. "One with needs, who runs through women faster than wildfire through dry brush."

Averting her gaze, he scrubbed a hand over his jaw and rolled his shoulders as though he were now the one who was uncomfortable. "If I have an itch, I scratch it. Plenty of ways to do that without getting entangled in a relationship. Satisfied?"

"Not by a long shot." She drew in a deep, fortifying breath. "Why not me?"

Kimi had seen him in plenty of relationships and was even aware of several of his one-night stands. She wanted her chance with him, but he didn't seem interested in her, like she was defective.

"I promised Jacy. Agreed you were off-limits."

That burst the bubble of her anger. She had a big tumbleweed of feelings for Takoda caught inside her, trying to sort out whether she was in love with him, and he'd promised her brother that he'd never be with her? "When?"

Please, please don't let it be right before he died.

"When isn't the point. He made me swear and I did. Don't ask me to break my word."

Something akin to pain filled her chest. She folded her arms, hoping to stifle it. "I don't believe Jacy would still expect you to keep that promise. Not if what you truly want is for me to be safe and happy."

"I guess we'll never know since he's not here to tell us for himself. This isn't easy for me, you need to know that, but... There's a line with you, Kimi, and I can't cross it."

Chapter Six

As Kimi stormed out of the kitchen, Takoda turned his back, refusing to watch her leave. Emotions he did *not* want to feel swamped him. Filling him. Flooding him. He could barely breathe.

That kiss. He could still taste her, despite trying to wash it away with coffee. And the way she'd felt in his arms, pressed against him. So right. Like they might fit together.

Belonged together.

But he had overstepped, way, way across the line. Now he had to figure out how to pull back.

Tak picked up a muffin and devoured it. Then he ate another. He was ravenous. The only problem was, he wasn't hungry for food.

Cleaning up the crumbs from the counter, he shoved inappropriate thoughts of making love to Kimi from his mind and forced himself to focus on the very pressing problem involving Thomas Wheeler.

Last night, Tak had updated Logan on what had been happening. His buddy had checked out Kimi's house and got a statement from the neighbor, Simpson. Today, they were going to meet at Wheeler's place. See if they could get to the bottom of things together.

Kimi returned to the kitchen fully dressed. But her expression was somber and all traces of passion and humor were gone. "I'm ready to go," she said without looking at him.

They left the house and got in his truck. Yesterday's precipitation had become steady snowfall this morning. He had to turn on the wipers to see the road.

"The muffins were good," he said. It looked as though she'd made a dozen but hadn't had any herself. "Thanks for baking."

She stared out the window. "Sure."

"Did you eat anything?"

"No. I'm not hungry. Only had some coffee."

They had ended things on a sour note, which was enough to ruin her appetite, but she'd had time to eat before he'd entered the kitchen. "Thinking about your dad?"

She nodded. "Yeah. I tried not to for a little while, but then you reminded me about meeting Logan."

The subject of her father was never a simple or easy one. Her feelings about him must have been all over, and Tak didn't want to reopen old wounds. They couldn't avoid talking about Thomas Wheeler forever, but they also didn't have to do it right that second either.

He switched on the radio.

A Morgan Wallen song came on, and Kimi sang along low to "I'm The Problem."

Tak's thoughts circled back to the mess Thomas had dragged Kimi into. One man following her and trying to snatch her purse was bad, but two of them in her house was serious trouble.

"We interrupt normal programming with an emergency bulletin," a radio announcer said. "Radar indicates a polar vortex moving in. A significant winter storm is expected to impact much of Montana and the entire northwestern region starting tomorrow in the late afternoon. Snowfall will range from four to potentially over ten inches in some areas. High winds causing the wind chill factor to plunge well below zero is expected."

Winters in Montana could be rough. Most of the time the snow started falling in September and stuck around through May. A fluctuation in temperatures was an understatement. It was not unheard of to have a forty-degree day followed by one that was subzero. Storms and arctic fronts were common, as were backup generators and four-wheel drives. But a polar vortex could be nasty.

Preparation could mean the difference between living and dying.

They arrived at her father's house early. Since there was no city traffic to deal with, Tak could get to most places in Cutthroat Creek and Bitterroot Falls quickly.

Tak parked in front of the one-story rambler that was situated on a large plot.

Logan wasn't there yet. Last night, the detective had sent a couple of officers, who were out on patrol in Bitterroot Falls, to Thomas Wheeler's, but he hadn't been at home or didn't answer.

Tak and Kimi got out of his truck and headed up the walkway.

Tufts of dense clouds drifted across the gray, midmorning sky, obscuring the sun. A drop in temperature from the incoming storm could already be felt. He zipped his fleece-lined leather bomber jacket against the frigid wind. Kimi wore sensible pants stuffed into fur-trimmed waterproof boots, gloves and the heavy-duty anorak she sported every winter.

Climbing the steps to the front door, Tak held out his hand and Kimi gave him the spare key she had. He pounded on the door a few times—as he had done yesterday when he was trying to track down her dad to ask about the note and retainer fee—and waited. No response.

He inserted the key and unlocked the door.

"Mr. Wheeler?" Tak stepped inside, with Kimi following behind him. "Are you here?"

Leaving the small entryway, he walked down the narrow hall and stopped in front of the living room. Kimi came up alongside him and covered her mouth with a hand.

The house had been ransacked, the same as hers. Torn cushions. Knocked-over furniture. Papers strewn across the floor. There were also the same holes in the drywall. Someone had been determined to find something.

In the light of day, the damage was devastating. Nothing was salvageable. Even the television set had been smashed.

Treading carefully into the living room, he pulled a pair of latex gloves from his jacket pocket. "Don't touch anything," he said to Kimi, and she nodded as she followed him.

A mucked-up crime scene ruined cases. Once, he'd been on an investigation where a rookie cop had contaminated evidence to the point that almost nothing was of any use to forensics, much less being able to stand up in court. After that, Tak made it a habit to always have a pair of gloves on him.

He searched the place, looking for any signs of foul play.

Someone had broken the windowpane in the back door. Glass shards covered the kitchen floor in front of the door.

"When I was here yesterday, looking for your dad, I didn't take the time to check out the back of the house." He'd been worried about leaving Kimi alone at the hospital for too long.

He had called the nurses' station to see if she was working a shift and had been told that she was, *unexpectedly*.

There was always the possibility she might not have felt well enough to stay and would've left early. If that happened, Tak wanted to be there to ensure her safety.

"I'm going to check the bedrooms," she said.

Tak followed Kimi down the hall. In all three rooms, the beds had been flipped onto their sides, mattresses sliced open, and wardrobes emptied.

A door closed toward the front of the house. Footsteps approached. *Two people.*

They were only expecting Logan.

Shoving Kimi behind him, Tak drew his gun.

"Takoda! Kimi!" Logan called.

Who was with him? "We're back here," Tak said.

Logan met them in her father's room. He was quick to give Kimi a hug. Another man entered. A uniformed officer from the Bigfork Reservation Police Department. "This is Lieutenant Joe Midthunder. He reached out to my department last night. Someone on the reservation filed a missing person's report for Thomas Wheeler two days ago. Joe hoped Thomas would show up, but then he missed something important yesterday. Something he never would've missed. I filled Joe in and invited him to join us today."

Kimi narrowed her eyes. "Who filed the report two days ago?"

"I'm afraid that's confidential," the lieutenant said. "The person would like to remain anonymous."

"Anonymous?" Kimi folded her arms. "What if they had something to do with the reason my father's missing? What if they have important information?"

The lieutenant shook his head. "They don't."

"Can you at least tell us what Thomas missed yesterday that was so important?" Takoda asked.

"I can't." The lieutenant shook his head. "It's confidential."

"Hold on." Logan raised a palm. "Before you hit him with the same list of questions I already asked, you're not going to learn anything besides the association between your dad and this individual who filed the report was personal in nature and not business-related."

Stiffening, Kimi breathed in, her jaw set hard. She didn't like this any more than Tak did, but he needed to get things back on track.

"There's a Midthunder with the Bitterroot Falls PD," Tak said casually.

"That's my daughter." The lieutenant hooked his thumbs on his utility belt. "She didn't want to work on the reservation." He swallowed hard. "With me."

Difficult relationships between dads and daughters was a theme today.

Logan cleared his throat and turned to Kimi. "Hey. How are you holding up?"

"Fine. I just wish I had some answers." She slid a glance at Lieutenant Midthunder.

"Understandable," Logan said and then turned to Tak. "How's your head?"

"Much better."

"Did you two find anything in this mess?" the lieutenant asked.

Tak shook his head. "We really haven't had a chance to properly search the place. I figured it was better to see if there were any signs of foul play and then wait for you."

"Once you give the okay, Logan, I'd like to look through his things," Kimi said. "See if anything he normally had on him or was fond of is here."

"Sure." Logan nodded. "You'll have to wait for forensics to dust for prints and then still wear gloves."

She nodded.

"Anything in particular you're looking for?" Lieutenant Midthunder asked.

"Um, well." Kimi thought about it. "He wears a signet ring on his right pinky finger that has the Wheeler family crest on it."

Her dad's side of the family was originally from England and could trace their roots back to the 1600s. The ring was supposed to pass to Jacy after Thomas died.

"His Zamberlan work boots," Kimi added, "and his notebook. Brown leather with strap wraps engraved with his initials. None of those things he'd willingly leave behind. So, I'm hoping if they're not here, then it means they're with him, wherever he is, and maybe he's all right."

"When was the last time you saw your father?" Logan asked.

"At Christmas. I was surprised he called me and invited me to lunch."

Strange. Thomas rarely called her. Never asked to see her. Not even during the holidays. Takoda should've been there for her, to talk it over, see how she was doing. Especially then. After Jacy died, they'd spent every Christmas Eve together, watching movies and cooking dinner before they exchanged gifts. It was one of the best nights of the year for him. He always looked forward to having her all to himself, even though he couldn't have her in the way he wanted, making it also one of the worst nights. To be so close to her while keeping himself at a distance.

Last year, he'd been all alone, thinking she was cozied up with DD.

If only he'd known. He would've swallowed his pride and gone to her.

Thoughts of that kiss threatened to derail his focus, but he blocked it from his mind.

"What did you talk about with your dad when you saw him?" Logan asked.

"Not much. Work. Mostly about his. He was leaving CCMC."

Thomas had worked for Cutthroat Creek Mining Company forever. They were the largest palladium mining company in the region. "Did he say why?" Tak asked.

"Only that he had gotten a lucrative offer from the Stracke Group. TSG deals in precious metals and was looking to open a mine in the area."

Lieutenant Midthunder watched Kimi intensely, like he thought she might be a suspect.

Another strange thing for Takoda to add to the list.

Logan took out his pad and a pen and jotted down notes. "Are you sure his leaving didn't have anything to do with the recent layoffs at CCMC?"

Kimi shoved her hands in her pockets. "He spoke for twenty minutes about how palladium was going to surge in demand and its price was about to skyrocket because congress was going to pass some bill to ban the import of certain minerals from the Russian Federation, specifically palladium. He went on and on about how he was finally going to cash in as the head of the exploration department for the Stracke Group. Twenty minutes of him talking nonstop about that before he even bothered to ask me how I was doing." She flicked a glance at the lieutenant before lowering her head. "Not that he really wanted the answer. He never mentioned the layoffs."

"Forgive my ignorance," Logan said, propping a fist on his hip, "but what's so special about palladium?"

"It's a shiny, silvery-white metal," Tak said, "that's an essential component in the automotive industry, used in catalytic converters. Also in electronics, dentistry and jewelry. I only know so much about it because I got stuck talking with Thomas once."

"After Jacy's funeral." Kimi looked at Takoda and grief filled her eyes. "Even then, Dad talked more about himself and his own life than his son's."

It might have been the selfishness in Thomas Wheeler, but Takoda always had the impression that the man didn't know what to say in awkward or difficult situations. So he'd fall back on something familiar he was more at ease discussing to fill up the quiet spaces in conversation.

"Did Thomas ever go looking for palladium on the reservation's land?" Tak wondered.

Midthunder shrugged. "Wouldn't have mattered. Thomas knew the tribal council would never agree to selling any rights or building a mine. We respect the land."

"Was he out there at Bigfork a lot?" Kimi asked.

"Depends on your definition of *a lot*, I suppose." Midthunder gave away nothing in his expression. "He had friends out there."

"Were you one of them?" Kimi asked. "Did you know my father well?"

The officer pursed his lips. "I knew him well enough to recognize that, as of yesterday, I should take the missing person's report seriously."

Tak glanced at Kimi. He was certain the same question running through his mind was going through hers. What was so special about yesterday?

"Was that it?" Logan asked Kimi. "Your father didn't say anything else to you?"

"Why did he want to meet in the first place?" Midthunder added.

"To wish me a Merry Christmas and to give me a gift."

Tak moved closer to her. "What was it?"

"A rare first-print edition of *The Wizard of Oz*. He used to read it to me and Jacy when we were kids. He also gave me a necklace with a colorful butterfly etched on the pendant. When I didn't show any excitement over it, he went so far as to take it out of the box and made a big deal of putting it on me."

In Sioux, Kimimela meant *little butterfly*. But in Algonquin, Kimi meant *secret*. Takoda had only ever heard Thomas call her Kimi. Maybe it was nothing. Maybe it was everything. "Sounds sweet of your dad. Sentimental."

Kimi arched an eyebrow, like the comment had sounded delusional. "My father isn't sweet or sentimental. He's smart. Shrewd. A gifted geologist and mining engineer, and the best surveyor able to find palladium where others didn't think it would be. He's many things, but sentimental isn't one of them."

Midthunder nodded in agreement.

Tak wished he could hold Kimi, but he settled for putting a hand on her arm.

She jerked her arm free of his touch.

Midthunder noticed but remained deadpan.

Also giving him a questioning look, Logan furrowed his brow at the interaction between him and Kimi.

Takoda shook his head at his buddy, a silent plea for him not to ask about it. The tension with Kimi was his fault. "Maybe your father gave you the necklace as a way of extending an olive branch." Deep down, he wanted that to be true, for Kimi's sake, but he doubted that was the reason. The timing of Kimi being in danger and her dad giving her that gift, when he hadn't bought her a Christmas present since she was fourteen, couldn't be a coincidence. "I'd like to see it." He hadn't seen her wearing it the past couple of days.

Maybe the necklace was at her house. The guys who had broken in hadn't gotten a chance to search upstairs.

"Good luck with that," she said. "Every time I looked at the necklace, it brought up a lot of conflicting feelings. I didn't want to throw it away and I didn't want to keep it either. So, I sent it to my mother. Figured she might actually wear it."

Aiyana had the necklace.

Tak groaned. "Is she still living with her companion in Spokane?" Aiyana detested the words *boyfriend* and *girlfriend*. She believed no one past the age of thirty should use such terms to define their relationships. It didn't sound mature or dignified.

Kimi nodded. "Yup. This guy seems to be sticking around."

More like Aiyana was the one choosing to do the sticking. From the stories Tak had heard, after the divorce, Aiyana hadn't been interested in being tied down again. Maybe it was really about finding the right person. "But you kept the book?" Tak asked.

"The necklace made me angry, to be honest. But I found having the book comforting. I guess because it was a reminder that my dad didn't forget about all the things we did together years ago. When I packed to stay at the hotel, I threw it in the bag for some reason. I started rereading one of the stories. Getting mugged dredged up a lot of old stuff for me."

That meant the book was at Takoda's house. They had one of the gifts Thomas had given her and maybe one clue that would get them closer to keeping Kimi safe.

"See if your mom will send the necklace to you," Logan suggested, "express mail."

"I shouldn't have to drag her into this." Her tone was defiant. Angry. Kimi took out her cell phone and started dialing. "I'm going to try my father again. How dare he put me in this predicament," she said, and Tak couldn't agree more.

She put the phone up to her ear.

The four of them stood silently waiting for the call to connect.

Ringing came from inside the room. Thomas's phone was there at the house. They all looked around, trying to pinpoint its exact location.

Takoda tracked the sound to a corner, coming from beneath a wardrobe. Lieutenant Midthunder helped him shove the two-door wardrobe to the side. The ringing stopped as the call went to voicemail, but the phone was there.

Kneeling, Tak pressed on floorboards. One gave way with a click as he pushed in. Then the board popped up half of an inch. He lifted it.

Inside the cubbyhole was a cell phone. He reached in, grabbed it and held it up.

The cell phone was covered in blood.

Chapter Seven

Inside the Bitterroot Falls police station, Officer Isabella Midthunder drew a sample of Kimi's blood for them to compare against what they'd found on the cell phone at the house. A DNA test would confirm if it was her father's blood.

Kimi was furious with her dad for dropping out of her life only to draw a big target on her back. But she hoped he was okay. No matter what their issues, she'd never want any harm to come to him. She loved him. As complicated and difficult as that love was, it was real.

If nothing else, he'd had the forethought to hire Takoda to keep her safe. Enlisting him meant all of IPS would do whatever they could to protect her. Maybe her father knew her well enough to know that if she ran into trouble, she might hesitate to ask for help.

The note and the retainer he'd sent to Takoda were insurance that her stubbornness wouldn't get her killed.

That was love, as flawed and confusing as it might be. Wasn't it?

Why couldn't it be straightforward and simple with the men in her life?

She glanced over at Takoda. Hunky, sexy, frustrating

man. The mixture of hurt and anger simmering in her chest made it hard to breathe.

Takoda was talking to Logan and Lieutenant Midthunder. They were out of earshot, but they had been working on getting representatives from the Cutthroat Creek Mining Company and the Stracke Group to come down to the station as part of procedure, to answer some questions regarding the case.

Both companies, surprisingly, were cooperating, without any red-tape delays, or giving Logan the runaround.

"All done." The officer put a piece of gauze on her arm and then a Band-Aid. She finished labeling the vial of blood.

The younger Midthunder was about Kimi's age. She wore her hair in a sleek bun and had a warm, kind demeanor. Unlike the lieutenant. Not once had she glanced at her father, and the lieutenant had steered clear of his daughter since entering the station. They hadn't even exchanged greetings.

Kimi found the tension interesting. But could she use it to her advantage? "You had such a gentle touch." She pulled down the sleeve of her sweater. "I know a few phlebotomists who could learn a thing or two from you."

The officer smiled.

"Do you mind if I call you Isabella?"

"Sure, but it's just Izzy."

"My father disappearing has been a lot for me. Being followed and attacked hasn't helped. The thing is, we have a strained relationship. You could even call it estranged. There's so much about his current life that he didn't share with me. That he kept hidden." Kimi scooted to the edge of her chair, getting closer to the officer. "Someone on the rez filed a missing person's report for my father. Before I did."

Izzy frowned. "Ouch."

"Exactly." Kimi nodded. Izzy got it. They were making a

connection. "Your dad won't tell me who it is and it's driving me nuts. The not knowing who. Or what their relationship is to my dad. I respect the fact that he's entitled to a private life. But his choices have put me in danger. I may never see him again." That was true, but she hoped that wasn't the case. "I don't even know who's after me or why. I feel like my father stripped me of power by putting me in the dark and in danger without even telling me why. The one thing that would make this horrible time just a little easier, is if I knew who filed the report and what they mean to my father."

Izzy flicked a glance at her own father before lowering her eyes.

"I know I'm asking a lot from you, and we only just met. But I need to take control of my life. My father, Takoda, now your father, who's using his authority to keep information from me that I have a right to know—they're all trying to help, but it feels like I'm being pushed aside." She looked at Izzy. "A name. Their relationship. That's all I need."

Looking up at her, Izzy said nothing.

Kimi grabbed a pen and a sticky note. She wrote down her cell phone number. "Think about it. Will you do that? At least consider it?"

Izzy hesitated. Slid another furtive glance across the room to her father. Lowered her head. She pulled off the latex gloves and tossed them in the waste bin. With a curt nod, she picked up the sticky note and the DNA sample. "I'll consider it," she whispered and walked away.

That was ten times better than a flat-out *no*. Kimi would take it.

PACING INSIDE THE observation room of the police department, Kim stared at Lieutenant Joe Midthunder. There was no guarantee that Izzy would try to help her and, even if she did, there was no surety she'd succeed.

A hundred different splintering emotions ricocheted through Kimi. What was the lieutenant hiding? Who was he hiding? Protecting? What gave him the right to decide she didn't have a need to know?

Takoda stepped in front of her, stopping her in her tracks and redirecting her attention. He shook his head. "Let it go." Then he mouthed, *For now*.

There he went, trying to tell her what to do, again. She narrowed her eyes at him.

He flattened his mouth in a grim line. "I'm on your side. Always." The sincerity in his voice almost made her want to forgive him for his rejection earlier.

Almost.

The door opened. Logan came into the room. "Representatives from both companies are here and supposedly eager to cooperate. We'll have to wait and see how true that is."

"It only took them four hours to show up," Kimi said, sounding far snarkier and more sarcastic than she liked.

Logan frowned. "At least we got a same-day response with representatives showing up here at the station, rather than us being forced to go to them, only to get bounced around from one office to the next. This is faster and more efficient."

"I'm sorry." She put a hand on Logan's arm. "You're right."

"Who did they send?" Tak asked.

"We have Phyllis Earle, the senior vice president of legal from the Stracke Group, and Nick Nason, the chief financial officer of CCMC. I'm not thrilled they sent a lawyer, but I expected it. The good news is the Stracke Group only sent one and not a team. All right, Joe, let's go question them."

"If you don't mind," Midthunder said, "I'd prefer to keep my involvement in the investigation discreet. No need to draw unwanted attention to the reservation."

"You mean to the person who filed the report," Kimi said.

The lieutenant didn't even glance in her direction.

"I'll go instead." Tak went up to Logan. "Sit in with you."

Logan considered it for a second. "Will you be in there as a close personal friend of Kimi's or as a professional?"

"Her father hired me to protect her. This is official IPS business. But we all know it's also personal."

The answer seemed to satisfy Logan, and he nodded.

After the two men left, Kimi pivoted on her heel and stared at Joe Midthunder. The man had turned his back to her, like she wasn't even there, and looked through the one-way glass into the interrogation room.

Since she hadn't grown up on the reservation, she didn't know him, but she'd heard of him. He was a hard man but a fair one. Didn't speak unless he had something important to say. And that when you were around him, it was better to listen than to speak.

To hell with that.

First, her father had spent years avoiding her and Jacy like they were mistakes he wanted to forget. Whenever they had talked, it wasn't about anything real. Anything that mattered, at least to her. She had so many questions for her father that she might never get to ask.

Kimi marched up beside Midthunder, ready to get some answers from someone.

"You should listen to your friend," he said, his voice low, his gaze focused on the other room as Logan and Takoda showed Phyllis Earle in and got started. "Let it go."

"The only problem with that is, Takoda doesn't get to tell

me what to do and neither do you. Was it some woman my father was seeing who filed the report?"

Silence.

Her blood simmered, her face growing hot. "If it is, you can tell me, Lieutenant Midthunder."

"Call me Joe."

"Whatever you tell me will stay between us," she pleaded. "I won't share it with Takoda or Logan." Her dad wasn't the only one who could keep a secret. She just wanted the truth. "But I need to know. I need you to tell me for my own sanity."

He turned his head slightly, running his gaze over her face. The line of his mouth was firm, his sharp features unyielding the slightest bit to her honey-coated attempt at persuasion. "You don't know what you need." Hooking his thumbs on his belt, he returned to looking straight ahead. "And I can't give you peace of mind. No one else can do that for you."

Inflexible. Obstinate.

Grinding her teeth, Kimi had had enough of being stonewalled and dismissed where her father was concerned. "I deserve answers!" She caught herself, surprised by her own raised voice, and glanced at the interrogation room to see if they had heard her. No one seemed to as they continued with preliminaries, establishing things for the record.

"You do deserve answers, only not from me," Joe said coolly. "Misplaced anger solves nothing, but can destroy everything." His tone wasn't antagonistic or even condescending, which somehow only irritated her more. Turning, he faced her. Met her gaze and held it. "Be careful. In trying to find your father, don't lose yourself and the things you hold dear along the way." He looked back at the interrogation room.

"You sound like a fortune cookie, Joe."

Not a word in response, but she spotted the corner of his mouth hitch up in a slight grin.

Kimi wanted to scream in frustration, but she controlled herself. Anger had always been easier for her to manage than the alternatives.

Grief. Pain.

Love. The one-sided kind. For her father.

For Takoda.

Tears stung her eyes, but she refused to cry in front of this man. Straightening, she drew in a deep breath and did her best to focus on the discussion in the interrogation room.

"We did not poach Mr. Wheeler." Phyllis Earle sat poised, wearing a blue pantsuit that was nearly the same color as her eyes, and Kimi thought it was a bold choice for such a conservative-looking woman. She had chestnut hair that was streaked gray and pulled back from her face. "He approached us about a position. I was concerned that he would violate the noncompete clause in his contract with CCMC, which is standard in positions such as his in our industry. He assured us it wouldn't be a problem for him to be released from his contract without any worry that CCMC would seek injunctive relief or monetary or punitive damages."

Nodding, Logan took notes. "Did he have proof of this assurance?"

"No, he didn't."

Logan tilted his head to the side. "Then why take such a risk by hiring him?"

"The matter wasn't clear-cut. There were many factors to consider. Palladium is very rare, making it more expensive than silver, platinum or gold. Mr. Wheeler is a renowned geologist and mining engineer. With his exceptional expertise in pinpointing palladium, the board was willing to gamble on him despite my warning that things could get messy."

"What compensation package did you offer him?" Tak asked.

"Title as chief of the exploration department. A fifty-thousand-dollar signing bonus. Six-figure starting salary. In addition, very lucrative bonuses based on production benchmarks. We agreed to give him a percentage of the revenue on the back end, which is unheard of, but we were willing to pay for his talent. He also asked for something else that was unprecedented. Another stipulation in his contract was that we would consider any current or former employees from CCMC to fill our positions if they applied and didn't have a noncompete clause. I think he wanted us to lure their best folks away. Thomas must have had a big grudge against CCMC."

"Did you ever hear anything from CCMC, receive any legal threats from them regarding his noncompete clause after he was hired?" Logan asked, and Ms. Earle shook her head. "Would it be possible to get a copy of his contract?"

Ms. Earle picked up her phone and typed something. "My assistant will email it shortly."

Logan set down his pen. "When was the last time you saw Thomas?"

"Saturday evening at the gala we hosted in the Bitterroot Mountain Hotel ballroom. We made a big announcement about the first mine we're opening and introduced the entire team to the press. Thomas was so excited. At first. The chief of staff gathered the team backstage, ensuring we were ready to walk on stage when our names were called. Thomas was all smiles. Then he spotted someone near the curtain and his entire demeanor changed. His enthusiasm turned to nerves. After the announcement, it was like he vanished. I couldn't find him anywhere."

Leaning forward, Tak rested his forearms on the table. "Did you get a look at the person he saw backstage?"

She nodded. "It was a man. Tall. On the muscular side. He had facial hair. Not a beard. More of a heavy five-o'clock shadow. I remember him because he was wearing sunglasses at night indoors. It's a pet peeve of mine."

A chill ran through Kimi and she shivered.

Joe looked over at her. "Do you know the person she described?"

"The same man who started following me on Sunday and did this to my face the other day." She gestured to the bruises.

In the interrogation room, Logan's phone chimed and he glanced at the screen. "That was fast. I received a copy of the contract. That's all we have for you for now. If you hear from Thomas, please let us know."

Phyllis Earle stood.

"One more thing," Tak said. "What will you do if Thomas doesn't turn up? Do you have a replacement for him?"

"It would be a significant blow to the Stracke Group. We can start production on the first mine thanks to him. Fortunately, it looks as though it will be very profitable. Current projections forecast that the mine will be operational for at least twenty years. We had big plans for this region, but Thomas was the key to it," Phyllis said. "Now that he's officially missing, the board will have to come up with a contingency plan. It's a shame. Thomas was set to begin surveying a new area next week. If only he had shared whatever he was working on in his notebook before he disappeared." Phyllis shook their hands and left.

The brown leather-bound book her father carried everywhere. They hadn't found it at the house.

"What is it?" Joe asked her. "What are you thinking?"

"That notebook. Instead of using a laptop, like this is the twenty-first century, Dad preferred to write things down." Her mom had given it to him as a present years ago. Personalized with his initials. Whenever he filled it up, he simply replaced the insert with a new packet of paper. "He always had it on him. Maybe that's what those men are looking for. Is this all about palladium?"

"Possibly. It is a billion-dollar industry."

She thought back to the cell phone hidden in the house and the bloody handprint on it. She wondered how long it would take to get back the test results. "Do you think my dad is dead?"

"Not wise to speculate. The blood at the house might not have been your dad's. If he was injured and bleeding, why would he take the time to hide the phone and wipe away any traces of blood on the floor or the dresser? What I know for certain is that you were right about Thomas. He's smart and shrewd. He's a survivor."

But that raised an alarming question. "Well, if the blood isn't his, then whose could it be?"

Joe gave her a steely look. "That's what I've been wondering."

Chapter Eight

Takoda stayed seated in the interrogation room while Logan went to get the next representative. He pulled up the article he'd found about the Stracke Group. It accused them of going into working-class communities rich in natural resources across the globe and establishing a couple of mines. Once they'd been depleted, Stracke closed the mines, leaving the communities in worse conditions than they'd started, but all they cared about was their bottom line.

The deal they'd made with Thomas would've cost them a great deal of revenue. But if they had gotten their hands on his notes, finding the locations for the next mines, then eliminating him would have saved the expense of paying Thomas and potential litigation with CCMC. That would explain why they'd been willing to gamble on Thomas.

Billions were at stake.

What if the man with sunglasses worked for the Stracke Group? What if something went wrong and Thomas got away with his notebook?

The door to the interrogation room opened. Logan ushered in Nick Nason, the CFO of Cutthroat Creek Mining Company. They both sat.

"This is Takoda Yazzie, from Ironside Protection Services. He'll be sitting in on the interview." Logan went through preliminary questions, getting Nason to state his full name and title for the record since the interview was being recorded. "Not to offend you, Mr. Nason, but we were expecting someone from your legal department to come in. Maybe even the chief of staff."

"My thoughts exactly," Nason said. "But the CEO, Jeff Randolph, asked me to come. Lately, with all the bad press regarding the layoffs, it's been me and legal as the face of the company."

"How long did Thomas Wheeler work for CCMC?" Logan asked.

"A long time." Leaning back in his chair, Nason crossed his legs and smoothed down the front of his expensive-looking suit. "Almost thirty-five years. Longer even than I have been with the company."

Logan nodded. "Was he a good employee?"

"One of the best. He made a valuable contribution for many years before leaving."

"When was the last time you saw him?" Logan asked.

"The day he quit," Nason said. "He turned in his letter of resignation at the holiday office party, which was held on the twentieth. Made a big spectacle of it."

Based on what they'd heard of his reputation so far, her father sounded like the type who would've given at least two weeks' notice. Unless he couldn't for some reason. Had he resigned in the middle of a public office party instead of behind closed doors because it was safer?

Tak tried to connect the dots from the resignation to Thomas days later meeting Kimi to give her those presents. According to Kimi, her father even went so far as to put the necklace on her, as though he feared she might not bother to take it out of the box.

All of those things were connected: the resignation, the new job, the presents. They had to be. But how?

"Thomas spent over thirty years working for CCMC," Takoda said. "Any idea why he would he leave, especially so abruptly? Was it work conditions? Salary?"

Nason shoved a hand through his hair. It was thick and dark, less flecked with gray than Phyllis Earle's. He looked to be younger than the lawyer, maybe in his late forties. "Only Thomas could tell you for certain, but he did ask for several pay raises in the past five years. Every time, we increased his salary by two percent, and he always received a twenty-five-thousand-dollar bonus with each new target area he discovered for us."

They weren't paying Thomas what he was worth. A two percent raise didn't even keep pace with inflation. Takoda studied the CFO's face, his body language. "Twenty-five grand for a site that would bring in millions."

Nason gave a pleasant smile, though he couldn't quite manage to make his eyes look remotely pleasant. "I'm sorry. I didn't hear a question."

Takoda folded his hands in his lap. "Why wasn't Thomas paid more? Why wasn't he given perks and better bonuses?"

Nason rested his elbows on the arms of his chair and made a confident steeple of his fingertips. "In mining, it's a balancing act between risk and reward. The company takes all the risks and deals with the financial setbacks while keeping things operational. It was Thomas's job to lead exploration and find spots for new mines. Palladium is typically deeper and harder to locate and access than, say, gold or silver. Sometimes we won't get a highly conductive electromagnetic response over target areas. That's where Thomas came in. His sixth sense was uncanny. Reliable. If he told us where to dig, we usually hit paydirt every single time. But with the last two sites he selected, we were never able to confirm the presence of palladium or any other precious metal that we could've used. Consequently, we didn't recoup the expense of the exploration. Thomas cost us millions in addition to the waste of time and other resources."

"There's been talk in the town and articles in the *Bitterroot Beacon* about the recent layoffs," Logan said. "Is the loss in revenue from the failed sites Thomas picked the reason?"

"Yes, in part. We laid off two hundred workers because of him. We've also automated certain divisions with advancements in technology, and had to let another hundred and fifty workers go for that reason. Machines are cheaper in the long run. We had to reduce production costs. According to the chief of operations, Thomas had lost his magic touch. He became a dud. We allowed him to leave to mitigate our future losses."

Logan flipped through his notepad. "After the Stracke Group hired Thomas, he found a lucrative target area for them. The mine is projected to be operational for twenty years. I'm sure CCMC isn't happy about being wrong about him. Was anyone so bitter about that they might seek revenge?"

"Thomas found one mine for them." Nason shrugged, like that meant nothing. "It's only a matter of time before the Stracke Group realizes who they really hired. A dud."

"Maybe you'd like us to believe he lost his magic touch because it fits the narrative for CCMC." Logan closed his notebook. "Your company lost millions in revenue and laid off hundreds of people, only to watch your competitor celebrate a lucrative new mine thanks to Thomas Wheeler. Maybe someone in the company was so upset over seeing him produce for the Stracke Group instead of CCMC, they took measures to ensure the one mine Thomas found for them would also be the last."

Another pleasant smile that didn't reach Nason's eyes. "I hear a lot of speculation, but no proof. More importantly, no question."

Takoda refrained from shaking his head as he listened to Nason. The guy might be the chief financial officer, but he acted like a lawyer, only answering questions asked, deftly steering clear of being baited. "What's your background? What did you do before working for CCMC?"

"I was a lawyer with the securities and exchange commission. I was looking for a change and wanted to move back home to Montana. A friend of a friend recommended me for a position at Cutthroat Creek Mining and I've been with them ever since."

Explained a lot. "You didn't mention you were a lawyer," Takoda said.

"You didn't ask."

Both TSG and CCMC were being careful, which was to be expected.

"After Thomas hit paydirt for the Stracke Group," Logan said, "why didn't you sue him for breach of contract since he had a noncompete clause?"

Nason sighed. "I was hoping I wouldn't have to bring this up, but Thomas was not only a dud, quite frankly, he was dangerous to be around."

Takoda straightened. "What do you mean?"

"He was in debt to a loan shark," Nason said. "I assumed Thomas had a gambling problem based on rumors and his nickname—Wheeler Dealer. He became a liability to the company. There was a clause in his contract that stipulated if he was terminated for any reason, he would get a big payday. That was drafted before I came on board. We were happy to accept his resignation instead of shelling out more money to a lost cause."

Logan and Takoda exchanged a look. Neither of them had heard any whispers of Thomas Wheeler being in debt. Besides, only a fool went to a loan shark for money, and Kimi's father was no fool.

"That's a significant claim," Logan said. "Any proof to substantiate it?"

"Big Billy Burdock. Have you heard of him?" Nason asked, and both Tak and Logan nodded. "Burdock confronted Thomas on company grounds and assaulted another employee who tried to intervene."

Logan picked up his pen. "The name of this other employee?"

"After his nose was broken, the individual has made it clear that he doesn't want to have anything to do with Thomas or his troubles, but his name is Peter O'Donnell. We do have a recording of the altercation from a security camera." Nason took out his phone and quickly hit Play, as though he'd had the video teed up and ready to go. He set the phone on the table.

On the screen, Thomas Wheeler left a mine and was striding through the parking lot when Burdock hopped out of a pickup truck, ambushing him. Burdock was stocky and bald and smaller than someone might expect with the moniker Big Billy.

There was no audio on the playback, but it was clear they were having a heated conversation. If only Takoda could hear what it was about. The time and date stamp in the upper right corner showed December 15, 4:35 p.m.

In the video, Big Billy grabbed Thomas by his shirt and yelled at him. Pointed a thick, meaty finger at his face.

The loan shark had a nasty reputation, but desperate people still turned to him for help. Only to regret it later. There were rumors that if his clients didn't pay him what they owed, they would end up with broken bones. Sometimes family members were threatened. In worst-case scenarios, those clients who failed to pay disappeared.

No body, no murder charge. Convicting someone of murder without the purported victim's body in evidence was theoretically possible. But it was extremely hard to prove, forcing the prosecution to rely on circumstantial evidence. Also, where Burdock was concerned, no one was ever willing to testify against him.

For two minutes, the argument continued as Thomas raised a shaky palm and appeared to try and reason with Burdock.

Takoda noticed that in Wheeler's other hand, he was clutching a brown leather-bound book close to his side. The one with his notes about the palladium mines.

Then another man appeared on the screen. A guy wearing a hard hat ran over and made the mistake of trying to pull Burdock off Kimi's father. His back was to the surveillance camera, making it hard to identify him. Burdock punched the man in the face. The hard hat flew off from the impact of the blow, and the man cradled his face, which still wasn't visible, in his hands—maybe his nose was broken. Burdock shoved Thomas to ground, got back in his truck, and sped out of the lot.

Once the video finished, Nason said, "I'd be happy to forward this to you."

No doubt the finance lawyer would do so quickly.

Logan nodded. "Yes, we'll need it." He passed his number to Nason, and within seconds Logan's phone chimed with the receipt.

Tak crossed his arms, hating the fact they were left with

more questions than answers. "Mr. Nason, why didn't CCMC file charges against Burdock after the assault for battery, or the very least, trespassing?"

"Burdock is not a man to be trifled with," Nason said. "He was only on CCMC property because of Thomas. We don't want any problems around our mines or with any of our employees. Burdock is a man known for causing trouble. If Thomas went to work for a different company, then the loan shark would stay off CCMC property and away from our employees. No need to stir up more problems, antagonizing a ruthless thug by filing charges. The violent incident was only one more reason we were relieved to wash our hands of Thomas."

After Nick Nason stood and left, Tak and Logan rejoined the others in the observation room.

Joe turned to Kimi. "Did you know about your father's gambling debts?"

"No," she said, shaking her head, "but then there is a lot about him that I don't know. Whoever filed the missing person's report might know more. You should ask them."

"I will."

Kimi stared at Joe, her eyes narrowed, her hands clenched.

"Try to remember," Joe said, softening his expression and his tone, "I'm not the man you're furious with."

Takoda felt like he had missed something. The tension between Kimi and Joe was different, but not necessarily better.

She had a right to be upset, at her father, at him after the way he handled everything in the kitchen. *Tactless Tak strikes again*. But she didn't have a right to take it out on Joe. He was only doing his job, and his responsibility was to protect the people on the Bigfork Reservation.

"Now we have some leads to go on," Logan said. "I'll

start with questioning Peter O'Donnell. See if he caught any part of the conversation between Thomas and Burdock. We know the man who has been following you was at the Bitterroot Mountain Hotel on Saturday evening. He should be on the security footage. We may be able to get a good image of him and figure out who he is. As for Burdock, he's a known loan shark, with a couple of convictions for misdemeanors. We haven't been able to charge him with any felonies. Definitely the type of man who would break kneecaps if someone owed him money. Finding him might be tricky, but I'll make it my top priority."

"Can we see the video Nason showed you?" Kimi asked.

Logan brought it up for her and Joe to watch.

Focused on the screen, Kimi tensed. When it came to the part where Burdock got violent, she cringed.

Logan stopped the playback of the recording. "I'm sorry you had to see that."

So was Tak. She might have a difficult relationship with her father, even be angry with him for putting her in this deadly situation, but Takoda was certain that if anything bad happened to Thomas, it would hurt her.

DISBELIEF CLOUDED EVERYTHING. Kimi wasn't certain what was true anymore. She reeled from the video. Was her father a gambling addict? Indebted to a vicious loan shark?

She would've sworn it wasn't possible. Until she'd watched Burdock threaten her father.

"In the video, Dad is holding the notebook that Ms. Earle mentioned," she said. "I didn't see it at the house. The men who tossed my place and Dad's might've been looking for it. He keeps all his research notes in there. I'm sure whatever location he was going to survey next would be in his notebook."

Takoda nodded. "That would make it worth a lot of money."

He was right. So much money that it might be worth killing to get it.

Someone cleared their throat, and everyone looked at the doorway. Chief Edgar Macon stood in the hall. The man was burly with a barrel chest. His graying hair was cropped tight and low. He strode into the room with the full force of his authority sucking up the air around them.

"Logan, we need to have a word about the Wheeler case. In private."

"Should Joe be a part of the conversation?" Logan asked.

"No." The chief looked around the room. "Excuse us."

Joe led the way out. Kimi and Tak followed him down the hall. The door to the observation room closed.

"What do you think that's all about?" Kimi asked.

"No way of knowing," Joe said. "No need to speculate. You two appear to be very chummy with Detective Powell. I'm sure he'll fill you in."

Raised voices came from the observation room. The heated conversation was short. Chief Macon left, not making eye contact with them as he stormed past.

A few seconds later, Logan joined them at the end of the hall, looking flustered and shell-shocked. "I'm off the case."

Surprise slid through Kimi like cold water rushing in her veins. "What? Why?"

"I wasn't given a reason." Logan shook his head, his eyes still dazed, his cheeks red. "The chief made it clear he didn't have to give me one."

"Who is taking over the case?" Tak asked.

Logan rubbed his forehead. "No one."

"But my father is missing," Kimi said. This was all so surreal. "Joe has a missing person's report, and I filed one with the BFPD. You can't just drop it. This is an official case."

"Not anymore." Logan's jaw clenched as he glanced at them. "I was *ordered* to stand down. If the blood on the phone turns out to be your father's, then the chief might possibly reconsider. He emphasized *possibly*. Until then, no other BFPD resources are to be used on the Thomas Wheeler case."

Kimi heaved a sigh and then pivoted toward Joe. "What about you? You'll continue to investigate, won't you?"

"My authority is limited to Bigfork and, as I've already told you, I don't want to draw unwanted attention."

"This is unbelievable." She threw her hands up in the air. "So, you all are just giving up?"

"I'm not." The sincerity in Takoda's voice drew her full attention. "We'll figure this out together, with the IPS team. Protecting you means finding out what happened to your father."

"But we both recognize it's useful to have someone with a badge to help," she said. "You've pointed out to me numerous times where IPS had to rely on law enforcement to get a warrant."

Takoda said nothing in response.

What argument could he make? The power of a warrant was a mighty thing, and as capable as IPS was, they didn't have the authority to get one.

"You still have a badge working on your behalf," Joe said coolly.

"What are you talking about?" Kimi asked, not filtering the irritation from her voice.

"*He*," Joe said, pointing a finger at Logan, "was kicked off the Thomas Wheeler case. Not the Kimi Redbird Wheeler case. The guy with the sunglasses may have been after your dad, but he also followed you. Attacked you. If Takoda can't convince the hotel to share the footage from the night of the Stracke Group gala, Powell can still get a warrant without mentioning Thomas. And Burdock trespassed on private property and assaulted someone in addition to your dad. That gives Powell a reason to look into Burdock, too. Maybe the loan shark's flunkies are after you. Who knows. But while the good detective is questioning Burdock, if Thomas's name happens to come up in a discussion, I'd call that a happy coincidence."

As far as Kimi was concerned, there was nothing happy about any of this. But she supposed she couldn't find a hole in his logic.

"No matter where this leads," Tak said to her, "I'm in this with you. Not because of the retainer from your dad. And not because Jacy would haunt me if I didn't help." He stopped, not actually telling her why.

Leaving her to wonder. But she believed him.

The one thing she was sure of was that he wasn't going to abandon her this time, and he wasn't going to give up.

"A word of caution," Joe said, lowering his voice to a whisper. "Whatever the reason behind Ed Macon ordering Logan to drop the case, it's a problem. I suggest you find out how big of one if you're going to pursue this."

Kimi followed Tak's gaze across the bullpen to the chief's office. Ed Macon was sitting behind his desk, on the phone, staring at them.

Was the chief of the Bitterroot Falls PD dirty?

Or was the problem much worse?

Chapter Nine

This was an all-hands-on-deck kind of scenario. Gathering the rest of the Ironside Protection Services team was essential and Takoda didn't waste any time doing it.

Not only had Eli, Bo, Chance and Autumn shown up, but the entire crew came to the Wolverine Lodge. Logan and Summer, a lawyer who made her mark in the area with a prominent case. Chance's significant other Winter also joined them, along with her colleague Declan Hart. Both Winter and Declan were DOJ Division of Criminal Investigation special agents. Kimi finally got to meet Bo's girlfriend, Nora Santana, a previous IPS client.

Even Jackson Powell, Logan's brother came. The US marshal lived in Missoula. They usually only saw him for big events or for brunch on occasion when he was free.

All their lives intersected and intermingled, and they had become more than coworkers or friends. They were family. In a time of need, they stuck together and had each other's backs.

The Wolverine Lodge was conveniently located for everyone, and the food was great. Also, their table received a couple of plates of appetizers on the house. Summer and Logan were sort of local celebrities after they'd stopped a local company from selling a product that was poisoning people. IPS had helped Summer to comb through the mountain of discovery material. In the end, she'd received a huge settlement to compensate those who had gotten sick.

They had pushed several smaller tables together in the bar section of the restaurant. Service was faster for their large group when they placed their orders through the bartender and picked things up as they were ready, bringing everything back to the table themselves.

Watching Kimi light up at seeing the crew tugged at Takoda's heart. She needed them all more than ever: their kindness, their support, and their love.

He hadn't realized how much she had missed out on after he had distanced himself, and thereby also the group, from her. New relationships, engagement parties and meeting relatives from out of town, the holidays, group dinners and Sunday brunches. Kimi hadn't participated in any of it because of him.

Takoda felt like the biggest jerk.

Going forward, he vowed to himself that no matter what happened between him and Kimi, never again would he put her in a position where she felt that she had to alienate herself from all these people who cared about her.

Once Kimi had gotten through hugging everyone and catching up on their lives, they dug into their food and delved into the nuances of the situation with Thomas Wheeler.

"Have you reached out to your mom yet?" Summer asked.

Kimi nodded. "I called. Left several messages and sent her a text." She shrugged. "Now, I have to wait. Unlike my father, my mom is good at calling back. If not within the same day, then by the next at the latest. Unless she's hiking or camping somewhere with lousy cell service."

Worry furrowed Kimi's brow. Takoda wanted to rewind

the clock a few minutes to when she was smiling and happy to be surrounded by trustworthy people determined to help her. Not focused entirely on the dire details of their predicament.

Maybe if they all put their brains together, they could bounce around theories and get one step closer to figuring out what on earth was going on.

"Kimi, if your dad was hiding, any idea where he would go?" Jackson sat across from her. He'd been quiet since he arrived, taking everything in. Studying every answer and response like he was just as eager to uncover the truth.

A professional habit none of them could break.

Kimi shrugged. "He's lived in Bitterroot Falls all his life. I know when my mom was pregnant with Jacy, they talked about moving to the Bigfork Reservation, where she grew up, but they decided against it for some reason. But I know he's not there staying with anyone."

"How can you be sure?" Jackson asked.

"Lieutenant Midthunder from the reservation PD is looking for him, too. Someone there filed a missing person's report, but he won't tell me who." Kimi looked down at her food, her shoulders tensing.

Tak ached to comfort her, but he was always more cognizant, more careful, around the group.

"That must be hard." Seated on the other side of Kimi, Nora put a hand on her arm. "While you wait for your mom to send the necklace," Nora said, changing the subject, "at least you have the book your dad gave you. It might be the key to a lead, right?"

"Where my father is concerned, anything is possible." Kimi slid a look at Takoda.

He pulled on a hopeful smile. "I think the probability it's important is high. I don't buy it was a coincidence he gave you the book and necklace, then disappeared a few weeks later without it being connected."

"I still can't believe the chief pulled you from the case," Declan said to Logan. "With zero explanation."

Logan grimaced and tipped his beer up to his lips. Summer put a hand on his back and rubbed. "The sooner we can get the DNA samples analyzed the better," Logan said. "If the blood turns out to be Thomas's, I'll have a fighting chance of getting it reopened."

"The DCI lab will run it faster," Winter said. "One of us can take it over and have it processed."

"I'll do it," Declan offered. "Tonight."

"Are you sure?" Winter asked. "I don't mind going."

The DCI lab was an hour-and-a-half-drive away in Missoula.

"Go home with Chance," Declan said. "This single guy will take the hit."

Autumn glanced at Declan. The look had been so quick, so subtle, so full of sympathy, that if anyone hadn't been paying close attention, they would've missed it. Tak didn't think there was anything going on between the two since Autumn had a boyfriend. The professor was notably absent tonight, as usual. But part of Tak believed Autumn and Declan would've made a better match.

"How about if you let this single guy do it?" Jackson offered. "I was going to hang around for a few days since I have time, but I can run it to the lab. Sleep at home there. Come back tomorrow and pitch in any way I can to help find Kimi's dad."

"Appreciate it," Declan said. "But if you're coming back tomorrow, you should probably count on staying with Logan and Summer. A nasty storm is coming in. Supposed to hit by late afternoon."

"Hey, Chance, how well do you know Ed Macon?" Takoda asked. Chance was in charge of the IPS Big Sky office, had been in Bitterroot Falls the longest, and had worked on a couple of cases with Macon. It was because of him that IPS had cemented such a strong professional relationship with the BFPD. "I'm trying to wrap my head around why he'd pull Logan from the case the way he did."

Chance finished chewing and wiped his hands on a napkin. "He has a solid history of being trustworthy and on the up and up. I've never heard any whispers of corruption. *But* I do think anyone could be compromised under the right circumstances."

Dissenting opinions rose around the table for a few chaotic minutes.

"Not you," Winter said. She kissed Chance's cheek. "You could never be corrupted. Not for money or power. You're too good. I daresay everyone at this table is."

"What about for love?" asked Autumn, a forensic psychologist who'd once worked as a profiler for the FBI. "I think most of you would do anything to protect the person you loved. Even if it meant compromising yourself. Am I wrong?"

A couple of heads lowered, along with some forks, but no one disagreed.

The hairs along the back of Takoda's neck rose. The bustle slowed, along with everything inside him. The din muted and everyone at the table around him faded, even Kimi. Setting his glass of water down, he surveyed the room. He wasn't sure what he was looking for, and maybe it was nothing.

Look harder and you'll see, Jacy said, his voice razor-sharp.

Two things Tak never ignored: his instincts and the voice

of his dead best friend. Rubbing the back of his neck, he scanned the room again, slowly this time.

Then he spotted it. *Right there.*

At the end of the bar, the section in a corner with dim lighting. Tak's gaze clashed with a cold, dark stare in the mirror behind the bar. A man dressed in a black business shirt and slacks, sitting on a stool. Not a big guy, like the one Kimi had described who'd followed her. This man was tall, lean and hard, the outline of sinewy muscles obvious in the shirt that fit him like a glove. His hair was cropped so low, a tattoo on the back of his head was visible.

The guy cut his gaze from the mirror and picked up his drink. More tats across his knuckles.

Takoda wanted to dismiss the sensation of alarm firing up his nerve endings as paranoia. Perhaps an overreaction. But the feeling wouldn't leave him. In fact, it only intensified the more he thought about it. The mysterious stranger had a distinct hardness about the eyes, one that marked someone devoid of goodness, or empathy, or some might even call it a soul. Sure, he'd crossed paths with bad people and that was part of the reason he couldn't shake this.

Not when he had a nagging sense of familiarity. Tak had never seen him before, but he had encountered his particular type.

Deadly. Someone who would not hesitate to take a life if it got them closer to achieving their objective.

Tak didn't want to inadvertently provoke anything, so he shifted his gaze from the man. Even though he remained hyperaware of his presence, he hoped like hell that guy was not some new giant X factor in their current problem set.

The situation they were dealing with was already big and complicated and didn't need to get any messier. Thomas had hired Takoda to protect Kimi, but the exact nature of the danger, how deep it ran, the number of people involved, and the source of the threat still needed to be cleared up.

Takoda forced himself to tune back into the conversation at the table.

Bo wrapped an arm around Nora's shoulder, and she looked at him like he was the greatest person on the planet. "Autumn made a good point. We'd bend the rules to keep the people we love safe."

Tak turned his attention to Kimi and an ache sliced through him.

She's just my best friend's little sister, he tried to remind himself. Nothing more.

After the kiss this morning, one that had been mutual, making it impossible for him to dismiss his part in it, he was finding it harder to ignore his feelings for her.

Takoda needed to help her, protect her, and not cross the line again.

He flicked a glance at the bar. The tattooed stranger appeared entirely focused on his drink. But Tak knew better.

"Big difference between bending rules and breaking the law," Eli said. "The chief of police made a detective drop a case for no good reason. The question we should be asking is, if Macon is such a good cop, how could he be compromised?"

Chance took another bite of his food, looking around the table. "Well," he said, his tone suggesting the possibility was real, "his wife works for the Cutthroat Creek Mining Company. In human resources."

"Great." Kimi sighed. "How long has she been there?"

Chance frowned. "Maybe thirty years."

"We've got to dig into it," Eli said. "CCMC might have gotten to the chief of police, coerced him or bribed him to drop the case. If they did, we need to know."

Bo nodded. "I agree, but proving it will be hard, and it'll take time. The kind of time Kimi might not have. We should simply operate on the assumption that he's dirty, for now, and once we know she's safe, then we can revisit it. Since the DNA will be processed at the DCI lab, for the sake of expediency, whether or not Macon is on CCMC's payroll doesn't change the landscape other than restricting Logan. We get to the point where someone is caught and can be arrested, I say we call DCI. Meaning you two." Bo gestured to Declan and Winter, and both special agents grinned.

"On the bright side," Logan said, "we were able to get hotel security footage. It didn't shed much light on what happened to Kimi's father, but we were able to pull an image of the man who's been following her. No warrant necessary. Now, we just have to figure out who he is."

"I may know someone who'd be willing to help." Chance set his fork down. "On my last IPS business trip, someone from the Denver office introduced me to a hacker. Guy named Orson. No last name given. Wicked talented. He has a facial recognition program that puts what law enforcement can do to shame, and in less time. But it'll cost us."

Another twinge crawled across the back of Takoda's neck. He looked up and caught the man at the bar staring again. This time the guy held his gaze, steady without blinking, as he finished his drink. Pulled a wad of money from his pocket. Dropped a couple of bills on the bar.

Declan leaned close to Takoda. "What is it?"

Always discreet and alert, Declan had similar instincts, easily picking up on trouble.

"See the guy at the end of the bar. The one with the tats," Takoda whispered, and Declan nodded. "He's been watching us for some reason, and I'm telling you it's not a good one. He's going to try to leave, but we're going to ask him a few questions instead."

Tak and Declan both rose from the table just as the tattooed stranger leisurely lifted himself from the stool and threw on a slim-fit wool coat.

"Where are you going?" Kimi asked.

"Be back in a minute. Need a drink?" Takoda asked, already moving when she shook her head. Takoda went around one side of the table to cut off the guy while Declan approached from the other side to outflank him.

The stranger slipped a hand in his pocket and turned, facing them. He stood still and shook his head once. A sharp and clear motion of warning.

Takoda's gaze dropped when the man flashed the inside of his coat, the hand in the pocket raised slightly, subtly. He noticed the rigid, telltale outline of a gun pressing against the inner lining of the stranger's coat pocket. Not simply a gun. From the length of it, the shape, and the fact only the man's fingers barely fit in the pocket, it was one with an attached sound suppressor.

Plenty of folks in Montana carried a gun.

A *silencer* changed the game. It meant this guy was a professional. A mercenary. A hired gun. Killing a person *was* the mission.

Tak halted several tables away from the man.

Declan spotted it, too, and stopped moving.

The gun wasn't pointed at Tak or Declan. It was aimed in the direction of their table. At Kimi. Where the others sat, five of them with their backs to what was transpiring—all of them vulnerable to being shot.

Impotent fury flooded Tak, hot and fierce. He stood rooted to the spot, not daring to even twitch a finger when there was a gun trained on the people he loved.

The deadly stranger leveled his gaze at him and smiled, the expression full of menace and meaning.

That guy had the upper hand, quite literally with his finger on the trigger, while Takoda and Declan were at a severe disadvantage, even though they had the numbers and firepower on their side.

This was no bluff. No test. It was a checkmate. If they pressed this and tried to confront him, Kimi could take a bullet. Any of their friends or number of innocent bystanders in the restaurant could be killed.

Then chaos would ensue and all bets would be off.

Not going to happen. Not if Tak had the power to prevent it.

With his blood boiling, he watched the man ease backward out of the bar. Staring at them, the stranger strode through the waiting area that was empty and past the hostess station. As soon as the stranger shoved through the front door of the restaurant and headed down the stairs, where he wouldn't have a shot at the bar, both Tak and Declan took off after him. They each drew their weapons along the way.

The cold, hard steel of his Mk 23 in Tak's palm fortified his determination to get that guy. He heard the heavy footfalls of some of the others from their group pounding close on his heels. The unmistakable sound of someone chambering a round into their gun echoed behind him. They burst through the door of the restaurant and raced down the front steps.

Chance, Eli, Winter and Jackson had sprung into action, joining them. Bo's and Logan's instinct would've been to stay at the table, to safeguard their significant others and, of course, Kimi.

Using a hand signal, Takoda directed everyone to split up. Immediately, they fanned out in the parking lot, covering every direction. They peeked in vehicles. Checked every dark corner. Searched behind the restaurant.

No cars sped out of the lot. No sound of anyone running in retreat.

And there was no sign of the tattooed stranger who'd had the audacity to threaten their entire team. To point a gun at Kimi. The man had done so without an inkling of fear. Only a deadness in his eyes and a smile on his face.

In his gut, Takoda knew that this tattooed guy might be the greatest threat.

The one and only consolation was that in the stranger's boldness, he'd exposed himself to the security cameras in the restaurant. Now, they could get a picture of his face to pass to the hacker, Orson. Hopefully, he was as talented as Chance claimed because Takoda doubted the stranger would pop up in normal databases.

This mess Thomas Wheeler had set into motion and dragged them all into kept growing, changing and shifting. Getting deadlier every step of the way.

Kimi had already been followed, attacked, her home tossed and just been in the crosshairs of a new player on the board. All in two days.

Thomas, what have you done?

Whatever happened next, Takoda needed to be ready for it.

Chapter Ten

Tossing in bed, Kimi couldn't sleep. Not for lack of trying.

At first, she was cold in just the T-shirt, so she'd put on the sweatpants that she'd deliberately neglected to wear this morning. Just to mess with Takoda. Or tempt him.

Probably both.

But now she was too warm and still cold at the same time.

She was exhausted, mentally and physically. Being mugged and followed and worried if her father was dead or alive was draining.

Everything could be boiled down to one central problem. She was angry and scared.

Mostly scared. One hundred percent terrified the trouble chasing her was going to catch her and try to kill her.

Not without a fight.

Some people froze when they were frightened. Not her. She usually swung first and asked questions later. As she got older, the jabs became more verbal in nature. Her mom used to say that she should've named her something that meant little warrior instead of little butterfly.

Her phone rang. She glanced at the screen. *About time.* "Hi, Mom," she answered. "Thanks for finally calling me back."

"Kimi, sweetie, you left three messages. Is everything all right?"

Each voicemail had been vague but conveyed a sense of urgency. Every time she tried to think of what to say, it sounded complicated in her head. And scary. The last thing she wanted to do was worry her mother when she had no answers, no idea what was going on, or what had happened to her father.

Too many people were already touched by this. Tonight, the entire IPS team and their significant others had gotten sucked in, too. If she could keep her mother out of it and safe, then she would.

"You know the necklace Dad gave me that I sent to you?"

"Yeah, sweetie. What about it?"

"I need to get it back."

"Oh, I knew you'd come around and want it someday. I know your father is a difficult man to understand, but he loves you."

"Could've fooled me."

Her mom tsked. "Stop that. With the family you're born into, you have to take the love people are able to give and make peace with it."

Kimi lay back and stared at the ceiling, thinking of Takoda. He was loyal. Passionate. Not only in the romantic sense, but in the depth of his convictions.

She suspected a lot of women were attracted to that dangerous air he possessed. But for any of them catching him and holding on to him was the challenge.

"You know," her mom said, "there was a time when you and your dad were really close. You were about nine or ten, and Jacy was a teenager only interested in sports and girls. But you were daddy's little girl. The two of you would collect rocks and test soils and make up codes. Work on those jigsaw puzzles for hours. Do you remember?"

Her heart squeezed. They used to leave each other coded messages and put together 5,000-piece puzzles while her mother baked, painted and played music. Those were the best times. "Yeah. I do. As long as I was interested in something he loved, it was great. The minute I asked him to do something I wanted to do, then he suddenly didn't have the time for me."

Slowly, resentments had fueled anger, and that anger had built a wall between them. One where they'd stopped talking to each other about the things that mattered. Stopped making time to spend together. Letting distance creep in like a terminal disease.

Where was her fight then? Where was her dad's fight? She was just a kid. Wasn't it on him?

"I hope the fact that since you want the necklace back, it means you're ready to forgive your father for all his mistakes and start over."

Nope, sorry to disappoint you, Mom. "Tomorrow, can you send it to me overnight mail?"

"Oh, sweetie, I wish I could, but the necklace is at home."

"The house here in Montana?"

"No, home as in Spokane."

Of course. Davey's place was now her mother's home. "Where are you?"

"Davey and I are still in Hawaii. Didn't I tell you?"

Kimi stifled a groan. "No, Mom. You didn't."

"Well, we are." Her mother's voice was full of glee. "For two more weeks. The weather is perfect. We went scuba diving today. Tomorrow, we're going surfing."

"That sounds like fun." It really did. At least, she was far away from any danger. "Mom, it's important I get the necklace, for reasons I don't want to explain right now, but I need it ASAP."

"Then I guess you're going to have to go get it. You know the address. A spare key is under the big flowerpot with the winter pansies. The code to the alarm is 3543. And the necklace is in my jewelry case in the top-right dresser drawer."

Davey's place was a retreat outside the city, situated atop a mountain on ten serene acres, with a gorgeous view of Spokane Valley, Liberty Lake and Newman Lake.

"Okay." It was Kimi's fault for not keeping the necklace in the first place. She wasn't a kid anymore and she couldn't keep blaming her dad for the status of things between them. Maybe it was time to forgive old grievances. Figure out a way forward with her father. If he was still alive. And if she survived whatever trouble he had gotten her roped into. "I miss you."

"I miss you, too. You should've come out and spent Christmas with us."

"Intrude on the love bubble during the holidays?" She'd visited them once, not realizing what she was walking into with her mom and Davey. They couldn't keep their hands off each other. The idea of being a third wheel again made Kimi cringe. "No, thanks."

"You're my little warrior, not an intrusion. Not ever. I've got to go, sweetie. Davey made reservations for a romantic dinner on the beach, and he doesn't want us to be late."

"What time is it there?"

"Seven."

Three hours behind. "I won't keep you. Enjoy dinner."

"I will. Love you, sweetie, and I hope you'll think about reaching out to your father. It is a two-way street. You and Thomas used to share so much. In a lot of ways, you're both alike. I'm sure you can find common ground."

That common ground was a part of a different life. Her dad was much closer to someone else. "Hey, Mom, do you know if Dad was seeing anyone on the Bigfork reservation?"

"I don't know. We haven't spoken since Jacy's funeral. But it's possible. He knows a lot of people out there. Geology takes him everywhere. I've got to go."

"Bye. Love you."

She hung up and rolled over. Her arm hit something hard. The hardbound copy of *The Wizard of Oz* her dad had given her. After all the commotion at the restaurant, with some armed man watching the group, they had forgotten about the book.

Everyone's focus had shifted to a potential new threat. To make matters worse, the security cameras outside the Wolverine Lodge had been disabled, which most of the group believed substantiated Takoda's theory that the mysterious man with tattoos was a professional. And not the good kind. They had gotten a partial image of the man's face from the surveillance system inside the bar, but the guy had acted aware of the cameras and never turned directly toward them.

Takoda was probably awake in his room waiting to hear back from Orson, the hacker Chance had reached out to in the hope of identifying Mr. Sunglasses and Mr. Tattoos.

Besides, she had doubts about whether the book would even lead to a clue. It was entirely possible her dad had given her a first-edition collection of folktales to remind her of better times between them. When they had been close, like her mom had said.

Sitting up, she grabbed the copy of *The Wizard of Oz* and flipped through the pages slowly. Maybe her father had hidden a message inside. She searched the pages for any markings, any dog-eared sections. Perhaps a handwritten phrase. A word. A number. Any clues scribbled on the inner margins.

Zilch.

She sucked in an irritated breath.

KISS, Kimi. Jacy's voice was loud in her head. *Keep it simple, silly.*

A principle in the military and one her brother had used all the time.

Keep it simple. She ran her hand over the cover of the book. Single-layered foiling. The pages had silver-edged gilding. Then she noticed the way the light from the bedside table lamp hit it. How the edges of the pages shimmered.

Like…palladium instead of silver?

She opened the front flap and examined it. The pastedown had a geometric pattern. There was something about the 3-D shape, but she couldn't pinpoint what was bothering her.

On the title page, there was no note. Struck her as odd. During her formative years, her dad had given her plenty of books, mostly about geology and cryptography, but he'd always inscribed them with her name, the date, the occasion, and signed them.

Kimi turned back to the pastedown and smoothed her palm over the geometric-patterned paper. The notion of damaging a book, a first edition no less, went against the way she'd been raised, but desperate times… She reached into one of her bags and pulled out a metal nail file.

Going slowly, she eased the stainless-steel tip under the corner edge of the leaf attached to the inside of the cover. She shimmied it along the edge until the entire endpaper that had been glued to the board was loosened. Nothing. No hidden message for her.

"This is pointless," she muttered to herself, ready to hurl the book across the room.

Don't stop, Jacy said. *Keep digging.*

Something inside Kimi calmed. "Okay, Jacy."

She flipped the book and opened the back flap. Stared at the same geometric pattern. She ran her palm over it. As smooth and level as the front pastedown. She repeated the process of loosening the endpaper from the board. She peeled back the pastedown. Once again, nothing.

Her dad had given her the book for a reason. It wasn't to remind his thirty-year-old daughter of her childhood. Of that, she was certain.

Kimi held the book and looked at the spine. Opening the front and back covers, she studied the joint, the small groove that ran vertically down the book itself, between the boards and the spine. She opened the book further, bending the joint, and held it up to the light.

Something was in there.

Picking up the nail file, she held the book closer to the light. She shoved the metal tip under whatever was glued inside, pried it loose, and it fell on the nightstand with a clink.

A key. She stared at it. Not anything standard with simple cuts and grooves for the lock in a regular door or to a car. This was smaller than that. Flat. Brass. With unique and intricate toothlike cuts. She'd never seen one like it.

Of course, there was no note telling her what the key was to or what she was supposed to do with it.

Thanks, Dad.

Clearly, her father didn't practice the principle of keeping it simple.

She didn't know what the key might unlock, but Takoda would probably have a good guess.

Swiping the key from the nightstand, she hopped off the bed and went to the door.

Nerves fluttered in her belly and her thighs tingled, all at the thought of seeing him. She hesitated with her hand on the knob.

Being here in Tak's house, sleeping right down the hall from him, the memory of kissing him in the kitchen this morning, was making it impossible for her to continue to pretend.

The butterflies in her tummy, the tingles, the achy, tight feeling that started at her scalp and spread throughout her body, the hot rush of attraction she felt whenever she was in the same room with him. All the visceral physical reactions to him that she was tired of ignoring.

She thought back to the way he'd looked at her in the kitchen. After the kiss. After he told her about the ridiculous promise that he'd made to her brother and intended to keep.

There's a line with you, Kimi, and I can't cross it.

What if she moved the line? Found a way to erase it.

Kimi shoved down her sweatpants and stepped out of them, leaving on the oversized T-shirt with nothing underneath. She tucked the key inside one of the socks she wore and made a decision.

There were plenty of things in the world to be afraid of, and her father had only added more to the list. But when it came to Tak, he was no longer something to fear. Neither was everything he made her feel or want. Not even the possibility of rejection frightened her anymore.

She wanted Takoda Yazzie, and it was up to him to determine what he would do about it. For her, there was no more denying her attraction to him or their chemistry.

No more pretending.

Chapter Eleven

The surveillance footage of the Bitterroot Mountain Hotel the night of the Stracke Group gala showed Thomas running out of the hotel, getting into his two-door, 2002 Ford Bronco, and hightailing down the road. The man with sunglasses was in pursuit.

Within the bounds of bending the rules, Logan had pulled the CCTV footage within a three-mile radius of the hotel for the night Thomas disappeared. Passed it to Takoda.

Sounded like a lot, but in Montana, the CCTV coverage was limited in the largest cities of Billings, Missoula, Great Falls, Bozeman. A drop in the bucket in comparison to some of the most surveilled places in the country like DC or New York. But in Bitterroot Falls and Cutthroat Creek, the number of closed-circuit cameras was sparse, outnumbered by traffic cameras, which were mainly at the busiest intersections.

Takoda had reviewed the footage a dozen times. Both Thomas and the man in pursuit made it beyond the radius of coverage. Only a partial license plate number was visible on the other man's vehicle. A single digit and a letter: 6A. North Dakota plate with the front one not displayed.

Slapping his laptop closed, he cursed the situation. He cursed Thomas Wheeler for endangering Kimi.

And he cursed himself for making the one promise to Jacy he regretted.

But Tak was alive, with a chance for regrets and wants and desires he couldn't slake, while his best friend was buried six feet deep.

"It was supposed to be me," he muttered. "Not you."

Chance had recruited them to join Ironside Protection Services, along with Bo and Eli, all from the RED HORSE Unit. Tak and Jacy had planned their transition from the air force together. To be here in Bitterroot Falls. Close to Kimi. To get her out of trouble when she needed help.

Now, he was following through on the plan for them both.

The knock at his door pulled him from his thoughts.

Kimi.

"Give me a minute." All he had on was a pair of boxer briefs. It was late and he'd hoped she was getting some rest.

He slipped into his jeans, fastened the button and threw on a fitted T-shirt.

A quick glance around to be certain he hadn't left anything embarrassing out, like the photo of her he usually kept tucked away in his wallet. The candid one Jacy had taken the summer before he died.

In the snapshot, Kimi was sitting on a yellow blanket in a field of wildflowers that stretched for miles. The vivid colors of the grass, the flowers, the blanket, her dress, those cowgirl boots she loved so much, contrasted against the backdrop of the snowcapped peaks and the brilliant blue sky. But what had been breathtaking about the photo was her. Kimi in a sexy, purple sundress with thin, delicate straps, her raven hair caught in a soft breeze, her head thrown back in laughter. The 3x5 photo was too small for a frame and a smidge too big to fit his wallet just right. The photo Takoda looked at so often, the edges were crinkled and starting to fade.

Why hadn't Jacy sent a digital version?

Fortunately, he had remembered to put it back in his wallet after he'd stared at it earlier tonight, replaying the mindblowing kiss they'd shared.

He padded barefoot across the room and opened the door. "Tak."

The sight of Kimi standing in his doorway wearing a T-shirt—an even shorter one than this morning—was too much for his willpower tonight.

Geez, just put him out of his misery right now.

"Anything wrong?" he asked.

"I can't sleep. Mind if we talk for a bit?" She peered up at him, the look on her face so warm, so alluring, so… He couldn't quite pinpoint what he saw in her eyes, but whatever it was, he liked it. A lot.

"Yeah, of course." He went to step out into the hall, but she squeezed by him, pressing her soft body against his as she entered his room.

His heart started racing again.

It was so bizarre how his pulse stayed as steady as a ticking metronome when gunfire and explosions sounded off around him or when he chased down a man who had threatened his loved ones, but the second Kimi touched him, his heart beat double-time, pounding frenetic in his ears.

"Let's go to the living room," he suggested. "I can make you a cup of tea or hot chocolate." Anything to get her out of his bedroom.

Staring at him, she chewed her bottom lip, and for some reason, it was the sexiest thing ever. "No, thanks."

"I'll even light a fire."

Her gaze slid to the fireplace in his room.

Another design decision he thought had been ideal at the

time, but he wasn't so sure anymore with Kimi half dressed, standing a few short feet from his bed.

"Light it in here," she said, throwing out the words like a challenge.

"What did you need to talk about?"

She crossed the space separating them and put her palm on his chest. "Have you ever thought about us? Together? Wondered what it would be like if I was yours? And if you were mine?" she asked, and everything inside him tensed and tightened. "Even for one night."

All the time. He couldn't keep her out of his head. The reason none of his relationships lasted was that none of those women could hold a candle to Kimi.

She was so close to him, he felt the soft, feminine heat from her body. Inhaled the scent of honeysuckle in her hair, mixed with the delicate smell of soap on her skin. "Please, don't do this."

"Do what?" Her palm slowly slid up his chest. "We're only having a simple conversation."

Then this conversation was going to test his hold on his less-than-stalwart restraint. Nothing about his deep feelings for her, his desire for her, what he wanted to do with her, was simple.

Backing away, he broke the physical contact between them, but the tension in the room, the electricity in the air, only intensified. He plopped down on his bed and dropped his head into his hands, elbows on his knees. "This is the opposite of simple."

"You make things harder than necessary." She strode over until she was standing in front of him.

He stared down at her sock-covered feet. "Probably."

"I want this. You want this, don't you? So much easier to give in to this thing between us. I don't know, call it chemistry, attraction, whatever. All I know is it's overwhelming when I'm near you, and distracting, invading into my thoughts when I'm not."

"But there's a line," he said, sharp and firm.

"Yeah, yeah, you told me." Kimi stepped in between his legs.

He sat upright to avoid touching her, which had been part of her plan. As soon as he did, she straddled him, sinking down on his lap, her bare thighs pressing against his legs, and wrapped her arms around his neck. He could tell from her eyes, the way her gaze caressed his face, and her light brown cheeks flushed, that her attraction to him was as intense and immediate as his for her. Like radiating from a stoked fire.

"What are you doing?"

"Moving the line." She crushed her lips to his and kissed him.

There was nothing slow or tentative about it, all hunger and urgency, and his brain misfired. She slid her tongue into his mouth, and he groaned, accepting the invasion willingly. Goodness, she knew how to kiss, and he was lost as to why the thought of her doing this with someone else riled him so much.

She rocked her hips against him. Hips that moved in the most aggravating and satisfying way. Before he could process what was happening, his arms were around her and he was kissing her back with all the passion and yearning that had been building inside him.

The sensation of her sweet mouth and her supple body was making him lose his mind. His raunchiest fantasies had nothing on reality. In everything he imagined with her, he often glossed over kissing her. Jumping ahead to the steamy parts where they weren't wearing any clothes. Now he realized that it had been a serious mistake. Colossal.

Her lips on his, their tongues tangling, the way she poured herself into the kiss while pulling his need to the surface, stoking his craving for her, was the hottest thing he'd ever experienced. That spoke volumes considering he lost track of the number of lovers he'd had throughout the years, some of their faces a blur.

Everything about Kimi caught his blood on fire. Her beautiful face, those finely sculpted features, her silky hair, her soft skin, the way she smelled, how she felt in his arms. This incredible, intelligent woman who brought every cell of his body to life with her touch.

This was hell. Or heaven.

Takoda couldn't be certain. She had him spinning in circles and spiraling out of control. He was losing this battle.

His body tightened, straining with want. He grabbed those soft, undulating hips to either stop her or bring her closer, but he slipped his hand under her shirt. His palm glided over her spine along warm, smooth skin. Then lower to her backside.

Her *bare* backside.

Tak jerked his hands away from her like he'd been scalded and wrenched his mouth to the side. "Kimi," he warned, gritting his teeth against the pure pleasure and sheer torture throbbing through him. "You're not wearing underwear." This test was too great, and he was going to fail. "We agreed."

"We did." The same look she had at his door flashed in her eyes again, and this time he could name it—determination and desire. "But your bedroom isn't a common space."

"I need you to back off." His voice pained, his tone pleading.

"Tell me you don't want me." She trailed a string of kisses

across his jaw, down his neck, rocking her hips against him, and he shuddered. "And I will."

He was speechless, unable to lie, unable to utter a single half-truth.

Her lips returned to his, and every reason why she shouldn't be in his arms evaporated. Gone like a wisp of smoke in the wind.

Takoda strained upward, holding her, kissing her harder, plunging his fingers in her hair. He gathered the hem of her T-shirt in his fist to strip it off her, and his doorbell rang.

He stilled, his mouth leaving hers, and she went rigid. His heart was pounding, his breath ragged. Sighing, she dropped her forehead to his shoulder.

The spell was broken. It was a sign. They needed to stop.

The doorbell rang again, three more times, in quick succession. Someone wanted his attention, and it didn't seem as though they were going to leave until they got it.

"I have to answer the door," he said.

"I know." She rolled off to the side, and his body ached at the loss of her on top of him.

Grabbing his Mk 23 from the holster on the floor, he got up and went to see who dared to ring his bell after eleven o'clock at night. After he and the other guys had started working for IPS, they'd each bought a plot of land, not too far from one another. As engineers, they'd designed their homes with the best security features. Privacy film on bullet-resistant windows. External doors made of ballistic steel that could withstand prolonged blunt-force attacks and stop a bullet. Not to mention state-of-the-art security systems with motion-activated lights and security cameras.

He went to the wall-mounted panel near the door. Turned off the alarm. Brought up the camera view of his porch. It was the last person he expected.

Heaving a breath, he opened the front door. "Hey, Dan. What can I do for you?"

Doctor Dan stood with his coat open, showing his green scrubs, his hands stuffed in his pockets. "Is she here?"

"Yeah." Tak stepped aside, letting him in.

Kimi was in the kitchen, standing on the other side of the counter that blocked the lower half of her body.

Tak locked the door and switched on a light in the room. "I'll give you two some privacy."

"No need," DD said. "I won't be staying long."

"What are you doing here?" Kimi asked.

"I went to the hotel, looking for you, but you had checked out. So, I went by your house. I noticed your car parked at your neighbor's. Mr. Simpson told me you were with Takoda. I can't say I'm surprised. I just wish you had been honest with me," he said, his tone scathing.

Talk about awkward. Being privy to their conversation from his bedroom, with the door open, would have been far more comfortable than being quite literally in the middle of it. Tak eased back a bit.

Kimi folded her arms. "I was honest. Always. I know how this looks."

"I thought you didn't need a babysitter."

"I don't. But it turns out I do need a bodyguard."

"So, I was right," the doctor said. "You're not safe. The reason I went looking for you instead of simply calling was because I was worried you might be in some sort of danger. A man snuck into the women's dressing room at the hospital. Broke into your locker. Candace walked in on him. He shoved her into a wall. We had to call the police."

"Oh, my God." Kimi put a hand to her throat. "Is she okay?"

"She will be. No injuries, but she's shaken up. I just

wanted to be sure that you're all right." Dan glanced at Tak. "I see you're right where I thought you'd be. At least, I don't have to worry about you anymore." He turned for the door, hesitated, and looked back at her. "Remember when you told me you kissed him." Dan gestured with his head to Tak. "And you couldn't understand why I wasn't upset?"

Kimi's shoulders twitched, as though she were inwardly squirming. "Because you felt a kiss didn't matter. You were just relieved I didn't sleep with him."

Dan shook his head. "That's what you assumed. I had hoped that while we were on a break, you would sleep with him. Satisfy your curiosity and then we could move forward without me wondering when you two would eventually hook up." Dan stared at her, his face hard, his eyes sad. "I mean, he's the reason you broke up with me, isn't it?"

"There were a lot of reasons."

"But he was one of them, at the very top of the list. Right?"

"Yes." She looked away from the doctor. "But what I feel for him goes beyond curiosity," she said to Dan but now looked Takoda straight in the eyes. "It's been much more than that for a long time, but he doesn't feel the same." She cut her gaze back to Dan. "I never would've cheated on you and, just so you know, the number one reason on my list was that we weren't a good fit. I'm sorry if I hurt you."

"I'm not hurt," Dan snapped, his tone defensive. "Only annoyed. I'm a great catch, Kimi. This is your loss. Not mine." He opened the door, hustled down the porch steps and disappeared into the cold darkness.

Taking a deep breath, Takoda locked up and reactivated the alarm. Everything Kimi said was sinking in, seeping in the cracks and crevices inside his chest. Slowly, he strode into the kitchen and approached her. "I do have feelings for you. Strong feelings."

"They're not the same as mine. Not even in the same league. If they were, nothing would stop you from being with me, and I don't mean just some reckless moment where I'm throwing myself at you. One that you could later dismiss and regret." She hiked her chin up at him and shook her head. "I mean, really be with me. Instead, you want to cling to some promise to Jacy. When this was never his intention. I have to believe that. The only thing that should matter between *us*, is any promise you make to me. But it's not because…" Her eyes turned glassy and she shrugged.

There were things she didn't know. About him. About how Jacy died.

"Kimi." He reached for her, but she backed away.

A tear leaked from the corner of her eye and rolled down her cheek. Something painful twisted deep in his gut.

She swiped at her eyes. "I don't want talk about this anymore."

Relief trickled through him at ending this conversation, but he hated leaving things like this. Unsettled. Uneasy.

Her unhappy and on the verge of tears. Because of him.

Not knowing what to do or say, he fell back on the mission. "Tomorrow, we'll work on tracking down Big Billy Burdock and question Peter O'Donnell about the altercation outside the mine. Okay?"

"No, we won't," she said, her voice firm, her shoulders squared. "Logan or one of the other guys will have to do it."

He leaned a hip against the counter. "Why is that?"

"My mom is in Hawaii for two more weeks. Tomorrow, we're going to Spokane to get the necklace. *Together.*"

She'd spoken to Aiyana. It would've been nice to know that when she'd knocked on his door.

"Nope," Tak said. "It's a five-hour drive." One way, and a polar vortex was going to hit tomorrow. Driving a long distance in bad weather was enough for him to worry about. He had better check his truck, make sure he had all the essentials. "You can stay at Chance and Winter's place while I go get it." She'd be comfortable and, more importantly, safe on the Lady Luck Ranch. Plenty of armed ranch hands lived on the sprawling property. No one would get to her there while he retrieved the necklace.

Kimi folded her arms. "Only one of us knows the address."

"Simple enough to find with a quick internet search." He could have it in under a minute. Not necessarily a good thing how personal data such as home addresses and phone numbers were easy pickings unless you took steps to protect your privacy.

Thinking it over, the ease with which someone could pull up Aiyana Redbird's address made the trip somewhat risky. Anyone watching him take Interstate 90, heading West, might assume that was where he was headed. They wouldn't even have to tail him either.

"What about where to find the key to the house and the necklace? Or the code to the alarm? Since a Google search won't tell you any of those things, I guess it means we're taking a road trip, together."

Tak heaved a breath. Fighting her on this would be futile. "Fine, you can go, but you've got follow my rules. Nonnegotiable. You do what I say, when I say it, no questions asked, and you've got to wear body armor."

"Are you kidding?" she asked, and he shook his head. "Why do I need body armor?"

"We don't know why these men are after you or how far they're willing to go to get whatever they're after. Desperation can push people to extremes. Then there's the guy with tattoos. He won't hesitate to shoot. *Nonnegotiable*, got it?"

"Okay," she said, raising both palms. "I'll follow the rules."

"We'll leave first thing in the morning." Last time he'd checked the weather, the snowstorm was supposed to hit around late afternoon. They should be able to make it back before the worst of it hit. "Grab the necklace and come straight back. No overnight stay." Though he'd ensure they were prepared for anything. "You should go back to your room and get some sleep."

She slinked forward, drawing closer. "I didn't get a chance to tell you everything I wanted to say."

He assumed they were done with that topic. "It's late. Maybe we shouldn't get back into everything tonight." This was a no-win situation for him. "It's like you want me to prove how I feel about you even if it means breaking my word to your brother." He owed Jacy so much, at the very least, to honor his wishes.

"Generally, that's how a relationship works, Takoda. Two people show each other how they feel. Or it isn't real. But that's not what I'm talking about." Kimi crouched down, pulled something out of her sock and dropped it on the quartz countertop with a *ting*. "I found it in the book my dad gave me. Hidden in the joint along the spine."

"Way to bury the lead earlier." He picked up the key and stared at it. Three words were stamped on it: Do Not Duplicate.

"Any idea what it opens?" she asked.

"A safe-deposit box." This kind of key couldn't be mistaken for anything else. He turned it over. "Number 317." He frowned, thinking it through. "But, of course—"

"We don't know which bank or where?"

"Exactly." Too many possible banks to count and Tak doubted it would be a local one. No telling how far Thomas had driven to open a safe-deposit box.

"There has to be a way to find out."

"Possibly." Tak hoped so. "Since Thomas was being so careful, I don't think he had an automatic monthly payment for the safe-deposit box. I can get Eli to dig into your dad's finances for the last year and see if he made a payment to a bank equal to the amount of a year-long rental fee for a box. But if your dad paid in cash, then there won't be a digital trail."

"I can't shake the sense this is so much bigger than we realize," she said.

"No matter what it is, I'll keep you safe. I'd sooner die than let anything happen to you."

Kimi took a deep breath and shivered. "Which terrifies me. I don't want you to get hurt." She looked away from him. "Why would my dad drag me into the middle of this? Does he care about me at all?"

"Of course, he does. Otherwise, he wouldn't have hired me to protect you."

"Then why didn't he just talk to me when we had lunch? Why all the deception?"

Thomas was a difficult man to understand, but he wasn't cold or ruthless. He was sort of nerdy. Socially awkward. But struck Tak as good-natured. Kindhearted. Wouldn't-hurt-a-fly type of man. Not one who would throw his daughter to the wolves to save himself.

"Maybe he was ashamed. Maybe he hoped things wouldn't come to this." There was a reasonable explanation, one that didn't negate a father's love for his daughter. Perhaps Tak had an idealistic perspective since he imagined his parents had been perfect. His family was loving and protective. Honor meant a great deal to them. All his relationships were framed by those core values. "Don't worry." Tak reached out and caressed her cheek. "We'll keep taking this one step at a time and figure it out. *Together.*"

Kimi gave him a sad, soft smile.

And a hard-hitting punch went straight to his chest, cracking something wide open inside him.

The key was the only solid clue Thomas had left for Kimi. One way or another, they were going to find the bank and the safe-deposit box the key unlocked. They had to.

Chapter Twelve

Thanks to an intensification of the polar vortex, arctic air moved in faster than anticipated. It didn't help that they'd driven directly into it either. Despite the storm coming in early, they had crossed the border into Washington in great time, with no delays on the road.

Takoda had packed the truck as though he were prepping for Armageddon. Blankets. Battery-operated lanterns. Binoculars. An EMT trauma kit. Meals ready to eat. Water. Flares. Bolt cutters. Just-in-case overnight bags. Plus, whatever else he had that she didn't know about. He'd wanted them ready for anything.

That included forcing her to wear a bulletproof vest. Not as bad as she had expected it to be. No thick, clunky, sweltering piece of Kevlar. Under her sweater, she wore a concealable ultrathin body armor T-shirt-style vest. Level IIIA, whatever that meant. Something to do with the type of bullets it stopped. It was flexible and lightweight, allowing her to move freely. He'd also given her a crash course, explaining the differences between soft and hard body armor.

The vest she had on was designed to stop all kinds of handgun rounds while the hard type was heavier and offered more protective power against rifle rounds. The fact he'd insisted she wear one at all meant the man with the tattoos had spooked Takoda Yazzie, and that truly frightened her.

The long, uphill driveway to the house stretched before them as they slowly drove through the layer of snow that had accumulated. Kimi found it relaxing to watch the big, heavy, white flakes fall and dance in the fierce wind, but she wasn't eager to get out of the warm truck.

Davey's and her mom's vehicles were sitting in a single file in front of the attached one-car garage.

Tak stopped behind their cars and threw the gear in Park. "Why doesn't one of them keep their vehicle in the garage?"

"They use it for storage. Holiday stuff. Mom's art supplies. Davey's home brewery."

Glancing around, he left the engine running. "I don't like it. The house is so exposed."

Kimi looked out the window. The trees were set far back from the house, which was situated on a large, cleared plot. The opposite of Tak's place. He'd chosen to build his custom home nestled in the woods on the three-acre parcel of land he'd handpicked, only clearing trees to make way for construction.

The strategic placement wasn't something she had ever considered.

His phone rang. The caller ID popped up on the dashboard. Unknown number.

He tapped an icon on the screen, taking the call. "Takoda Yazzie."

"This is Orson. Chance gave me your number last night. He thought it would be faster to contact you directly when I found something."

Kimi and Tak exchanged a look. Hope welled in her chest. They needed a break.

"I take it you did."

"Yes," Orson said, "and *not yet*."

Interesting way of phrasing it, Kimi thought.

"I'm in my truck," Tak said. "I'd rather not talk here. Let me get inside."

"Two minutes. I'll call back."

"Make it ten," Tak said.

"Ten it is." Orson hung up.

Tak shut off the engine and put on his jacket, leaving it unzipped. Setting his cowboy hat firmly on his head, he turned toward her. "Hang back a second," he said, putting a palm on her arm and giving her a hard stare.

Her belly quivered under the heat of that steady gaze. When he looked at her like that, the only thing she could think about was how it would feel to have his hands all over her.

If she loved him—and she was *in love* with him—wasn't she entitled to at least one night in his arms? One night he wouldn't look back on with regret.

Tak hopped out of the truck, shutting the door. He took the binoculars from his jacket pocket and walked around, scanning the area.

Waiting for him, Kimi slipped on her winter gear—knit hat, down-filled parka, gloves—and tugged the hood of her coat over her head. A few minutes later, Takoda appeared outside the passenger-side door, squinting against the pelting snow.

He opened the door for her, letting in a biting rush of wind. Kimi climbed out of the truck, set her foot on the running board and slipped. She might have fallen out of the truck if not for Tak catching her, wrapping his arm around her and setting her down.

"Oh, thanks." With her palm on his solid chest, she glanced up at his handsome face and laughed off the instant heat the close contact made flare.

He grinned. "You okay?"

She nodded. "Yeah. Clumsy of me."

Keeping his arm around her, he shouldered the door shut and tried to shield her from the whipping wind and fierce fall of flurries as they trudged the rest of the way up the long driveway.

"Aren't you freezing with your coat open?" she asked.

"I want to be able to draw my weapon quickly if the need arises. A little cold for a couple of minutes won't kill me."

"No, but it might give you pneumonia."

Another grin that had her using the wind as an excuse to snuggle closer.

They crossed the yard to get around to the front door.

"The key is under that flowerpot," Kimi said, pointing to the largest one that was painted blue.

He lifted it and grabbed the key. "Not the best hiding spot." He unlocked the door, held it open, ushering her inside, and closed it with the next gust.

The alarm beeped, thirty seconds of warning to let the homeowner disarm the system.

Out of the freezing cold, she stomped her feet and shoved her hood back before stepping farther into the house. She went to the security panel and entered the code, and the beeping stopped.

"Let's get what we came for," he said. "Where is the necklace?"

Tugging off her gloves, she led the way through the house. It had a large, open floor plan, with the bedrooms at the back. They passed the dining space with its oversize sliding-glass doors overlooking the valley. She understood why her mother loved being out there. The place was a rare gem. Beautiful and peaceful.

Though to her, she preferred Takoda's house and view.

His land felt different. Sunrises and sunsets were the best. He'd picked a great spot. No matter the season, it was a picture-perfect postcard of a slice of heaven.

Since the last time she'd been in Spokane, Davey had given her mom free rein to redecorate. It looked like a completely different house. New furniture and curtains, fresh coat of paint. Artistic touches of Aiyana Redbird hung on almost every wall. Her mother had a special gift to be able to touch a person's soul with her paintings. The great Thomas Wheeler, with his magical sixth sense, could find palladium. Even Jacy had been gifted. Her brother could build anything.

Kimi always wondered if she had a gift. On the rodeo circuit, she'd recognized she had a little talent and a lot of luck. Maybe it was healing people. Jacy inspired her to become a nurse, but a career in medicine felt like her true calling.

In the primary bedroom, she went to the dresser and turned on a floor lamp beside it. Opening the top-right drawer, she found the jewelry case exactly where her mom said it would be. The necklace was in a velvet-lined section of the box. She held it up by the chain and the oblong pendant dangled. Fine silver glinted in the light from the lamp, and she looked over the intricate, colorful etching of a butterfly. No denying it was pretty.

The phone rang. Unknown number again. Orson.

Takoda set the cell on the dresser and put the call on speaker. "What do you have?" he asked, taking the necklace from her.

"The photos of both persons of interest you guys sent were pretty worthless. The sunglasses covered most of one guy's face. Since you said that he's been spotted over the past several days, I tapped into the surveillance footage of the local gas stations. Not many between Bitterroot Falls and Cutthroat Creek. Cross-referenced his image with one you gave me of his vehicle. Found him. Of course. Everyone goes to a fueling station eventually and they all have cameras. His name is Fred Foley. He works for Red Sentry Stronghold."

Takoda stopped examining the pendant, his brow furrowing. "The private security firm?"

"Yep. His vehicle is registered to them as well."

"Then someone must've hired him," Kimi said.

"There's another person on the line?" Orson asked.

"Yes, sorry," Tak said. "Kimi Wheeler. She's the woman I was hired to protect. It's just the two of us."

"Next time, state if the call isn't private at the beginning," Orson said, his tone sharp with irritation. "I breached Red Sentry's firewall. Didn't take much effort. I would *not* recommend their services. Anyway, Red Sentry assigned Foley to work for a shell corporation. While I was in their system, I noticed he's not the only one. Steve Higgins is also on the same contract."

"I was attacked by two men in Kimi's house. Now we know who the second guy is." Tak fiddled with the pendant, a dull *snick* sounded and a hidden mini flash drive slid out.

They exchanged a quick glance.

"Any luck finding out who owns the shell corporation?" Takoda asked.

Orson went into explaining shell corporations, dummy companies, and the layers of protection.

On a closer look of the flash drive, she noticed it wasn't a regular USB but a Type-C—the kind you could pop into an android phone.

What on earth had her father put on it?

"The owner has taken several clever steps to hide their

identity," Orson said. "But I got a name for you. Bill Burdock."

"The loan shark?" Kimi wondered aloud.

With a similar puzzled expression, Tak slipped the flash drive back into its hiding place and handed it to her. She tucked it away in the pocket of her jeans.

"Since Red Sentry is based in North Dakota and these fellas are out-of-towners," Orson said, "I took the liberty of finding out where they were staying. You're welcome. First, they were checked in at the Goldeneye Inn off Route 93, just outside of town. The inn looks like a dump, but then they upgraded big-time to the Bitterroot Mountain Hotel two nights ago."

Goose bumps erupted over her skin. "They knew I was staying at the BMH. What would've happened if you didn't bring me to your house?"

Tak put a hand on her forearm, and his touch calmed her fear.

"Thanks, Orson," Tak said. "At least with some names, we know who we're looking for and can get the cops to pick them up."

Logan was free and clear to bring in Foley and charge him for mugging her. Too bad they couldn't prove that Higgins had broken into her house, but surely Logan had enough to question him. "What about the third guy?" she asked. "The one with the tattoos."

Orson whistled. "Talk about tricky. None of the photos that you guys sent had a good shot of his face. Running through my regular facial recognition program wouldn't have worked. So, I had to get creative. You all stated you had never seen him before. I figured he was from out of town also and had to sleep somewhere. The Goldeneye and Bitterroot Mountain Hotel were a bust. The next closest place was Lariat Suites. Hacked their front desk camera and bingo. He checked in yesterday morning. Rented a black Lincoln Navigator from the Missoula airport."

"The first day this guy is in town, finding me is at the top of his list of things to do?" Find her? Question her? Hurt her?

"I think it was about simply finding you," Tak said. "He was scoping out the group. Seeing what he was dealing with. Just one bodyguard or several." Takoda scrubbed his hand over the scruff on his jaw. "Orson, please tell me this means you have a name for this guy."

"Now we've reached the *not yet* part I mentioned earlier. The thing is, I dug up five different names with licenses and passports for him. All aliases. Names of dead people. His true identity is unknown for now. This guy is a ghost."

Kimi stared at Tak. His brow wrinkled with worry.

"What does that mean exactly?" she asked with a sinking sensation in the pit of her stomach.

"It could mean a couple of different things. He has a powerful friend somewhere, looking out for him. Or…" the hacker said, dragging out the word and the suspense, "he did an excellent job of erasing his identity at a very early age. But if he's an active professional, like you suspect, then someone knows about him. In either case, the next best place for me to look is in the dark folders of government agencies. FBI, Homeland Security, CIA. See if I can get a hit on him with the better photos I have from the motel. I've cracked some of their systems before, but I'm talking years ago. Don't get me wrong, I can do it again. The trick is doing it without getting caught. They've wised up and are smart enough to lay traps for people like me who can get through. May take longer than you like. But it'll be double my original fee to do it."

Kimi shook her head. *Too much money*, she mouthed.

"Give us a minute," Tak said. He muted the call. "It's worth it to know who we're dealing with. Right now, whoever this guy is, this ghost has us at a disadvantage. I don't want you to worry about the expense. If Chance won't cover the cost from IPS funds, then I'll pay the bill."

Part of her wanted to hug him for his generosity. A more practical part of her wasn't sure it was the best way to proceed. "It's a lot of money." They had already burned through the retainer, plus used IPS funds. Orson was expensive. Thorough and fast and worth it, but expensive. "There's also risk to Orson by hacking into government sites. Knowing the name of this ghost won't tell us who he's working for or minimize any threat he might pose." Shaking her head, she remembered something Bo had said last night at dinner. "It doesn't change the landscape of what we're dealing with." A dangerous man. Knowing his name wouldn't make a difference. "I say, let's focus on Burdock. See if Logan or IPS can find him and tell us what is going on."

She could tell by his grimace that he didn't like it, but he nodded.

Tak took the call off mute. "Orson, we're going to hold off. For now. If we change our minds and decide we need you to press forward, we'll let you know."

"No problem. Here's my number." The hacker passed it along and Tak programmed into his phone. "Remember, it will take time, and I'll need my fee wired in advance."

"All right. Understood. Thanks." Takoda ended the call. "I want to get out of here and on the road." He turned off the lamp and peeked through the curtain out the window. "It's really starting to come down. You can see what's on the flash drive after we hit the interstate."

As they walked back through the house, Tak's head swiveled as he looked out every window they passed. Near the front door, he pulled a curtain back and looked around outside while she set the alarm. The security system began the one-minute countdown before it was activated.

He stepped outside first. Kimi pulled on her gloves, crossed the threshold, and shut the door. A blast of snow whooshed over her.

She locked it. "Ready?" she asked, pointing to the heavy flowerpot so he could lift it and she could replace the key.

He held up a fisted hand, instructing her to hold in place and be quiet. A military gesture she had seen enough times in movies to understand its meaning.

Takoda scanned the area, and she hoped it was out of an abundance of caution, and not because anything was actually wrong.

How much and how far could he see with the awful wind blowing the heavy snowfall, obscuring their vision a few hundred feet from the house?

Time stretched, each second that ticked by an agonizing eternity as she shivered in the cold. Finally, he lowered his hand and lifted the flowerpot.

"What was it?" She set the key down on the perfect, snow-free circle of concrete.

"Not sure." He put the pot down. "I had a feeling, not sure how to explain it. And with the wind, I can't see if there are any other footprints in the snow besides ours." Slipping an arm around her, he ushered her off the stoop. "Just being careful."

She shoved her gloved hands into her pockets and was about to take a breath of relief when he glanced back over his shoulder and then urged her to hurry across the yard.

A shiver rushed down her spine, like the icy fingers of

a ghost. "What's wrong?" she asked over the howl of the wind, anxiously trying to look behind them.

In response, he drew his weapon and shoved her forward ahead of him.

It was the only warning she received before he yelled, "Run!"

A clap of thunder cracked through the roar of wind and one of the flowerpots on the stoop exploded.

Not thunder. The boom was a gunshot.

Gunfire kicked up snow around them, bright muzzle flashes erupting through the snowy haze.

She bolted across the yard, heading for the driveway, praying she didn't slip. Snapping a fast look over her shoulder, she spotted them. Two muscular men in black had emerged from around the other side of the house, bounding through the snow. One she recognized—her shadow with sunglasses, Fred Foley. The other guy must've been Steve Higgins.

Takoda fired back, the shockingly loud sound of his weapon, so much closer to her, splitting the air. She made it to the driveway and raced down the slick pavement.

Gunfire pinged off metal, sparks flaring in the swirling gusts of snow. She screamed. Cringing, she ran, trying to make herself as small a target as possible, covering the back of her head with her hands. Her breath caught in her lungs, jammed there as she braced for the shattering sound of more gunshots.

Bullets slammed into the side of Davey's car, setting off the alarm. Her mom's headlight burst. The muscles in Kimi's stomach tensed until she felt sick.

Fear coiled in her chest, throbbing behind her sternum, but not for herself. *Tak, please be okay. Please.*

Looking over her shoulder, she saw Takoda. He was on

his feet, hustling in her direction as he fired back at the two men.

"Don't stop!" Takoda called out.

Kimi didn't need to be told twice. More shots came in quick succession. She scrambled along the driveway. Her heart knocked against her ribs as she approached the truck. She hit an icy patch and slipped. Throwing her arms out to her sides, she regained her balance. Pressed on. Didn't slow down.

A buzzing came from behind her, grew louder and louder, and then swooped right over her head. Kimi glanced up into the falling snow. A drone streaked past her and then flew higher, ascending, circling back toward the gunfire.

The truck's lights flashed on, the engine starting remotely with a satisfying grumble. She hurried around the front of the truck, to the passenger-side door, flung it open, and climbed inside. Slamming the door closed, she watched Takoda shooting back.

One man in black dropped, but he was still moving, crawling through the snow.

Tak raced to the truck and hopped in behind the wheel. Everything inside her released. He jerked the gear into Reverse and sped down the driveway. Snow kicked up around them, spitting into the air.

Tak put a hand on her shoulder and shoved her head down behind the dashboard. Once the rear tires hit the street, the rear end of the truck fishtailed in the snow with a screech. He slammed the pickup into Drive, stomped on the accelerator and zoomed down the street.

He checked the rearview and side mirrors, but something caught his attention outside her window and then he swore.

"What now?" she asked, staring up at him, crouched in an awkward position.

"I just spotted a black Lincoln Navigator parked on the other street at a higher elevation. It has a view of Davey's property."

"The ghost?"

He shook his head. "I can't be sure. I only caught a glimpse of the vehicle."

"The drone."

"Drone? What drone?"

"There was a drone that flew right over my head. Someone had to be operating it. Sure wasn't the guys shooting at us."

Takoda swore again.

"Is it safe? Are they following us?"

He checked the mirrors once more. "I think we're okay. I shot one of them. Probably slowing them down. If the ghost was out there, too, then he'll make time to get the drone before following us." He shifted in his seat and groaned.

As she glanced over at him, she noticed his arm. His sleeve had a hole and there was blood.

Panic threatened to squeeze the air from her lungs. She forced herself to breathe. "You're bleeding."

"I'm aware. Consequence of being shot."

"We need to pull over." She scanned the street for a spot where they could stop. "I have to check you."

His gaze bounced up to the rearview mirror. "No. I want to make that light," he said, pointing at the traffic signal.

Reluctantly, she nodded as he stomped on the gas, racing through a yellow light that was turning red, and made a hard left onto the access road that would eventually lead out of town.

"Tak—"

"No! We can't stop. They found us. Even though I was laser focused on ensuring we didn't have a tail on our way here. But they still popped up. Must have spotted us taking I-90 and pieced it together. We can't stop. Not yet. Not until we're a good distance away and I know you're safe. I'll be fine." He gave her a calm, reassuring glance that did little to quell her growing worry for him.

Chapter Thirteen

Pushing the speed limit as much as he dared on I-90 East, Takoda focused on the road, keeping his grip steady on the wheel despite the excruciating pain in his arm and situational awareness vigilant.

No tail.

Not that they needed to follow close behind them if those men thought they would be headed back home.

"You're losing blood," Kimi said, her voice calm. "I need to check the wound."

"Not yet." She'd already been exposed to crossfire back at the house. His injury would have to wait.

"The storm is getting worse. We have to stop anyway. Driving through it with you injured is nuts. We need to find somewhere I can examine you and we can ride out the blizzard until it's over," she said, but he didn't respond. "Tak!"

She was right. He would be useless to her if the bullet had hit an artery and he passed out from blood loss.

"Okay." They would cross the state line into Idaho within minutes. "It has to be in a large city. It'll make it harder for anyone to find us." They'd reach Post Falls first, but he'd prefer one that was bigger. "We'll head to Coeur d'Alene. On your phone do a Google search. Look for a hotel, but not right off the freeway. And we need a parking garage close to it. In case they search the lots of the hotels, they won't see my truck parked there. Probably faster if you pinpointed the garages first."

Nodding, she said, "Got it." She took her phone from her coat pocket. It didn't take her long. "I found something. A city parking garage in the heart of Coeur d'Alene near the lake. There's an inn about a five-minute walk away."

Five minutes in this weather with a gunshot wound, hauling supplies, would feel like fifty. But they had no choice. "All right."

The adrenaline pumping through him cooled and the pain in his arm bloomed as they drove sixteen minutes, a little less than fourteen miles, before she directed him to get off the interstate.

"Take exit 13," she said, and he did. "At the bottom of the off-ramp, make a right."

He followed her directions to the garage and parked on the second level even though there were spots on the first. Gritting his teeth against the pain, he grabbed the EMT kit housed in a discreet black backpack. Then he stuffed a couple of MREs and water in one of the overnight bags and locked the truck.

"Give me the pack," she said.

"No, I've got it."

"This isn't the time to be chivalrous. You're hurt. I can carry the kit on my back with no problem since I wasn't shot in the arm and can hold one of the overnight bags. That'll free you up to cover us if necessary." She held out her hand, eyes gleaming with a resolve that wouldn't take *no* for a response.

Her insistence to help him meant more than he cared to admit.

Not wanting to push himself until he knew how bad his

injury was, he swallowed his pride and let her take the trauma kit.

She slid her arms through the straps, putting the pack on her back, and took the lighter overnight bag. Snaking one of her arms around his waist, she held on tightly to him.

"Nothing wrong with my legs, you know."

Her only response was to roll her eyes.

The cold, biting wind ripped through him as they trekked the quarter mile through the snow to the Arrow Point Inn.

He took money out of his pocket and stuffed the bills in her hand. "When we get inside, you go to the front desk and get us a room. I'll hang back," Tak said, and she glanced at his bullet hole and blood on his jacket. "Pay in cash and register under a fake name so we can't be tracked." The way things had escalated back at the house, turning into a shoot-out, he didn't want those men to know where to find her.

"Got it."

Inside the warm entrance, he took the overnight bag from her and headed to the sitting room adjacent to the foyer while she strode up to the front desk. Takoda kept Kimi and the front door in his sights. An older man at the desk was all smiles as he chatted with her, only glancing over once in the direction of the sitting room. Tak tipped his Stetson in greeting and the white-haired man appeared satisfied.

Six minutes later, Tak met her at the staircase.

She held up the key to room twelve. "Come on. Second floor."

They headed up the steps.

"Did he ask why I didn't check in with you?"

"Before he could, I told him you were in a bad mood." She removed her hat and gloves. "Triple whammy of the snowstorm hitting early, low blood sugar, and that we had a fight. He was very sympathetic."

"As beautiful as you are, I'm sure he was."

She grinned at him.

He followed her to the last door at the end of the hall and stared at the placard. "The bridal suite?"

"The place is empty. Off season and the storm. And I did say he was sympathetic."

She unlocked the door. They stepped inside the large room and dropped their bags.

The four-poster, king-size bed dominated the space. He looked around. Outdated wallpaper. Original hardwood floors. Floral designs on the area rug and comforter fabric. Adjoining bathroom. Gas fireplace. A small bistro-style table for two with chairs was tucked in a corner near a window and the fireplace.

They could've done much worse.

"A little chilly in here," she said, rubbing her hands together.

He set his hat on a nightstand. "Since the place is empty, they probably have the temp set low to save on the heating bill."

After she took off her coat, she started the fire. "It should warm up in here relatively quickly." She pulled her sweater over her head and quickly stripped off the body armor vest, leaving her in a tank top and bra. A sigh of relief slipped from her lips and she stretched. Kimi came over to him and helped him ease his jacket off. She studied the jacket sleeve. "There's no exit hole. The bullet is still in your arm."

Meant she'd have to dig it out. It was going to hurt like hell.

"We can go to the hospital," she offered. "When I was looking for a place for us to stay, I found one. Twelve-minute drive from here."

"Plus, there's the time it'll take to get the truck and the

wait to be seen. We both know a gunshot wound has to be reported to the police. Unwanted attention we don't need. You can take care of it."

"I can, but I only mention it because there won't be any anesthetic in the kit."

At least she didn't offend him by asking the question that was clearly on her mind.

"Don't worry about me. I can handle the pain."

Pursing her lips, she riffled through her purse and took out an elastic hair tie. Gathering her hair up, she put it in a messy bun and secured it with the black band. She grabbed the med kit and put a hand on his lower back, steering him into the bathroom.

Lowering the toilet seat lid, she said, "You know the drill."

He sat, eager to get it over with.

Kimi handed him a packet of pain reliever tablets and a bottle of water.

While he popped the pills and washed them down, she laid out supplies on the counter and tugged on latex gloves. Turning to him, she unbuttoned his flannel shirt.

"I've got it," he snapped.

She slapped his hand away and peeled the shirt off carefully. Underneath, he wore a long-sleeved compression thermal that fit him like a second skin. "I'm going to have to cut it off." Crouching down, she rummaged through the bag. "Great. No scissors."

He unsheathed his MAMU knife he had secured at his waist, flipped it in the air, catching it by the blade, and offered her the handle. "Be careful. It's very sharp."

Taking it, she smiled, and as usual, the sight left him breathless.

She plucked the material away from his skin and sliced.

The knife slashed through the shirt with ease. She did the same with the back. As she slowly peeled off the sleeve from his injured arm, he gave the other side a simple tug and it fell.

Leaning over, she inspected the wound. His skin prickled with warmth at her proximity.

"The good news is the bullet isn't near your brachial artery. I'll remove it and then clean the wound. Take off your pants."

What? "Why?"

"It's going to bleed. A lot. It'll ruin your jeans."

Nodding, he said, "Okay." Deep down, he wondered if it was a bad idea. Having on fewer clothes around her was never good.

"Right now, I'm in nurse mode. Chop. Chop." She clapped her hands, snapping him into action.

Kicking off his boots, he unzipped his jeans and stripped out of them. With only his boxer briefs and socks left, he sat back down.

Her gaze raked over him, landing on the holstered Ruger strapped to his ankle before bouncing back up to his face. The entire time her expression read *pure professional*.

Grabbing a towel, she draped it over his lap. She opened the packaging of the sterilized forceps. "Can't rush this. I'll need to go slowly. It's better if we don't stop once we get started and get it done."

"Go ahead. Just do it."

"Here we go." She shifted his arm toward the light, peered closer, and stuck the forceps in the wound.

Agony flared white-hot. Shutting his eyes, he gritted his teeth and focused on breathing. As she dug around, trying to get a hold on the bullet, the pain splintered and bloomed. He clutched his knee, went somewhere else in his mind.

Heard the ocean, felt the warmth of the sun and grains of sand beneath his feet, saw Kimi on the beach, smiling at him. Holding his hand. Stroking his face. Calling his name.

"Takoda, I got it."

He opened his eyes to see her holding the bullet with the forceps.

"It's all in one piece," she said, dropping the bloody slug in the trash and the forceps in the sink. Blood poured from his wound and she pressed a piece of gauze to it. "Ready to irrigate it?" She grabbed the saline solution.

"There should be hydrogen peroxide in the kit."

"Saline is better. Hydrogen peroxide can damage the skin, and it'll only delay healing. Trust me, I know what I'm doing."

"Sorry. You're the expert," he said. "You know, Jacy always thought medicine was your calling. I think he was right."

Her brow wrinkled in doubt. "Really?"

"Yeah. He said you had healing hands. After you breezed through your degree and I saw how much you loved being a nurse, I thought you'd go on to med school. Become a doctor."

Something flashed across her face as she held his gaze, and then it was gone. "Brace yourself."

Freezing-cold saline blasted into the wound.

"Geez!" Clenching his jaw, he fisted a hand. "That hurt worse than taking out the bullet."

She dabbed at the blood leaking from the hole in his arm. "Stitches won't be possible. These kits don't usually come with sutures." She held up a skin stapler. "Breathe through it."

He nodded. Instead of shutting his eyes this time, he stared at her face while she worked.

Kimi held the sides of the wound together and pressed in the first staple.

A sharp pang arced through him and he ground his teeth. Found his center as he looked at her, memorizing every detail. Her smooth, light brown skin. The way the light hit her, bringing out the hints of brown in her hair and flecks of copper in her eyes. The sultry curve of her lips. How intently she focused. The steadiness of her hands.

She was so beautiful it made his heart ache.

"All done," Kimi said.

He looked at the three staples in his arm. Barely felt the last two.

She wet a washcloth with warm water, cleaned the blood from him, stroking his skin with such tender care, and leveled that bright brown gaze on his face. He fought a rush of need, a familiar struggle, but found it hard to suppress. It was then he realized this attraction, this desire, had been seeping into the cracks and fissures of his armor like the water that freezes inside a rock, expanding and breaking it apart.

Lowering his head, he was at a loss, his restraint so close to shattering.

"Just in case," she said, placing a hemostatic dressing over the wound with adhesive. "It'll prevent any further bleeding."

"You did a great job. Thank you."

"Anything for you." She gave him a quick kiss on the lips.

Surprised, pleasantly, he stilled. "Please, don't tell me you give all your patients kisses."

"Why? Would it make you jealous?"

"Yes." The word slipped from his mouth without thinking.

Grinning, she plucked off her gloves. "Well, I'm all out of lollipops." She kissed him again. "So lucky you."

A knock sounded at the door.

Tak grabbed his gun from the holster on the floor and was on his feet.

Kimi put a hand on his chest. "Relax. It's only Jim. He offered to bring up some chili to get your blood sugar up. He didn't want me to have to deal with Mr. Grumpy Pants in the bridal suite."

Narrowing his eyes, he followed her to the door. "We have MREs."

"Ugh. That's not real food."

"May not be good, but I guarantee it's real." He checked through the peephole, verified it was the older man from the front desk and no one else was in the hall. Then he nodded.

She opened the door and he stayed behind it, gun in his hand. "Thank you so much, Jim. This is really kind of you."

"The sooner you can get your husband in a good mood, the better. This is a family recipe sure to please the pickiest eater. Enjoy your night, nuzzled up close in the best room in the house."

Kimi stepped back, holding a tray of food. Two bowls of chili covered with plastic wrap, bread rolls, a bottle of sparkling apple cider and two mugs.

Tak shut the door. "Husband, huh?"

She shrugged. "I told him we were married. Anne and Guy Drury."

"Guy? Very original. Whatever story you spun certainly worked to win him over."

She set the food on the table. "I was convincing when I spoke about you being my husband." Looking up at him, she flattened her hands on his bare chest. Skimmed her fingers back and forth over his skin.

His insides churned with need. "What exactly did you say?"

"That we were newlyweds." Her hand slid up to the base of his neck. "And we were coming from my mom's house." Her thumb slid over his chin and jaw.

Each gentle stroke was driving him wild. "And?"

"There was a fight. An ugly one. And for a few frightening moments, I thought about what it would be like to lose you." Tears glistened in her eyes, and his heart squeezed. "It would kill me, Takoda." She stepped closer, bringing their bodies flush. "One of us, both of us, could've died today. I don't want either of us to leave this world without knowing what it's like for us to be together. But with no regrets."

Risking his life, facing death, never bothered him. Not until Kimi. His existence was punctuated the day he'd met her, everything redefined—there was simply before Kimi and after Kimi. She was the reason he wanted to plant roots in Montana. In Bitterroot Falls. To be near her. It was impossible for him to say when he'd fallen in love with her. The only thing he knew for certain was that every day he wasn't with Kimi, he felt a stab of hunger for her and found nourishment at the very sight of her.

He wanted her and not for one night. A lifetime with her wouldn't be enough.

Wrapping his arms around her warm body, he cupped her face in his hand and let go of every good argument about why he should stay away from her.

Awareness, attraction, need—something electric vibrated in the air and licked over his skin. She rose on the balls of her feet, bringing his mouth to hers, and the last bit of control holding him back crumbled. All his rules, the promises he'd made to everyone else, faded away.

Tak inhaled her scent, drawing her closer. She kissed him harder, deeper, while her hands went exploring. Lifting a leg, she caught it behind his knee. Rubbed and writhed her body against him, luring him in and turning him on like no one else.

She drew one palm slowly down between them, slipping a hand in his boxer briefs and cupping him. "You were shot, had the slug removed without any anesthetic, the wound stapled, and you're still *up.*"

"I've never been so up in my life."

She squeezed, and he groaned. "You like my touch?"

"You have no idea what that does to me. What you do to me." He kissed her, taking possession of her mouth, running his hand over the curves of her body. Heat overwhelmed him. Easing his lips from hers, he caressed her face. "I want you. This. Us." He met her gaze, and she smiled, lighting up parts of him that he didn't even realize existed. "No regrets," he vowed.

Chapter Fourteen

The bubble of euphoria gradually leveled off in the after-glow. Kimi nestled her head on Takoda's chest. His good arm was wrapped around her, holding her close as they lay in bed, their legs tangled. Every muscle in her body was relaxed. She'd had sex before, but this was the first time she'd ever made love. Experienced something so deep, it moved her heart. Touched her soul. Made her want to connect in every way possible to another.

To him.

Tak played in her hair and brushed his lips across her forehead. "How do you feel?"

"Relieved." Finally, he'd made love to her, and he wasn't running away from her afterward. They were going to do this. Be together or try to, anyway. "And happy." Which was strange, considering everything else going on. "But I should be asking you that." She leaned up on her elbow and looked down at him. "How's your arm?"

"Sore, but it'll be fine."

"You should ice it. There was an instant cool pack in the kit." She went to get up, but he tightened his grip on her.

"Later. I don't want to ice it now."

"Then what do you want?"

He cupped her breast and kissed her. "I'll give you three guesses."

She smiled. Reaching over him, she grabbed his wallet from the nightstand that he'd put there before they had gotten too far earlier without using protection. "Let's see if you have any more condoms." Apparently, he had some on him at all times. *Wildfire through dry brush.* Well, not anymore. Now, he was hers. Opening his billfold, she noticed a photograph hidden inside. "What's this?"

"Don't look at that," he said, trying to take it from her.

Sitting up, she leaned away from him. "Carrying around a picture of an old girlfriend?" Jealousy spiked through her and she instantly wanted to burn it. Kimi pulled out the photo and shock washed over. It was of her…when she'd had a picnic with Jacy. Their last picnic together. "Why didn't you want me to see it?"

He sat up and shrugged. "It's embarrassing. That I've been carrying your picture around for years. Looking at it, at you, way more than I'll ever admit."

Her heart ballooned to near bursting. All this time, he'd had a thing for her, and she hadn't realized. "How did you get this?"

"Jacy sent it to me. With a note that simply said I had *missed out on the best day.*"

She smiled. "It had been a great day. Perfect weather. Warm and balmy. The only thing missing was you," she said, thinking back on it. "Funny thing is, when he took this picture, we were talking about you. Jacy was trying to convince me to leave the rodeo circuit. Stay home. Go into medicine. I said, *Marry Takoda and have a few kids.* Pretended to be joking, and I laughed. That's when he snapped the photo. But I was secretly serious. A fantasy I didn't think would ever be reality because you never showed the slightest interest in me. And do you know what Jacy told me?"

"Stay away from me?"

"No. He told me I could do a lot worse than you. That you were a good man, the best guy he'd ever known, and he couldn't think of anyone else he'd rather have as a brother. I thought that was his way of giving me his blessing."

It is time. Jacy's voice in her head was clear but faint. *Time for me to stop standing in the way.*

Kimi smiled, hoping it really was her brother talking to her, telling her he thought this was right. "I had planned to test the waters with you when you got back from the deployment, but then…"

"Jacy died."

She nodded. "I just don't understand why he would make you promise not to be with me when he was giving me the green light. At least, I thought he was." It still made no sense. "When did he ask you to give your word not to touch me?"

"After I first met you and he saw the way I looked at you."

"What?" she said in disbelief. That was a lifetime ago. "I was barely a woman, running wild, looking for trouble. Jacy had been right, back then, to keep us apart." Neither of them had been ready for anything serious. Takoda had still had lots of wild oats to sow, and she'd needed to figure out who she was, what she wanted. "Jacy didn't send you a photo of me and him, the two of us together. I think he sent you this picture of just me as his way of releasing you from your promise." They had both grown and matured and understood what was at stake.

"A part of me felt like he was teasing me. Taunting me with that picture of you, looking so sexy. So beautiful. Which would've been cruel. Jacy was never cruel. I should've known better. Your theory makes more sense."

"Yes, it does." She leaned in and kissed him. "And you don't have any more condoms."

Squeezing his eyes closed, he groaned.

Kimi figured she'd torture him for a couple of hours before letting him know she had an emergency stash in her purse.

"Hey, um, we need to talk." He shifted in the bed, angling toward her, and took her hand in his. "There's something I need to tell you." His expression turned serious.

Taking a deep breath, she prepared herself. As long as he didn't have a secret wife somewhere, whatever he needed to tell her, she could handle it. "What is it?"

"It's about Jacy."

He hesitated. A long time.

So long, she flattened her hand on his chest. His heart thudded against her palm. She would've sworn the look on his face was fear mixed with sadness. But whatever made him afraid, scared her, too. "Please, just spit it out."

"You don't know everything about his death," he said, his tone grim.

She tensed. "The air force hardly told us anything at all because it was classified."

"Yeah, um, I can't tell you everything, but I can tell you what I should've four years ago. We were supporting a spec op mission in Syria. The day it happened, we were building a bridge. One of us needed to keep watch while the rest of the team worked on construction. We drew straws. It was supposed to be Jacy." His voice hollowed. "But I'd hurt my ankle on our HALO jump into the target area."

Jacy and Tak had told her enough for her to understand the dangers of a HALO jump. The parachute had to be opened at a low altitude after free-falling for a period of time. It required a special military oxygen delivery system. They'd pointed out an example to her once in a scene in a Tom Cruise film.

"Your brother wanted me to swap places with him. He said I should take point and secure the perimeter. Since I was a better shot, and with my bad ankle, I agreed to do it. Everything was clear. For a while. They were almost done when armed insurgents snuck up on our position. I… I took out as many of them as I could, but one slipped past me. Got through." Tak lowered his head. "The guy had explosives. Blew the bridge." His voice strained, cracking. "Jacy didn't make it out. Because of me. I failed to keep him safe. Jacy and one other guy died. On my watch."

The details, the words, the description of how she'd lost her brother sank in. Then the devastation on Tak's face hit her.

"Takoda," she whispered, pressing a palm to his cheek. When he lifted his head and met her eyes, there was so much unspeakable sorrow in them, it broke her heart into a hundred sympathetic pieces. Tears she hadn't realized were building fell, rolling down her cheek. "It wasn't your fault."

"But it was. I let him down. He should've been the one protecting the perimeter. I was supposed to help build the bridge. It should've been me who died that day. Not him."

Throwing her arms around his neck, she drew him into a tight hug. "Stop. It isn't true. You two had a dangerous job. Part of what made you both heroes was how you accepted the risks, knowingly putting your lives on the line for this country. I loved Jacy, and I miss him every day. So much so, that sometimes I swear I can hear him talking to me."

Tak eased back and looked at her with tears in his eyes. "Yeah? Me, too."

"I know he loved you and would've traded his life for yours. Without hesitation. You did the best you could."

"My best wasn't good enough."

"How many others survived?"

"Seven."

"You have to remember the ones you saved." More tears fell as she kissed him. "I can't believe you've lived with the weight of this on your own." For four years. "Jacy would've wanted you to make it. To live without carrying around guilt or survivor's remorse. So that you could be here. With me."

Pulling him down to the bed, she hugged him, holding him in her arms, stroking his head. Showing him how much she loved him.

They stayed that way for a long time, minutes, maybe close to an hour, until his grip on her loosened.

She shoved back the covers, went to the bathroom, and freshened up. Coming back into the bedroom, she noticed the necklace gleaming on the floor in the firelight. It must've fallen from her pocket when Tak was peeling off her clothes and tossing them wherever.

Kimi threw on clothes and picked up the necklace. "Let's see what's on the flash drive." She sat at the table.

"Better be good considering I took a bullet for us to get it." After he half dressed from the waist down, he joined her and removed the plastic wrap from the food.

She plugged the Type-C flash drive into the phone and accessed it. "There's one document. Named 'Worst-Case Scenario.'"

"I'd say this is it." He ate a spoonful of chili. "Wow. This is really good, even at room temp."

Clicking on the document, she opened it and let out a sound that was half sigh, half grumble.

"What is it?" he asked.

She turned the phone toward him so he could see the screen. "It's never simple with my father."

"It's just columns of numbers." Taking her cell phone, he studied it. "Not a phone number or coordinates. What the hell is it?"

As soon as she saw the number sets with dashes between the digits, a flood of memories from her childhood came rushing back. "I think it's a code that uses an Ottendorf cypher."

Tak popped open the cider and filled their mugs. "Pretend like I don't know what an Ottendorf cypher is and explain."

"It's a cypher that's a series of numbers used with a known piece of text from a book to hide a message."

"Okay. So, obviously the book is *The Wizard of Oz*. How do we use it to break the code?"

"I'll need pen and paper."

Tak hopped up to get some and Kimi dug out the book from her overnight bag.

"Here we go." He'd found both in the top drawer of the nightstand and handed them to her.

She put the phone on the table and pointed to the first number set: 10-2-4-1. "Each set of digits corresponds to a letter. Ten is the page number." She opened the book, turning to it. "Two is the second line on that page. Four tells us to go the fourth word in the line, and one means the first letter in that word." She jotted down the letter G. "Each column should spell out a word. We just have to get the rest of the letters and put the words together."

While she deciphered the code, she ate her bowl of chili. By the time she was done eating, they had the message.

Glacier Ridge
Timber Trail Bank
Safe Deposit Box

Takoda looked up at her. "We'll go first thing in the morning after the roads are cleared. Glacier Ridge should be about a four-hour drive from here."

She nodded, grateful the necklace and book had led to something concrete. But the thought of what they might find in the safe-deposit box filled her with dread.

Chapter Fifteen

The landscape was so familiar to Kimi as they drove
through Glacier Ridge. The mountains, the city, the build-
ings, the streets, the river. "I feel like I've been here before,
but I don't ever remember coming here."

"Maybe you did when you were a kid. The Glacier Na-
tional Park isn't far from here."

Takoda made a right and US Route 2 turned into 9th
Street.

"I think there's an ice cream shop a couple of blocks down."

Sure enough, they passed the Sweet Retreat Creamery,
and she got a sinking sensation in her stomach.

Once they reached the Timber Trail Bank, Tak parked and
cut the engine. "Call your mom. Find out. I need to check
in with the guys and get an update anyway."

A coldness prickled her skin, raising goose bumps. "I
don't think I want to know."

Tak squeezed her hand. "But you need to know. Your dad
picked this bank for a reason. We need to know what it is."

He was right. Calling her mom to ask wasn't about her
feelings, it was about the bigger picture. One they needed
clarity on.

She dialed her mom at the same time Tak made his call.

"Kimi?" a groggy voice answered just before the final ring.

"Hi, Mom." She glanced at the time on her phone. Eleven a.m., which made it eight in Hawaii. Not wicked early. She put the phone back to her ear. "Sorry for waking you."

"Is everything okay? Did you get the necklace?"

Her brain went back to the horrible scene in the snowstorm. Gunfire. Running. The fear. Takoda getting shot. The bullets that tore into her mom's and Davey's cars.

Grimacing, she tipped her head. They didn't need to know right now. It would only cause them both to worry. Who was she kidding? They were going to freak out and then panic, wondering if she was going to be okay.

"There's so much I need to you tell, Mom," Kimi said, "and I promise that I will. But right now, I have to ask you something. It might sound odd, but have we ever been to Glacier Ridge?"

"Glacier Ridge?" There was rustling on the other end of the line, like her mom was moving around, getting out of bed. "Oh yeah, a couple of times when you were little. Your dad took you and Jacy up there. Hiking. Fishing. My goodness, that was so long ago. What made you think of that?"

"Do you remember where we stayed?"

"Oh, um, a cabin in the woods. Right next to the Flathead River where you guys went fishing."

"Was it a rental?"

"No, it was a family cabin. Thomas's aunt owned it. Jean McGregor. She barely ever used the place."

"Please tell me you remember the address."

Her mom laughed. "Of course not. Actually, I don't think I ever knew it. I spent the time at an artist's retreat, painting and doing yoga. Why do you ask? Is everything okay?"

Far from it. "I don't want to keep you. You're probably wishing you had a hot cup of coffee in your hands right now."

"You know me too well."

Kimi shut her eyes, wishing she could spill her guts about it all. "Go get caffeinated. Enjoy your vacation, Mom. We'll catch up and I'll fill you in on everything soon. I promise. Love you."

"All right. Love you. Bye, sweetie."

Disconnecting, Kimi turned to Tak. He was wrapping up his call, but she tapped him on the arm.

"Hold on, Jackson," Tak said. He put his hand over the mouthpiece. "What is it?"

"My dad used to take us up here, hiking and fishing. We stayed at a family cabin right off the Flathead River. At the time, it was owned by my Great-Aunt Jean McGregor. That's all my mom knows."

His eyes flashed with understanding. "Hey, I need you guys to find an address. ASAP." Tak relayed the details. "On second thought, Chance connected us to a hacker, Orson. He'll be able to find it the fastest. I'll call—" Takoda listened for a moment to whatever Jackson was saying. "Okay. Just let us know as soon as you hear anything back." He hung up. "Chance is there at the scene, too. They're going to reach out to Orson. Take care of payment."

"Why are you talking to Jackson?"

"He's pitching in, helping out. I called Logan, but he couldn't talk now because he's dealing with the forensics team. So he passed his phone to his brother."

"Forensics? Is this about the blood at my dad's house?"

Takoda shook his head. "No, but results did come back from the DCI lab. The blood on the phone we found was from two different people. One sample belonged to your dad. There's a fifty percent DNA match to yours," he said, and her heart sank. "There was no match to the other person in the database."

Whose blood was it? Was her dad hurt? Was he even still alive? "Then what's with forensics?"

"They found Big Billy Burdock. Murdered. One shot to the chest and one to the head. Execution style. Looks like he's been dead more than twenty-four hours. Closer to forty-eight. They won't know for certain until the medical examiner looks at him."

She swallowed to fight back the fear slithering through her. "Maybe I wasn't at the top of our ghost's list of things to do when he got to town. What if killing Burdock was?"

He cupped her face in his hand and the total concern in his eyes pinched something in her chest. She was in danger, but as long as he was with her, so was he. Takoda had this fierce protective streak that touched her and worried her. She knew without a doubt he would die to protect her, but she couldn't ever let it come to that.

"Let's find out what's in the safe-deposit box," he said. "I don't want to sit out here."

They climbed out of the truck. Heading for the bank, she adjusted the body armor vest underneath her sweater. Inside, they found the customer service desk.

"Good morning," a young woman with a sleek ponytail said. "What can I do for you today?

"Hi," Kimi said. "I'd like to access a safe-deposit box."

"I'll need your box number and identification please."

Kimi unzipped her purse and handed over her license.

"Thank you." The young woman clacked away on her keyboard. A moment later, she narrowed her eyes at the screen and then flicked a glance back up at them. "I'm sorry. I need to speak to the bank manager." She spun her chair around, got up, and made a beeline for a middle-aged guy in an office.

"What do you think that's about?" Kimi whispered.

"Did Thomas ever get you to sign any paperwork for the box?"

She shook her head.

The young woman returned. "Mr. Pegg will help you." She pointed back to the office. "He has your driver's license."

Takoda put a hand on her back, and they went to the office.

"Hello, I'm Clive Pegg. Please, shut the door and have a seat," he said, and they did as he asked. "You'd like to access box 317?"

"Yes. I have the key."

"This is highly irregular," Mr. Pegg said. "I know your father, Thomas. We spent summers fishing together in Flathead River when we were younger. Over the years, we've seen each other whenever he came up. I met you and your brother once. Gosh, you were a tiny little thing. Younger than my girls." His gaze wandered, and he smiled as if remembering. "Last month, Thomas came in and asked for a discreet, somewhat, uh, how shall I say it…"

"Irregular," Tak suggested.

Pegg smiled wider. "Yes, Thomas made a discreet, irregular request. He opened a safe-deposit box. Wanted you to have access. But he told me he couldn't bring you in and have you complete the necessary paperwork at the time. He asked me if you ever came in with the key to grant you access. I agreed to help him. He gave me a picture of you, to ensure no one could come to the bank impersonating you. Thomas seemed particularly concerned about that. Anyway," Mr. Pegg said, placing four forms on the desk in front of her, along with a pen, and her driver's license. "I verified your identity. The picture on your license matches. Just sign the forms." Leaning forward, he lowered his voice. "For my records. Backdate them for me, if you will, and I hope we can keep this just between us."

"Of course. When did my father open the box? I'll use that date."

"December tenth."

Nerves made her hand tremble when she picked up the pen. Quickly, she signed and dated the forms, feeling unnerved about the process.

"Thank you. I'll show you to the box." He escorted them out of the office and guided them along the way.

"You mentioned how you and Thomas spent summer's together," Takoda said. "His aunt had a cabin around here. You wouldn't happen to know the address, would you?"

"Had? Mrs. McGregor still does. Thomas used it as his address when he opened the four boxes."

Bulging her eyes in surprise, she slid a furtive glance at Tak and mouthed, *Four?*

"Thomas wanted you to have access to all of them," Mr. Pegg said, "but you'll need the keys."

But they only had one.

"The address?" Tak asked. "Of his aunt's cabin?"

Pegg showed them into a secure back room. "It's 202 Bad Rock Way. Take 9th Street to Glacier Ridge Road. Make a right. Only one way to turn on Bad Rock. Last cabin. Right on the river. I was over on Wildcat Lane, the street just before it." He stepped up to box 317 and inserted his key. "Ms. Wheeler."

Kimi inserted her key, and they unlocked the door.

"Take your time." Mr. Pegg left them in the room, closing the door behind him.

There were boxes of varying dimensions, this one was the largest size. She guessed it was 10x10.

Takoda took it out. "It's heavy." He set the box on the long table and flipped the lid up.

She stared at a breathtaking amount of cash, large bills bundled in neat stacks. "How much do you think is in here?"

"Beats me." He picked up a stack and thumbed through it. "Two hundred grand. Maybe more."

"We should count it."

They started taking the stacks out, lining them on the table. At the bottom of the box, there were three more keys.

"We'll have to get Mr. Pegg to open the other boxes. Do you think it's more money?" she asked.

"We'll need to check and see."

"And if it is? What are we supposed to do with it?"

"Leave it here, for now. No way we're walking out of this bank with any cash, not knowing where it came from, especially with those men after you. This is probably what they're looking for."

Her stomach clenched and a wave of nausea hit her. She tore her gaze from the money and looked up at Takoda. "What has my father gotten us involved in?"

Chapter Sixteen

Almost one million dollars.

By their rough count of the money in the first box combined with what appeared to be a similar amount in the other three boxes, Thomas Wheeler had close to one million dollars in cash stashed away in Glacier Ridge.

What concerned Takoda more was that Thomas hadn't used the money to pay Big Billy Burdock and get the loan shark off his back. Or that money could've helped him stay hidden if he was in fact hunkered down somewhere. Why leave it in the bank for Kimi to find?

And what had happened to Thomas Wheeler?

Snowflakes drifted across the windshield as Takoda followed Clive Pegg's instructions. He made a right, turning down Bad Rock Way.

At the end of the single-lane road, one solitary cabin sat along the riverbank. The snow-covered, frozen landscape was beautiful in a stark yet serene way. In the summertime, with the sound of the rushing river weaving through the mountains, it must have been gorgeous. No car was parked in the driveway, but there was an unattached garage.

If Thomas Wheeler was there, Takoda hoped they didn't find him dead inside the cabin. That was the absolute worst thing that could happen.

Takoda would prefer not to find him at all. Then at least there would still be the possibility he was alive somewhere.

Slowly, he turned off the road, down the driveway, but stopped before getting too close to the cabin. "Let me go inside first and clear it."

If her father was there but not alive, he sure didn't want her to see his corpse in whatever state it might be in. The stuff of nightmares that would haunt her forever.

She leaned back in her seat, her expression smooth, but her eyes hardened. "I'm going with you."

"Kimi, I don't—"

"I know what you're thinking. But I'm a nurse. I've seen dead bodies before," she said matter-of-factly. "Whatever we find inside, I can handle it."

This incredible woman had a backbone of steel. He loved that about her.

Loved everything about her.

"Seeing the dead body of a stranger is different. This is your father," he said, and she looked away from him. "And if those men found him, they might've done things to him to get him to talk." Tak was certain she had never seen anyone who'd been tortured, and he didn't want her to start now.

"I don't think we have to worry about that."

"Why not?"

"The curtain moved. Whoever is inside is alive. I hope it's him, so I can kill him myself for putting me through all this." She grabbed the door handle, but he caught her arm, stopping her from getting out.

"Hold on," he ordered, drawing his gun. "We're not going to do anything rash. We don't know what we're walking into. I go in first and you stay behind me. Got it?"

"Yeah, I understand. But I'm not useless."

"I'd never think that."

"When we were at my mom's house, you were worried something might happen, but you didn't give me a chance to help you."

"Help me how?"

"Give me a gun. Like you said, we don't know what we're walking into. If my dad is in there, it doesn't mean he's alone."

And their presence was no longer a surprise.

Takoda hesitated, considering it for only a second, before he bent and withdrew his backup gun from the top of his left boot. He handed her the Ruger LCP Max.

She pressed on the end of the slide around the muzzle with her thumb and forefinger, pulling it back to expose the chamber, making sure the first round was loaded. Released it. Leveled her eyes at him. "I'm good to go."

"I'm impressed."

"Did you really think my brother didn't teach me to shoot and handle myself?"

Of course I did, Jacy whispered in his head.

Takoda grinned. "I should've expected nothing less. Follow me and stay close behind me."

He shouldered out of the pickup. Shut the door with a quiet *snick*. Rounding the truck, he met her on the passenger side. The sheet of snow around the front of the place was pristine and untouched. He wanted to leave it that way. They approached the cabin from around the side.

Staying in the tree line, they swept wide, avoiding the front door and heading instead for the garage. His heart pounded in his ears, but through that dull sound, snow crunched beneath their footsteps. Coming to the unattached garage, he peeked through the transom window at the top of the door.

One vehicle parked inside. Not a two-door Ford Bronco. A red Jeep Wrangler.

Going around the side of the house, they moved in silence. The river came into sight, frozen from the subzero temperatures of the snowstorm. Right before they reached a window, he raised his fist, signaling her to hold. The curtains were open. He peered inside. The shadow of a person moved across the living room to the other side of the house, toward the front door.

Kimi's breath crystallized the air beside him.

He gestured with his head for them to continue around back, where they found footprints in the snow. A pile of chopped wood covered with a tarp. They eased up to the back door. He tried the knob. Locked.

Crouching on the balls of his feet, he slipped his lock-picking tools out of his pocket and got to work on the pin tumbler. Kicking the door in would've been faster, but he didn't want to draw gunfire to their position. Quickly, he popped the door open. They crept inside, and he shut it closed. With Kimi right behind him, they both swept through the mudroom to the kitchen, their guns up, at the ready.

The house was warm and full of golden light. They treaded lightly through the kitchen, which was empty. The smell of food permeated the air. No signs of violence. He stopped behind a wall, his shoulder pressed against the casing of the hallway.

Footsteps shuffled. Whispering in the next room.

Takoda peeked around the casing.

"There!" a woman called out.

The double barrel of a shotgun swung in his direction. Takoda scrambled to the side, sliding Kimi out of the way along with himself just in time.

A massive boom tore into the air, blasting out a window.

Chapter Seventeen

A cry stuck in Kimi's throat as adrenaline rushed through her veins.

The shotgun pumped.

Throwing an arm out in front of her, Takoda held her in place. "Thomas! Stop!"

Was her father there? Was he the one shooting?

Another shot shook the walls, blasting a gaping hole in the Sheetrock next to Tak's head, and a scream escaped her. That had been so close. Inches from hitting him.

She swallowed hard, fighting back the fear clawing through her.

"It's Takoda Yazzie! I'm with Kimi."

Silence.

"We're alone. Put the gun down. We're going to come out." Takoda shifted toward the hole and Kimi grabbed his arm, yanking him back from harm's way.

WHAT IF HER dad wasn't in his right mind? He could panic. Pull the trigger out of fear. A knee-jerk reaction that could kill Takoda.

"It's all right," Tak whispered to her. He glanced through the hole. "No more shooting. Okay?"

Then Takoda eased into the hall with his gun down at

his side. He beckoned to her to join him. Drawing a deep breath, Kimi stepped out and faced the living room.

Her father stood near the front door, wearing a baggy black sweater and jeans, with a shotgun shaking in his arms. A woman with glasses, stringy blond hair framing her face in a bob, cowered behind him. Slowly, he lowered the barrel toward the floor.

"Dad?" Her heart swelled. No matter the situation, no matter the past grievances, seeing him filled her with an inexplicable sense of hope.

"What…what are you doing here?"

She ran to him and threw her arms around him in a hug. "Thank God. You're alive."

At first, he didn't touch her, then one arm closed around her in a tentative embrace that reminded her of the distance between them. The lack of affection and warmth.

The secrets.

"How did you find me?" Dad asked.

"We followed the clues you left until we ended up at the Timber Trail bank in Glacier Ridge." Kimi let him go, glancing at Takoda when he stepped deeper into the room and up beside her. "The town seemed so familiar, like I must've been here before, and then Mom confirmed it. Clive Pegg gave us the address."

Dad gaped at them, his jaw trembling, as if he was processing their presence. His blue eyes were wide, his hair longer than usual and unkempt, his frame leaner. At seventy-two, he was vibrant and healthy, with a youthful energy the last time she'd seen him. But the man in front of her looked frail and weary, his hair more gray than brown now, as though he had aged a decade in mere weeks. Setting the shotgun down, he rested the barrel against the coffee table beside his leather-bound notebook. That was when she noticed his right hand was bandaged.

The woman behind him appeared to be in her late forties, maybe early fifties. She was wringing her hands, her features taut with terror and uncertainty. It wasn't until the woman's panicked stare landed on the gun in her hand that Kimi realized she was still holding it.

Kimi slipped the weapon into her coat pocket and that seemed to reduce the fear on the woman's face.

"I—I didn't think you would remember this place," Dad said. "You were so little the last time I brought you and your brother." He shoved a shaky hand through his hair. "But you shouldn't have come here. It isn't safe. We just need to buy ourselves a little more time. A few days. Just until next week. Tuesday. Maybe Wednesday."

A prickly tangle of emotions churned within Kimi as she rocked back on her heels. "Shouldn't have come? After everything you put me through, that's what you have to say?"

"What are you talking about?" Dad asked. "Did something happen?"

"A lot happened! There are men after me."

Worry etched into her father's expression as he pivoted toward Takoda. "I hired you to look after her. Protect her. Make sure nothing happens."

"Dad! Don't put any of this on Takoda. I'm alive because of him, after you put me in danger." Stiffening, she beat back the burn of tears suddenly stinging her eyes. "What is going on? And who is this?" Kimi waved a hand at the woman.

"This is Wendy Johnson." Her dad put a hand on her arm, urging her forward.

"Your girlfriend?" Kimi asked.

"No." Wendy shook her head. "We're colleagues. We work together at CCMC."

"Thomas, you owe us some answers." Takoda's tone was far gentler than hers. "Since you took off, Kimi has been followed, mugged, her house broken into, and we were shot at yesterday."

Wendy gasped. "Oh, no."

"Takoda took a bullet protecting me," Kimi said.

His face fell and he bowed his head, but her father didn't respond. This was how their conversations went. He shut down the second it veered into territory that was messy or serious or difficult. What they needed to discuss now was all the above.

"We found the money in the four safe-deposit boxes." Takoda's tone was soft and firm at the same time. "What are you wrapped up in? Does it have something to do with the loan shark, Burdock?"

Dad nodded. "Billy is involved, yes."

"Do you owe him money?" Takoda asked. "We were told you have a lot of debt and needed to pay him off."

Her dad's gaze snapped up, his expression confused, shocked. "Owed him money? I'm not in any debt."

"You should tell them," Wendy said. "They've come this far."

"But they shouldn't be here at all." Dad turned to her. "I left you the money just in case you needed it. A worst-case scenario. I don't want to drag you into this any deeper. This is serious business with dangerous people."

"Burdock is dead," Takoda said flatly. "He was found murdered."

Wendy staggered like she might faint. "We're out of time." Trembling, the woman wrapped her arms around herself. "They're going to kill us next," she said, her voice cracking with a sob.

"No, no, no." Her dad put his face in his hands. When he

looked back up, he was ashen. Shaking his head, he clutched Kimi's shoulders and urged her toward the door. "You have to go. Please. You can't be near me. It isn't safe for you."

"You're unbelievable." Kimi wrestled her arms from his grip. "No place is safe for me *because* of you. We're not going anywhere until we get answers. If you want us to leave, then start talking."

Her dad sighed. "This is so much bigger, uglier, than I first realized. I don't know where to begin."

Takoda put a hand on her father's shoulder. "If this isn't about you being in debt, what is it about?"

Wendy dropped down onto the sofa. "Money laundering."

Kimi flickered a shocked glance at Takoda. By the look on his face, neither of them had expected that one.

"About eighteen months ago," her father said, "the projections of palladium from previous target sites started increasing. Slowly. But steadily until they were much higher than I ever estimated. I spoke to the director of operations about it. Unable to answer my questions, he referred me to Nick Nason, the CFO. Nick pushed me off for months." Dad sat at a small table on the side of the room. "Then one day he came clean with me, or at least I thought he did."

Pulling out a chair, Kimi took a seat opposite him. "Clean about what?"

"He told me the company was in financial trouble. Prices of palladium had fallen. They were in a lot of debt and, to cover it, they had started siphoning money from the pension fund. But Nason had a plan to get everything on track. Erase the debt. Restore the retirement fund. It was all predicated on taking the company public right before the congressional bill is signed. A wave of retail investment would make CCMC whole. But he needed to make the books look financially solid. At the time, he didn't get into the specifics.

If I didn't go along with it, he told me the company would face bankruptcy, mass layoffs would happen, jobs and pensions would be lost."

"So, you agreed to go along with it," Takoda said.

He nodded, and Kimi reached over the table, taking his hand in hers. His face softened with surprise. They weren't the hand-holding type, but he just looked so beaten down, so lost. Regardless of their issues, he was a good man with a good heart.

"No one was going to get hurt with Nason's plan," Thomas said. "In fact, it would help people. Then Nick coerced me to start meeting Burdock, way out in the middle of nowhere, to do pickups and bring bags of money back to the company. Insisted it was an essential part of the plan. Not long after that, the numbers in the quarterly reports started climbing. Way off. Too high. And not just for projected palladium, but for revenue."

"What did you do?" Kimi asked.

"I confronted Nason. He yelled at me to keep my mouth shut, my head down, and go along with the plan. Otherwise, thousands would lose their jobs if CCMC filed for bankruptcy. But it felt wrong. *Dirty.* I demanded to know the truth. And he told me."

Dad pulled away from her and propped his elbows on the table, dropping his head in his hands. "About laundering money for a drug cartel. That Burdock made the introduction to the Estrada cartel. How their cut of blood money bolstered the company, and they were hiding it with inflated palladium projections. But he needed me to find a new target area, rich in palladium, before the IPO, to solidify the financials. The board and top shareholders wanted independent verification of minerals at the new target area. They must've gotten suspicious of the inflated numbers. Once I knew the cartel was involved, I refused to cooperate."

Kimi touched his arm. "Did he threaten you?"

"Nason told me about an offshore account he opened in my name. That he'd been funneling money into it to make it look like I'd been taking cartel money on the side. To frame me as a bigger accomplice in all this. He thought he could strong-arm me into finding more palladium for them. But I said *no*. Nason went so far as to have Burdock threaten to assault me at work. Still, I refused."

The video Nason had given them. Everything the CFO had told them had been designed to mislead.

"Is the cash in the bank drug money?" Takoda asked.

"Since the offshore account was in my name, I cleaned it out, but didn't know what to do with it."

Takoda stepped closer to the table. "If CCMC is going public with shady financials, then others in the company must know."

"Of course," Dad said, nodding. "The COO and CEO."

"Is that why you made your resignation so public at the holiday party?" Takoda asked.

"It stopped them from coming after me immediately and directly," he said, "though, I think Nason was the only one among the higher-ups who knew the details about the cartel's involvement."

"They know there's a significant amount of money coming in from somewhere." Wendy leaned forward, putting her arms on her thighs. "I overhead Jeff Randolph, the CEO, mention something about plausible deniability to Nason. The less they know, the better in case things ever hit the proverbial fan. Once the company goes public, there's a lot of money to be made, especially after Randolph gets his cousin to push through the bill banning the import of palladium from Russia."

Kimi had read about how Senator Yates was a staunch supporter of American mines and protecting Montana jobs, but not once had she seen one word about him having a personal connection to CCMC. "Senator Yates and Randolph are cousins?" she asked.

"Twice removed, but yes," Dad said. "CCMC needs one more mine with verifiable minerals. And fast. That's why they're so eager to get their hands on my notebook. They must think you have it." He looked at Kimi. "Or hope that you do."

Takoda scrubbed a hand over his jaw. "Nason needs the book. Not Burdock. So why would a loan shark set up shell companies to hide the fact he hired private contractors to go after Kimi?"

"Shell companies?" Wendy stood and slipped her hands in her pockets. "That sounds like Nason's MO to me. If he could forge documents and open an offshore account in Thomas's name, surely he could do the same with shell companies in Burdock's name. It would keep Nason's hands clean if the paper trail led to someone else."

Dad sighed. "The hole I was in with Nason kept getting bigger and darker. I didn't know what to do. Then the FBI approached me." He reached into his back pocket and pulled out a business card. "Special Agent Kirk Kehoe" was written on the front. "I thought that was the way out. Kehoe persuaded me to learn as much as I could about the cartel, how much money was being laundered, to enlist someone in the finance department to help me get account numbers and stuff."

Kimi looked at Wendy Johnson. "So, you went to her."

Wendy nodded. "Thomas dragged me into this. But it

sounded noble. Stopping illicit activity. Crippling a money laundering arm of a drug cartel. Getting CCMC back on the path of the straight and narrow."

"That's how Kehoe sold it to me." Dad glanced up. "But he waited until Wendy and I were in so deep, knowing way, way too much, before he started talking about us testifying and the need to go into the witness protection program. He didn't mention one word about any of that when he first approached me."

"They never do," Takoda said. "It would've scared you off. Made you reconsider."

"Darn right, it would've." Dad slapped a hand down on the table. "We want to sever the connection between CCMC and this drug lord. We want to hurt the Estrada cartel. But the price is too high doing it the FBI's way."

"If I leave," Wendy said, "I don't know what'll happen to my property. That land has been in my family for generations. I don't have kids, but the land means everything to me."

"I won't become someone else." Dad raked his hair back with a hand. "Change my name. Give up my life. Give up the people I love. The work I've devoted my life to." He shook his head. "I won't do it."

Kimi sighed. "You won't continue to work for Nason and the cartel. You won't finish what you started with the FBI. What's your plan?"

"To be free." Her father stared at her, his eyes gleaming with familiar grit and determination. "With Nason, it's all lies. They still laid off hundreds of people. Even if the IPO and new retail investment was enough to save CCMC, there's no walking away from the cartel. Nason made a deal with the devil. Once you're in, you're in until you die. It's impossible to salvage CCMC, the jobs, the pensions, without continuing to wash the cartel's blood money. And with the FBI, it's a different kind of manipulation that makes you sacrifice everything in the end. So, Wendy and I decided to knock down the entire house of cards."

Takoda glanced between Thomas and Wendy. "But how?"

"We made copies of the real quarterly reports," Wendy said, "evidence of the company's actual financial status, and Thomas's true technical readings of the amount of palladium in the mines and sent everything to the shareholders."

Kimi shook her head. "I don't understand. How will that help?"

"The shareholders will demand an audit by an independent third party," Dad said. "The IPO won't happen next week. It'll be an unstoppable domino effect that'll bring CCMC down. With the company bankrupt, they won't be able to launder any more money and Nason won't need me or my notebook. It's the only way to be free of the cartel and the FBI. In my contract with the Stracke Group, I negotiated a position for Wendy and stipulated a clause that they try and fill their upcoming positions with current or former CCMC employees. I didn't tell them CCMC was going to go under. They couldn't guarantee the last part, but they agreed to try to offer them jobs. Wendy and I just needed to ride it out, stay in hiding until enough dominoes fell."

Though fearing for his own life, her father had done everything he could to help innocent CCMC workers. To give them a chance at continued employment and a fresh start with the Stracke Group.

"But why give me the necklace, the book cipher, the key, Dad?" Why involve her in this at all?

"Because you're the only one…who could figure it out."

"The coded message?" she asked.

Frowning, Dad brushed his knuckles across her cheek,

a show of emotion so out of character, Kimi was taken aback. "All of it. I even hid a phone in my house that had mine and Wendy's blood on it. If anything happened to me, to us, I needed someone to know. To piece it together. No matter how big the puzzle is, Kimi, you could always solve it. Even if you were angry at me, disappointed in me, hurt by the wrong thing I said, you never could resist a puzzle."

Unfortunately, that was true.

Takoda stilled, his head tilting like he'd heard something.

"What is it?" Kimi asked him, goose bumps erupting on her skin.

"I'm not sure." Rubbing the back of his neck, he hurried to one of the front windows and peeked out the curtain. "There are fresh tracks in the snow. Someone's here," Takoda said, and a coldness slipped through Kimi's veins.

"Oh, no." Wendy pressed her hands to her chest. "They found us."

Kimi and her father stood as a faint buzzing whirred.

Takoda swore. "Drone." The grimness of his tone sent a shiver down her spine. Hurrying from the window with his gun drawn, he made a beeline for her. "We've got to leave."

Someone kicked in the front door.

"Get down!" Takoda was in action as the words left him, jumping in front of her and shoving her down.

Then bullets shattered the windowpane.

Chapter Eighteen

Foley swept inside the cabin, shooting.

As Takoda returned fire, he made sure Kimi and Thomas were down.

Bullets sliced through the air, puncturing drywall. A round slammed into Wendy Johnson, spinning the woman 180 degrees. The second slug hit her in the back. Her eyes rolled into the back of her head. She swayed and toppled forward.

Takoda dropped to his knee and fired low, catching Foley in the gut and shin. A guttural cry left the man as he fell.

Out the corner of Tak's eye, he saw Kimi and her dad crawling under the table.

Taking aim, Takoda shot Foley in the wrist before the man could squeeze off another round. The Glock hit the floor, and Foley screamed out in agony.

Takoda rushed toward the door, staying low, and kicked it shut. "Go hide in one of the bedrooms and stay there," he said to Kimi.

She clutched her father's arms and brought him to his feet. Thomas's gaze fell to Wendy, his features twisted in anguish, and a sob escaped his mouth. While Kimi dragged her father away from the dead body and into a bedroom, Takoda turned his attention to Foley.

He snatched the lamp from the end table and used his

fixed blade to slice the cord. Foley was writhing and swear-ing. The blood on the floor from his gut was nearly black. The bullet had hit the liver. Foley didn't have long to live. Tak flipped him over onto his stomach, drove a knee into the guy's back, and tied his wrists behind him, eliciting an-other cry of pain. While the man was still breathing, Tak wasn't giving him a chance to take another shot.

"How did you find us?" Tak asked, and when Foley didn't immediately answer, he pressed his knee into his back again.

"Stop! I'll tell you," Foley said, and Tak eased off him. "A tracker on your truck. The other guy put it there. The one with tattoos. Told us where to find you."

"Who is he?"

"I don't know."

Tak refocused. At any minute, Higgins would try to breach the cabin. The only surprising thing was that it hadn't happened yet. Takoda ran in crouched position, heading to-ward the back door.

Scrambling into the kitchen, Tak knelt, his back pressed to a lower cabinet. He pulled a smoke grenade from his pocket. After the ambush at Spokane, he was better pre-pared.

The most likely spot for Higgins to enter was through the back door. A classic tactic for the enemy to cut off all points of escape and close in.

Tak had a view of each door, front and rear, including the one to the bedroom, where Kimi and her father were hiding. Ready to pop smoke and open fire, he stilled.

The air had grown quiet. No buzzing from the drone. No sound of footsteps through the snow.

Silence. Just the steady beat of his heart in his ears.

Had they given up and left? Was it over?

One thought slid through his mind as cold fear slid

through his veins. The back bedroom was situated in the corner of the house, with windows on two different sides.

Tak sprang to his feet. Another wave of adrenaline surged through him, propelling him as fast as he could go to the other side of the house.

Racing to the bedroom, he flung the door open.

A gunshot rang out. The bullet ripped into Thomas's abdomen, and her father doubled over.

"No!" Kimi screamed.

Higgins was at the riverside window, gun in his hand, and Takoda lined up his sights.

Another shot split the air.

But Tak hadn't pulled the trigger yet.

Higgins made a gurgling noise, clutched at the bloody wound in his throat, and fell backward with a thud into the snow.

Kimi stood, the gun shaking in her grip.

Takoda hurried into the room.

Thomas was holding his abdomen. His lips were moving, but no words came out of him, like all the air had rushed from his lungs.

Dropping the gun, Kimi ran to her father's side.

A red laser dot popped up on Kimi's chest and danced. A high-powered guidance laser from a weapon.

Tak lunged, grabbing Kimi.

A gunshot whispered overhead. Shattered glass from the west-side window sprayed across the room.

Pain bloomed in Tak's elbow as they hit the hardwood floor. He rolled, covering her with his body, protecting her head with his arm. A sharp exhale rushed from her lips across his face.

Thomas clutched his chest with his other hand and collapsed right before a second shot whispered through the room.

The shooter was using a sound-suppressed sniper rifle. The ghost was still out there.

"Dad?" Kimi's voice was shrill.

The air was quiet. No more shots were fired.

"Stay here. Don't move," Takoda ordered.

Crawling on the floor, he yanked the bottom of the curtains, closing them on the riverside window, which was nearest. Then he crept across broken glass to the west window and did the same thing, obscuring the shooter's visual of the room.

Leaping to his feet, he picked shards from his palms and brushed glass from his pants.

Kimi scrambled to her father. "Tak, give me your knife!"

Unsheathing it, he handed it to her. She sliced through her father's sweater, and beneath it he wore body armor. *Kimi's body armor.* A bullet had lodged in the chest.

Panic gripped his heart. "You gave him your vest?" She must've removed it and got her father to put it on right after the two of them had run into the bedroom to hide. Kimi was a quick thinker, especially under fire. Though Takoda would've preferred it if she had kept the vest on rather than putting her life at risk, even to protect her father.

"I thought he was in more danger than me. I was right."

Blood trickled from the top of the vest across Thomas's neck.

Tak unstrapped the vest and removed it.

Kimi gasped at the sight of the blood leaking from the wound. "The armor was supposed to protect him!"

The vest stopped the bullet Higgins had fired, only knocking the wind out of Thomas. But this… "Rifle rounds are different." Level IIIA armor would slow down the slug, but it'd still penetrate the vest.

Thomas raised a bloody hand and cupped her face. "I'm sorry. I failed you. As a f-f-father. You. Jacy."

"No, Daddy." Tears fell from her eyes. "You didn't."

"Made s-so many mistakes. Forgive me. Please."

Kimi stared at the wound. "Nothing to forgive."

"Go…go. Bigfork. I love you. Always."

"We've got to stop the bleeding," Kimi said, her frantic gaze flying to Tak. "We need the med kit."

The sniper could still be out there. But every second Tak delayed meant another second of unchecked bleeding for Thomas.

He had two smoke grenades and could use them for cover.

"Okay." He picked up the Ruger and shoved it into her hand. "Just in case. I'll be right back." Tak ran to the front door.

Pulling the pin, he tossed the first grenade outside. A thick cloud of white erupted. He darted from the cabin and sprinted through the snow. No potshots taken. Yanking the next pin, he chucked the grenade. Another white cloud bloomed, obscuring him.

He made it to the truck. Snatched the med kit. Bolted back to the cabin without the sniper firing a single round. Takoda hoped it was a sign the ghost had cleared out after shooting Thomas.

In the bedroom, Kimi had her hand over the wound, applying pressure.

Thomas was still, his eyes closed, his head had lolled to the side.

Oh, no. Was he too late?

Tears spilled from Kimi's eyes. "Daddy!"

SEATED AT THE kitchen table, Kimi was quiet, her brain in a fog. The house was abuzz with activity, sheriff's deputies swarming everywhere.

A protective sheet covered Wendy's and Foley's dead

bodies in the living room. And she was responsible for killing the man outside. She'd pulled the trigger to save her father and herself, but it still wasn't enough because there had been a sniper.

The thought of her father made her heart hurt.

She'd finally connected with her dad—gotten real answers, affection, a heartfelt apology, all the things she'd yearned for from him—only to watch him get shot.

No more tears came. Her eyes were swollen and ached from crying. She was numb. Her limbs were heavy, like her veins were full of lead.

Takoda had cleaned her face and hands. Held her. Let her cry at the unfairness of it all.

Kimi's phone chimed. A text message. She took her phone from her pocket, but she felt disconnected. Like she was having an out-of-body experience.

Looking at the screen, she didn't recognize the number. She tapped on the message and read it.

This is Izzy. The missing person's report was filed by your father's son. Your half brother, Michael. He knew something was wrong when your dad missed his sixteenth birthday.

Takoda cupped her face and wiped her cheeks. She touched her eyes and her fingers came away wet. Tears. She was crying again and didn't even realize it.

"What is it?" he whispered.

She showed him her phone.

He read the text and set her cell on the table. Crouched in front of her. Held her hands. Pressed his forehead to hers.

More tears fell and he wiped them away.

Takoda didn't say anything. What could he say that would

take away her pain or answer her new questions or help her to understand this newest bombshell secret? Tak gave her what she needed instead, his support and his comfort.

A deputy handed Takoda a blanket and he wrapped it around her shoulders.

The same deputy turned to the sheriff. "Have we gotten their statements yet?"

"No, and we're not going to," the sheriff said, his narrowed gaze sliding over Kimi and Tak. "We were ordered not to question them."

"Who has the authority to give you that order?"

The telltale *thwump, thwump, thwump* of a helicopter cut through Kimi's daze, drawing her attention, along with everyone else's, outside the kitchen window. Kimi hoped that she and Takoda had made the right decision.

"You're about to meet him," the sheriff said.

The sleek black helicopter touched down on the expansive field of snow on the side of the house. The door slid open. A man wearing a blazer with FBI stenciled across the front in yellow letters climbed out. Jackson Powell hopped out next.

Kimi looked up at Tak.

"I don't know why Jackson is here," he said, answering her unspoken question.

They had found the card for the FBI agent who had tried to force her father to testify and then go into witness protection. Kirk Kehoe was the only person they knew who might be able to help fix this. So, she called him.

The FBI agent strode into the back door, through the mudroom, into the kitchen. Even if he didn't have on a jacket announcing who he was, he had an air of authority that immediately commanded attention.

Holding a folder in one hand, the agent went up to the sheriff and offered his other hand. "Special Agent Kirk

Kehoe. Thank you for securing the scene. I trust my requests were respected."

The sheriff handed him something. Her father's leather-bound notebook in an evidence bag. "They were," the sheriff said. "We reported four dead bodies, instead of the three we've got, like you asked, and didn't question these two. Mind explaining?"

"I do mind. This is my case. End of explanation," Kehoe said simply. "Now, I'll need the room. Excuse us."

The sheriff pursed his lips, eyes narrowing to slits, but he and the deputies began to vacate the house.

Jackson came into the room and stood beside the federal agent. His US marshal badge hung prominently from the chain around his neck, and he wore a windbreaker, too, with his agency's name stenciled on it.

Once they were alone, the FBI agent turned to Kimi and Takoda, who remained standing. "I'm Special Agent Kirk Kehoe. We spoke on the phone."

Kimi couldn't treat her father's chest wound. The body armor had slowed the bullet, preventing the slug from going as deep as it otherwise would have. He needed to be mede-vaced out of there. The FBI agent was the only one they knew who had the power to make it happen quickly without wasting time. When they spoke on the phone, with her frantic over her father's life hanging in the balance, she agreed to honor whatever conditions he would set in exchange for his help.

"Your father is in stable condition under a false identity. The sheriff's department is going to report that Thomas Wheeler was found dead on the scene here. I believe you both already know Jackson. He's a deputy US marshal assigned to my special joint task force, called Operation Big Sky Guardian. Our job is to bring down the Estrada cartel.

Stop their drug smuggling, human trafficking and money laundering in this country by disrupting their supply chains and networks. Our focus is their base of operation in Canada, which uses Montana as their entry point and distribution hub."

"Are you the reason Chief Ed Macon made Detective Logan Powell drop this case?" Takoda asked.

The special agent nodded. "Yes, I am."

Takoda pivoted to Jackson. "When you came to dinner the other night, you were working. You were there as a marshal." Statements. Not questions.

"I was also there as a friend," Jackson said.

"Did he...?" Her voice was hoarse, her mouth bone-dry. Kimi swallowed and cleared her throat. "Did Agent Kehoe send you to Bitterroot Falls the other night? Did he ask you to see if I knew where my father was?"

Sighing, Jackson lowered his head. "Yes, he did."

Kehoe eased forward in front of Jackson. "You're aware your father was working for us?"

"I'm aware you baited my father with promises of getting him out of a bad situation, only for him and Wendy Johnson to later learn you wanted them to testify and go into witness protection. To upend their lives and take them away from everyone and everything they've ever known."

"I never lied to your father."

"You misled him. Same as Nason. To get what you wanted."

"Nick Nason and I are nothing alike," Kehoe said. "He doesn't care about this country, or the people he hurts, or if the money that pays for his lavish lifestyle comes from a cartel that kills tens of millions of people with drugs. Not to mention the human trafficking. Trust me, you don't want me to go into the ugly details of that sordid business."

"Look at me." Takoda stepped up to the agent. "I suggest you change your tone and back off or this conversation is finished."

"I've done you a big favor," Kehoe said. "*Huge.* So, this isn't over until I say it is."

"This is important," Jackson said. "We have a serious problem. Lives are at stake."

"She had to watch as Wendy Johnson was murdered, and her father almost died in her arms. She was nearly killed!" Takoda pointed a finger at Jackson. "Don't tell either of us what's at stake."

"My apologies for getting off on the wrong foot." Agent Kehoe sat next to her at the table. "What you've been through is awful. I'm sorry you've had to experience any of it." The smooth-talking agent looked at Takoda. "Please, sit," he said, gesturing to a chair.

Takoda shook his head once. "I'm good."

"Suit yourself," Kehoe said. "Your father promised to help us get Nason, and Ms. Johnson was supposed to provide financial information regarding the cartel. Account numbers that we could track and monitor to see how Estrada moves their money. We still need that information."

"My father won't testify. He won't go into witness protection."

"I understand," Kehoe said. "But I also told you over the phone that my help, protecting your father, comes at a price."

"What do you want?" Takoda asked, his voice like cold steel.

"I want Ms. Wheeler to contact Nason. Offer him the notebook." Kehoe set her dad's book on the table. "When you meet, get him talking. We need him to incriminate himself. Get him to boast about the cartel, but more importantly, about taking CCMC public. If we can establish intent, we can charge him with a multimillion-dollar pre-IPO fraud scheme. Then we can use the charge as leverage. Get him to flip on the cartel and provide us with all the information Wendy Johnson was supposed to give us."

Kimi shook her head. "You have to be kidding. First, you put my father in this position that nearly got him killed. Now you expect *me* to help you?"

"Let's get something crystal-clear, Ms. Wheeler. Nick Nason put your father in this position. Pressured him. Coerced him. Used him. Nason got him entangled with the Estrada cartel. And Nason got him shot. He may as well have pulled the trigger and put the bullet in your father himself. I offered Thomas protection. A way out of this mess. We're the good guys here, trying our best, risking our lives to bring down the bad guys. Like Nason. Like the man who shot your father. Like the Estrada cartel."

Kimi clutched the blanket against the cold shiver that ran through her. Squeezing her eyes closed, she considered it. "I don't know." Her father was alive, fighting for his life. She just wanted to focus on him recovering.

"I'm the only thing standing between your father and the next bullet that will kill him," Kehoe said. "As far as the world is concerned, he's dead. We can keep it that way. Once he's released from the hospital, I can have him moved to a DCI safe house here in Montana. Where he'll stay until we eliminate the threats to him. Then he'll be free and clear. But that puts you on the hook to deliver for me."

She looked around the room. "I need time to think about it."

"There is no time," Jackson said.

Kehoe nodded. "He's right. If you're going to help us, it has to be done today."

"Whoa." Takoda raised his palm. "Why today? What's the rush?"

"It was a good thing Jackson went to dinner the other night." Kehoe's hard gaze swung between Kimi and Takoda. "He got a look at the guy at the bar. Passed us the pictures you pulled from the surveillance cameras."

Takoda frowned. "But the pictures were lousy. Grainy. You couldn't see the guy's face, and a hacker we hired couldn't identify him."

"Your hacker didn't need to because I already know who he is." Kehoe put the folder on the table, opened it and took out a clear picture of the ghost's face. "His name is Alvaro Aguilar. He's the top hitman for the Estrada cartel. They don't dispatch him to collect money or fetch notebooks." Kehoe tapped her dad's brown-leather book. "When they unleash this monster, it's only for one purpose. He's cleaning up loose ends. Burdock. Your father. Wendy Johnson. If he finds out Thomas is still alive, he will come back to finish the job." The agent paused, letting that sink in. "We're aware your father set certain things in motion to stop the IPO of CCMC. The news is going to break any day. When it does, the impending bankruptcy of CCMC will be announced. Then the Estrada cartel won't have any need for Nason. He's a dead man walking unless we can flip him first and get him to agree to testify against the cartel. Time is of the essence."

Kimi took it all in and one thing struck her as a red flag. "Wait a minute, how would the cartel know that there are loose ends? That my father, Wendy or Burdock could be a threat to them. I mean, isn't it business as usual for them? Why is this Aguilar even here?"

"After your father jumped ship from CCMC and went to work for the Stracke Group, there was no movement on the part of the cartel. I thought we could still pull this off, bring Mr. Wheeler and Ms. Johnson around to see our perspective. It wasn't until your father and Ms. Johnson deviated from the plan by running, which forced me to reveal their identities to the joint task force. So that we could track them down and come up with plan B."

"That's when the cartel took action?" Kimi asked.

The special agent's expression turned grim. "Forty-eight hours after I briefed the task force about your father and Johnson and the need to find them, Aguilar landed in Missoula."

Understanding dawned, and a cold rush prickled beneath her skin. "Are you saying you have a leak in your task force?"

"Yes," Jackson said. "We have to assume the cartel knows the identity of each member of the task force as well as any assets we've discussed in the group."

Not only was her father in danger, so was Jackson.

"Was Thomas's plan to stop the IPO discussed?" Takoda asked.

The agent nodded. "Yes, but Nason is still alive. For now. Today might be our last chance to get to him. Only Jackson is assisting me with this. No one else from the task force, to be on the safe side. And no one from the task force, other than Jackson, will know your father is alive. Help us get the man who ruined your father's life and nearly got him killed."

Kimi took a deep breath. Her father might not want her to work with the FBI, but he and Wendy Johnson would want her to do what she could to stop the cartel. And this was the only way she could protect her father until it was safe for him to go back home. "I'll do it. Under one condition."

"I think I've already gone above and beyond for you and Thomas," Kehoe said. "But what is it?"

"Nason doesn't get full immunity. I know you'll give him

a lesser sentence or something." She wasn't naive. "But he doesn't get off scot-free. I want justice."

Agent Kehoe gave her an appraising look, then offered his hand. "You have a deal, Ms. Wheeler."

Kimi looked at Jackson. "Can I trust this man to keep his word?"

"Yes. We are the good guys here. He'll keep his word." The sincerity in Jackson's eyes and voice swayed her.

"Okay." She shook the agent's hand.

Kehoe took out a flip phone, setting it on the table, along with a phone number written on a piece of paper. "Call Nick Nason. Set up a meeting. Tell him you've got your dad's notebook and will give it to him. But you want one hundred thousand dollars in cash and for him to leave you alone. No more being followed. Attacked. Or any further attempts on your life."

"Why ask for the money?" she wondered.

"Nason is filth. If you don't come across as greedy as him, he won't buy it."

Takoda finally sat. "What if he says he needs more time?"

"Then tell him you'll offer the notebook to the Stracke Group. Nine o'clock is the deadline. I guarantee he'll agree to the meet."

"But…" Kimi swallowed. "It'll be a trap, won't it? I mean, for us."

"Yes. Both sides will set traps. We just have to be better than him."

Takoda took her hand and held it. "I'll be with you. Every step of the way."

Nodding, Kimi picked up the phone and made the call to Nason.

Chapter Nineteen

The closed palladium mine came into view. Takoda parked behind two black SUVs. Nason had brought plenty of company. But they hadn't expected him to be alone.

Nick Nason was like a hyena. A vicious scavenger that profited from the work of others and hunted in a pack.

Also, Orson had given them a heads-up. The hacker was painstakingly thorough and had tampered with Red Sentry's system, creating an alert to notify him if any other personnel were assigned to the same contract as Foley and Higgins. Even though Burdock was dead, the shell company allegedly in his name hired four more men today. Marked urgent and high priority. Confirmation that Wendy Johnson had been right about Nason using Burdock to cover his tracks with Red Sentry.

Orson passed along pictures, names and background information on the four new Red Sentry security personnel. Typical credentials; prior military or law enforcement. The one guy they were worried about was Ulysses Oldman. He had a unique designator beside his name, no background information readily available, and was the highest paid man on the contract.

Their best guess was he had Special Forces training. Regardless, the goal was to take extreme caution, protect

Kimi, and get out of there unharmed with a confession from Nason.

The only hitch was if Nason talked, then it definitely meant DEFCON 1 and Nason didn't intend for them to leave the mine alive. They'd already suspected as much and had prepared for the worst.

Why else choose the deserted mine as the meeting place?

The perfect location to dispose of bodies.

They climbed out of the truck and got their bearings. Tak had brought Eli and Bo as backup. Chance, Winter, Declan and Logan were with Agent Kehoe and Jackson in the chopper, waiting to swoop in and apprehend Nason. Then close in on the mine and come to the rescue if necessary. They just needed the signal.

No security personnel was outside. On the slow drive in, Eli had scouted the surrounding area with a dual-screen, binocular-infrared and night-vision device. Military-grade. Eli had given the all-clear outside.

They each had a pair of dual binoculars as part of the plan.

"Get him talking," Takoda said, coming up beside Kimi. "Play to his ego. For men like him, it's always a weakness."

"How will I know when he's said enough?" she asked.

"We'll tell you," Eli said. "Something you won't mistake. Then we'll try to make a graceful exit."

Kimi unzipped her coat and touched the collar of her sweater, where Kehoe had put the wireless listening device. The higher and more exposed it was positioned, without being detected, the better.

Tak caught her hand. "Don't mess with it."

"I'm trying not to." She took a deep breath. "Nerves."

"Give us a minute," Tak said to the guys, and they gave them a little space. He put her palm on his chest. "Focus on talking. We'll do the rest. Remember, if things kick off, take cover. When there's no cover?"

"Drop."

People would aim for body parts, not the dirt. Though she was armed, he hoped there wouldn't be a need for her to use the weapon again. She'd already killed one man. Kimi was a healer, and the weight of taking a life was heavy on her shoulders, dimming the spark in her eye. If he could spare her from going through that tonight, he would.

"If the plan doesn't work," she said, "if anything happens—"

Leaning down, he cut her off with a kiss.

TAKODA REALLY KISSED HER. All mouth and muscle as he brought his arms around her. Threw his whole body into it. Those lips crossing over hers, deepening the kiss with each pass. His tongue licked against hers, drawing a moan up her throat. His fingers slipped into her hair and he held her close for more until there was a pulsing inside her, around her, as if the air came alive, and her nerves settled, replaced with a familiar hunger that burned through her.

He broke the kiss and stared down into her face. "I'm so in love with you that I'd be lost without you. I won't let anything happen to you."

"The feeling is mutual. I'm not worried about me." She curled her fingers into his sweater, her nails scraping the body armor he wore beneath it. "Don't die in there. Promise me."

It was unfair, unrealistic, to ask him to give his word about something like that when there were so many factors beyond his control. But she needed some reassurance or she wouldn't be able to go through with this.

"I'll do my best for you." He brushed his lips over hers. Another soft, warm kiss. "Let's get this done."

The lock on the main double doors had been cut so they could get in. Lanterns had been placed along the dirt floor for illumination, giving the main entrance an eerie glow. Bo had given them all emergency light sticks that they could activate with a snap.

As a teenager, she had been in a mine once with her father.

She didn't like it then and she didn't like it now.

The musty, stale air was so strong with the hint of mold, she nearly choked. An arching ceiling soared overhead. The rock walls trapped the cold temperatures. A constant chill filled the air, even in the summer. Now, it was freezing, their breaths crystallizing in the air.

Wires ran the length of the wall, connected to small lights that either no longer had power or deliberately hadn't been turned on.

No one went in guns blazing, though, the guys had their weapons drawn at their sides. They were all playing it cool, but she was anything but. Her heart was racing, a dull headache pounding in her temples.

Kimi had a gun just in case. She never imagined—despite the training with her brother that prepared her—she'd have to kill someone one day. Taking a life was no easy thing, even in self-defense, and she had to learn to live with it. But everything was overshadowed by her concern for her father and what she had to do next with Nason. Protecting those she loved was second nature, and she was ready to use the gun or any other means to keep them safe.

Following the glowing lights along a slight curve in the path, taking them deeper so the front doors were no longer visible, they came to an opening, where they found Nick

Nason and his four goons standing to one side. Bright lanterns had been set around the space. Two tunnel openings were further back. Beyond one of those, she spotted light reflecting across the surface of a huge pool of water.

An abandoned mining cart sat at the opening of the other tunnel, blocking the entrance. Their footsteps echoed through the damp space as they approached Nason. This entire situation had her on the verge of wanting to jump out of her skin, but she focused on talking.

"Nason, where's the money?" she asked.

One guy tossed a duffel bag at Eli's feet. She couldn't remember his name. The only person Takoda demanded she steer clear of no matter what was Ulysses Oldman. At six-four and two hundred and fifty pounds, he was the biggest guy in the room, making him easy to pick out.

Kneeling, Eli unzipped the bag and pretended to check it. He slipped the strap on his shoulder as part of the ruse, no doubt prepared to drop it at the first sign of trouble.

The meeting spot was tight. Close quarters where rock walls and gunfire didn't mix. Bullets would ricochet. Anyone could be killed. She hoped that meant Nason wanted to avoid a shootout.

"Where's the notebook?" Nason asked.

Kimi took it out of her coat pocket and held it up. The notebook shook in her hand. She tried to stay calm, an impossible task.

"Hand it over," Nason said.

"First, I want to know why you roped my father into your scheme instead of leaving him alone."

"He asked too many questions and started demanding answers."

"You could've stonewalled him. Spun some story. But you didn't. Instead, you deliberately dragged him in deeper.

Coerced him to pick up the drug money from Burdock. You made him a target."

Nason shrugged. "Thomas had a big, weeping heart. It was his Achilles' heel. He made it so easy for me to play him. He was willing to keep his mouth shut and do as I told him if he thought he was saving jobs and pensions. The fool that he was didn't even want anything for himself. Why not get him to do the dirty work? The less interaction I had with the Estrada cartel or Burdock, the better for me."

"Did you really believe laundering drug money was going to save the company? Or was it always just about you lining your pockets?"

Nason laughed. "I didn't get the brilliant idea to *save* the company by taking it public with the IPO until Randolph found out what I was doing. He was livid until he saw how lucrative it is to be in business with the cartel."

The guy was a talker, which didn't bode well for them.

She looked around, trying to figure out where to take cover. "Then you realized with the fake financials and the IPO that you could make even more by scamming investors?"

"When Randolph confronted me, I was forced to think quick on my feet. That's how I do some of my best work. I know the ins and outs of what the SEC is looking for when a company has an initial public offering. I know the loopholes. The things they miss. The IPO is just the start. Once the bill is passed in congress, the price of palladium will skyrocket, the company will eventually be made solvent, and then there'll be that much more Estrada money I'll get to pocket." He grinned, looking like a ghoul in the lantern light. "The notebook. Now."

Kimi glanced at Takoda. Did they have enough?

"We're golden," he said with a nod.

Swallowing hard, she tossed the book into the center of the space and shuffled deeper into the room. "The layoffs, the pensions you put at risk, did that mean anything to you?" A part of her needed to know if this man had a heart. A soul.

"Sure, it did. The infusion of cartel money was just on the books. When I had to lay off people anyway, Thomas became a thorn in my side, and I cared very much about that. The daily irritation I endured at seeing his face, hearing his voice, suffering his complaints and pleas to help the workers. *Ugh*. Grated on my nerves. He had to go." Nason stepped forward and picked up the notebook and thumbed through the pages. "Now that I have this, I have zero regrets he died slightly sooner than anticipated."

All this man cared about was stroking his ego and raking in more cash. He didn't care about anyone except himself. Nason wasn't simply dangerous, maybe he was evil. But he was definitely heartless.

"A hundred grand isn't enough. I should've asked for more," Kimi said, edging closer to the mining cart. "Because of you, my father and Wendy Johnson are dead! Their lives are worth more."

"Shoulda, coulda, woulda." Nason strode toward the exit.

Kimi put her hand up to her mouth, hiding her lips. "He's leaving," she whispered into the mic.

"Thomas and Wendy outlived their usefulness," Nason said. "And so have you." He looked back at his goons "Take care of them and that bag of money is yours."

Then all hell broke loose.

One second everyone held their position, not making any sudden moves. In the next second, everyone shifted. Guys drawing knives and lunging, and chaos ensued.

Kimi kissed the dirt as Jacy would've called it, dropping to the ground and rolling toward the steel cart.

Gunfire erupted. Tak and the other guys went for the lights first, shooting out the lanterns.

Darkness was their friend. The Red Sentry thugs would be blind while Tak, Eli and Bo would be able to see with the dual-screen binoculars.

Bullets pinged and bounced off the walls and the steel mining cart behind her, each muzzle flash illuminating the free-for-all in the space. Kicking. Punching. Blades slashing.

Water splashed—someone must've fallen into the huge pool in the first tunnel. From the sounds, two men were fighting in the water.

Staying low and flat, she trembled, trying to ignore the churning in her gut and the rippling tension that made her blood run cold at the thought of Takoda or any of their friends getting hurt.

A bullet brought a chunk of the rock wall down near her, and a scream slipped from her lips.

More blows were exchanged in the darkness. Someone was grappling on the ground. An anguished roar echoed through the chamber.

Light flicked on in the tunnel with the pool, an emergency glow stick beaming bright. Another stick illuminated near the exit.

Kimi snapped one of her chem lights and tossed it into the center of the space. Frantically, she looked around. Several of the Red Sentry goons-for-hire were down. Eli was wet, but on his feet. Bo was slowly climbing to his feet, out of breath.

She spotted Tak.

Ulysses surged forward, hiking his shoulder into Takoda's midsection and hefting him off the ground before slamming him into the rock wall. The men grappled and fell to the dirt, rolling and grunting and punching.

Dread curled her stomach. Bo and Eli raised their weapons. But they didn't dare shoot. The movements were too jerky, quick, and Takoda could have just as easily been hit.

Then a gun went off, making her flinch.

For a second, no one moved. No one seemed to breathe. Horror raced through her.

Ulysses was on top of Tak. Both simply lay there. Still. Quiet.

Panic welled inside her. "Takoda."

But Ulysses moved, and Kimi's heart stopped. *No.* Ulysses must've been the one to shoot. The wrong man survived.

A small cry squeezed from her throat. Anger, pain, fear— all fired through her. She jumped up, needing to get to Takoda, to claw that brute off him. To kill Ulysses with her bare hands.

Bo caught her by the arms, stopping her as Ulysses started to rise like some villain from a horror movie. But then his body was shoved to the side.

His *dead* body.

Takoda sat up with a groan. A rush of overwhelming relief drove Kimi to her knees. He was alive.

A FIERY PAIN bloomed in his abdomen. Takoda pressed his hand to his side, where Ulysses had cut him. His vision blurred, but he saw Kimi clearly when she launched herself at him, throwing her arms around his neck.

"Ouch," he grunted.

She eased back. "You're hurt. Let me see."

He removed his hand

Kimi lifted his sweater. "He stabbed you."

"More of a slash, really." Takoda sucked in a sharp breath through the pain. "I don't think it's too deep."

"But you're wearing body armor." She applied pressure to the wound.

His chest tightened at the look of worry on her face. "It's bullet resistant. Not knife resistant."

She gave him a sad smile and kissed him.

Eli sloshed through the chamber, soaking wet.

Bo put two fingers to his ear. "They got him. Nason is in cuffs as we speak. Winter and Jackson are headed inside."

Mission accomplished. One step closer to stopping the Estrada cartel and getting Thomas back to Bitterroot Falls, living the life he wanted.

Takoda took Kimi's hand and stared in her eyes. "As I was fighting that guy, I realized he was better than me. When I hit the ground and he had the advantage, all I could think about was you. Doing my best, surviving, for you. Kimi, I've been in love with you for a long time. Can't-see-straight, get-ridiculously-jealous-when-you're-with-someone-else kind of love. I want to marry you," he said, and she gaped at him. "But we can wait. I mean, I'll do it right. Make sure you're happy and ready and then I'll pop the question with a big ring. I just know without a doubt that this is right and I needed to tell you."

"Yes!"

"What?"

She kissed him. Leaning in, she kissed him deeper. Pain flared in his gut and he groaned.

"Sorry," she said. "Yes, to all of it. No waiting necessary. But a ring would be nice."

If he could see her smile every day for the rest of his life, he'd be the luckiest man on the planet. "You got it."

You better marry her, Jacy said low, so faint like a whisper in the wind.

The words, his best friend's voice, whether real or imagined, brought him peace.

Peace that Jacy would approve, be happy for them, and wish them well.

It was a good thing, too, because Kimi was it for him. She was his forever.

Chapter Twenty

Kimi wasn't sure how she was going to get through today—her dad's fake memorial service.

Thomas Wheeler was alive and recovering in a hidden location in Montana, one unbeknownst even to her. She hadn't seen him since her dad had been medevaced out of Glacier Ridge. The hardest part was that they couldn't tell anyone the truth. Not friends. Not family. Not even anyone in IPS. Everyone had to believe that Thomas Wheeler was dead.

It was the only way to ensure his safety until the threat with the Estrada cartel was eliminated.

A very real, very deadly, threat. Nick Nason had been taken into custody. Special Agent Kehoe had been smart enough to hold him in a cell and not move him until Nason flipped, giving them all the information they needed. Account numbers. Amounts. Timelines. Details they could use to establish a pattern and track other cartel funds.

As soon as Nason was exposed, in the process of being transferred to a different facility, someone—Alvaro Aguilar—put two bullets in him. One in the chest. One in the head.

The CEO and COO of the Cutthroat Creek Mining Company were charged with the pre-IPO fraud scheme. Kimi was able to give her dad's notebook to the Stracke Group. Hundreds of people were going to be hired by them instead of losing their jobs. Her dad might not have been able to save CCMC, but he had preserved the livelihood of so many in the town.

Kimi looked over at Takoda sitting behind the wheel of his truck as he parked in the church's lot. The tension inside her released. With him at her side, she could get through anything.

Over the past week, they'd been in his house, sharing one bedroom. Gone was the frustration and denial. No more pushing each other away. No more holding back. He kept telling her how much he loved her. How wrong he'd been for waiting so long to act on his feelings. How right he believed they were together. Takoda wasn't going anywhere. She could count on him to be there for her always. As her husband. One day.

Tak hopped out, crossed the front of the truck and opened her door for her. Taking her hand, he helped her out, shut her door and held her. Pressed his forehead to hers. Stared in her eyes. "Ready?"

He was her rock, and she was going to lean on him now.

"No, but I don't want to be late for his service. Besides, Mom and Davey are already inside." They'd left twenty minutes earlier. "We should go in."

He kissed her, took her hand, and they interlaced their fingers as they walked.

The weather was beautiful. Warm enough to melt the ice on the ground. The sky was a bright blue and cloudless. The breeze was gentle. Her father would be pleased with it.

She also hoped that he approved of her donating the money from the safe-deposit boxes to the American Institute of Professional Geologists to be used for scholarships.

Her dad would want some good coming from the money, to help people, especially if it paved the way for there to be more geologists in the world.

They rounded the corner. Kimi stopped. The entire crew was there, waiting outside the church. Chance and Winter. Summer and Logan. Autumn. Declan. Nora and Bo. Eli. Even Jackson.

"I can't believe you're all here," she said, determined not to cry.

"Of course we came." Summer hugged her. "You lost your dad, and you need us. We're here for each other, through all of it."

"The highs and lows," Chance said. "The good weather and the storms."

Guilt and appreciation swelled in her chest. She wished she could tell them the truth. One day, she hoped they'd understand.

She was lucky to have them.

They all huddled around her and Kimi had never felt such an overwhelming outpour of love and support. This was the true meaning of family.

Kimi and Takoda entered the church. She did her best to get through the greetings and hugs and condolences as they made their way to the front of the nave.

At the second row, she went to join Mom and Davey when the woman seated in the first pew stood, turning to her.

"I'm Lena. You're Kimi, right?"

She swallowed hard. "Yes."

"This is Michael," Lena said, and the young man in a dark suit stood up.

He was so tall for a sixteen-year-old, and it was surprising how much he looked like Jacy when he'd been that age.

"Hi." Kimi offered her hand.

Michael hugged her instead. A tight, genuine embrace that lasted far too long.

"It's nice to finally meet you," she said. "I hate that it's under these circumstances, but I hope we can spend time together and talk." Start building a relationship.

"Me, too. I have so many questions for you and stuff to share."

She bet he did. "It's the same for me."

"Would you sit with us?" Michael asked.

Drawing in a deep breath, Kimi nodded. She squeezed Tak's hand, and he didn't let go. They both went to join Lena and Michael.

Nerves slid through Kimi as she stared at the large photo of her father on the memorial board. She'd pushed off going to the rez, despite his wish, not knowing what to say, how to start the conversation that her father should've initiated. Thankfully, the minister came out, went to the pulpit, and she began the service.

Tak leaned in. "Great timing," he whispered in her ear.

Grinning at how he seemed to read her mind, she couldn't agree more. She loved him so much.

The minister gave a moving sermon and praised her father's good qualities. People shared stories about her dad. Most of them were funny, but all of them highlighted how he was such a passionate and kind man.

"Now, Lena, Thomas's partner, would like to sing a song."

Agent Kehoe had stressed the importance to Kimi for everyone, absolutely everyone, to believe her dad was dead. If they could keep him alive, protected, it would be worth it in the end. She hoped he was right.

Michael reached under the pew and pulled out a guitar.

With a smile, Lena took it and stood in front of the nave where someone had set up a microphone for her.

"Thomas loved this song. He loved Montana. He loved the land here," Lena said. Then she sang "Montana Melody" by LeGrande Harvey. Not only was she a skilled guitarist but also had a hypnotic voice.

Montana, Montana, my home.

Everyone clapped once Lena finished.

When she returned to her seat, Kimi turned to her. "That was beautiful. Truly."

The minister stood at the pulpit. "The family has chosen Kimimela Anne Redbird Wheeler to speak on their behalf."

Takoda gave her hand another quick squeeze.

Kimi got up and went to the microphone. "Hi. I really wasn't sure what to say about my dad. Then my mom told me to just speak from the heart. So, here goes. My father was a brilliant geologist. A braver and stronger man than I ever realized. Fearless in his convictions. He was a fighter, determined to live his life on his terms. There are so many things that he taught me and that I learned to love because of him. Hiking. Fishing. All about codes and ciphers. And puzzles. I will work on a puzzle no matter how big or how long it takes. Or how difficult it might be. I definitely inherited his tenacity," Kimi said, and everyone laughed. "In many ways, my father was an enigma to me. I only wish that I had had more time to figure him out." She promised herself that when she saw him again, things would be different. She would try harder. "Even though our relationship was strained and distant at times, in the end, I never felt closer to him. Or prouder of him. I love him. He will be greatly missed."

Once the minister wrapped up the service, everyone

stood, preparing to go to the repast in the auxiliary part of the church.

Lena touched her arm. "Can I speak to you for a minute, in private?"

Kimi nodded to Tak that it was all right. Michael stepped over to the side, but he wasn't alone long. Her mom and Davey went straight over to him.

"I wish we could've met before today," Lena said.

"Dad asked me to go Bigfork. He didn't get a chance to tell me why. Then again, I don't know if he ever would've told me. Do you know why he didn't tell me about Michael?"

"That's what I wanted to talk to you about. Your father was hesitant to have a child with me. He was so worried that he'd mess it up. Then one day he said to me, 'Lena, if we can't change, learn from our mistakes, grow and become a better person, what's the point of this journey?' After Michael was born, he told Jacy first. Your brother got very upset."

Kimi imagined the conversation and it was easy to see Jacy exploding.

"He felt like your dad was trying to replace you two. Start over," Lena said. "He told your father that if he loved you, Kimi, then he wouldn't break your heart by telling you about Michael."

That knocked the wind right out of her. But she could see it. "I was fourteen. Hormonal. Confused about so many things. My relationship with Dad was difficult. Fracturing at that point. It would've been a big blow to me. Back then. But not now."

"Thomas didn't know how you'd ever take it, but he believed Jacy knew you better than he did. So, he promised not to tell you. Since I respected that, when Michael filed the missing person's report, I asked Joe Midthunder not to tell you either. He conveyed that it was hard for you, not knowing who filed the report. I'm sorry about that. Your dad loved you, both you and Jacy, so much. Thomas just didn't know how to mend what was broken between you guys."

"It wasn't entirely his responsibility," Kimi admitted. "Not after I became an adult. I should've put in more of an effort. I regret that. But I'm glad we finally connected." She had a chance to forgive him, to accept the love he was able to give. One day, they would get their fresh start.

"Thomas wanted half of his ashes spread on Bitterroot Mountain and the other half on Bigfork. The weather is supposed to be just as nice tomorrow as it is today. We'd like to do it then. Would you and Aiyana be able to join us? Thomas would've wanted that."

Agent Kehoe assured her the cremated remains were fake, the kind they use in Hollywood. Having a memorial to sell the idea was one thing. Spreading was like a final goodbye.

"Lena, if you don't mind, could we wait? Say, a year?"

Her father should be back home by then. Kehoe thought it would be much sooner since he was activating a deep cover asset within the Estrada cartel. Jackson was hopeful they'd be able to pull off Operation Big Sky Guardian.

Kimi's fingers were crossed.

"I thought getting to it would be better, but we can wait. I'm in no hurry to say goodbye to him." Lena wrapped her in a warm embrace.

Kimi hugged her back. "Is it okay if I speak with Michael?"

His mom waved him over.

"I have something for you." Kimi opened the purse Jacy had given her. It went with every color and every outfit, in her opinion. She took out her dad's signet ring with the Wheeler family crest. "Dad would've wanted you to have it."

Smiling, Michael slipped it on his finger. "His ring."

"It's your ring now."

"Thank you."

Kimi noticed people exiting through the side door that led to the auxiliary building.

"Are you staying for the repast?" Michael asked.

"Yeah, I am."

"Would you sit at our table?"

She nodded. "Sure." It was time she got to know her little brother. They could exchange numbers and set up a day to spend time together one-on-one.

Lena and Michael headed off through the side door.

Turning around, Kimi found Takoda waiting for her. She slipped her arms around his waist.

He drew her closer. "You did great."

"Think so?"

"I know so. How do you feel about having another brother?"

"Strange. But in a good way. The more family," she said, glancing over at their motley crew, who had shown up for her, who she loved, "the better." She put her head on his chest, soaking in his warmth.

"I was thinking we should take a trip," he said.

Looking up at him, she smiled. "Just the two of us? On a warm, sandy beach?" Where he was going to propose, down on one knee, with a ring.

"You read my mind." He got that soft lovey-dovey look that was just for her. Then he kissed her quick and hard, making her tingle from her scalp to the soles of her feet. "I love you, Kimi. You're perfect. Well, perfect for me. We belong together."

"I was trying to tell you, but you were being stubborn. Next time, listen to me sooner."

"I promise." Grinning, he caressed her face, and his fingers slipped into her hair.

She loved his touch. Craved it. "I'm going to hold you to that, mister."

"I wouldn't have it any other way."

* * * * *

Look for Big Sky Manhunt
*the next thrilling installment of
Juno Rushdan's bestselling
Harlequin Intrigue miniseries
Ironside Protection Services*

*On sale April 2026
Wherever Harlequin Intrigue
books and ebooks are sold.*

And catch up with the previous titles,

Big Sky Slayer
Big Sky Safe House

Available now!

COMING SOON!

We really hope you enjoyed reading this book.
If you're looking for more romance
be sure to head to the shops when
new books are available on

Thursday 26th February

To see which titles are coming soon, please visit

millsandboon.co.uk/nextmonth

MILLS & BOON

LET'S TALK

Romance

For exclusive extracts, competitions and special offers, find us online:

- **f** MillsandBoon
- **X** @MillsandBoon
- **⬤** @MillsandBoonUK
- **♪** @MillsandBoonUK

Get in touch on 01413 063 232